For the Love of Maggie

"Oh, Maggie, it's all mixed up in my head. It's love, and uplifting, almost a reverence. . . ."

"Don't revere me, Lars!" she said crossly. "I'm human, sometimes too much so, I fear."

She unbuttoned his shirt and ran her hands inside, her palms gliding across his broad chest. The silken wiriness of his hair tickled her hands, sending a shiver over her body. She leaned to him with parted lips.

The familiar heaviness stole over her as his kiss stirred her blood. One big hand cupped her head, holding her mouth firm against his. The other stroked her back and shoulders. Gently, he stretched her out on the blanket. "Sweet Maggie . . ."

She murmured deep in her throat, and arched her body off the ground as he began to remove her clothes. It occurred to her for the first time that they had never made love at night. Somehow that seemed fitting. Their loving was an openness, a thing done in light and the spill of sunshine, nothing secret or furtive, nothing held back.

The warm breeze caressed her nakedness, and Maggie lay back with her eyes closed, waiting with pounding heart. . . . Then he was back, hands gentle on her shoulders, his lips demanding.

*   *   *

Would it be Lars, at last? What of handsome Jonas, and the persistent Andrew? Or would Lord Ramage have his sadistic way after all? Maggie would have to learn to separate the urgencies of passion, the tremors of desire, and the dreams of love. When her mind and body weakened, her heart would be all she'd have. Dare she dream of love and trust her fragile heart?

Love's Daring Dream

Patricia Matthews

PINNACLE BOOKS • LOS ANGELES

LOVE'S DARING DREAM

An original Pinnacle Books edition, published for the first time anywhere.

First printing, May 1978

ISBN: 0-523-40346-1

Cover illustration by Lou Marchetti

Printed in the United States of America

PINNACLE BOOKS, INC.
One Century Plaza
2029 Century Park East
Los Angeles, California 90067

For my sons, Michael and David,
who have a bit of the Irish;
And for Patrick, Danny, Kathy, and Connie,
who have a bit more!

LOVE'S DARING DREAM

The springtime bud now opens to the sun,
And frozen winter hearts may hope at last,
And I face toward the future for I know,
That there is nothing for me in the past.

Before me lie dark forests still unknown,
And I must face the challenge and the fear.
Will I be strong enough to walk this road?
To hold together that which I hold dear?

And when I've found my way, when I have won,
Must I forever work and strive and scheme?
Or will I find someone to share my load,
Will I be free to know love's daring dream?

Chapter One

In the year 1852, Ireland was in the black grip of the Great Potato Famine. Half of the population existed on the edge of starvation.

And so it was with the Donnevan family.

In the bedroom of the poorly furnished two-room cottage, Maggie Donnevan crouched on the far end of the rough bed, her knees drawn up close to her body, and her head bent forward. Through the thick waterfall of brown hair, she watched as Kathleen, her sister, placed her belongings in the tattered remnant of an old apron, and tied the corners to form a bundle. It was a pitifully small bundle, to contain all the worldly possessions of a girl of eighteen. The salt sting of tears burned Maggie's brown eyes as she stared at it.

It wasn't right! It wasn't fair!

She raised her gaze to her sister's face. Framed

1

by black hair, it was a beautiful face, even with the planes and hollows caused by near-starvation. The body beneath was beautiful, too—too slender now, but with full breasts and flaring hips. Maggie bit down on her lip to keep from crying out and put her head down upon her knees, feeling the firm push of her own budding breasts against her legs and feeling the shame deep inside her; the fear that she was going to be beautiful too. Men would desire her, also. Kathleen's fate might be hers as well. Maggie pushed away the thought, and swallowed her tears, trying to keep her voice steady.

"Kathleen, must you? Must you do it? We can get along. Things will get better. I know they will!"

Kathleen smiled sadly, a smile that did not quite reach her gray eyes. She moved to the bed, and sat down next to Maggie. She stretched out a hand and began to smooth the younger girl's hair. "You've heard little Kevin crying in the night from the pangs of hunger in his belly. You've looked into Mum's eyes, when the men come home hungry, and there is no food to give them. What I am doing is for the best. There will be one less mouth to feed, and I will be able to bring you things, money and food. Lord Ramage has promised me this."

Maggie stared into Kathleen's eyes. Kathleen was resigned. She had made up her mind. She was going to suffer that awful man to . . .

Maggie's mind could not complete the thought. And all because Kathleen was pleasant to look upon; an object to be bought and paid for; to be used for a man's pleasure for a time, and then probably cast aside. Even at sixteen, Maggie understood this much.

Maggie threw herself into her sister's lap, and gave in to the tears clogging her throat. "Why are you doing it, Kathleen? Why, why?"

Kathleen leaned over and kissed the top of Maggie's head. "I've explained that as best I can. Because it will keep us from starving, dear. So that we, the Donnevan family, can *live* awhile longer."

There was only one window in the thatched hut that the Donnevan family called home. Through it, Maggie could see the coach drawn up outside; it was very large and very black. It made her think of a funeral coach she had glimpsed once when a member of the landed gentry had died. Maggie could hear the horses snorting and stamping as though impatient to get away. The black coach stood out in sharp contrast to the green, rolling Irish countryside stretching away into blue mists.

Her mother and father stood across the room, away from the window, their faces turned aside. Her mother's face was grooved with lines of sorrow as she clutched six-year-old Kevin to her skirts with one hand. Her father's face might as well have been carved from gray stone, for all the expression he showed. His eyes were bleak and unseeing.

Maggie watched despairingly as Kathleen walked quietly past her parents' backs; she paused for a moment as if waiting for a word, any word, and, when none was forthcoming, she turned and walked out of the low cottage door. As the door closed behind her sister, Maggie made a vow to herself—Kathleen's fate would *never* happen to her.

Kevin set up a dreadful howling and tried to tug away from his mother's skirts, but Nora Donnevan pulled him back and bent to him, attempting to hush his cries. John Donnevan turned away and rummaged in the almost-bare cupboard for the half-filled poteen jar. Both of them seemed oblivious to the fact that their oldest daughter was leaving this house to become the mistress of the man who owned the land they lived on, who owned their very existence.

Maggie stared at them, eyes flashing with a growing fury. "How can you?" she shouted, her voice cutting through the smoky room with shocking suddenness. "How can you let her go!"

She ran to her father, and yanked at his sleeve. Without changing expression, he shoved her roughly away.

"You will not mention her name again in this house," he said harshly. "She is going into a life of sin. A strumpet, that's what she's become. She is no longer a daughter of mine." He set the poteen jar on the broken table with a thump, and dropped down onto the low wooden stool next to it.

Tears streaming down her face, Maggie walked stiff-legged up to the table, and faced him.

"She's doing it for us. For me and Kevin and Patrick and Danny and Mum and you. Yes, *you*, too. So we won't starve. She's doing it for us. How can you talk about her like that?"

He glared at her. "Shut your mouth, girl! I am the man here, and I expect my children to show me proper respect!" He took a swallow of the poteen and slammed the jar back down onto the table. "Aye, that's what comes of letting a girl-child run

4

too free," he muttered. He glanced accusingly at his wife. "I've told you and told you, Nora, to control this girl. Now look at what we've wrought, a mouthy wench who talks back to her own pa. If you can't control her, I'll be forced to take my belt to her!"

Maggie looked at her mother for support, but the older woman lowered her eyes and withdrew, as surely as if she had left the room. Only her twisting hands, fiercely pulling at the worn material of her apron, gave away her inner feelings.

Maggie knew and feared her father's anger, but she had an anger of her own now, and had gone too far to stop. In her short span of years she had never been so angry. In that moment she hated her father. He was a stupid, arrogant man, who considered women little better than cattle, and treated them as such. Maggie had long since realized this. Now it had to come out!

"You revile Kathleen, and call her names, yet where did the money come from that made the porridge with which you filled your belly this morning? From Kathleen, whom you call a strumpet!"

Nora Donnevan raised her thin hands as if to ward off the spill of bitter words coming from her daughter, but Maggie, ignoring the look of pain in her mother's eyes, could not stop.

"You are too proud a man, you say, to have a daughter who lives in a state of sin, and yet you aren't too proud to accept the food and drink bought with the money from this same daughter, all the while pretending you don't know from where it comes! A fine, proud man you are, a . . ."

5

Maggie's words died in mid-sentence, as her father, with a bellow of pure rage, pushed the wooden table from him with a mighty shove that sent it crashing halfway across the room, and lurched erect. Kevin wailed with fright.

Maggie felt her throat tighten with fear. Her father would strike her now, as he had so many times before, and his hand was heavy, particularly when affected by the drink, but she had said what she must.

She watched him as he stood there, weaving slightly, his face flaming. She refused to shrink back as he took one step toward her; and then an amazing and frightening thing happened.

John Donnevan's expression changed. It was as if he had forgotten what he intended to do; as if he was looking inward to something only he could see. Then, an expression of horror and pain twisted his mouth into a grimace. Clutching his chest with both hands, he fell forward to the floor like a stunned ox, his big body hitting the floor with a dull, thudding sound.

Nora Donnevan sank to her knees by his side. Maggie could do nothing but stand and stare, frozen motionless by the shock of the moment. She only stirred when her mother looked up at her, all expression wiped from her face, her eyes like clear, blue glass.

"He's dead," she said in a flat voice. "Himself is dead." A spark glowed in her eyes suddenly. "The guilt will always be on your head, Margaret Donnevan, you being the death of your own father!"

Maggie opened her mouth to deny her responsibility, then stopped herself as she saw her mother lower her head. The woman rocked back and forth, making a keening sound of grief. Tears fell like slow rain on her dead husband.

Maggie tied the patched, white apron over her least worn dress and carefully combed her thick, brown hair. She felt drained and listless, not really up to coping with the condolences of the neighbors, whose voices she could hear as they gathered in the other room and in the yard.

Yet, it was the custom—a wake must be held for John Donnevan, so that he might be properly put into the ground. His spirit must be put to rest, even if his family was sorely tried in the process.

It would have been a poor wake but for Kathleen, as the Donnevans, like all their neighbors, had little or no food even for themselves. Kathleen had prevailed upon Lord Ramage to send victuals and drink, so that the Donnevans would not be shamed. Maggie wondered wryly what John Donnevan would have thought of this—the man he hated, and the daughter he had scorned, providing the means for his final goodbye.

Maggie took Kathleen's note from her pocket and smoothed it flat, touching the writing with her finger, as if seeking the presence of her sister in the hastily scrawled words:

My Dearly Beloved Sister,
I am sorry that I cannot be at your side to help you bear the burden of the next few days; but His Lordship states that I am too recently arrived to be let leave so soon, and since I know how our brothers feel toward me, it is perhaps for the best.

His Lordship, out of the kindness of his heart, he states, made arrangements to send both victuals and drink suitable for the occasion, in amounts sufficient to feed a goodly number of mourners. Keep some aside for the family, for the neighbors will eat your cupboards bare. Give my love to Kevin, and to Mum, if she will accept it. I will try to keep in touch with you.

Your Loving Sister, Kathleen.

Word that there would be proper food and drink at the Donnevan wake had spread, and the house and yard soon filled with mourners. Maggie noticed that among their neighbors and relatives were many who had not spoken to her father in years, and some who had called him a hard, cold man to his face. It was strange how the prospect of a good meal could wipe out the memory of a man's wrongdoing, she thought cynically; but when she saw the thin, pinched faces and the hungry eyes around her, Maggie could not fault them. A hungry belly knew no right or wrong; it simply cried out to be filled.

The older women were wailing and beating their breasts with their closed fists, and a great clatter and chatter was going on between people who had not seen one another in some time, but all eyes were casting expectant glances at the roadway. Maggie knew they were wondering when the food and drink would arrive; and, truthfully, so was she. She knew that her mother would be shamed if they had nothing to offer the mourners.

Her two brothers, Patrick and Daniel, great

lumps both of them, stood sullenly on either side of their mother. They wouldn't offer to help with the serving, Maggie knew; they were too like her father, believing that menial work was for women. She gave them a disdainful look, and Dan, the youngest, caught her eye and looked away sheepishly. Sometimes she had hopes for Dan; he had a life to him, a more understanding nature that Patrick lacked, but at the moment she despaired of him, too. Life with John Donnevan had instilled in them a lack of consideration for women.

A shout went up behind her, and Maggie turned to see a cloud of dust approaching down the roadway. The cloud resolved into Lord Ramage's black coach.

Using her elbows, Maggie forced her way to the forefront of the crowd. There would be too many willing hands to unload the food. She wanted to be certain, as Kathleen had told her in the letter, to put some aside for the family's use.

She reached the coach door, and her presence kept some kind of order, as the food was handed out. There were loaves of bread; rounds of cheese; several fowl; and wonder of wonders, a suckling pig, already roasted. In addition, there were several jars of poteen. A great chorus of sighs greeted this wondrous sight.

Maggie, in all the confusion, managed to get some of the food into the bedroom, where she hid it under the far corner of the bed. Then, feeling that she had at least provided for tomorrow, she returned to the mourners, who were by now already sampling the poteen, with a corresponding rise in spirits. Sean Dougherty had pulled out his fiddle, and the wailing of strings sang out the plaintive strains of a ballad that spoke of long-lost heroes in a day when Irishmen were masters of their own destinies and their own land. After the ballad, Maggie knew, would come the jigs and the reels, and the guests, made mellow by full bellies and the effects of poteen, would dance away the night. There would be little rest for anyone this night, but Maggie knew she would have to put Kevin to bed soon and hope that he would be able to sleep through the noise.

Maggie stood on tiptoe in the crowded main room, straining to catch a glimpse of her mother, who had been kneeling by the side of her husband's bier since early morning. In the flickering light of the two candles—one at the head and one at the foot of the bier—Maggie could see her father's body laid out, with his hands folded over his chest. Beside him knelt the small figure of Nora Donnevan. Maggie felt a flash of exasperation. John Donnevan had treated her mother shamefully; pushing her down and keeping her down, making her something less than a person. Why should her mother now punish herself like this?

Brushing her hair out of her eyes, Maggie made her way through the mourners until she was at her mother's side.

"Mum, come away now. Come rest yourself, do. Have a wee bite to eat before the food is gone."

Nora Donnevan mutely shook her head, and went on telling the worn beads that slipped through her fingers like the wasted years of her life.

Maggie gave a great sigh, born of both anger and guilt. Why, oh why, couldn't people act like rational beings? Why all this self-torture? Her mother's hand tugged at the skirt of her dress, and Maggie realized that the woman wished her to kneel beside her. She shot a quick glance at her father's cold, white face, and shuddered. She bent down to release Nora Donnevan's thin fingers from the material, and gently shook her head. She would not be a hypocrite. In her heart, Maggie knew that she was not sorry that her father was dead.

The hours crept on, and when the food was all gone, many of the mourners returned to their own cottages; except for a few still drinking and others so overpowered by drink that they slept where they had fallen.

Finally, only Nora Donnevan remained by the bier, still kneeling by her husband's body. It was all that Maggie could do to get the woman to cease her vigil and retire for what was left of the night. When Maggie left the bedroom, Nora Donnevan was staring with blind eyes at the low, thatched roof.

Maggie stood for a moment in the other room, wondering where her brothers were. Her glance strayed to the body of her father, then jumped away. She felt stifled, hemmed-in, and couldn't stay in the house another minute.

Just as she went out the door, Patrick barred her way. At twenty, he was the eldest of the Donnevan children. Even though the poteen had slumped his broad shoulders, at six-feet-four he towered over Maggie. His red hair was disheveled, and his blue eyes were glazed by drink.

He stood swaying before her. "Why ain't you with Mum, little sister?"

"Why aren't you?" she snapped.

"Sure, and it's the men of the family now we are, me and Danny boy. It's the man's place to see to the mourners."

"Whisht! Swilling poteen, you mean. You stink of it, Brother!" She made a face of disgust. "And Mum's finally lying down, since you're all that concerned."

"It's that damned Kathleen's fault! Himself wouldn't be dead but for her. She's brought shame to the Donnevan name—"

"Whisht! Don't you be damning Kathleen, Patrick Donnevan! I notice you, and Brother Dan, haven't spurned the food and drink she sent. So, watch what you say. I'll listen to no bad words about our sister."

She stormed off, leaving Patrick staring after her, openmouthed.

Maggie had eaten only a few bites of food all day, but she had no hunger even now. She picked her way through the sleepers on the ground, and walked out into the field, the field that had yielded only two edible crops in six years.

It seemed to Maggie that she could not remember a time when each year they hadn't lived in dread of the blight destroying the potato. Actually, it had begun in the autumn of 1845. The small farmers of Ireland existed on the potato; they knew little of other crops. Not only did it feed humans, but the tubers, too small for people, were used to feed hogs, cows, and fowl. Aside from milk, the potato was the mainstay of the table; even their bread was baked from it.

The Donnevan farm consisted of three acres, for which they paid Lord Ramage a yearly rental of ten pounds an acre. In the good years, they grew enough potatoes to feed the family for an entire year, hopefully with a sufficient amount left over to pay Lord Ramage's rent, and for clothing and drink.

Since 1846, the good years had been few. The potato would grow and look all right when freshly dug, but before it could be eaten it became a mass of corruption and rot, emitting a foul stench when cut open. John Donnevan had been "hanging gale"—letting his rent fall in arrears—ever since that disastrous first season of 1845–46. Even the few good years were not enough to enable them to catch up with the back rent.

So, when this year's crop also failed, the Donnevans were not only starving, but Lord Ramage had threatened to evict them unless they paid the money owed him.

But for Kathleen's sacrifice, they would now be living under a tree somewhere. A common practice of the more calloused landlords was to simply tear a tenant cottage down and move it, if the tenant balked at being evicted. Lord Ramage was certainly capable of such an action.

Only about half of the mourners attending the long wake appeared at the desolate cemetery the next morning when John Donnevan was put into the ground. There was much weeping and wailing by those attending, but Maggie could not find any tears in her to shed for her father. Her only memories of him seemed to be unhappy; she could not, though she tried, remember him as ever being kind and loving.

As the priest spoke the services in a monotone, Maggie felt only impatience for it to be over, impatience and bitterness. The bitterness stemmed from the fact that the cemetery was on Lord Ramage's property, also. The cemetery was small, fenced in, and the spot where John Donnevan was buried was crowded into a tiny corner against a fence, as though Lord Ramage begrudged the space.

Not only do we not own the land we farm, Maggie thought; *we don't even have a burial plot for our dead. Somewhere, some place, there has to be a better life than this!*

When it was finally over and the mourners began to leave, Maggie was confronted by a belligerent Patrick, red-eyed from weeping and dreadfully hungover. He said accusingly, "I didn't see you shed a single tear for Himself."

"You, and the rest, shed enough tears," she said tartly.

"It's a hard woman you are, Maggie Donnevan."

"I'll do my mourning in my own way, if you please."

Maggie turned away toward her mother, and helped the weeping, black-clad woman into the cart for the ride home. The cart was only large enough for Maggie, her mother, and Kevin. Patrick and Dan walked along behind it to their cottage.

Nora Donnevan hadn't spoken a half-dozen words since the stroke had felled her husband. When they arrived at the hut, she went straight away into the other room and stretched out on her back, staring blindly up at the low roof.

It was up to Maggie to put the noon meal on the table. Fortunately, there was still some of the roast pig left from the wake, and two loaves of bread. Maggie could save the food she had hidden for the coming week. She started a low fire in the hearth, feeding it with peat moss. She put chunks of meat into a pot and hung it over the fire to warm. Kevin tagged after her disconsolately, sniffling. Maggie did her best to comfort him, but she suspected he was much too young to feel any great sense of loss and was merely emulating his elders.

Patrick and Dan were at the table, reviving themselves with mugs of poteen. The men, two years apart in age, could have been twins insofar as their great size and bulk were concerned, but Dan more resembled Maggie in coloring, having the same brown hair and eyes, and his features were finer than Patrick's.

The pair talked as though Maggie wasn't even in the room.

"Poor Mum," said Dan.

"Sure, and 'tis a great shock to the poor woman," Patrick said. "Kathleen doing this terrible thing, then Himself's death."

Maggie turned from the hearth. "I told you I'd listen to none of your blatherings about Kathleen, Patrick!"

Patrick scowled at her. "Then don't listen, Sister. A fine one to talk, you are. Mum mumbled something to me about you talking up to Himself, stirring him into a great rage. 'Twas then he fell dead.

That, then, is on your head, making you no better than your sister!"

"I said nothing to him that should not have been said before!"

"He was our pa, Maggie," Dan said, "and you should have obeyed him. It is the way."

"Maybe it's time some of our ways are changed. Like the pair of you, sitting there drinking, instead of out working. If that had happened long ago, Kathleen might not have been forced to shame the Donnevan name!"

"That's not fair, Maggie!" Dan protested. "You know there's no work. The good Lord knows Patrick and me have tried, and we're not proud. We'd work at anything!"

"Enough!" Patrick roared, and thumped the table with his fist. "We don't have to be explaining ourselves to the likes of her!"

At the thunder of Patrick's voice, Kevin began to cry, and Maggie seized the excuse to escape for a minute, shooing him outside into the yard to play. She stood watching as Kevin became absorbed in playing with a stick.

She was a little ashamed of her sharp tongue. Despite their many faults, her brothers were hard workers, when work was to be had. But there simply *was* no work. For every job that came available, there were a hundred workers clamoring . . . no, begging for it!

Maggie sighed, wiping her sweaty brow with her apron. She stared off into the green, misty distance. Such a lovely land it was, Ireland; but she knew it was a deceptive beauty, a death trap for all too many. She had heard that people were leaving Ireland by the thousands, emigrating to the Land of Promise—the United States.

But passage to America cost money, a great deal of money. Stories had begun to trickle back that the Irish weren't so welcome as they had been at first. They had brought pestilence and cheap labor with them, and the Americans were becoming hostile.

What did it matter? Why was she thinking such thoughts? The Donnevans couldn't even put food on the table, much less pay ship passage to another country!

Maggie hadn't realized how much she would miss Kathleen. The two girls had always been close, and, until now, had never spent a night apart. The missing was like an ache inside Maggie, an ache that would not go away, no matter how hard she tried to banish it.

Two weeks after the funeral, the black coach pulled up outside the cottage. Patrick and Dan pretended not to see it and walked off in the other direction. It was left to Maggie and Kevin to unload the baskets of food. As the last basket was unloaded, the coachman coughed. When Maggie looked up at him, he disdainfully handed down a sealed letter.

He said, "I was told to await an answer."

With trembling fingers Maggie broke the seal.

Dearest Maggie,

Oh, how I miss you, dear sister! It seems an eternity since I have seen you.

I have asked Lord Ramage for permission for

you to visit with me. He has to go to Galway City on business, and will be absent for four days. He said that, since he would not have to look upon you, you might visit me in his absence, so long as you are gone upon his return.

He will leave three days hence. Immediate upon his departure, I will dispatch the coach for you, if you will agree to come. Please, do, dear Maggie. Think of it, four whole days together! It will be heaven to see and talk to you. You cannot know . . .

Here some words had been crossed out, and Maggie could not make them out.

Quickly she read on:

If you consent to come, no return letter is necessary. Just tell the coachman yes or no. I do pray your answer will be yes.
Your Loving Sister, Kathleen

Clutching the letter to her bosom, Maggie turned shining eyes up to the coachman and said in ringing tones, "Yes! Oh, yes!"

The coachman gave a meager nod, flicked the reins, and the coach clattered away.

Naturally, when Patrick and Dan found out about the proposed trip, they were dead set against it. Maggie turned a deaf ear to their threats and pleas. She was going to visit Kathleen, nothing could dissuade her!

In desperation, the brothers turned to their mother and tried to get her to forbid Maggie to go.

But Nora Donnevan had retreated more and more into herself. She seemed scarcely aware of anyone around her, had to be cajoled into eating, and hadn't spoken a word in days.

The evening before the coach was to come for her, Maggie took a bath and brushed her long hair. A note of caution sounded in her mind as she studied herself in their one broken mirror. During the brief time of Kathleen's absence, she seemed to have ripened very fast. Her breasts were larger, fuller, her hips more rounded. With Kathleen sending food regularly, she had been eating more, and had undoubtedly gained a pound or so.

Maggie felt a chill. She had never laid eyes on Lord Ramage, but his lechery and cruelty were well-known about the countryside. It would not do to have him see her as desirable. She had no illusions that possessing Kathleen would keep His Lordship from preying on other young girls and women.

And even though he was supposed to be absent, Maggie did not wish to take the risk of his early return. Besides this concern, Maggie felt ill at ease with her burgeoning womanhood. Glancing at her reflection in the bit of glass, she let her hair obscure her face, for even that part of her body was changing. She didn't like the full, pouting look of her lower lip, of her hazel-brown eyes fringed with thick, dark lashes. She felt that they promised something, something she was not yet ready to deliver. Only her nose, short and slightly tilted at the end, seemed the same.

"I don't want to grow up," she muttered. "I don't! I don't!"

She had only two dresses. One, an old dress of Kathleen's, was too large for Maggie, frayed and patched many times. But it was voluminous enough to conceal the outline of her body. Maggie put it on and felt better.

The next morning Maggie, looking like a ragamuffin in the large dress, and carrying a few toilet articles wrapped in a kerchief, was out in the yard waiting for the coach long before it was due. Behind her, the cottage was closed and silent. Her older brothers had not spoken to her. Kevin had wanted to come out and wait with her, but Maggie made him remain inside. That was her only regret about being away—Kevin and her mother would have to fend for themselves.

Because of this she had wavered several times in her decision, then had decided it might be good for Patrick and Dan to assume the responsibility for the family while she was gone.

The black coach came. The liveried driver made no move to get down from his high perch, and Maggie had to open the door and climb in herself.

The distance to Ramage Castle was not far, and all the way they traveled on land belonging to Lord Ramage. There were no villages, but they did pass farm after small farm, the fields empty and weed-grown. People came out from the many huts they passed and lined up to watch the coach roll by. On all the faces Maggie could see envy, and many were openly hostile. In addition to his cruelty, his callous disregard for the welfare of his tenants, Lord Ramage was English, and the Irish hated their English masters with a passion that burned hotter than their peat fires.

Maggie shrank back into the corner of the coach, fearful she would be seen and recognized.

Soon, the coach turned off the main road into the private drive leading up to Ramage Castle, where it squatted on a hill overlooking the surrounding countryside. Maggie put her head out the door to peer ahead.

She had to admit that it was a sight to behold, a huge, gray mass of stone, with turrets and battlements. To Maggie, it seemed forbidding, malevolent. It was at least a hundred years old. It was also, she was soon to discover, uncomfortable—drafty, difficult to heat, with stone floors as hard as iron underfoot.

But none of that really mattered, for Kathleen was there to welcome her. The sisters embraced, tears flowing unashamedly.

Kathleen was pale, though a bit plumper than Maggie remembered her, and there were faint circles like shadows under her eyes. Even as glad as she was to see Maggie, Kathleen had a tormented, almost haunted look about her.

"How is it here, with him?" Maggie asked in a whisper, afraid she would be overheard. The castle swarmed with servants; she couldn't understand why any household should need so many servants.

"Why, it's grand here, Maggie! You see, have you ever seen a dress so grand as this?" Kathleen said in a high, carrying voice.

She spun around slowly for Maggie's inspection. It was a lovely garment, of rich, green velvet, with puffed sleeves, and a full skirt sweeping the floor. Maggie did think that the bodice was cut a *little* low.

21

"And the jewels! You should see the jewels His Lordship lavishes on me. A fortune! And servants . . ." Kathleen swept a hand around. She was smiling gaily, yet Maggie sensed a forced, false note to it. "All I have to do is call, snap my fingers, and whatever I want, they bring. And Maggie . . . that rag you're wearing. It's a disgrace for the sister of the mistress of Lord Ramage to be so attired. I have countless gowns now. I'm sure one would fit you. Come. . . ." She beckoned Maggie toward the staircase.

"No, Kathleen," Maggie said softly. "I'd rather not, but I do thank you, anyway. You've seen me in this dress before, it's an old one of yours. If you can abide me in it, I'd rather keep wearing it."

"Yes, Maggie, I see," Kathleen said in an equally soft voice. She darted a look around. They were alone in the great hall at the moment. "My little sister is growing up, and wise enough to realize it."

They dined alone in the huge dining room that evening. The table alone was as large as the Donnevan cottage, or so it seemed to Maggie.

The food was marvelous, with enough to feed six people. There was a mutton pie, several fresh vegetables, and berry tarts for dessert. There was even a bowl of boiled potatoes.

Maggie said in amazement, "These potatoes are delicious! But where did they come from? Whisht! I thought the blight had ruined all of this year's crop."

Kathleen shrugged. "His Lordship had them brought in from the North. 'Tis only Galway and surrounding counties that were destroyed by the blight this year." Kathleen's eyes had a bright

22

shine, and her speech was slurred. There was a large decanter of port on the table, and she had been imbibing heavily, eating very little.

Maggie sensed the depth of despair and depression in her sister, but Kathleen would not discuss her life here, except on superficial terms, and always veered the conversation away each time Maggie broached it.

Maggie spent the night in a bedroom all her own, with a huge four-poster—the softest bed she had ever known.

The next three days both delighted and depressed Maggie. The only times Kathleen showed any animation was when they were away from the castle, and then she would only talk of the time before she came here, and only in terms of longing. Every night she drank herself into a stupor.

They spent a large part of each day in the forest that grew almost up to the edge of the castle grounds.

"His Lordship's personal hunting preserve, for him and his friends," Kathleen explained.

It was nice in the forest, which teemed with deer, hares, and other wild creatures. Once, they saw a magnificent stag on a rise across a small stream. Apparently sensing their presence, the stag stood with his horns high, frozen in place for a timeless moment, so still that Maggie thought of a great painting.

Then he whirled and disappeared into the underbrush with two bounds.

Maggie let her breath go. "What a beautiful creature!"

"There are many such in this forest. They seem

to sense when His Lordship is absent and they are in no danger. They seem to actually feel a kinship with me. But many nights His Lordship comes back from the hunt in a foul temper. They manage to hide from him. A good thing that is. He kills anything that moves." Kathleen's voice rasped with bitterness. Then she shook her head, turned a smile on Maggie, and linked arms with her. As they strolled along, she said, "I love it here. It's peaceful, and all the creatures are wild and . . . free."

These were the delightful periods to Maggie, the walks through the woods and the good sister talk, as delightful as the return to the castle was gloomy. As soon as they entered the courtyard, Kathleen's mood turned as gray as the castle walls.

Their last night together arrived all too soon. Maggie was to take the coach home early the next morning. Neither girl had much appetite that evening and ate little supper. To make matters worse, it had rained during the day, and they had not been able to walk in the forest.

The night was chill, and the girls huddled before a blazing peat fire in the library, sitting together on a bearskin rug before the hearth. Kathleen had brought in a decanter of port and two glasses. On this, their last night together, Maggie shared the port with her sister.

Maggie looked around the large room, marveling at the shelves of books, all the way to the ceiling along three walls. She felt a stab of envy. She had always loved to read, and had constantly hungered for books, borrowing whatever she could find. She'd had little schooling and had been taught not much more than the rudiments, but being bright, she had learned quickly, and had gone on to add to her own knowledge.

"So many books!" she said. "How I would love to read them. Has Lord Ramage read *all* those books?"

"It's likely," Kathleen said with a shrug. "His Lordship is an educated man, and spends much of his time here, reading and drinking his French brandy. . . ."

"Sometimes a book and a bottle of brandy," said a sneering voice from the doorway, "are better company than some wenches!"

"Oh, no! Lord in Heaven, no!" Kathleen whispered.

Maggie jumped to her feet, whirling around. In the library doorway stood a man of striking good looks. He was tall, broad of shoulder, and narrow-hipped; his coloring was fair, his hair snow-white, yet he could not have been more than thirty-five years of age. His light blue eyes were as chillingly cold as lake ice, and his full, sensual mouth was very red, causing Maggie to wonder if he painted his lips. Yet, as handsome as he was, as commanding a presence, there was something repellent about him. It was as if the man was all gloss, all handsome surface with no more depth than a painting, which he resembled, as still as he now stood.

He was splendidly dressed, with a ruffled shirt, dove-colored trousers snug over his thighs, and black riding boots. Over it all, he wore a black, lined cape.

Now he moved, raising his hand in a languid gesture. "What, Milady Kathleen, no greeting for the master of Ramage Castle on his return? No rushing into his arms with tears of delight? I must confess to being sorely disappointed." His voice was cruel and mocking.

Kathleen, now on her feet, stammered, "I . . . I was not expecting your return until the morning, Your Lordship."

"I can imagine. I returned early purposely, wishing to view the sister of whom you have talked so much." His cold, haughty gaze moved over Maggie. Then he dismissed her with a flick of his wrist. "Now that I have seen her, I cannot say I am overly impressed. I have seen beggars better dressed on the streets of Dublin."

"Maggie, this is Lord Ramage," Kathleen said quickly. "Your Lordship, this is—"

"Do not bore me with introductions." Again he made the flicking motion with his wrist. "Out, the pair of you. I wish to have some of that French brandy now. Which does not mean, madam, that I will forsake your bed this night." Ignoring Maggie as though she didn't exist, he raked Kathleen with a burning gaze. "The wenches of Galway are a sorry lot. At least here I can partake of beauty, tho it be a cold beauty."

Chapter Two

Hurried down the drafty halls by Kathleen, Maggie felt scalded by shame and humiliation. To be thus dismissed, like some kitchen slattern! Like some barnyard animal beneath His Lordship's notice!

She recognized the contradiction here. She had dressed to look her worst, as unattractively as possible, and now she was angry that Lord Ramage had taken one glance and dismissed her with a contemptuous gesture.

Knowing this did nothing to mitigate her anger in the least. She said hotly, "What a terrible man! How can you bear being here with him? Sharing a . . ." She felt her face flush, but she blurted it out, "Sharing a bed with him!"

" 'Tis not easy, dear sister," Kathleen said with a sigh. "He is indeed a terrible man, you cannot know how terrible until you . . ." She broke off, looking away. "But it is a price that must be paid."

"It's too terrible a price! I'd rather starve than have you do this!"

"I'm sure you would, Maggie dear." Kathleen squeezed her hand. "And so would I. But there are Patrick and Dan to consider, and don't forget little Kevin and Mum. The others might survive, but Kevin and Mum could not survive another winter of starvation."

There was such a look of desperation on Kathleen's face that Maggie knew it would be useless to argue. Her sister was resigned to her fate.

At the door to the bedchamber Maggie had been using, Kathleen kissed her, and said in a tight voice, "Good night, dear Maggie. Sleep well."

With a cry Maggie embraced her fiercely, weeping. Kathleen held her for a momnt, making soothing noises, then disengaged herself. She went down the hall with dragging footsteps.

Still weeping, Maggie watched until Kathleen turned into the master bedroom. Sleep well? How could she sleep, knowing full well what would be going on in Lord Ramage's bedchamber?

With an angry sound, Maggie dashed the tears from her eyes and went into her own room. For the first time she wished there was a lock or a bolt on the door.

"His Lordship won't permit any doors or bolts to be installed on any of the bedchamber doors," Kathleen had explained. "He says that, as master of Ramage Castle, he should not be forbidden entry to any room here."

Candles were glowing in the room, a peat fire in the hearth.

In a gesture of defiance—defiance of what, Maggie was not sure—she removed all of her clothes, and stood naked before the tall mirror. Then she tried to view herself as a man might.

She had indeed blossomed early, and as she turned in front of the pier glass, she saw round, high breasts, a long, flat waist, rather slender hips, and long, well-shaped legs. If she grew any more, she was going to be a tall woman.

She looked critically at her skin, which had an olive cast. She was not white-skinned, as were Kathleen and her mother. Still, her skin was smooth and unblemished, and was suitable to her brown hair and hazel-brown eyes. She supposed that a man might find her appearance pleasing.

Her hands, Maggie thought, were her worst feature. She gazed at them. Narrow, long-fingered, true; but coarse and reddened from hard labor, the nails broken.

Yet there was strength in those hands. The hard work had toughened her. At most labor she could do a full day's work equal to a man's. . . .

"Damme, I was right in my surmise," said a drawling voice behind her. "Under those beggar's rags dwells a beauty, a tempting morsel indeed."

Fright made Maggie gasp, and she spun around. Lord Ramage leaned against the doorjamb, his gaze bright, bold, and arrogant. Maggie felt the cold grip of panic in her belly, and then the hot flush of shame. She made a desperate lunge toward her clothing, but Lord Ramage, moving with a quickness she would not have thought possible, was there before her, barring her way. "I thought I would confirm my suspicions of your hidden charms, my lush beauty." A hot spark sprang to life in the depths of his cold eyes. "You are as fetching as your sister. I wonder if your blood runs hotter? Methinks I shall soon discover that for myself."

Maggie, almost out of her mind with fear, made a move to dart around him, but he clamped a hand cruelly around her wrist. Maggie screamed.

He gave a careless shrug. "Scream all you like. No one will dare come. I am master here, and there is no one to gainsay what I do behind these walls."

He bent her arm behind her back, and brought her against him. He smelled of brandy and horse. Maggie tried to turn her head away, but his mouth descended upon hers, and she could feel the hardness of his manhood stirring against her belly.

His lips were hot and wet, and with a strength born of revulsion she managed to wrench her head aside. The scream that came tearing from her throat was piercing.

Lord Ramage laughed. "Save your breath, girl, 'twill do you no good."

Again, he brought her hard against him. Maggie fought him, but his strength was too much. Inexorably, he forced her step by step toward the bed.

"Let her go, Your Lordship."

Lord Ramage went rigid. Still holding Maggie close, he turned.

Kathleen, in a long white nightgown, stood in the doorway, hands out of sight behind her back. Her head was back, her eyes bright with purpose.

"How dare you, madam?" Lord Ramage said

harshly. "Everything in this house belongs to me, and I will use it as I see fit!"

"Not Maggie, not my sister. Your bargain, sir, was with me. Now, let her go."

He threw back his head and laughed. "And if I don't?"

"Then I will kill you," Kathleen said steadily.

She took her hands from behind her back. In one she held a long-bladed kitchen knife. She gripped the handle in both hands and raised it. "I will kill you with this."

He grew very still. "You would not dare. You know what will happen to you should you harm me."

"I would rather die than see my sister despoiled by you! For the love of God, sir," she cried, "she is but a child!"

The change from threat to pleading caused Lord Ramage to laugh again. "Begging now, are you? It will serve you no purpose, dearest Kathleen. You have pleaded with me before, if you will recall. A child, you say?" He glanced at Maggie, holding her at arm's length. "Damme, she seems no child, but ripe for the plucking." He looked around, and his breath caught.

Kathleen had advanced on silent feet, the knife once again raised high. "You are right, I well know that begging avails me nothing with you," she said in a tense voice. "But be warned, sir, I am not afraid to use this knife."

Softly, he said, "I believe you would use it."

"For Maggie's sake, I would."

Slowly, Lord Ramage let go his grip on Maggie.

She stepped quickly back, eyes fixed on the pair confronting each other.

"She's nothing to me, just another wench." He strove to make light of it, but was not completely successful. "Since you feel so strongly, I will leave your precious sister be, you have my word on it." His gaze fastened on the contours of Kathleen's body glimpsed through the almost sheer nightgown. "Our bargain still holds?"

Kathleen nodded, lowering the knife. "Our bargain still holds."

"Very well, madam. I command your presence in my bedchamber at once." He started for the door, then turned back with his cold smile. "And without the weapon, madam, if you please."

Kathleen dropped the knife, and covered her face with her hands. Maggie hurried to embrace her. Through her own sobs, she whispered, "Thank you, Kathleen. Thank you, thank you!"

Kathleen lowered her hands. Her eyes were dry, but dark with torment. She gripped Maggie's hand fiercely. "I will leave word with the servants. The coach will depart at dawn. You must be ready to go. You must not stay here a moment longer than necessary."

"Stricken, Maggie said, "I won't even get to see you in the morning to say farewell?"

Kathleen shook her head. "No, this is farewell." She kissed Maggie on the cheek. "Goodbye, dear Maggie."

Maggie held her. "Must you go to . . . to him?"

"Yes, I must." She freed herself from Maggie's grip.

She turned then and left quickly, closing the door firmly behind her.

Maggie slept little that night. Several times she awoke with a start, certain she heard a muffled scream from down the hall; or was she having nightmares?

Kathleen paused outside the door to Lord Ramage's bedchamber. She shivered in the thin bedgown and slippers, as a draft blew along the stone corridor, setting the wall torches to flickering. Kathleen squeezed her eyes shut. She wanted nothing so much as to run, to flee this dreadful place. It was a feeling she had experienced every night since that first awful night in His Lordship's bed.

"My dear Kathleen," said his cruel, mocking voice from the other side of the door. "Do not keep me waiting. You know how it angers me."

Kathleen started, eyes flying open. Lord Ramage seemed to possess some mystic ability, to be able to sense her presence beyond a closed door. Perhaps it was her fear of him. She understood that wild animals, the predators especially, could actually smell fear in a frightened person.

She steeled herself for what was to come, and opened the door.

The large bedchamber was illuminated by two candles burning on each side of the bed. Lord Ramage stood between the door and the bed. He had already removed his clothing, and stood naked waiting for her.

Kathleen turned her head aside. She thought that it was this that disturbed her the most. There was

33

something obscene, and terribly humiliating about it. It was always something of a shock to Kathleen to see that lean, powerfully muscled body topped by snow-white hair. She closed the door and stood with her back against it.

His coldly handsome face remained calm, untroubled, but his soft voice was venomous as he said, "You know you're going to suffer for balking me in my desires, do you not, dear Kathleen? Nobody defies me in my own castle! You know that."

"Yes, Your Lordship, I know that," she said dully.

"Yet you did defy me, knowing full well the penalty you would pay. Damme, I must admire your spirit. It will be a challenge for me to crush it. I'll see to it that you have no more spirit than a worm when I send you crawling from this castle. You may depend on it!" He gestured commandingly. "Now, remove your garment."

Kathleen obeyed, pulling the nightgown over her head.

Lust flamed in his eyes, and his manhood stirred to life. "Damme, you *are* a fine figure of a woman. But for that I would have sent you back to starve with the other Irish trash in your hovel. Come here, wench."

Again, Kathleen obeyed, moving toward him on leaden feet.

When she was within arm's reach, Lord Ramage lashed out with one hand, the back of it striking her across the cheek. On one finger he wore a heavy diamond ring. The diamond cut into her flesh, and the blow set her head to reeling. Again, he struck her, this time across the other cheek.

The brassy taste of her own blood filled Kathleen's mouth. She would not let herself cry out; she would not give him the satisfaction. Once more, he hit her, this time with his fist high on the cheekbone. Kathleen felt the skin split. This time the pain was so intense that a keening cry escaped her.

"Ah, that should mark that beauty of yours for days to come," he said gloatingly. "Now, onto the bed with you!"

Only dimly aware of what she was doing, Kathleen moved to the bed and fell across it, wishing for unconsciousness. She fell on her side. Lord Ramage seized her arm and turned her onto her back.

"Don't swoon on me, madam. I want you fully aware." He took one nipple between thumb and forefinger and squeezed brutally.

Again she screamed.

From afar, she heard his mocking laughter. She scarcely felt his weight as he came down on top of her, and she felt nothing as he penetrated her.

From the beginning, the very first night, it hadn't been just the brutal treatment that so humiliated and degraded her; it was the impersonal manner in which he took her. He might have been a machine, showing no awareness whatsoever of her as a person.

Kathleen had been a virgin that first night, with no experience and little knowledge of men. Yet, she had long been aware of the urgings of her body, and had suspected that her blood ran hot.

True, she had sold herself, sold herself into sexual slavery in return for sustenance for her family

35

However, she had been prepared to give as well as take.

Lord Ramage had never given her the chance. When she had first glimpsed that handsome, muscular body, as beautiful as a finely wrought sculpture, her heartbeat had quickened, and she had waited in quivering anticipation.

And then he had been on her like a ravening animal, inside her in a twinkling, without so much as a word or gesture, and never once did he look into her face. In that moment something had gone dead inside her.

When his lust was spent, Lord Ramage had struck her across the face, and said in icy contempt, "Damme, you are a cold bitch!"

Whatever he had killed inside Kathleen never revived, and she remained dead, looking forward to his sexual assaults as a dreaded ordeal.

Now his breath left him in an explosive snort, and he collapsed atop her. After a moment he rolled away.

"Cold. Damme, cold as plunging into a lake at winter, and I've always heard that Irish women are hot-blooded in bed."

Kathleen, more aware now, held herself tense for another blow.

Instead, he shoved her roughly. "Find yourself another bed to sleep in tonight, madam. I do not want you freezing my bed the remainder of the night."

He gave her another push, and Kathleen crawled out of bed and crept like an old woman, crept like a wounded creature, naked and shivering, down the drafty hall to an empty bedchamber. Yet she knew she wouldn't sleep this night, not until she heard the coach in the morning, carrying Maggie away from this place, and out of Lord Ramage's reach.

Maggie was up and dressed long before first light, and a rap on the door summoned her to the coach. She saw no one in the halls as she walked on tiptoe down the stairs and outside.

As the coach pulled away, she looked back. The morning was gray as death, Ramage Castle fog-shrouded. Even as she looked back, it was hidden by the mist.

Almost six months passed before Maggie saw her sister again. There were no more notes, and if it had not been for the regular food deliveries, she would not even have known if Kathleen was still alive.

During this time, the Donnevan family existed in a state of wary truce. The brothers had learned not to speak ill of their oldest sister upon pain of a tongue-lashing from Maggie.

The boys still went out looking for work, but there was none to be had. Maggie had to admire their persistence in the face of failure, and tried to be kinder and more thoughtful of them when they returned, empty-eyed and discouraged at the end of a day of fruitless searching. The one consolation was that, thanks to Kathleen, their bellies were filled. And Kevin seemed to be happy enough. The color had returned to his newly filled-out cheeks, and he laughed and chattered as he followed Maggie about the cottage as she performed her chores.

But Nora Donnevan was steadily deteriorating.

She had lost all touch with reality, and had to be hand-fed. The only times she showed awareness were during the weekly visits to John Donnevan's grave.

The result of this was that, subtly, slowly, Maggie was becoming the head of the household. Even Patrick and Dan, except when they thought their male pride was being trod upon, began to look to her for guidance.

Maggie's seventeenth birthday came and passed, without any notice whatsoever. She would have expected that from the boys, and her mother in her present condition; but Kathleen had always been a great one for remembering birthdays. To not receive even a note from her hurt Maggie deeply. It also increased her fears for Kathleen.

Three weeks after Maggie's birthday, Nora Donnevan expired in the night, in her sleep. Maggie had sensed it coming and was not surprised. She had prepared the boys for it. She immediately dispatched a message to Kathleen at Ramage Castle.

Maggie existed in a state of numbness during the preparations for the funeral and the wake. If she felt any grief, it was locked away deep inside her.

Again, she was concerned about Kathleen. There was no reply to the message, and no word since. Maggie felt anger stirring in her. At least Kathleen should have the decency to send a note of condolence!

At the cemetery, listening with the small group of mourners as the priest intoned the funeral service, Maggie was shaken out of her benumbed state by a stirring and a muttering from the people around her.

Heads craned around, and Maggie followed their glances. Her heart gave a great leap as she saw the black coach drawn up in the road outside the cemetery. A woman dressed in black was getting out of the coach. Now she turned and started toward the gravesite. Although she wore a heavy black veil, concealing her features, Maggie knew it was Kathleen.

Instead of coming to stand with the Donnevans, Kathleen stood a distance apart from the mourners, until the services were completed, and the mourners began to depart. They went with curious, sidelong glances at the woman in black. Kathleen stood without moving.

Maggie whispered to her brothers, "It's Kathleen. Come with me to speak to her."

Patrick shook his head. He said firmly, "No, we'll be having nothing to say to her. Come on, Dan." He nudged Dan with an elbow, and they walked off without looking back.

Maggie glared after them. *Damn the pair of them! Stubborn, pigheaded, blind! . . .*

A hand tugged at her sleeve. "Maggie, is that Kathleen?"

Maggie smiled down into Kevin's upturned face. "Yes, Kevin." She took his hand. "Let's go talk to her."

Kathleen stood rigidly as they approached, not lifting the veil.

"Kathleen, I thought you weren't coming."

She started to take Kathleen into her arms, but her sister warded her off. "There's not much time, Maggie," she said in a low voice. "I have to return to the castle at once. His Lordship forbade me

39

coming to Mum's funeral, he wouldn't even allow me to send an answer to your message. But he's gone off for the day, so I slipped away."

Maggie desperately wanted to see her sister's face, wanted to reach out and lift the veil, but something told her that the thick veil was worn as more than just an expression of grief. There must be marks on her face. For the first time since her mother's passing, Maggie was suddenly close to tears. In a choked voice she said, "They're gone now, Mum and Himself, Even you, Kathleen, you are gone from us!

"But there are still the four of you. You have to think of yourself, Maggie, and our brothers," Kathleen said fiercely. "That's really why I'm here."

Maggie stared. "I don't understand."

From the reticule on her arm, Kathleen took a small, kerchief-wrapped bundle. "Here." She placed it in Maggie's hands. "I want you to take these. There's more than enough for passage to America. The four of you must leave this accursed country!"

Still staring, Maggie said, "Without you?"

"Yes, without me. It has to be that way."

"But . . ." More puzzled than ever, Maggie glanced down at the bundle in her hands. Quickly she untied one corner and folded the kerchief back. She gasped. A fortune in jewels glittered in her hands. She knew little of precious stones, of their value, but she knew that, if these were real, they were worth a lot of money.

Kathleen snatched the bundle from her, her head swiveling about fearfully. She hastily retied it. "No one must see. No one must know, not even Patrick and Dan. You're resourceful, Maggie, you can convince them to go without telling them where the passage money came from."

"But where *did* those jewels come from?"

Kathleen hurried on feverishly, "I've figured it out. Sell the jewels, Maggie. Don't let them cheat you now. You can do it. Then buy passage to America. Not the East Coast, not New York. So many of our people have migrated there that they're being turned back unless they have in their possession a thousand American dollars. Go around the Horn and to the West Coast. It will cost more, but it is still a new country out there, and opportunities abound." She gave a harsh laugh. "I've been thinking on this for some time, and have listened carefully to His Lordship and his English friends. They think it a great jest that Irish people are going to the Land of Opportunity, only to be turned away." She gripped Maggie's hand tightly. "Promise me you'll go, as soon as possible. It's late spring now, and I've learned that most ships sail for America in the spring and summer, because of the winter storms."

With a flash of intuition, Maggie knew. "Kevin . . ." She touched Kevin on the shoulder. "Go join your brothers." She nodded toward where Patrick and Dan waited by the family cart. As Kevin started to protest, she said sharply, "Mind me now, go on along!"

Kathleen leaned quickly down to embrace her little brother, pressing her face to his, then gently pushing him away.

41

Kevin went, kicking up clods of dirt with his toe.

Maggie looked at Kathleen, trying to see her eyes behind the veil. "You stole those jewels from Lord Ramage, didn't you?"

"It doesn't matter. I want you to sell them and go. Today, tomorrow, the minute you can. Maggie, you have to find a new life for yourself and the boys. That's worth any price!"

"And the price you pay. . . . What will he do when he learns?"

"It'll be a while before he finds out. He had them hidden in the library, and I chanced to see him looking at them one day. Maggie, don't you understand? To people like the Donnevans, it's a fortune, it's life. To a man as rich as Lord Ramage, it's nothing!"

"But he will find out eventually. Then he'll have you charged with theft."

Kathleen was shaking her head. "He has too much pride for that. He would never admit publicly that his mistress dared take something of his, and by that time it won't matter, anyway. You'll be gone."

"Then why don't you come with us? That way you'll be out of his reach, too."

"No, no! The minute he finds me gone, he'll suspect something is amiss, even if he doesn't know the jewels are gone. Then he'll come looking for me. His Lordship is a very possessive man. He flies into a rage when something of his is taken from him. He'd come looking for me at once, long before we could get away. But if I'm back when he returns, he'll suspect nothing. If he finds out I've been gone, I'll tell him I had to attend Mum's funeral. He'll be furious at my disobeying him, but he'll get over that."

"Kathleen, he will find out eventually. I'm afraid for you."

"If the four of you are long out of his reach, I care not what he does to me. It will be well worth it. If you don't do this, all I have been through will be for naught."

The timbre of Kathleen's voice told Maggie that it would be useless to argue further. She had her mind set on this, and nothing was going to dissuade her.

"I will do as you wish, Kathleen, but with a heavy heart. You will never be out of my thoughts and prayers. I will write to you. If fortune smiles on us in the New World, perhaps you can join us."

"Perhaps. I would like that." Yet there was a distant note in Kathleen's voice, as if she was withdrawing, as if she was already dead to her sister and brothers. "Now I must go. I have lingered overlong as it is." She reached out and hugged Maggie fiercely. "I love you, dear Maggie. Maybe, in time, Patrick and Dan will come to think more kindly of me. God go with all of you," she said in a choked voice. Then she was gone, almost running toward the coach.

Maggie stood watching until the coach vanished from her sight. Then she turned a determined face toward the cart, and her waiting brothers.

Kathleen's words had implanted a sense of urgency in Maggie's mind; and as she cooked and served the boys their supper, she tried to think of how best to approach the subject of emigration.

Patrick was the first to finish his meal. He started to push back from the table.

"Wait, Patrick," Maggie said sharply. "There's something we have to talk about, all of us, including Kevin."

The other two boys stopped eating, and all three stared at her in surprise. Under their combined stares, Maggie's resolution faltered.

Then she remembered the sacrifice that Kathleen was making, and steeled herself to plunge ahead. "We have a decision to make. We have to leave here. We have to . . ."

"Leave here?" Patrick interrupted. "How can we leave here? Sure, and this has been our home for as long as I can remember!"

"What kind of a home is it now?" she said scornfully. "A place of hunger and death. But for Kathleen, we would have starved to death long since!"

A thoughtful look on his face, Dan said quietly, "Where did you have in mind for us to go, Maggie?"

She took a deep breath. "To America."

"America!" Patrick roared. "You're addled, dear sister. To go to America would cost a fortune!"

"I will manage it. My promise on that."

"*You* will manage it? You're a slip of a girl. Passage to America for the four of us would cost a hundred pounds or more. Aye, you'll manage it!" Patrick's booming laughter sounded. Then he became still, his eyes burning into hers. "I'm after thinking you mean it."

"I do mean it. Have I ever made a promise to any of you that I didn't keep?"

"But how will you get the money?"

Maggie wouldn't bend. "That, I'm not going to tell you. There's no reason for you to know. All I want is for the three of you to agree to go. . . ."

Kevin broke in eagerly, "I'll go, Maggie!"

"Silence!" Patrick thundered. "You're but a tad, you have no say in this." His fierce gaze clung to Maggie. "It seems to me you're getting mighty uppity for a lass of only sixteen."

"Seventeen. I just had a birthday that none of you took heed of."

"Seventeen, then." He made a gesture as if brushing away a fly. "Sure, and you're taking a lot on yourself, telling us what to do. As the eldest, I'm the man of the Donnevan family now!"

"And a grand job you're doing of it!" she retorted. "I'm not telling you, Patrick. I'm asking. Don't you see, it's the only way for us. In America, we can make a fresh start. I've read of great fortunes being made. Working together, we can do the same."

Softly now, Patrick said, "Does Kathleen have a hand in this?"

"Leave Kathleen out of it!" Then she voiced a silent plea to Kathleen for forgiveness, and said, "You claim Kathleen has brought great shame to the Donnevan name. I should think you'd be happy to be far away from her."

Patrick opened and closed his mouth, then simply stared at her, speechless. Maggie never removed her eyes from his, until he finally dropped his gaze, looking down at the table.

"Maggie," Dan said, "I think you're right. We will never get anywhere here. Even when the potato famine is finally over, what can we do but grub away our lives? I'm with Kevin. I think it will be a grand adventure, starting a new life in a new country. There's a gold rush out in a place called California. I heard that gold nuggets are lying on the ground, a fortune there just for the picking!"

Maggie started to debate with him about that. Hunting for gold wasn't exactly what she had in mind, but now wasn't the time to discuss that. First things first. She had to convince them to go with her.

Looking at Patrick's lowered head, she said quietly, "Patrick?"

His head came up. His face was red and angry. "Why be asking me? Seems to me you've all made up your mind. What does my say count?" He came to his feet, almost toppling the rickety old table. "Aye, just because I'm the oldest, I don't have anything to say!"

Turning, he strode out of the cottage and into the night.

"Patrick, wait!" Dan called after him.

Maggie stayed him with a hand on his arm. "Let him walk it off, Danny. You know how impulsive and quick to anger he is." Inside, she was exultant. She knew now that Patrick would come around. He would grumble and drag his feet, and put as many obstacles as possible in her way, but in the end he would be with them.

The Donnevans would face the future together, whatever it held for them.

All the Donnevans except one.

For a fleeting moment Maggie was torn asunder by grief for Kathleen. Then she resolutely forced all thoughts of her sister from her mind.

Chapter Three

A month short of Maggie's eighteenth birthday, she and her brothers stood at the rail of the 140-ton brig, *Indian Princess*, as the vessel crept north up the California coast. The ship's destination, San Francisco, was, according to ship gossip, only a number of days distant.

It had been a long, dreary voyage. Maggie had thought it not possible to experience a more miserable existence than she had known in Ireland, but she had been badly mistaken.

The long voyage across the Atlantic from Limerick, Ireland, on board the schooner, *Shannon's Way*, had been their first ordeal. The passengers had been crowded below decks in terrible conditions; there had been no privacy; their food had been little better than slop; and the air had been foul with human excrement and vomit.

The destination of *Shannon's Way* had been Charleston, South Carolina. Most ships carrying Irish emigrants to the United States sailed to New York, but Maggie well knew that they wouldn't be welcome there.

In Charleston, they had boarded the *Indian Princess*, joining the ten other passengers already on board. The *Indian Princess* was out of Boston, with a cargo consisting of house frames and shingles, plus sixty thousand feet of sawed lumber, badly needed commodities in San Francisco, Maggie was told.

Crude bunks had been constructed below, put together with raw lumber. Maggie understood that the bunks would be dismantled in San Francisco, where the planks sold for ten dollars a board foot.

Maggie was the only female passenger, and her brothers rigged up a curtain made of old sailcloth around the bunk, assuring her of a measure of privacy.

The food was somewhat better on the *Indian Princess*, and the captain, a shrewd New Englander, made numerous stops at ports along the way for provisions and fresh water for the casks.

But even with better food and less cramped living conditions, the voyage had been far from comfortable. They ran into several storms. One such storm, encountered as they rounded the Cape, lasted for two days, and several times Maggie had been sure that the ship would capsize or be driven to the bottom by the tremendous waves. The boys, especially Patrick, suffered spells of seasickness, although Maggie seemed immune to the complaint. In addition, Patrick bedeviled her constantly to tell him her plans. As eldest, he said, he had a right to know.

But Maggie couldn't tell him what she didn't know herself. She only knew that somehow, some way, they would manage to find some gainful employment, or some business that they could build together.

When they finally approached the continent of North America again, the weather grew calmer, their progress smoother and faster. Those suffering from seasickness began to revive, and now that San Francisco was nearing, all talk concerned the gold fields.

Even Patrick became excited. He told Maggie, "I was talking to a couple of the boyos about the gold strike, in what they call the Mother Lode. They said that gold is so plentiful, you can just pick it up off the ground by the bucketfuls!"

"Have these boyos been there yet?" she asked tartly.

He said in astonishment, "Of course not, little sister. That's where they're going now."

"Then, how do they know this to be true?"

"They've been told by others who have been there. That's where everybody is heading. Aye, I'm glad we came now, Maggie. Sure, and I can hardly wait to get to the gold fields and make us rich!"

Maggie gave a little snort and turned away to avoid discussing it further. Hunting for gold wasn't what she had in mind. She had heard all the stories, too, but her innate common sense told her that most of them were highly exaggerated. The gold rush had started in 1849, and it was now almost four years later. If there was any gold left, it would not be lying about for the picking.

She had never told the boys where the money for their passage came from, nor how much she had. She had sold most of the jewels in Limerick for just under a thousand pounds, and had six hundred pounds left. It should be enough, if she used it wisely, to start some business endeavor.

Maggie had kept several jewels, one a large diamond. She carried them in a small pouch attached to a chain which hung around her neck, the pouch snug between her breasts.

Maggie's first sight of California was dismaying. It was July now, and all she could see were brown hills, with only a few patches of greenery here and there. The ship sailed into the port at Los Angeles for provisions and fresh water. All Maggie saw were a huddle of miserable adobe huts, and the ubiquitous brown hills. In the distance was a blue smudge, which she took to be a range of mountains.

So unlike Ireland, green Ireland. Even during famine and hardship, Ireland was always green. She felt like weeping, but stoutly refused to do so. Was all of the West Coast to be like this?

No passengers left the ship in Los Angeles, but one new man came on board just before departure time. Maggie was leaning on the rail on the land side, and she eyed him curiously, as the small boat moved out from shore and came alongside the ship.

The new arrival stood up, waiting for the Jacob's ladder to be lowered. He was tall, thin, not young, probably in his mid-fifties. His hair was bright red, streaked with gray. He was a homely individual, and Maggie thought he was dressed oddly. He wore a faded red flannel shirt, that looked more like a man's undergarment than a shirt. Bright red suspenders held up black, stiff-legged britches stuffed into high, flat-heeled boots. The only baggage he had was a dirty canvas bag slung over one shoulder. On top of his head was a large, broad-brimmed hat, greasy from much handling.

He clambered awkwardly up the Jacob's ladder, and over the railing. He took two lurching steps, and Maggie noticed that he had a pronounced limp. Now he removed the hat, and leaned over the railing to spit a brown stream into the water, his prominent Adam's apple bobbing.

Maggie averted her gaze in disgust. Snuff, he had a mouthful of snuff. What a filthy habit!

Maggie remained where she was as the ship got underway, creeping slowly out to the open sea.

Suddenly a brisk breeze stiffened the sails, and the vessel listed slightly to port. Maggie gripped the railing to keep from losing her balance.

A figure careened into her, bumping her away from the rail. She would have fallen if her arm hadn't been seized in a pair of calloused hands.

"Beg pardon, little lady," said a whiskey-coarsened voice, with a slight Swedish twang. "Yah. Always clumsy as an ox on these things. I never seem to get my sea legs, as the sailor boys put it."

It was the man she had seen boarding a short time ago. Up close, his face had a dour, melancholy cast. His eyes were a faded blue.

"You should watch where you're going!" she retorted.

For a moment he glowered at her. Then he removed his dirty hat, bobbing his head. "Yah, I should. I sure am sorry, little lady."

He didn't look the least bit sorry, Maggie thought. Yet there was something appealing about his long, sad face, and Maggie, belatedly remembering his limp, found herself relenting. She said, "It's all right. I don't think I've found my sea legs either, and I've been on this boat, and another one, nigh a year." She felt herself coloring slightly. A lady didn't use the word "legs" in the presence of a man.

He didn't move away. Instead, he leaned on the railing a respectable distance away. "Came around the Horn, yah?"

"Yes."

"I know just how you feel. I made that dreary trip myself four years back."

He pronounced "just" with a "y", and Maggie hid a smile behind her hand. "Then I gather you're not a seafaring man by trade?"

"A sailorman? Nah! I'm a Scandie."

"A Scandie? What's that?"

"It's what the fellers in the logging business call a Swede or any Norski from the old country, come to work as loggers in Maine or Minnee-sota. Timber's about all logged over back there, that's why I came out here. Name's Olaf Yorgenson, little lady. J-o-r-genson."

Maggie found herself smiling again at his odd accent. He stuck out a huge paw, and after a moment's hesitation, she took it. "I'm Maggie Donnevan."

"Yah, an Irisher. I thought so. Don't often see a lady such as yourself bound for the gold fields. With your husband, be you?"

"No, I'm not married." She added hastily, "I'm traveling with my brothers."

"Going to look for gold, are they?"

"I . . ." She paused. "I'm not in favor of it, but Patrick, my oldest brother, has his heart set on it."

"Yah, got the gold fever. Everybody has, it seems. Dad-damned fools, you ask me." He snorted. "Any gold a man gets this late he works for, less'n he's lucky and makes a new strike. And that ain't too likely." He spat a brown stream over the railing.

Maggie again felt revulsion, but she was interested now. This was the first person she'd talked to on board who didn't have dreams of making his fortune looking for gold. "That's not where you're going?"

"By Thor, nah! Nah, I'm on my way back to God's country."

"Where's that, Mr. Jorgenson?"

"Washington Territory. I'm in the logging business, and *that* boom is yust starting up there."

"I hope the country's nothing like this," Maggie gestured toward the shore. "It seems that all I've seen for weeks has been dry, flat, brown land."

"You can be sure it's nothing like this up yonder." He waxed enthusiastic. "Up around Puget Sound, my country, it's green, green all the year round. Green forests, with trees so thick a man can't ride a horse into them. So thick it's almost

55

nighttime in there at high noon. Little lady, there's hundreds of square miles of virgin timber up there, yust waiting for the cutting."

"You're in logging, you say. What do you do?"

"I'm a bullwhacker. I was a faller—that's the man who stands on one end of a springboard, his partner on the other end, and chops away until the tree is about to fall, then leaps free. One day my axe slipped, and I chopped off two of my toes. That ended my days on the springboard. I couldn't keep my balance anymore. So I became a bullwhacker. Bothers me some to walk, but I manage it."

"I'm afraid to ask, but what's a bullwhacker?"

Olaf Jorgenson laughed. "I drive a team of oxen pulling logs along the skidroads to the water."

Maggie threw up her hands, laughing. "Whisht! No more! I don't understand half of what you're saying! But tell me this, Mr. Jorgenson—"

"Call me Olaf, please, little lady."

"You talk about a timber boom, and say it's just beginning. How much money would it take to start in the logging business?"

"Depends on how big a business you're talking of. For a small outfit, what we call gypos—that's an independent bunch who cuts trees here and there, then sells the logs to the sawmill operators—for that, if you don't need oxen, it don't cost much. Yust enough to buy axes, saws, a few other pieces of equipment, then the pay of whatever loggers you need."

"Could you give me an estimate of how much?"

"Oh, for that kind of an outfit, maybe five hundred dollars, somewhere around there."

Maggie's mind was struggling to convert her

hoard of pounds into dollars. She said absently, "Is that what you're planning on doing up in Washington Territory, Olaf?"

"Nah. I'll go back to bullwhacking. By Thor, I'd like to have my own logging crew, but I can never save up enough cash. Course some men are natural-born to work for others all their natural lives. That's me. I did think maybe Lars and me . . ." His face lit up. "That's my boy. Twenty-one, he is now. A fine lad, and the best faller I've ever seen in action. But my wife, Helga, she got bad sick this past year." His face settled back into its melancholy lines. "It's her lungs, the doctors say. The damp weather and fog up there ain't good for that. That's why I'm down here. I brought Helga down and found a place for her to stay out in the desert. To pay for our passage and money for her to live on took all the money Lars and me had saved. . . ."

"Oh, I am sorry, Olaf," Maggie said in quick sympathy. She placed a hand on his arm.

"It's all right, little lady," he said gruffly. "I yust hope Helga gets well, is all."

"So do I."

"That's right thoughty of you, Maggie." He patted her hand.

Suddenly, Maggie was seized from behind, lifted off her feet, and set down with a jarring thump a few feet away. Patrick, eyes blazing, stepped in front of her. "You keep your hands off my sister, old man!"

Olaf Jorgenson bristled. "Old man, is it?" He doubled his fists. "If it's a fight you're after, young feller, by Thor, I'll oblige you!"

"Oh, Patrick, don't be such an oaf!" Maggie snapped. "We were having a friendly conversation, Mr. Jorgenson and me, and you come charging in like some blithering idiot!"

Patrick looked chagrined. He fumbled for words. "Well, it's my job to be seeing after you now that Himself is gone, and from where I stood . . ."

Maggie set her lips. "Patrick!"

Patrick ducked his head. " 'Tis sorry I am, Mr. Jorgenson, but a man has to look after his women-folk!"

"Next time, Patrick, be sure I *need* looking after before you jump in!" Maggie snapped.

Olaf Jorgenson was still unappeased. "By Thor, I don't like some young whelp accusing me of something like that. I may be yust a plain logger, but I got my principles, and I got a wife and son. I'm a family man!"

Olaf still looked mad enough to fight, and knowing Patrick's temper, Maggie intervened again. "Patrick is impulsive, Olaf. He has a way of jumping before he thinks."

"You'll learn better out here, young feller. You go around with that chip on your shoulder, and some of these tough coots here will gun you down. Good day, young lady. Tell your brother Olaf won't be bothering you again!" He started away.

Maggie called after him, but he limped on. She whirled on Patrick. "Now see what you've done! The first time I've made a friend on this whole dreary voyage, and you have to insult him!"

"I said I'm sorry. But you are my sister, Maggie, and just a wee colleen. Sure, and it's my duty to be looking after you."

58

"I don't need looking after. When are you going to learn that? Now go away, go back to your gold-crazy friends, and leave me alone!"

It wasn't until later that Maggie realized Olaf Jorgenson had planted an idea in her mind. It blossomed, the closer they came to San Francisco. She tried to talk to Olaf about Washington Territory again, but he was still offended; he was courteous, but no longer friendly.

Maggie sighed to herself. Men, the best of them were a difficult lot!

Yet her spirits were up. They were nearing the end of the long voyage, and what glimpses she got of the coastline were heartening. The sere brown hills had given way to rocky cliffs and shorelines of powerful beauty. Atop the rocky heights, wind-twisted trees were outlined against green scrub, and as they progressed farther north, the trees grew thicker and taller until there were veritable armies of them marching up the hills that rose high above the Pacific.

On the morning they entered San Francisco Bay, Maggie and Kevin were standing at the railing. Earlier, they had run into a dense fog—an increasing occurrence as they had moved north—but it was now lifting, and bright shafts of sunlight were breaking through to illuminate the city of San Francisco as she rested on her green bed of hills. The north shore across the bay was thickly forested, and Maggie eyed the trees with interest. *Whisht, but they are tall! Who would have thought that any of God's green things could grow to such a height!*

59

She was deep in thought when Olaf's gruff voice said beside her, "Yah, it rains more here than down below, little lady. That's why it's greener. The farther north you get, the more rain and greenery."

She looked at him, pleased. "Olaf! I'm happy you're friendly to me again!"

He smiled sheepishly. "Yah. I got over my mad at your feisty brother." He spat over the railing. "Besides, I like you, little lady, and I decided 'twasn't your fault your kin has a big mouth." He gazed toward the shore. "And soon as I can find a ship going north, I'll be on my way back to God's country. That cheers a man up some."

"Olaf, I'd like to ask you something. You said you'd go back to work bullwhacking when you got back up there. Who for?"

Olaf shrugged. "Whoever'll hire me. I was working for Jake Fargo's crew. Lars, he's still working for Jake. I can probably get my old job back."

"If I . . ." Maggie paused, trying to phrase it just right; "Suppose I, and my brothers, were to go to Washington Territory and start our own logging company? Would you go to work for me? We would certainly need someone with your experience to guide us."

Olaf gaped at her in astonishment. "*You!* You start a logging outfit? Why, you're only a slip of a girl!"

Maggie bridled. "I'll be eighteen soon, and I've heard that girls grow up fast here."

Grave now, he nodded wisely. "Yah, that's true. But a woman giving orders to a bunch of loggers? Don't know how they'll take to that. Besides, it would take money, and you with no experience . . ."

"I think I have enough money to start. Olaf . . ." She put her hand on his arm. "At least think about it? What can you lose? You'll earn wages. If I can't make it, you can always get another job. You said jobs up there were plentiful."

"That's true." He studied her, blue eyes thoughtful. "By Thor, I think you mean it. You've got the sand and the spirit. And you're smart, you'd catch on quick." He spat a brown stream. "My boy, Lars, we always work together."

"That's no problem," she said eagerly. "You said he was the best . . . what was it?"

"Faller. And that he is, but there may be a hitch there. I don't know how he'd take to working for a woman, either."

"There's a way around that. If the men balk at taking orders from a woman, Patrick can give the orders."

"Nah, nah!" Olaf took a step back. "I ain't taking orders from that mouthy young feller. A fly-off-the-handle gent like him could get us all killed. Fact is, I don't know how long he'd last himself. It's a dangerous business, logging. Don't know how many men get killed ever year."

"Then you give the orders. You can be my . . . what would you call it? Superintendent?"

"In the logging business, we call it 'bull-of-the-woods,' or boss logger."

"You can be my boss logger, then. I'll see to it that Patrick behaves." She fell silent, looking off.

"What's wrong, Maggie? One minute you're all afire with this idea. But now you look like somebody yust dumped you into Puget Sound."

"Patrick. He's going to be a problem. He's dead

set on hunting for gold. I'm going to have trouble changing his mind."

"If you can't stop him from that, how are you going to keep a leash on him if'n you go logging?"

"That would be different. If I can get him to agree to go up there," she set her chin, "he'll also agree that I'm in charge."

"Although you ain't said right out, it strike me you've got the money, not your brothers."

"That's right. My brothers don't even know about it."

"Seems to me that whoever holds the purse strings calls the tune."

"I'm afraid that when I mention my plans to him, Patrick will go charging off to the gold fields on his own. He's stubborn as a pig."

Olaf grunted. "By Thor, I'd let him go. He'd be no great loss."

"Oh, no!" Maggie's voice was firm. "We Donnevans stick together. I promised that to myself, and my sister."

Olaf nodded. "Can't fault you for that. I admire family loyalty." A hint of mischief showed in his eyes. "Say, I yust thought of something. You have any snakes in Ireland?"

Maggie glanced at him in surprise. "Irish folklore is full of tales of dragons and snakes, but in all of Ireland there are none that I know of. The legends say that St. Patrick drove them out."

Olaf grinned wickedly. "I have a suggestion for you then. . . ."

Although the surroundings were beautiful, Maggie was, to some extent, disappointed by San Francisco. The sight of the great bay with hundreds of ships of every description at anchor fascinated her. But the houses sprawling across the hills mostly looked jerry-built, and a lot of construction was going on. She was told that a fire had recently burned most of the city to the ground, a not uncommon occurrence, and it was being rebuilt again. She could see why the demand for lumber was so great. She was also told that there were many fine mansions on the hills farther inland, but she didn't see them. She was determined not to remain in San Francisco longer than was necessary. She had yet to tell her brothers of her plans.

The waterfront teemed with rough types. Almost every man she saw wore a weapon of some kind. Drunken sailors and miners staggered along the streets, and it was with some difficulty that they were able to finally find clean lodgings not far from the waterfront.

Patrick was eager to start for the gold fields. "The others who came with us on board ship are leaving as soon as possible, Maggie."

She hedged. "We all need a rest first, Patrick, from the long sea voyage. And I have to do some shopping."

"We shouldn't wait a minute, little sister. The gold may all be gone before we ever get there!"

"For all you know, it is gone already," she retorted. "After all, the first discovery of gold was in forty-eight, and that's a long time back."

Despite Patrick's grumblings, Maggie and Kevin spent two days wandering through the stores, buying necessities, thus avoiding her two older brothers during the day. But every night Patrick drummed at her about the gold fields, threatening to go off on his own. Since he hadn't a shilling to his name, Maggie wasn't really too worried by his threats.

On the third morning, Olaf Jorgenson sought her out. He had found passage on a small ship sailing in two days time for Washington Territory, its final destination a town called Port Townsend. "I have asked, Maggie, and they have room for you and your brothers. Have you told them yet?"

"Not yet." Maggie sighed. "It's cowardly of me, I know, but I've been putting it off."

"Well, I made up my mind. I'll throw in with you, if you still want, me and Lars. He'll do what his pa wants. But I'm sailing on that ship."

Maggie squared her shoulders. "Book passage for us, and I'll give you money to start buying the equipment we need. I'll have it out with Patrick and Dan today."

Olaf looked at her curiously. "You're that sure, are you?"

Maggie wasn't all that sure, but she said, "I'm that sure."

She collected her brothers and told them they had to have a serious talk.

Patrick smiled broadly. "Well, and it's about time. Aye, that it is!" He rubbed his hands together briskly. " 'Tis a fortune we'll soon be having, we Donnevans."

Since their rooms were so small, Maggie led them down to the dock area where they found a fairly isolated spot. Then she faced them, hands on her hips. "We're not going to the Mother Lode, Brother Patrick."

Patrick was thunderstruck. "What are you saying, lass?"

"We're not joining the other fools rushing off. A hunt for fool's gold, some call it. Haven't you seen the derelicts on the streets here? They spent everything on their search for gold and found nothing. Now they're penniless, poor creatures."

"They didn't have the Donnevan luck."

Maggie stared at him unblinkingly, a wry smile lifting the corners of her mouth. "I'd laugh, Patrick, if it wasn't so tragic. Look back on our life. Any Donnevan luck has all been bad."

"Maybe they didn't work hard enough," he said obstinately. "You know we're hard workers, Brother Dan and me."

"Hard work has nothing to do with it. It *is* all luck, finding gold. It's all a gamble. No, the Donnevan clan is going to where the real treasure is."

Hands on hips, he challenged her, "Sure, and where is that, little sister?"

"Washington Territory. We're going into the logging business."

Patrick was struck speechless. It was Dan who said, "Logging business? Are you daft, Maggie?"

"Look at this town." She swept a hand around. "The gold rush and the fires leveling San Francisco every few months have created a great hunger for building materials, for lumber. In Washington Territory, there are thousands upon thousands of giant trees, all there for those who have the will and the experience to cut them. And the sawmills there will buy all the logs we can supply, at good prices."

Dan said, "But Maggie, you said 'experience.'

What experience at logging do we have? None, I'm thinking."

"I met a man on the ship, Olaf Jorgenson. He's been a logger all his life. He's agreed to go to work for us, give us the benefit of his experience."

"Us?" Patrick sneered. "Not me. I'm looking for gold, be sure of that, Maggie Donnevan."

"How?" She faced him squarely. "You don't even have the money to buy a pick and shovel."

"I'll make out. And what are you after using to start this logging business?"

"I have enough funds. I got us this far, didn't I?"

"It strikes me you're taking a lot on yourself! Aye, a mere colleen telling us what to do. Who's going to run this logging business?"

"I am. I want that understood from the start. I can do it, with or without you, Patrick. But for me you'd be back in Ireland, eating rotting potatoes. I want the Donnevans to stick together."

Patrick was shaking his head. "You'll be going without me."

"Dan?"

Dan looked imploringly at his brother, and received a stony glare in return. With a sigh he said, "I'm with you, Maggie."

"Me, too!" Kevin chimed in.

Absently ruffling Kevin's hair, Maggie said, "Well, Brother Patrick?"

"No. I've made up me mind."

"We need you, Patrick. Would you let little Kevin here face the perils of a wilderness without your strong shoulder to lean on?"

"How can you say that to me?" he cried. "It's your doing, none of mine!"

But Maggie felt a tiny throb of triumph. He was weakening; for the first time he sounded unsure. He had always adored Kevin, was very protective of him, and the thought of being separated from his young brother must be painful.

Maggie remembered Olaf's half-humorous suggestion. She said, "Do you know what a rattlesnake is, Patrick?"

He peered at her suspiciously. "Rattlesnake? Aye, I've heard of such creatures. What are you saying?"

For as long as Maggie could remember, Patrick had been terrified of anything that crawled. Hating to take advantage of this in him, she hardened her heart. "I'm told that the land around the Mother Lode country abounds in rattlesnakes. Thick as your arm, as long as a man is tall, and deadly poisonous. They have rattles, I'm told, but by the time you hear the sound of the rattles, it's too late. They strike like a lightning flash."

He scoffed. "Sure, and it's a tall tale you're making up, Maggie Donnevan."

Dan was grinning, and Kevin was laughing behind his hand. It had always been a great jest to them that brawny Patrick, afraid of neither man nor beast, should be absolutely terrified of crawling things. She glared at them, and they immediately sobered.

"No, Patrick, I am not making up tales. It's the truth I'm telling you. If you don't believe me, ask any man who has been there. Many of the gold hunters, I'm told, kill them and make belts of their skins."

Patrick gave a great shudder. Maggie continued,

"But up in Washington Territory, there's hardly a snake to be found, and those few, as harmless as kittens."

Patrick heaved a great sigh. "You win, little sister." He reached out to pull Kevin against him. "It's not me wish to see the Donnevan clan separated. And little Kevin here will need someone to see that he grows up to be a man." He tried one last sneer. "You, to be sure, will be so busy making our fortunes in this logging business."

"And so will you, Patrick." Maggie concealed her feeling of triumph. "To succeed, we'll all have to work very hard."

Then she smiled widely and stepped up to kiss him. For the first time in Maggie's memory, Patrick, never overly affectionate, swept her into his arms. Now that she had won, Maggie had to fight back tears.

He said gruffly, "You didn't think I'd be after letting you all go off and leave me, did you lass?"

A few short weeks later, on board a small frigate, the *Chinook*, Maggie stood at the rail and watched the shoreline of Washington Territory glide past. The bluffs towering above the beach were all covered with giant trees, growing so thickly that she couldn't see but a few feet into the dark forests. In other places, the trees came almost down to the water.

"Are we sailing off Washington now?"

Olaf Jorgenson, leaning beside her, spat a brown stream into the sea. "Yah. That's Washington Territory you're seeing, Maggie."

Maggie shivered. "It looks so dark back in there. It's almost frightening!"

Olaf chuckled. "You ain't seen the biggest ones yet. Wait until we start sailing through the Strait, and then around Puget Sound. That's where logging first started up here, along the coast of the Strait. Ships, especially them new clipper ships, always need logs for spars. There, they found the best timber for spars ever before seen. I was working around there when I first arrived. By Thor, it was something! Took a whole crew a whole day yust to clear the underbrush around a tree afore cutting."

"This Port Townsend where the ship's going . . . is that good logging country?"

"Nah." He shook his head, and spat. "It's a little bitty spit of land, long since logged off. They have a fort there guarding the entrance to the Sound. It ain't nothing much but a seaport town. Saloons and whores, mostly. A spree place for seafaring men. A dad-damned rough lot, all of them." He grinned. "Not that a bunch of loggers are much better. They all come in there to spend their pay and carouse. I've heard it said that so much whiskey has been spilled on the streets of Port Townsend that it's soaked down ten feet into the mud. And mud it is. Rains so much up here, the streets are mostly mud puddles." He wrinkled his nose. "It does stink, Port Townsend, no denying that. But anyways, Maggie, that ain't where the good logging is at."

"Then where, Olaf? Where is the best place to start?"

"Down around the Kitsap Peninsula," he said judiciously. "That's located down the Sound aways.

A couple of sawmills built there the last year or so, and thriving. Pope and Talbot built the best one at Port Gamble. Fact is, they built and own the whole dad-damned town. They're always willing to buy logs from independent loggers."

"We'll have to get on another boat at Port Townsend?"

"Yah. These sailing vessels don't like to venture too far down into the Sound. They sometimes have trouble finding a breeze to sail out again. Sometimes they have to hire a boat with steam to tow 'em out into the Strait." He spat. "Then, new paddle-wheelers are the coming thing. They don't need wind. Ain't but a few hereabouts yet, but they're the coming thing, you can bet your wad on it!"

"I just hope we bought enough equipment in San Francisco for us to get started," Maggie said worriedly.

"What you haven't got we can buy in Port Townsend. The onliest reason I advised buying in San Francisco is 'cause you'd save money buying there, even after paying the freight charges up here. Everything, even victuals, is higher by far here in the Territory."

Maggie was still concerned. What she hadn't told Olaf, what she hadn't told anyone, was the fact that her funds were rapidly dwindling. She'd had all the English pounds changed into dollars in San Francisco. After buying axes, saws, and the other items Olaf recommended, and paying their passage to Port Townsend, she had less than four hundred dollars in cash left. If she had to buy much more equipment, she would have nothing left but the few jewels in the bag between her breasts.

Olaf had reassured her on two things. "Like I already said, you can get along without a team of oxen at first. This spot I know about, we can roll the logs right down to the water. And, long as you can feed them, you won't have to pay whatever loggers we hire until you sell your first batch of logs."

"This Port Townsend sounds rough and pretty dangerous for the likes of us. Will we have to stay there long?"

"Hope not. My boy, Lars, is supposed to meet us there. Leastways, I writ him to. I been thinking on it. He'll likely take to you and be glad to work for a different crew, without me ordering him to. Two years now we both been working for a coot, name of Jake Fargo. A tough, mean sonofabitch." Olaf had long since stopped apologizing to Maggie for his rough language. "He'll work a man from can to can't, dawn 'til dark, and then try to cheat him out'n his proper wages, if he's able. Many men working in the logging business can't count too good. My boy now, he's got quite a bit of schooling," Olaf said proudly. "So Jake can't cheat us. Not only is Jake mean as a badger, but he's a big booger. Big as your brother Patrick, or my boy, who ain't no midget. Yah, I've seen Jake Fargo hammer a man into the ground with those fists of his, then put the hobnails to him. Or bash his head in with that pickaroon he carries."

"Hobnails?" Maggie looked puzzled.

"Big-headed nails, on the soles of a logger's boots. Helps him climb a tree, keeps him from falling off a log when herding them along in the water."

"This Jake Fargo uses hobnailed boots on men he fights?" Maggie asked in horror, envisioning the results of such an action.

"That he does, Maggie."

She shuddered. "He sounds like a terrible, cruel man!" She was afraid to ask what a pickaroon was.

"Yah, that's Jake Fargo, all right."

A few days later, Maggie stood again at the railing as the *Chinook* sailed into the Juan de Fuca Strait. The ship hugged the south shore, and Maggie gazed in wonder and awe at the thousands upon thousands of great trees marching from the edge of the shore as far as the eye could see. It was a wondrous sight calculated to make a person feel very small and insignificant in the face of God's handiwork.

The day was bright and sunny, if a little chill, and to the south she saw a towering range of mountains, capped by snow. For the first time she felt doubt about the wisdom of coming here. The forest looked impenetrable. How could something as puny as mere man cut down those giant trees? In a way, it seemed a shame, almost a sacrilege, to bring those trees crashing to earth, trees that had stood for years, only God himself knew how many.

Maggie shoved such thoughts from her mind. Others were cutting down trees, and making fortunes, so why shouldn't the Donnevans?

The voyage through the Strait was rough. The wind was strong, and time after time they passed through rain showers. Sometimes the rain was so heavy Maggie could see only a few yards away from the ship. But when they rounded a point of land and turned south, the wind ceased to buffet the ship; the land protected them.

It was mid-afternoon when Maggie stood with Olaf and Kevin at the railing to watch as the *Chinook* rounded the headland and sailed into the sheltered harbor. Their first sight of Port Townsend was not encouraging. There was a single waterfront street, with about thirty buildings, all constructed of pine boards, thatched with shingles, canvas, and wood slabs. A high bluff ran parallel to the street, and on top of the bluff Maggie saw two three-story buildings. One was still under construction. The other, while completed, was as yet unpainted.

Her face must have mirrored her dismay for Olaf laughed heartily. "Yah, that's Port Townsend. 'Bout the biggest village along Puget Sound. Wait until we step ashore. Yah, 'tis said that newcomers can recognize Port Townsend, even on the darkest night, by the stink."

Maggie was hesitant about asking what he meant, and he didn't enlighten her further. There was one rickety wharf, on wooden pilings, extending out into the small harbor like a finger. The *Chinook* came to a stop, bumping hard against the splintered wooden edge of the wharf. A number of people, all men, Maggie saw, were gathered for the arrival of the ship. They shouted raucously, and hoorahed, many waving bottles.

"Yah, they're soused," Olaf said. "The coming of

a ship is still a great event for the people of Port Townsend."

"Is there a place to stay?" Maggie asked.

"They were building a hotel when I left. Should be open by this time. I'm sure they'll have lodgings for a lady such as yourself, Maggie. Ain't ever day a lady arrives here. The females venturing here are mostly whores."

Only one other ship was docked, a smaller but longer sailing vessel, with two cannon mounted on deck. Olaf jerked his thumb at it. "Revenue cutter. Since Washington Territory became part of the United States, the Treasury Department got right interested in collecting duty on British whiskey being smuggled in. That there cutter was sent here yust before I left." Olaf laughed. "Onliest thing I ever heard it catching was an Indian canoe bringing down a keg of French brandy."

Patrick and Dan had already collected the family's meager belongings, and the Donnevans and Olaf went down the gangplank to the wharf. Olaf had advised leaving their logging equipment on board until tomorrow.

Ribald comments were aimed at Maggie by the motley collection of men. Maggie clutched her reticule, containing the rest of her money, to her bosom. Olaf, Patrick, and Dan formed a sort of protective shield around her as they moved toward the shore.

Olaf kept craning his neck this way and that. "Where's that boy of mine? He was supposed to meet me here."

Now Maggie wrinkled her nose as she caught a whiff of the rank odors Olaf had mentioned. Then they reached the street, which was nothing but wet sand, with no sidewalks, and Maggie saw where the smell was coming from. A dead horse lay in the middle of the street, swarming with flies, and farther on was the partly decomposed carcass of a dog.

Maggie held her nose. "Whisht! Why don't they take those dead animals away and bury them?"

"Who'd do it? Nobody gets paid for that." Olaf shrugged. "You around long enough, you get used to it . . ." He broke off to bellow, "Lars! Daddamned, boy, I thought something had gone amiss with you!"

He limped on ahead toward an approaching young man, bigger even than Patrick. He had a rough jumble of blond hair, laughing blue eyes, and a ruddy complexion. The two big men came together in a jarring embrace, and pounded each other on the back.

As Maggie and her brothers stopped beside them, a beaming Olaf faced around, one big hand still gripping the youth's shoulder. "This here is my boy, Lars."

Starting with Maggie, Olaf introduced the Donnevans one by one to his son.

Lars' face turned red as he doffed his hat to Maggie. He smiled somewhat shyly at her, and his gaze never left her face while he mumbled greetings to the rest of the Donnevan clan.

At least he doesn't use snuff, Maggie thought. She was astonished, then angry at herself. *Whisht!* Why should she care whether or not this big lummox used snuff?

A silence fell as the introductions were concluded, and Maggie was becoming increasingly uncomfortable under Lars' steady regard.

Then a drunken voice shouted, "Girlie, I'll pay twenty dollars! A whole month's wages!"

With a start Maggie looked around. They were ringed by at least twenty rough-looking men, all in different stages of inebriation, and all were staring at her hungrily.

A second man shouted, "I'll go thirty, all in gold!"

And yet another said, "Fifty, girlie. I'll up the ante to fifty dollars!"

Maggie, dismayed and frightened, realized they were talking about her. They were bidding for *her*!

At about the same time Patrick also realized what was going on and erupted with a bellow. "I'll break the next man in half that opens his filthy mouth! That's me sister, you guttersnipes!"

Dan stepped up beside him. "You have to fight me, too."

Then Olaf and Lars ranged alongside the two brothers. Olaf said, "Yah, me and my boy, you'll have to fight us all for dirtying the little lady's name!"

"They're Irishers!"

"And Scandies!"

"We don't need their kind here. Let's slaughter them, boys!"

And with that, bedlam broke loose. The two Donnevans and the two Jorgensons charged at the men who had been bidding for Maggie's favors, huge fists swinging.

Maggie seized Kevin by the hand and managed

76

to find a path through the milling mob, momentarily unnoticed in the diversion of the fight. She put her back up against a rough plank building. Kevin kept trying to slip out of her grasp and join in the fight. Maggie finally had to cuff him alongside the head to quiet him.

She returned her attention to the men. Her four defenders were giving a good account of themselves, men falling left and right under the hammer-like blows of their mighty fists. Surrounded on all sides, they stood back to back, Patrick and Dan paired, and the Jorgensons likewise. Patrick's face was alight with the joy of battle, and Maggie, knowing his love of a good fight, was sure he had already forgotten the cause of this one.

But they were outnumbered at least five to one. More, Maggie saw now, for other men were hurrying up, many carrying clubs.

The four couldn't stand up very long against the overwhelming odds. Even as she thought this, she saw Olaf go down, and now they were only three.

And what would happen to her, if all four went down? Would these ruffians then turn on her to vent their anger, and their lust?

Chapter Four

Lieutenant Andrew Kane, standing at the bow of the revenue cutter, the *Rambler*, had observed the docking of the *Chinook*. He could hardly miss it, he thought sourly, since the scroungy group of men on the wharf set up such an unholy racket.

He smiled faintly, gray eyes amused. The arrival of the *Rambler* at the Port Townsend wharf was generally ignored by the citizens of the town. The presence of the revenue cutter in the Puget Sound area was a source of irritation for the residents, as well as a cause of much merriment. Both facts were understandable, if not pleasing, Andrew thought, his face somber and scowling now, above the smouldering pipe in his mouth.

One local wit had written a piece and hung it on the wooden bulletin board, on the main street, from which the citizens of Port Townsend received their news, there being no newspaper as yet. The piece had galled Andrew as he read it: "The revenue cutter, *Rambler*, does best at chasing wild Indians and porpoises. Since little revenue is gained by the U.S. government from either of these activities, it is a wonderment what gainful purpose she serves us. True, there was a rumor last month that she ran down and captured an Indian canoe carrying a keg of French brandy. It must remain a rumor, since Port Townsend never saw the keg. It therefore must be assumed that the crew of the *Rambler* consumed the brandy. The cutter and her crew are also adept at running her aground on rocks. The best thing to be said for her navigator is that the cutter rarely runs aground on the same rock."

Andrew had been incensed when he read the broadside. Yet he had to admit that it was truthful enough. The crew that he was stuck with knew about as much seamanship as a team of oxen. Since the government pay was so low, men could earn much more logging or at commercial fishing; so Andrew was stuck with the dregs. They were mostly sots and layabouts, and usually he had to hire a completely new crew every time the cutter came into Port Townsend, which meant that he never had a crew long enough to whip them into shape.

A tall, well-built man of twenty-seven, Andrew Kane had soft brown hair and hard gray eyes. Most women found him handsome, with his high cheekbones, straight well-modeled nose, and a somewhat rakish smile. He was reckless by nature, prone to instant decisions and damn the consequences.

His mother, a gentle but high-spirited Southern lady, often said that Andrew had been born with the devil in him. And his father, a North Carolina tobacco planter, had breathed a sigh of relief when Andrew had agreed to attend the newly opened naval school—now called the Naval Academy—at Fort Severn in Annapolis, Maryland. It had seemed to Andrew's father that he spent most of his time getting Andrew out of one escapade after another.

As for Andrew, he had been seeking a life of adventure on the high seas. It wasn't long before he realized that he had made a serious mistake. He chafed under the strict discipline of naval life. A man of some brilliance, he had graduated from the naval school with high honors and was awarded a lieutenancy. But he was *still* a lieutenant. Unhappy with military life, a rebel at heart, he had made enemies and enraged his superior officers by often questioning orders.

And that was why he was now on a revenue cutter cruising Puget Sound. He had disobeyed one order too many, and had been sent to this godforsaken place, when Washington Territory became part of the United States and the Treasury Department decided to establish a branch on the Pacific Coast. Since the Department had no sea force of its own as yet, it occasionally asked the Navy for help when an officer was needed to command a revenue cutter in some distant place. Andrew's superiors had been glad to be rid of him, and Andrew had been happy to go. Surely there would be some excitement and adventure in a raw, frontier country such as the Northwest.

Again, he had been mistaken. It was a tedious existence, dull and joyless. Life at sea on board the *Rambler* was sorry enough, but shore time was little better. About all a man could do was drink and gamble, and that became boring also after a time.

Andrew liked women, and the women to be found in Port Townsend were either married and matronly, or slatterns and whores. The other small port towns on Puget Sound were no better. He would have been delighted to find a married woman with a shapely ankle and a roving eye, but alas, none were to be found. Damnation, some of the Indian maidens were more comely than most of the white women here, but Andrew, so far, had shied away from this sort of entanglement.

Since the logging business had begun to flourish, there were bad feelings between the whites and the Indians, and he did not relish the prospect of becoming involved in an imbroglio over some Indian wench. Twice, since Andrew had taken over the *Rambler*, there had been skirmishes between whites and Indians, and the *Rambler* had been employed to help defeat the Indian warriors. Andrew did his duty, even though he did not approve of the use of the government ship in such a cause. The Indians had inhabited this land back into the distant past, and now the white man was invading their domain. But then, nothing about the world was fair; Andrew had learned this long ago.

To further complicate Andrew's life, the customs agent sent to Port Townsend by the Treasury Department was a sonofabitch, in Andrew's opinion, and dishonest in the bargain. Andrew was almost positive that the man was salting away much of the customs money he collected on liquor imported from the British across the Strait. The trouble was, Andrew couldn't prove it. He knew that it would do no good to contact anyone in Washington. Any message sent hinting at the agent's possible dishonesty would either be dismissed as spite on Andrew's part, or filed away and forgotten. Washington Territory was too far removed from the nation's capital for the department to go to the expense of sending anyone to investigate the charges. They were likely content to be collecting *any* money.

And that reminded him. He had to report to the agent. He was several hours overdue, having brought the *Rambler* into port that morning. The fact that he had nothing to report had little to do with it. Aside from behing a bastard and dishonest, the agent was a martinet, and demanded that Lieutenant Andrew Kane report to him at the conclusion of each cruise.

Andrew sighed, straightening up from where he'd been leaning on the railing. He checked to see if his uniform was reasonably presentable. That was something else that displeased him. Andrew liked fine clothes, and the designer of the Naval officer uniforms must have been a dunce, and color blind as well. The twin rows of brass buttons on the uniform jacket corroded quickly in this damp climate unless they were polished regularly, and the billed cap reminded Andrew of a duck's bill. He detested the cap so much he refused to wear it, and the customs agent was always castigating him for being out of uniform.

He also took the Navy Colt from his holster and checked it. It was not unusual for him to be challenged by some roughneck fired up with rotgut, and it was simpler and less messy to warn the challenger off with the Colt, instead of hammering him into the ground with his fists.

The crew had all gone ashore, and were probably drunk by now. Andrew had ordered one man to stay behind to guard the gangplank. He was sullen at being handed the onerous chore, and Andrew knew he probably had a bottle stowed away somewhere, and would be at it before his commanding officer was out of sight. Failing that, he would likely desert his post as soon as Andrew was gone. In either case, there was little Andrew could do about it.

Shrugging, he trotted down the gangplank and started up the wharf. For some time he had been dimly aware of shouting, the sounds of a brawl, but since brawls were commonplace along the waterfront, he'd given it little thought.

Then he turned the corner of a building and took in the melee in a glance. Three big men were under attack by about twenty other men and were losing by sheer force of numbers.

Andrew started to detour around them when his glance was caught by the sight of a girl and a small boy crouched back against a building. The girl was clutching the boy, who appeared to be about seven years of age, to her skirts.

Andrew's gaze lingered on her. By God, she was a beauty, the prettiest female he'd laid eyes on since coming to Puget Sound—long, dark brown hair, a strong but sensual face, and a fully developed figure despite her obviously tender years. Some instinct told Andrew that she was the cause

of the fight, or at least some man involved in it was
hers. He squinted, trying to make out if she wore a
wedding ring. But her left hand was buried in the
boy's shirt, and Andrew couldn't see. Surely she
wasn't the lad's mother; she wasn't old enough.

What the hell, Andrew thought.

He drew the Colt and fired it twice into the air,
spacing the shots out by a few seconds.

All action froze, and he instantly had everyone's
attention.

Smiling, Andrew drawled, "I don't know what
this is all about, gents, but suppose we break it
up?"

One man took a few belligerent steps toward
him. His cheek was skinned, and his large nose
leaked blood. "Just because you be a Navy officer
don't give you no law and order authority here in
Port Townsend, Kane."

"*This* gives me all the authority I need, my
friend." Andrew cocked the pistol and aimed it at
the man's belly. "Now suppose you all go back to
your drinking or whatever it was you were doing.
You're frightening the little lady over there."

The man sneered. "Who says she's a lady?"

"I do, friend." In two quick steps Andrew
reached the man and laid the pistol barrel alongside
his head. The man sighed softly and crumpled to
the ground.

Andrew straddled the prone body and pointed
the Colt at the others. "I've got four bullets left.
I'm a dead shot, as most of you must know. Now if
you don't scatter pronto, I'm going to start shooting . . . at legs. Who's brave enough to risk a bul-
let-shattered leg? Eh?"

The group broke up, some taking off at a dead run. In a few minutes only the three big men were left, plus the few who lay unconscious on the ground.

Andrew motioned with the Colt. "What are you gents waiting for?"

"Oh, no!" The girl stepped away from the building. "They're with me." Her speech had the lilting rhythm of the Irish. Her color heightened as Andrew stared into her hazel eyes, but she spoke firmly. "It was the others started it. They ..."

He waved his hand. "You don't have to tell me. They're good at insulting a lady." He holstered the Colt. "They don't see that many of them up here, and they forget how to act around a decent woman."

One of the big men stepped forward, and Andrew could see that he was very young despite his size. "By Christ, 'tis meself that will be teaching the buckos!"

"Will it now?" Andrew eyed him with amusement. The lad's lip was cut, one eye was puffy, and rapidly blackening, and the skin on the knuckles of both hands was split. "You're a big one, right enough, but it seems to me that the odds were pretty heavy against you. And you look like you've been battling a crosscut saw."

"The devil take the odds!" The young man glared at Andrew out of his one good eye. "You saying that Patrick Donnevan can't take care of his sister?"

"Hush now, Patrick." The girl placed a hand on her brother's arm. "It's thanking the nice man we should be, not talking back." She smiled, showing a dimple and white, even teeth. "I'm Maggie Donnevan, sir, and this one here is my brother, Patrick. That one is Brother Dan. The wee one yonder is Kevin."

"My pleasure, ma'am." Andrew bowed his head. "Lieutenant Andrew Kane. I was happy to be of service."

The girl had half-turned, looking toward where the third big man, with a blond cowlick, was helping another man up from the ground. "Is your father all right, Lars?"

"I think he'll be—" Lars started.

"Yah. I'm fine. They didn't put the boots to me, and it takes more than the fists of drunken louts to keep Olaf Yorgenson down." Olaf pushed away from Lars and set a weaving, limping course for Maggie. His face was cut and bleeding. After two steps he staggered and almost fell. Lars rushed to help him, and Olaf waved him away. "I'm fine, boy. Keep your dad-damned paws off."

As Maggie started to introduce the Jorgensons to Andrew Kane, a blustery voice bellowed, "What's going on here?"

They all turned to see a short, plump man striding importantly toward them. He wore a black suit, a stovepipe hat, and had muttonchop whiskers.

"Damnation!" Andrew muttered.

The man skidded to a halt before Andrew. "I saw what happened, Lieutenant! What was the meaning of all that? You have no authority to keep the peace. In fact, you have no authority at all on land. You know these people resent us already. Now, you've made it worse. What is your explanation, sir?"

"You, sir, can go to hell!" Andrew said, and started off with long, swinging strides.

The fat man hurried after him, short legs pumping. "Wait now, Lieutenant Kane. You can't walk away from me like that! You're under *my* orders here, you understand?"

Maggie, wondering what it was all about, stared after the pair as they disappeared into the throng of men on the street, the short man still waving his arms and shouting, and Andrew Kane ignoring him.

She turned to Olaf. "Who is that dreadful little man?"

"Ah-h, that's the new customs agent." Olaf was putting a fresh dip of snuff into his mouth. He grimaced as the tobacco burned the cuts on the inside of his lips. "Dad-damn, that smarts!" He turned his head and spat. "As I was saying, that there is the new customs agent. The *first* one on the Sound, and folks don't take too kindly to his being here. 'Sides, he ain't too well liked, considering he's mouthy, like most little fellers, and likes to throw his weight around. The other one, the young Naval feller, he's in charge of that revenue cutter out there. Nice enough gent, from what I hear, but he ain't too well-liked neither, cause of what he is. But I guess he came along yust in time to save our hides. . . ."

Patrick grunted. "Speak for yourself, Jorgenson. Me and me brother were doing fine and dandy!"

"Against twenty men or more?" Olaf snorted. "Young feller, you are the cocky one. You've got a

88

comeuppance due you, and this here is the country for it!"

"All right, you two, that's enough! Whisht, how are we all going to work together, if you two keep bickering? Olaf . . ." Maggie linked arms with Olaf and gave him a beguiling smile. "How about those lodgings you promised? I could use a good wash, and a change of clothes."

"Lodgings, yah. But a wash, that I ain't too sure about." Olaf grinned. "This ain't San Francisco, young lady. Nothing fancy here, and what there is, is dear. Lars and me, we usually sleep out. You brung the sleeping bags, boy?"

"I brought them, Pa."

"Oh . . . I ain't told you yet, Lars. We're going to work for Maggie here. She's starting a logging outfit of her own. That all right with you?"

Lars, cheeks coloring, avoided looking at Maggie. "That's fine with me, Pa."

"Thought you'd be happy to be rid of Jake Fargo and his crew of thugs."

As they started up the street, Olaf continued, "Since we'll all be sleeping out for awhile in the woods—tents, o'course, but on the ground still—anyway, it might not be a bad idea if you bought sleeping bags now, Maggie. That way, your brothers, except'n the little one, can sleep out tonight, and save money. It may take me a couple of days to find passage for us on down the Sound."

"How about more men, Olaf?"

"Likely we can hire what we need down there. Always a few yust been fired for being drunk. Save paying passage for them."

"Fired for being drunk?" Maggie was dubious.

"That don't mean they ain't good loggers. But there ain't much in the way of entertainment around the logging camps. A man can get all tightened up and ready to bust loose, he been working for months without any fun. So he's likely to go looking for whores and drinking likker—"

"I'll be after thanking you to watch your language around my sister," Patrick said angrily.

"Hush now, Patrick." Maggie placed a restraining hand on his arm. "My ears aren't all that delicate, and I'm sure I'll be hearing much worse than that out here."

"That," Olaf said, "you can bet your wad on. Here it is." Olaf halted, gesturing. They were standing before a two-story building made of raw planks. "This is the best lodging Port Townsend has to offer." He spat into the street. "Truth be known, it's the only inn in the whole dad-damned town!"

A crudely painted sign hanging lopsidedly over the doorway proclaimed it to be: THE TRAVELLER'S REST. Maggie hid her dismay, shuddering over the thought of what it must be like inside. Still, she was going to have to become accustomed to poor accommodations. And how, she scolded herself, could it be any worse than that hovel back in Ireland?

Briskly, she turned to Olaf. "I can manage from here. It's getting late. You take my brothers to buy our sleeping bags. I'll give you the money."

"Nah, I have enough. You can pay me back later."

"About supper . . . is there an eating place where we can all meet for a decent meal later?"

"Nah." He waved a hand. "The places here serve

slop. Why don't I buy us some victuals, and we can cook our supper somewhere along the beach, over an open fire. I'm a dad-damned fine cook, you'll find. Wasn't so late, we could catch us some fish for supper. All you have to do here is drop a line into the water. Maybe we can do that tomorrow."

"Let's hope we don't have to stay over tomorrow."

"That, I can't promise. But I'll do my dad-damnedest."

Olaf took Patrick and Dan in tow and hustled them off up the street. Lars fell in behind, looking back at Maggie as he walked away.

Maggie took Kevin by the hand and marched inside the inn, carrying a small wicker bag with a change of clothes. The lobby was small, and there was no front desk, only a small table, at which sat a scrawny, bald-headed man. Doors to the right opened into a saloon. The sound of loud voices was almost deafening, and Maggie had to raise her voice to make herself understood to the man at the table. At first he told her there were no rooms available. But when Maggie said, "I can pay," he reared back and looked up at her.

"Well now, a lady such as you seem to be, ma'am, I'd hate to turn out into the street." He stroked his weak chin with grimy fingers. "One room left, five dollars the night. In gold."

The price was outrageous, and Maggie knew it. She held a rein on her temper. "And hot water for a bath?"

The man shrugged. "Only thing I can do for you there is to give you a bucket and send the lad there back to the kitchen for hot water. I'm the only one here. Can't leave my post," he said virtuously.

Maggie, tight-lipped, gave him a five-dollar gold piece, and held out her hand. "The key, please."

After a moment's hesitation, the man dug a brass key out of his pocket and gave it to her. He said sullenly, "Last room on your left, upstairs. If you're staying tomorrow, pay me in the morning, first thing."

"Whisht!" Maggie sniffed. "You'll not need be worrying about your due, sir."

Kevin took the bucket, and the man gave him directions about how to find the kitchen. Maggie went upstairs and down the dark hall to the end. The room was about what she had expected—long, narrow, with one bunk against the wall only large enough for one person, one straightback chair, a wooden washbasin with a cracked mirror over it. The only light and ventilation came from a small window, with a wooden shutter. At least there were enough blankets on the bunk so she could make a pallet on the floor for Kevin. The window overlooked an alley, and the air from outside was so foul-smelling that Maggie hastened to close it, then lit a stub of a candle set in a saucer on the washbasin.

Kevin came lugging a bucket of water. Maggie sent him back for another. "I'm going to bathe while you're gone, so knock on the door and wait until I tell you to come in."

"Aw-w, Maggie." Kevin's grin was mischievous. "I've seen you without clothes before."

Maggie looked at him in astonishment. "Where?"

"Back home. You and Kathleen both, when you were taking your baths."

"Why, you little imp! Peeking on us, were you? You've got the devil in you, Kevin Donnevan! Now be about what I told you." She aimed a slap at him, which Kevin easily avoided, scampering out of the room.

It was only then that Maggie let her laughter go. The little scamp! He was going to be hard to handle, yet she was so fond of him she could never really become angry with him.

She tested the water with her finger. It wasn't hot, merely tepid, but it would have to do. She poured it into the washbasin, then dug out a sliver of soap from the wicker bag.

Dan knocked on the door shortly after sundown. By that time Maggie was clean and refreshed, wearing fresh garments. She had scrubbed a protesting Kevin as well. She opened the door to Dan.

"Olaf found a good spot on the beach," Dan said. "I left them building a fire and came to fetch you and Kevin. You'd best bring a warm shawl, Maggie, as Olaf says it gets cold along the water at nightfall."

"I hope Olaf is as good a cook as he claims," Maggie said. "I'm starving."

Outside the inn, Dan led them up the street. Shortly, they were away from the buildings, and Dan guided them down to a wide, sandy beach. The air here was fresh and clean, tangy with the smell of salt. The thunder of the surf had the sound of slow, giant drums. Maggie breathed deeply.

There was one problem, she soon found. The

sand was soft and loose, and her tiny slippers sank with each step. "Whisht! Well, only one thing to do." She sat down on a huge, beached log, as white as bone. "You two turn your backs for a minute."

They complied, and Maggie began removing her shoes and stockings.

His back to her, Dan said, "Maggie?"

"Yes, Danny boy?"

"I'm glad you brought us here. I like it. I wouldn't say this in front of Pat. I think he likes it, too, but is too thickheaded to admit it."

Maggie laughed softly, pleased. "I'm glad, Danny. And yes, I think you're right about Patrick. He'll come around." She stood up, shoes and stockings in one hand. "You can both turn around now."

They continued on up the beach. In a moment Dan said, pointing, "There it is."

Maggie saw the flaring bonfire. They quickened their pace. Before long she could make out the figures in the firelight, and she heard voices raised in boisterous song. "Poteen!" she said in disgust. "Patrick got his hands on a jar of poteen!"

"It's English brandy, Maggie," Dan said shamefacedly. "And it really wasn't Pat. Olaf or Lars got it somewhere. Lars and Pat are getting along just dandy now, but Pat and Olaf are still prickly as hedgehogs."

Soon, Maggie could smell the mouth-watering odors of cooking food. As they neared the fire, she saw that Olaf was busy around the fire, and Lars and Patrick were sitting on the sand, backs against a chunk of driftwood, arms around each other's shoulders, singing. As Maggie watched, they broke off to take nips from a jug.

When Maggie and the boys stepped into the firelight, Patrick threw his arms wide. "Me little sister, and Danny boy!" In his clear baritone he began singing "Londonderry Air" at the top of his voice. After listening a moment to catch the words, Lars joined in.

Maggie decided it would be best just to ignore the pair of them. She and Kevin moved toward the fire. Olaf had three chickens spitted and turning slowly over the blaze.

"It smells delicious, Olaf."

"Yah." He turned his head and spat. "It'll soon be done. Here, boys, hand me that bottle afore it's all gone."

Lars handed him the brandy jug, and Olaf tilted his head back and drank deeply, his prominent Adams's apple bobbing like a cork. Maggie wondered idly how he could drink liquor like that without also swallowing the snuff in his cheek. She shivered in the chill breeze off the water, and sat down close to the fire, her knees drawn up. Pulling the shawl around her, she stared dreamily into the flames. For the first time in months, she felt relaxed.

She must have dozed off for a moment, for the next thing she knew Olaf was kneeling beside her. With a long-tined fork he was probing into the hot coals. He dug out several oblong objects, their skins charred black by the fire.

"What are those?"

"Potatoes, little lady." He grinned around at her. "Irish potatoes. You should know, coming from Ireland."

"But . . . *here?*"

"Yah. Lots of Irishers here. Many of them have farms along the Sound. One of them, so I was told, brought the potato over some years back. A lot of potatoes raised around here."

In a few minutes they were all eating hungrily from tin plates. The roasted chicken was tender and juicy, and the potatoes . . . Maggie broke one open and gazed in awe at the crumbly, white insides. In her haste to taste it, she ate a forkful before it had cooled sufficiently. It was delicious! It had been so long since she had eaten a potato not rotted by the blight that she could scarcely believe it.

For someone who had been accustomed to a heavy diet of potatoes all her life, then been denied them for several years, these were a literal delight. Maggie ate greedily and managed to snare another one from the coals before her brothers could gobble them all up.

Replete, she leaned back with a soft sigh. Now, for the first time, she was truly certain that her decision to come here had been a wise one. The potatoes were a good omen—nothing but good fortune would come their way henceforth.

She sat up, looking along the beach, then got to her feet. "I think I'll take a walk along the sand. I have to walk off all the food. You *are* a great cook, Olaf."

"You shouldn't be going off alone, little sister," Patrick said. "I'll walk by your side. . . ."

"You will not," she said sharply. "When are you ever going to learn, Patrick Donnevan, that I'm grown up and capable of taking care of myself?"

Andrew Kane was in a foul mood as he walked along the beach, his anger only deepened by the load of whiskey he had taken on back in town. He smoked his pipe savagely, trailing huge clouds of smoke behind him.

As usual, the meeting with the customs agent hadn't gone well. Andrew's stepping in to stop the fight had started it off on the wrong foot. Not that it would have mattered, anyway. He didn't like the man, and the feeling was mutual.

Still, Andrew knew that he should have stayed out of the brawl. As usual, he had been made foolish by the sight of a pretty face. And what had it gotten him? Nothing but trouble.

He stopped for a moment and looked out over the inlet, dark now, except for the faint phosphorescence of the breaking waves on the shore. He inhaled deeply the pungent, salty air.

One of the reasons Andrew had joined the Navy was because he loved the sea. His father's plantation in North Carolina was located near the Atlantic Ocean, and Andrew had learned to sail as a lad. He enjoyed being commander of the *Rambler*, but damnation, the customs agent was becoming ever more difficult, and Andrew knew that the day wasn't far distant when he would flare up at the bastard, probably deck him, and that would be the end of Andrew's command.

Of course, that wouldn't mean poverty for him. He could always return to North Carolina, or he could ask his father, a generous, reasonably well-off man, to send him funds.

Andrew was reluctant to do either. Much as he loved his father, he knew he would be unhappy under his father's stern discipline if he returned to work on the plantation. Andrew smiled slightly, his angry pace slowing. His father, who had been more than happy to see him away from the plantation, would not be overly delighted to have him underfoot again, a son he considered overly independent, with a strong taste for women and gambling. And if he accepted money from his father, he would feel tied down by the obligation, and Andrew hated feeling tied down.

No, he would not be returning to North Carolina, no matter what happened here. In most ways, he liked this country. There were many opportunities for a man with brains, drive, and ambition. If he was relieved of his command, Andrew felt confident that he could find something else connected with the sea. After all, *everything* here depended on the sea, in one way or another. About all of the merchandise, and most of the food staples consumed by the citizens of the Sound, came in by sea, and the things they produced went out the same way. The dizzying heights of the Rocky Mountains and the stretch of plains beyond civilization were too much of an obstacle for freight wagons to overcome. The westward pioneers had found a way through the passes, true, but many of them had perished, and those that had made it through had been forced to leave most of their household goods along the way. . . .

Andrew stopped short as he saw the glow of a fire some distance up the beach. He had no desire for human companionship this night; he wanted only to walk the beach until his anger and restlessness had calmed sufficiently for him to sleep.

He was about to turn, to retrace his footsteps, when he saw a figure coming toward him along the water's edge. There was sufficient light to make it plain that the figure was that of a female, and despite himself, his interest was captured. What woman would be walking the beach alone at night here? Virtuous women—God bless their plain faces—were all home safe in their beds, and the waterfront doxies were surely all pursuing their calling in the saloons. Perhaps it was some drunken wretch too sodden to know where she was going, but no, she was walking straight and true—with a lively step—flirting with the water's cold edge, and if he wasn't mistaken, humming under her breath!

Fully intrigued now, Andrew stepped back into the shadow of a huge fir at the edge of the sand. As he did so, the woman turned her face toward him—she was almost even with him now—and Andrew recognized her as the girl who had inspired the afternoon's melee; Maggie Donnevan, she had said her name was. What in the world was she doing alone without her brace of giant brothers?

He took a deep pull on his pipe, and found that it had gone out. Quickly, he took a sulphur match from his pocket, struck it on his thumbnail, and held it to the tobacco, drawing on it behind cupped hands, letting her see the light.

Maggie gave a muted cry, and drew back, poised for flight. There was a slight quaver in her voice, but she spoke out clearly enough. "Who is it? Who's there?"

Andrew stepped forward into the faint moonlight. "Why, I'm quite hurt that I go unrecognized. Surely you haven't forgotten the man who so gallantly came to your rescue this afternoon?" He could see the tension leave her.

"Oh, Mr. Kane, isn't it? I remember you, of course. But it's not that easy recognizing someone lurking about in the dark, now is it?"

She still sounded nervous, but Andrew was amused by the implied rebuke in her remark. The girl had spirit, if not a great deal of sense.

"You should be glad that it's me you have met, and not some drunken yahoo, like those who accosted you this afternoon," he said calmly. "What's the matter with those great brothers of yours, letting you walk alone at night? It would seem for all their size, their brains need a bit of stimulation. . . ."

Maggie drew herself up until she appeared nearly a foot taller. Her voice was sharp as she replied, "I don't need my brothers, or anyone else to tell me what to do, or where or when to do it, Mr. Kane. I make my own decisions, and if what I am doing seems foolish, 'tis only myself I have to blame."

Andrew found himself smiling, and realized that he was enjoying this. Arguing with a pretty girl was much more fun than arguing with the ugly customs agent.

She was going on, "I happen to come from a country where anyone, man or woman, can walk 'til the sun comes up, if they care to, and not a blessed soul will lift a hand against them. It's shameful that this place is so barbarous that a person must be on guard for—"

Andrew raised his hand against the spate of words. "Wait now! Wait now, ma'am. I was merely teasing. I didn't mean to rouse your ire. I

100

do apologize." He bowed low, and made as if to doff a hat. He looked up to find her watching him speculatively.

"You're from the South, aren't you? I mean, what you Americans call your Southern states?"

"I am indeed, ma'am, the sovereign state of North Carolina," he drawled. "But how would you conjecture that, all on your own?"

"Oh, despite what you appear to think of the Irish, I *do* have a wee bit of brains in my head, and ears to hear with, and eyes to see. Whisht! I don't have to be a genius to hear the strange way you stretch your words out, now do I?"

Andrew burst into laughter. The girl had wit!

He bowed deeply again. "Mistress Donnevan, once more my apologies. I certainly would not, for the world, have you think that I meant to disparage your intellect. During our brief conversation, I have been able to ascertain that your mind is every bit as beautiful as your lovely face and form, and that, as beauty goes, is considerable!"

He stood upright, a bit dizzy from the movement and the whiskey, to find her standing very close to him, her arms on her hips, and her eyes blazing.

"Oh, you think you're the clever one, don't you now? A gentleman, a man of education, having your sport with a poor, Irish lass who hasn't got all her wits about her! Well, I have something to tell you, fine gentleman that you are! I, Maggie Donnevan, have brought my brothers and myself from a place of starvation and sorrow, to a new world. For months we have endured storms, foul food, and disease to get here. I had the strength and the wit to do this, and I tell you that I have the

101

strength and the wit to do more, much more. I
have the strength and the wit to stand up to you,
and all the other no-good, poteen-drinking men to
get where I want to go. And I say to you, Mr.
Kane, that you, and others like you, had just better
not stand in my way!"

For a moment, startled by the violent outburst,
Andrew pulled back, and then a great wave of anger engulfed him. Just who did this girl think she
was? He had only been joshing with her, teasing
her a little. The gall of her! Without his help this
afternoon, she might well now be lying bruised and
battered in some alley, after being raped by a
dozen men.

He reached out and seized her shoulder. It was
firm and strong beneath his fingers, and he let his
fingers bite cruelly into her flesh.

"Now, just who is it that you think you are? Is it
the queen of Ireland we have here talking in such a
grand manner? If you will gather your vaunted
wits about you, you will recall that when I came to
your aid this afternoon, your champions were well
on their way to falling, every one of them. And
then what would you have done? How strong
would you have been when you had to face those
drunken, women-starved men, eh? Just how would
you have 'stood up' to their filthy bodies and lecherous hands? How, Mistress Donnevan? Damnation, how?"

With each question, he shook Maggie fiercely,
and her hair tumbled down and whipped against
her hot cheeks. She felt the icy stab of fear through
the heat of her anger, but the anger outweighed
her good judgment.

Her hand flashed out, and she struck him across the face with all her strength. Into the blow she put all her fear of her father, her hatred of Lord Ramage, and her fury at the race of men in general. Her hand stung from the blow, but Maggie felt a sense of satisfaction in having delivered it.

Her satisfaction, however, was short-lived, because with his free hand, Andrew hit her back. The impact jarred her head and addled her senses. To her dismay, tears flooded her eyes.

"'Tis no gentleman you are," she shouted. "To strike a woman . . ."

He looked at her with narrowed eyes, and spoke through clenched teeth. Again Maggie felt fear, as she realized that his rage was every bit as great as her own.

"Anyone who hits Andrew Kane, be it man *or* woman, had best be prepared to fight back!"

At these words Maggie kicked out at him, striking his shin with her foot, but in forgetting that she was shoeless, did herself more damage than she did him.

Andrew shook her violently, rattling her teeth, and then swung her up into his arms. Before she could even cry out, Maggie found herself sprawling across his broad shoulder—head and feet down, like a sack of meal—and he was moving across the sand with her; she could not tell in which direction.

In this undignified position, she found it hard to breathe, but tried to draw air into her lungs so that she could scream. Surely they would hear her back at the fire. Then the indignity of her situation was brought home to her. If she called for rescue now, if Patrick and the others had to come to her aid, she would be setting a precedent. She would lose the hard-won position of authority she was holding so tenuously. She had boasted that she could take care of herself. Well, she had better start now.

Then she was rudely dumped onto the sand, and before she had a chance to leap up, Andrew Kane was lying beside her, his two hands on her shoulders, and his heavy, booted leg thrown across both of her thighs. She was terribly conscious of the strength in those hands, and the heat and pressure of his thigh across hers filled her with something very close to panic.

She gulped air, and tried to gain for herself some measure of dignity. "All right," she said, "you are physically the stronger. I concede that with no shame. You can throw me down, hold me down, but there are other kinds of strength."

Andrew gave a harsh bark of laughter. "So now we are going to play word games, are we? You want to quibble and argue about the meaning of 'strength', go into the philosophical ramifications, eh? Well, I'll just wager you do, because then you've got to admit you're in trouble, eh?"

His face was very close to hers, and his breath was hot in her ear. She experienced the unreasoning fear of being confined, but fought against the urge to struggle, as she sensed it would only give him satisfaction.

Andrew, with the sweet scent of her hair in his nostrils, was undergoing a storm of emotion even greater than Maggie's. Grabbing the girl and throwing her down had been simple instinct. She had fought him, and he had fought back; but now, with her slender body pinioned beneath his leg, with the warmth of her flesh coming to him through the material of her dress, he could only think of how lovely she was, and of how hungry he was for a woman's body. Placing his face over hers, Andrew pressed his lips against her mouth.

Her breath was sweet as well-water, and her mouth tasted faintly of salt. As he pressed closer, Andrew could feel the soft, yielding mounds of her breasts against his chest, and in that instant, he became too aroused to think of any future consequences. There was nothing in the world at that moment except his body and hers.

Maggie, struggling for breath beneath him, seethed with conflicting emotions. She had never been kissed by a man, although occasionally, in what she thought of as a weak moment, she wondered what it would be like.

But she had never imagined this, this feeling of invasion, coupled with fear, and mixed in with a good portion of a strange sort of wild excitement.

His lips were hot, and met hers with a fierce kind of demand that she could not put a name to, but recognized nonetheless in some deep part of herself. His chest crushed her, drove the breath from her lungs, and she knew that he must be able to feel her breasts against him, just as she felt the weight of his chest on her.

This was beyond her experience. This she could *not* cope with. Admitting her fear, Maggie made a sound deep in her throat, and despite her prior intentions, she began to struggle against his hands, one of which had moved first to one breast, then to reach behind her. Against her thigh, where his leg crossed hers, she could feel a hard male insistence.

They struggled silently on the sand, for Maggie kept to her resolve not to call upon her brothers for help. Finally, she gasped out two words, "Please don't," but Andrew seemed not to hear them. He appeared to be near mindless in his passion, and Maggie, unfamiliar as she was with men, was frightened anew by the force of his desire, his need. He was like a great storm, or a tidal wave, sweeping everything before it. She had never felt so helpless.

She felt the buttons of her bodice give way, and the feel of his hot hands upon her flesh was both a terror and a pleasure. Again, she couldn't breathe as his lips sealed hers. Cold air struck her legs as he shoved her skirts upward.

Andrew released her with one hand, using it to fumble at his clothing, but Maggie's attempt to twist away was useless. She knew then that nothing was going to stop him. Even if she now cried out, it would be over before Patrick could gather his befuddled wits and reach her.

The actual act of entrance was almost anticlimactic. She felt a hard, hurtful thrust into her most private parts, but the pain was not unbearable; it was just the final step in what she thought to herself as an invasion of her being. He was moving above her now, faster and faster, his breath almost sobbing in his chest.

For just a second, his driving, blind, intimate thrusting came close to striking an answering spark in her own body, and then with a great groan, Andrew shuddered and collapsed his full weight upon her.

Startled by the sudden cessation of movement, Maggie lay still in shocked silence. Andrew made no move to roll away, but remained completely relaxed, breathing deeply like one asleep.

Finally, in impatience, shame and anger, she pushed at his heavy shoulders. Sighing, he rolled over onto his back. In the dim moonlight she could see the male part of him lying shrunken and still in the opening of his breeches.

Maggie was at a loss as to what to say or do. She felt shaken and bruised, but she could not see that this "great" experience had left her any different than she was before.

She felt an unpleasant wetness between her legs and upon her thighs, and she used her petticoat to wipe it away, grimacing as she did so. Then she noticed traces of blood upon the white linen of the petticoat. She felt tender and sore, but there was no lingering pain. She made an effort to straighten her clothing and hair, already thinking ahead to the moment when she must return to her brothers and the Jorgensons, at the fire. The buttons of her bodice were gone—lost forever in the sand, no doubt—but if she wrapped the shawl around her shoulders, they need not know. In fact, they *must* not know. She had suffered this indignity rather than relinquish her position of control, and it would be unbearable to lose it because of their finding out what had happened here.

Putting herself in some semblance of order helped her regain a measure of calm. Andrew, who until this moment had not moved, suddenly turned toward her. As he did so, he straightened his clothes, and began fastening his breeches. He seemed to be at a loss for words as much as she.

It was over now, and Maggie realized there was nothing to be gained from castigating the man. She even knew that her own culpability in starting the quarrel had triggered it. She also sensed, but did not understand, that he had been driven by an overwhelming need. It was the male in him. The man thing that she both hated and feared.

Still, her anger and shame would not let her leave it at that. "I hope you're satisfied," she said in a low, cold voice. "You've proven that you can abuse me physically. You've taken my maidenhead—"

"What!" Andrew raised his head, and before she could stop him, he reached forward and threw back her skirts. She swallowed her unspoken words, but before fear could fully possess her, he had found what he sought, and had pulled her skirts down again, carefully tucking the hem around her bare ankles.

His face looked pale in the semi-darkness, and his lips were drawn thin. "You speak the truth. You were a virgin." He drew back, and looked at her in apparent anger. "I normally don't apologize for my actions, madam, but for this night's work, I must truly say that I am sorry." He paused for a moment, then looked down at the sand. "I reckon you'll tell your brothers, and they will have every right to demand satisfaction." His voice was low and bitter.

Maggie, nonplussed at his sudden change in manner, couldn't think of any words to say but the truth. "I won't be telling them, for reasons of my own. You don't need be worrying yourself that they'll be coming after you to do you harm!"

Her voice had grown haughty at the last, and Andrew raised his head. "I'm not afraid of those great oafs, if that's what you're thinking. I was thinking about you, believe it or not. I may not always act the perfect gentleman, but I am not a complete and utter cad. I'll dally with any willing maid or matron, but I usually try to refrain from deflowering virgins!" He turned his head away and muttered, "It's unsatisfying work at best!"

Maggie heard his words, and despite the dull fatigue that was weighing her down, she could not resist one last word as she got to her feet. Pulling the shawl tightly around her upper body and shoulders, she leaned over and hissed at him like a cat. " 'Tis a liar you are, Andrew Kane! As well as a cowardly raper of virgins! You seemed to greatly enjoy the work while you were about the doing of it!"

Head high, and shoulders stiff, she turned toward the glow of the fire in the distance. Suddenly, she heard her name being called, and correctly guessed that Patrick had grown worried about her long absence. "Coming, Patrick," she shouted across the sand. "I'm coming!"

After a moment she realized that Andrew was walking close behind her. "I'll thank you to turn back," she said in a tense whisper. "You've caused me enough trouble and pain for one night!"

She was stopped by the firm but gentle pressure of his hand on her arm. "Just one thing." His voice was steady and serious.

"And what would that be?" she replied, putting all the outrage she could summon into her voice.

"What if I've gotten you with child?"

His words, spoken into the damp salt air, seemed to Maggie to be carved into the night like words of ice, the touch of which froze her heart and stopped her breath. There was a long silence as she struggled to breathe normally again.

"I will take care of that, when and if I come to it," she said faintly, not even knowing for sure what she meant. She pulled free of his hand, and walked toward the dying fire.

But after a few steps, against her will, she stopped and looked back. There was nothing to be seen. Andrew Kane had vanished into the night.

Chapter Five

The next day, the Donnevans and the Jorgensons rode the tide south down Admiralty Inlet on a small schooner—a vessel, Olaf said, that was mainly employed to transport passengers and small cargoes around Puget Sound. On board, also, were all of the equipment and supplies Olaf said they would need to start a logging operation.

Maggie looked back at Port Townsend dwindling behind them with mixed feelings. She had determined to put the incident of the past night behind her; yet she could not keep thoughts of the young Naval lieutenant from her mind. Willy-nilly, at odd moments, across her mind would flash images—brief memories of lips on lips, flesh against flesh—that caused her face to flame, and triggered her heart to panicky flutter. Sternly, she told herself that what had happened to her was not really

important in the context of the future of the Donnevan clan. The only real harm would come if she
should be with child, and that she wouldn't know
for at least three weeks. There was no use in worrying until then.

As the high bluff behind Port Townsend faded
from view, Maggie turned her face resolutely forward.

The schooner moved past Klees Rock, an ebony
knob jutting up out of the water, decorated with
purple starfish and wearing a skirt of iodine-colored
kelp. At times they were so close to shore, and the
water was so shallow and clear, that Maggie could
see huge, pink salmon lying head to current alongside the boat.

As the afternoon wore on, a blunt finger of land
appeared on their left.

"That there is Kitsap Peninsula, Maggie," Olaf
said, as they leaned together on the railing. "Port
Ludlow is coming up soon on our right. And look
at that."

"At what?"

"There, coming right down to the water. Them
big trees. Douglas fir. Yah, that's what we'll be logging. The best timber for selling."

Maggie looked to where he was pointing. From
this distance the foliage of the huge trees appeared
yellow-green in the sunlight, but were dark, almost
black, out of the sun. The broad, lower branches
drooped, the high branches curved up at the tips,
and the crowns formed perfect pyramids. The
boles were very straight and of great size. Even
from this distance Maggie marveled at the symmetry of the massive, cinnamon-brown columns.

Beside her, Olaf said, "Some of them trees are from two-hundred-and-fifty to two-hundred-and-eighty feet high, and measure from twelve to fifteen feet through at the butt."

As they sailed into the small harbor of Port Ludlow, Maggie could hear the sounds of hammering. Port Ludlow was just a small village. Trees had been cleared away in a half-moon near the water, and several crude wooden structures had been erected.

Then Maggie saw something that wrung a sound of surprise from her. On a promontory some distance south of the village, a great, two-story house stood in solitary splendor. Unlike the two she had seen on the bluff above Port Townsend, this one was completed, and painted. As the fading sun's rays struck it, she saw that it was a blinding white.

"Who built that great house? It looks so out of place, out here in the wilderness with nothing but crude huts about."

"That house? Belongs to a gent name of Jonas Kirk." Olaf spat over the railing, grinning. "Some folks say old Jonas has an empty attic. I say old, but he ain't any older than me, if that."

"An empty attic? You mean . . . a little crazy? Why do they say that?"

"By Thor, in a way it's hard to figure. 'Cause he's different from the others hereabouts, I'd guess. For one thing, he's an educated man. Number two, he's filthy rich. He's one of the rare ones who struck it big down in the California Mother Lode. He came up here and spent a small fortune building that big house. And the third thing is, he's married, to a woman less'n half his age."

113

Maggie shrugged. "Whisht! That might make him different, but I can't see why it makes him fey, as we say in Ireland."

Olaf arched an eyebrow at her. "That's what they say over there, is it? Well . . ." Olaf shifted position on the rail. "Could be it's his woman that's . . . uh, fey."

"Why? Because she's younger?"

"Nah. Not that so much. They lived in a tent whilst the house was being built. When it was finished, but not yet furnished, she took off for San Francisco."

"Ah, the poor man! She left him, left him all alone up there."

"Well . . . she left him, right enough, over a year back, and she ain't been back since. Yet, she didn't *leave* him, if you catch my meaning."

"No, I'm afraid I don't, Olaf."

"Well . . ." Olaf scratched the bristles on his long chin. "The way I get it, she went down there to buy furniture for the house. Almost ever time a ship comes up from San Francisco, it has on board a piece or two of furniture for Jonas up there."

Maggie asked, "And she's been gone that long, without once coming back?" Olaf nodded, smiling. "Now that I *do* find fey. Whisht!"

The schooner bumped gently against the wooden wharf jutting out into the small bay. Maggie noticed a number of people strung out along the wharf watching their arrival. Several, she saw, were Indians, both men and women. As Olaf and Maggie moved gingerly down the gangplank, followed by the others, a gaunt man with a flaming red beard came striding to meet them.

T̶h̶e̶ ̶ ̶ ̶ ̶ held out his hand. Olaf took it, and they pumped hands. With his other hand, the red-bearded man clapped Olaf on the shoulder. In a strange twang, he said, "Olaf, you old scandie, I'm glad to see ye! How's the wife?"

"Better now, Bill, down where it's dry." Olaf turned his head. "Maggie girl, this here is Captain William Sayward. He's a New Englander, from Maine, come out here seeking taller timber. He's got his own sawmill here. He's one of the men you'll be selling your logs to. Bill, Maggie Donnevan."

"How do you do, sir," Maggie murmured.

"A fine looking lady such as ye is always more than welcome here—" William Sayward broke off to stare. "Olaf, did I hear ye aright? *She's* going to be selling me logs?"

"Yah, that's right." Olaf was grinning hugely. "The little lady here is going into the logging business."

Sayward stared at Maggie a moment longer, and Maggie set her teeth, waiting for him to make the usual snide remark; but, unexpectedly, Sayward combed his beard with his fingers, and said, "Well, the good Lord knows, I can use all the logs I can get. I'll buy all you can bring me, ma'am."

"And at a fair price, Maggie," Olaf said. "Same price you'd be getting at the Pope and Talbot sawmill round at Port Gamble on the Hood Canal."

"I'd be happy to have you folks spend the night at my place," Captain Sayward said. "Not the best accommodations in the world, but the food is ample, and I'm glad for the company, you can be sure. Don't get many strangers in these parts yet."

115

At that moment a deep rumble of a voice shouted, "So there you are, Olaf! And you too, Lars, damn your eyes! So you brought your boy back to work for me, did you, Olaf?"

Maggie looked to see one of the biggest, and certainly one of the ugliest, men she had ever had sight of striding toward them along the wharf. The frail structure shook under his heavy tread, and his hobnail boots chewed up a spray of splinters. He was dressed in rough, filthy logger's clothing, that looked as if they had not seen a wash tub since their original purchase. It was apparent that at some time in the past his face had been badly slashed, leaving a long scar across his cheek and severing the tip of his great nose. With his small black eyes buried deep in flesh, and the severed nose resembling a snout, his face made Maggie think of a great beast of some sort.

Over his shoulder, held by one huge hand, rested a long-handled tool of some kind, with a sharply pointed head.

He stopped before Olaf Jorgenson, feet spread wide apart. "You know, scandie, I don't usually take men back who up and quit on me, but in your cases I'll make an exception."

"No need, Jake," Olaf said quietly, and spat a brown stream onto the planking. "My boy and I ain't coming back to work for you."

"What!" The big man's face reddened. "Then I'll see to it that no other logging outfit on the Sound will hire you! You'll have to haul ass back to that Norski country where you came from."

With a movement lightning fast for such a big man, he brought the strange looking object off his

116

shoulder and hurled it. It struck sharp point first into the planking between Olaf's feet, buried almost to the hilt, the long handle quivering.

Olaf hadn't moved a muscle. Now he said calmly, "You're a little late, Jake. I already have another job, both me and Lars. Yah, the little lady here," Olaf jerked his thumb at Maggie, "is starting her own logging company, and we're going to be working for her. Me and Lars." Now he looked at Maggie. "This here is Jake Fargo, Maggie. I think I told you about him, yah."

Jake Fargo stared at Maggie from little, glittering black eyes. He seemed speechless for a moment. "Her? Running a logging outfit! By damn, that's the funniest thing I've heard in a coon's age!" He threw back his head and laughed, great roaring laughter that boomed out over the water like a cannon shot.

Patrick stepped forward, bristling, fists clenched. "I'll be after thanking you to keep a proper tongue in your head when speaking before my sister!"

Jake Fargo's laughter died abruptly. "Why, you ain't nothing but a pipsqueak, a young tenderfoot. And an Irisher, to boot. By damn, we're being taken over by foreigners. Scandies, now Irishers!" He scowled blackly at Patrick. "You'd better learn something about Jake Fargo, boy, before you bare your fangs at me." He seized the handle of the object between Olaf's feet and easily plucked it free of the planking with one hand. He hefted it in his hand. "You see this? Many a man's skull have I split open with it. So ask around before you go making faces at me, younker."

He shouldered the long-handled tool and

117

marched off. Patrick, growling, took a step after him. Maggie stopped him with a motion of her hand. To Olaf, she said, "He's a terrible man, that one!"

"Yah, he's a mean booger, Jake Fargo."

"What's that horrible thing he's carrying?" Maggie shuddered.

"That? It's called a pickaroon. It's a logger's tool. The pointed head is driven into a felled log to horse it, move it by muscle power. So strong is Jake that I've seen him move logs it would normally take several men to bulge. Jake carries it with him everwhere he goes. Even in bed. Some say . . ." He laughed. "Some say he even keeps it close to hand when he beds a woman. He's known in these parts as Pickaroon Jake. But make no mistake, young feller . . . Jake means what he says." Olaf was suddenly serious. "He's killed men, a number, with one blow with that pickaroon." He added darkly, "We'll be having trouble with Jake Fargo. By Thor, we will!"

The next morning they started out early, walking north along the edge of the water, the men loaded down with their equipment. Olaf had hired one man in Port Ludlow, a tall, taciturn individual named Tom Reese. "That'll give us four men for fallers, soon as your brothers learn the ropes," Olaf explained to Maggie. "We'll hire buckers as we need them."

They were carrying tents, and enough food supplies for three weeks. The night before. Olaf had spent an hour showing Maggie the tools they would be using, and explaining their purpose.

Perhaps the most important pieces of equipment were six long-handled, single bit axes for the fallers, and the two cross-cut saws to cut the felled trees into sections. "Your big brothers can be 'buckers', sawing up the felled trees, until I think they have enough sense to wield an axe on a springboard without killing themselves."

There were two pickaroons—Maggie knew she would never look at one without a shudder—two wooden mallets, with thirty-six-inch shafts and hardwood heads five inches in diameter, that were used to drive wedges into sawcuts; and a cant hook for each man. The cant hooks—five-foot poles with a hinged, toothed hook on the end—were used to roll logs on the ground or in the water.

Maggie was curious about two other strange looking items. One was called a Böker, Olaf explained. "As you can see, girl, it's a wood and metal jack, taking its name from some German who invented it. It's used to move logs too dad-damned heavy to be manhandled. Böker levers, reversing when their locks slip, have broken many a logger's arm." The other item was called an undercutter. "It's used when a log's position is such that we have to saw underneath. That chisel-like end you see there is driven into the log's underside up to that curved indent. Then the saw, teeth up, o'course, rides in that there grooved wheel."

They were headed for a spot about three miles above Port Ludlow, where Olaf said there was a good stand of virgin timber, Douglas firs "as thick as fleas on a dog's butt."

A nagging concern was troubling Maggie as they made their laborious way along the shoreline. She questioned Olaf about it. "Don't we need permission from someone to cut trees in this place you're taking us?"

"Nah. This here is all mostly government land. Who's gonna know back in Washington City?"

"That sounds . . . well, dishonest."

"What's dishonest about it? It's done all the time, girl." Olaf spat a brown stream. "Lookee, there's a number of ways you can go about it. You could buy timberland, but I know you ain't got that much money. You could homestead a hundred and sixty acres, if you was a U.S. citizen . . . which you ain't. Neither am I. A way to get around that is to find some gent down on his luck, pay him a few dollars to file on the one-sixty, then turn it over to you to log. But that would still cost you, and the way I figure it, money's tight with you. Wait until you get some money ahead, then do it. Until then, don't fret about it. Hellfire, Jake Fargo has logged over hundreds of acres of timber that ain't his, and nobody cares. The thing you have got to understand, Maggie, is that with men like Captain Sayward, Talbot, and Gamble, hungry for logs for their sawmills, nobody cares where you fall them."

It was difficult going along the rugged coastline, and so they could proceed. Their heavy loads took a toll on the strength of all. Maggie marveled at Olaf being able to keep up, with his lame foot, but he never lagged behind once. Maggie was exhausted when they finally rounded a point of land, and Olaf stopped, pointing a finger.

"There, there's where the Donnevan Logging Company falls its first tree!"

120

The place where Olaf pointed was a small cove. Beginning almost from the waterline were hundreds upon hundreds of huge trees, rising up a gentle, trough-like slope nature had made in the hillside.

"We start at the bottom of the slope and work up, sliding the logs down into the water as they're cut. They'll glide down that slope easy as greased pigs, and we corral them in the cove, which is protected from the tides, until we're ready to move them to Port Ludlow and Sayward's mill."

They made their way along to the deepest curve of the cove, and the men got busy clearing the underbrush. By the time they had cleared a small camp area and the tents were set up, it was growing dark. There were three tents, one for Maggie and Kevin to share; the other two would house the men.

Olaf nodded in satisfaction and took a fresh dip of snuff. "First time I go into Port Ludlow to tell Bill Sayward to send his tugboat up for the first shipment of logs, I'll have him send some planks along. Then we'll floor the tents and make a sidewall a few feet up. Be snug and dry when it rains."

While the tents were being erected, Maggie and Kevin had scoured the shore for dry driftwood and now had a fire going. Leaving Olaf surveying the tents with self-satisfaction, Maggie trudged to the fire, and stood looking at the food sack Kevin had partially emptied before he had curled up on the sand, fetus-like, by the fire, and was now fast asleep. Maggie, although hungry, felt like doing the same. Never in her life had she been so exhausted.

"Ma'am . . . Maggie," said a soft voice behind her.

She turned her head to look into Lars' bright blue eyes.

"I know you're tired, Maggie. We all are. Pa sometimes expects too much of a woman, without really meaning to. He did that to Ma . . . but never mind that." Lars gestured sharply. "What I'm getting at, let me help you. We do have to eat, if we're to do a day's work tomorrow. I know you must be hungry, too. So I'd like to help. I'll build a framework to hang the pots on, and help with whatever I can."

There was a note of firmness, of authority, in the voice of the heretofore shy Lars that took Maggie by surprise. She said, "Thank you, Lars. I could use some help."

A spark of humor struck his eyes. "We'll fix Pa in the morning. He's always bragging about what a great cook he is. I'll see to it that he gets up and makes breakfast for us."

Maggie was shaken out of a deep sleep before daylight the next morning by a great bellow, "All out for the woods!"

Maggie groaned, wishing she didn't have to get up. Across from her Kevin made a grumbling sound.

"You go ahead and sleep, Kevin dear. You won't be needed, and I'll set a wee bit of breakfast aside for you."

Still half-asleep, Maggie put on her clothes, glad of the woolen skirt, jacket, and heavy shoes that Olaf had suggested she buy in San Francisco. It occurred to her that she wouldn't be needed either, but if she intended to learn the logging business, she was determined to observe every phase of it.

Once dressed and outside, she took a moment to look around. The morning was damp and misty, but the air was fresh and scented as no other she had ever breathed. Again, she experienced the feeling of wonder and awe, that she was never to lose, in the presence of these great trees. This rough, raw country had a terrible, fierce beauty that almost bruised the senses with its intensity.

She took a deep breath, and turned toward the fire Olaf had built. The men were all gathered around a huge blackened pot, from which Olaf poured thick, black coffee into tin cups. Then he dished out fried slabs of salt pork, fishcakes, and German potatoes onto tin plates. In a skillet resting on a bed of coals were biscuits; each man helped himself to several. Maggie was the last to be served, and she huddled close to the fire as she ate. Finished, she dozed for a moment before Olaf's great voice brought her upright. "All right, men, let's go fall our first tree!"

Lars and Tom Reese each carried axes and springboards, while Patrick and Dan toted crosscut saws. With an axe thrown over his shoulder, Olaf led the way up the slope several yards, occasionally stopping to clear away underbrush. Finally he halted near a towering Douglas fir. At a gesture from him, Lars and Tom Reese started chopping away the underbrush from around the bole of the tree. When it was all cleared, Maggie saw that the bole was close to eight feet thick at the base. She wondered how they could possibly chop through that much thickness of timber.

But as Maggie watched, she learned they had no intention of doing that. Following Olaf's directions, Lars and Tom Reese took up positions facing each other in front of the tree, then quickly chopped a narrow notch in the side of the trunk nearest them. In the early morning hush the sound of the axes rang out loud and clear, and Maggie thought the sounds could probably be heard for miles.

When both men had a notch cut to their satisfaction, they inserted the metal V-tips of their springboards about two-thirds of the way in, and about five feet from the ground, then climbed up onto them.

To Maggie's surprise, Olaf said, "Not high enough, boys. She's still too thick to chop through. Go up another five feet."

Standing on the springboards, the two fallers did as instructed. When Lars' notch was to his liking, he did something that both thrilled and terrified Maggie. He drove his axe deep into the trunk well above him. Then, clinging to the axe handle with one hand, he swung free while repositioning his springboard in the new, higher notch. For such a big man, he was as graceful as an acrobat, and he hung by one hand without any apparent effort. For the first time, Maggie was made aware of the fact that Lars was a man, not a boy.

And now he glanced at her, smiling. She had to turn her head away from the intensity of his blazing blue eyes.

When she finally looked again, Lars was grinning down at Tom Reese challengingly.

"Now Lars," Olaf called up, "don't be showing

124

off like a kid. That's a dad-damned good way to get somebody killed!"

"Never mind, Olaf," Reese said cheerfully. "What that young buck can do, I can do."

Reese drove his axe into the tree, and repeated Lars' feat, not so easily and not nearly so gracefully, but he managed it well enough. Now the two fallers were balanced on their springboards almost twelve feet above the ground.

Olaf said, "It takes two cuts to fall a tree this size, Maggie. A front undercut and a back cut. This is the undercut, o'course. Then they'll do a back cut, yust deep enough in to take away all support, and Mr. Tree will coming crashing down on this side, toward the water."

Maggie watched, fascinated, as the two fallers faced each other on their perches, Lars swinging his axe right-handedly, and Reese chopping left-handedly. The undercut was flat at the bottom, angled down about forty-five degrees at the top.

She was startled by something that happened when the cut was about sixteen inches deep. From the gap gushed a fountain of yellow-brown liquid. Both men apparently had been prepared for it, and leaped from the springboard to the ground before getting splashed.

Olaf called, "That's good, boys. We'll let her drain for a bit, while we have lunch. By then you should be able to resume cutting." To Maggie, he explained, "That's pitch, girl, crude turpentine. All these big trees have it. I saw a faller once get drowned in pitch cause he was ignorant and didn't know to watch out for it."

By the time they finished their lunch and had

rested for a bit, the gushing of pitch had dwindled down to a mere seepage. At Olaf's nod, Lars and Reese clambered like a pair of giant monkeys back up to their precarious perches. Again, the forest rang with the sounds of their axes.

The axes flashed with metronomic regularity in the sunlight. The two men chopped steadily, resting only for a few minutes an hour. Maggie marveled at their stamina.

It took almost four hours to finish their undercut. The incision reached more than halfway through the trunk, and was carved as smoothly as if it had been sculptured.

Then Lars and Reese removed their springboards from the front notches, and cut new notches in the back at approximately the same height.

After their springboards were positioned, Lars held up his hand. "Wait a minute, Tom." From the ground he picked up a small tree branch, sharpened it to a point with a few quick slashes of his axe, then strode down the slope about sixty feet. With one eye squinted, he glanced at the tree, then at the ground. Finally satisfied, he drove the sharpened branch into the earth, and labored back up the slope toward them.

Before he could mount the springboard, Olaf stopped him, growling, "I ain't much in favor of this showboating, boy."

"What do you mean, Pa?" Lars said in wide-eyed innocence. "We have to show Maggie that we know what's what about logging, now don't we?"

"Dad-damnit, Lars! Oh, shit." Olaf gestured in disgust. "Yust get on with it."

As Lars and Reese took their positions on the

back side of the tree, Maggie asked, "Olaf, what was that all about?"

Still grumpy, Olaf spat. "The way a tree falls is determined by the placing of the backcut to match up with the front undercut. A good faller can make his backcut so that the tree will fall in the exact spot he wants it to. Lars, he's yust showing off." He gave her a baleful glance. "And you know why, Maggie? 'Cause a comely female is watching, that's why!"

"It's no fault of mine. I didn't tell him to do it!"

"All the same, that's the reason." He turned to Maggie's brothers. "Everbody stand well back out of the way, over there." He pointed to a spot off to one side. "Yust because that idiot boy of mine says the tree'll fall where he wants it to, don't mean it will."

Maggie herded Kevin to the spot indicated, and Patrick and Dan followed. Both big brothers had been watching the operation in silent, open-mouthed wonder.

Now Patrick stuck out his chest, and said, "Sure, and it won't take me long to learn how to do what those boyos are doing."

Olaf snorted. "Longer than you think, young feller. Don't know how many men I've seen get killed by becoming fallers too soon. Yust remember, young Patrick, I'm bull-of-the-woods here. You get on the springboards when I say, not before."

It wasn't too long before Lars shouted, "Timber!"

He and Reese tossed their axes into the underbrush, and hurtled from their springboards, landing well out of the way.

There was a cracking sound, and Maggie watched in breathless awe as the giant tree began to fall, slowly at first, then gaining momentum until it struck the ground with a mighty crash. Maggie felt the very earth shudder under her feet. She felt shaken and subdued, as if she had just witnessed the death of a giant. The air was redolent of pitch, which Maggie could not help but think of as the tree's blood.

Lars came bounding down the slope to the spot where he'd driven the branch into the ground. The others followed him, even Olaf limping along behind. With his axe Lars swiftly trimmed the tree branches out of the way, then squatted down. He gave a shout of triumph, and stood up.

"See? Right on the button!"

They crowded around. It could easily be seen that the tree, in falling, had struck the sharpened branch and driven it into the ground. The men clapped Lars on the back, yelling congratulations. He looked over their heads, seeking Maggie's gaze.

But Maggie stood apart, gazing at the felled giant of a tree, at the moment unaware of anything else in the world.

That night, by candlelight in her tent, she penned her first letter to Kathleen since leaving Ireland:

My Dearest Kathleen,

Please forgive me, dear sister, for not writing sooner, but I have not really had much to write about. Not that nothing has happened to the

Donnevans, but up 'til now, most of it has been uncomfortable, tedious, and dull.

But today, today I feel like our life in the new world has really begun. We are in the logging business, Kathleen, and today I saw our first tree felled. How can I put into words what I felt? I felt pride, glory, and exultation, yet at the same time I felt humbled and saddened. Mere words cannot describe the great trees here, Kathleen. They stand high like gods, and today, I was responsible for killing one of those gods, a tree that has lived for a thousand years! Kathleen, when the men started to chop into it with their axes, it bled, bled just like a person with a terrible wound!

Yet, I cannot help but feel triumphant. I feel that the Donnevans are well-started on their way to a fortune. The logging business, so my bull-of-the-woods tells me, is on the verge of a great boom, and we are in at the beginning!

We are all well and thriving. Alas, I cannot tell you that our older brothers, especially Patrick, think any less cruelly of you, but I am sure he will mellow with time.

I hope that you are well, dear sister, and it is also my fondest wish that you will be with us once more. At the present time my finances are strained, but if we succeed as I pray we will, I will soon be able to send you passage money so you may return to the bosom of your dear ones. I dream of this every night. Perhaps by the time this missive has reached you, it will be possible.

You know, of course, that you have my everlasting gratitude, and all my love. Right now, I weep for your plight, and pray that it will soon be lightened.

Your Loving Sister, Maggie.

The next day, at first light they were at work again. Lars and Reese began on another tree, and Olaf showed Patrick and Dan how to chop away the branches on the felled tree until nothing remained but the trunk. Then he instructed them in the use of the crosscut saws. He gave each brother an eight-foot stick. "Measure the logs into sixteen-, twenty-four-, or thirty-two-feet sections," he explained. "Then saw them into those lengths. That's the lengths the sawmills like."

As soon as they got into the swing of it, Patrick and Dan handled their saws well. The only problem was that Patrick stopped now and then to look wistfully at the tree where Lars and Reese were chopping.

The third time she saw Patrick stop sawing and straighten up to stare at Lars and Reese on the springboards, Maggie went over to him and hissed, "Get back to work, Brother! You have a job to do, do it!"

With an injured air, Patrick replied, "Just getting the crick out of my back."

"You are not! You're envious, wanting to be up on those springboards!"

"Sure, and why shouldn't I be? It's our company, ain't it? I can do as good a job as those boyos!"

Maggie sighed. "Sometimes, Patrick Donnevan, I think you have porridge for brains. When the time comes for you to be a faller, and you'll be a good

130

one, I'm sure, Olaf will tell you. In the meantime, Brother, bend your back to the saw!"

She wandered over to where Olaf was busy trimming the branches from the second tree just felled. "Couldn't I help with that?"

"Nah." Olaf straightened up. "It ain't all that easy to handle an axe, not as easy as it looks. Don't worry, little lady. When we get going good, there'll be plenty to keep you busy."

Maggie still managed to find a job for herself. She and Kevin dragged the trimmed branches out of the way, to give easier access to the tree trunks for Patrick and Dan with their saws.

Within a few days, the crew had established a rhythm. Lars and Reese were felling two, sometimes three and four trees a day, depending on the circumference of the trunks. The two brothers, accustomed to the saws now, were able to keep up with the fallers.

When the felled trees were sawed into the proper lengths, Patrick and Dan, with Olaf supervising, gave the logs a hard push, and they slid easily down the gentle slope and into the water of the cove. By the end of the week, a trough had been worn into the ground, and the logs slid down even easier. By day's end, Maggie would stand on the beach, and gaze with pride at the growing number of logs floating buoyantly in the water.

One misty evening, Olaf said, "By the end of the next week, we'll have enough for Sayward to send his tug along and float 'em to his sawmill. You'll have your first logging money, Maggie. I'll make the trek down to Port Ludlow when we're ready and bring the tugboat up. Also, I'll scout around

131

and hire two more men for buckers. I think it's about time to break your brothers in on the springboards. Now don't worry . . ." He held up his hand as Maggie murmured a protest. "I'll see that they take it slow and easy, and that no harm comes to them. But they have to learn some time." He turned and looked back up the slope. A clearing now went some distance up, all the trees gone except for stumps. "I think I'll move our camp aways up the hill. The rains are starting now, and it'll be drier up aways. I've already picked out a nice, flat spot for our new camp."

Olaf followed through with his proposal the next day. While the fallers started on a new tree, the others took down the tents and moved them to a flat area about seventy yards uphill. Olaf had the tents pitched under the overhang of a squat tree, its low branches spreading out, forming a leafy roof.

"We'll leave this one stand," Olaf said. "Too short for good logs, anyways. From now it's gonna be raining most ever day. Those branches will give us some protection."

After the tents were up, he showed the brothers how to dig a trench in a U-shape to divert any water sluicing downhill around the tents. Then they dug a fire pit for cooking.

Olaf stood back and nodded in satisfaction. "Yah. Not bad. When I go in to Port Ludlow, I'll order some lumber sent down, and we'll wall the tents partway up. We'll make them tents real snug."

Olaf went to Port Ludlow, but for a different reason.

Maggie still couldn't resist going down to the beach twice a day, morning and evening, to look at

132

the collection of logs. On the morning of the day Olaf had selected to journey to Port Ludlow, she arose earlier than usual. Day was just breaking as she reached the beach.

She stopped at the edge of the water, staring in disbelief. She couldn't believe her eyes. When the truth finally struck home, she opened her mouth and screamed.

Within minutes all the men, half-dressed, came running down the hill toward her.

Patrick reached her first. She was still screaming. He shook her roughly. "Maggie! What is it, lass?"

She stopped screaming and pointed a trembling finger. "Look!"

All eyes turned to follow her pointing finger.

"The logs!" Maggie cried. "They're all gone! Not a single one is left!"

Chapter Six

"Dad-damned sonofabitch!" Cursing, waving his arms, Olaf limped up and down the beach.

Maggie, slowly coming out of shock, turned to him in bewilderment. "But what happened to them? Did the tide take them out into the channel?"

"Tide, my red ass!" Olaf snarled.

Maggie had never seen him so furious. He worked his mouth and spat, then looked startled when no snuff came out. Evidently, he had rushed from the tent before he could fill his cheek with his morning dip.

He came to a stop before her, glowering. "They've been stolen!"

"Stolen? But how, why?" she demanded. "And who?"

"Don't be thick-witted, Maggie. Why? Because

135

they're worth a hell of a lot of money! And how? They were quietly nudged out of the bay during the night while we snored away. And who?" He hesitated a moment. "Jake Fargo, who else? Yah, no other sonofabitch around these parts mean enough to do it!"

"And he just gets away with it? There's nothing we can do?"

"Nothing. How can we prove it? The logs don't have your name on them, do they? Jake floats them to a sawmill, says they're his, and who's to say different?"

An enraged growl came from Patrick, who had been listening with his fists clenched. "Sure, and we can descend on this Jake Fargo like avenging angels and get back what's ours!"

"Avenging angels!" Olaf glared at him in disgust. "Young feller, Jake Fargo has a crew of twenty men, and all are rough as they come. Jake would yust as soon order us killed as not!"

"No, that's not the answer," Maggie said slowly, still staring out at the empty water. For a moment despair seized her, draining her spirit; then anger and determination took its place. She set her lips. "We'll just have to get back to work, and work harder. There are still plenty of trees left. Soon as you all have breakfast, get back to work."

Slowly, the men turned away, all except Olaf who remained alongside Maggie, staring glumly at the empty cove. He said, "Yah, we can fall more trees. But we'll have to keep men on guard ever night, or Jake Fargo will strike again when we have a goodly number of logs."

"I think I have a better idea, Olaf. Your saying

that the logs didn't have my name on them made me think of it," Maggie said. "I've read somewhere that cattle ranchers in parts of the United States have had trouble with people stealing their animals. So they began using irons on their cattle, burning a brand into their hides. Why can't we do that? Then Jake Fargo couldn't steal them and claim them as his own."

Olaf stared at her, his mouth open slightly.

"Is there anything wrong with that idea?" she asked anxiously. "It wouldn't ruin the logs, would it?"

"Don't see why it should, so long as the brand's not burned too deep. Dad-damn, it might work!" He slapped his knee in glee. "Yah, you do surprise a man, Maggie!"

"All right," she said briskly. "You go into Port Ludlow today, as you planned. Have a brand made, with a . . . a big D. We need supplies, anyway. And the lumber for the tents. Also, you'd better hire two more men, for buckers, as you suggested. If we're going to increase production, it's high time Patrick and Danny became fallers." She refused to think about what it would cost and how seriously it would deplete her remaining funds.

Something of her thoughts must have been mirrored in her face, for Olaf said, "Bill Sayward is a nice gent. I'm sure, when I tell him your logs were stolen, he'll grant credit . . ."

"No," Maggie interrupted in a firm voice. "The Donnevans have had experience with credit. In Ireland, we call it 'hanging gale.' Once you get behind, you never catch up. I'll give you money to pay for what we need before you leave, Olaf."

Jake Fargo was pleased with himself. He had just sold the stolen logs to Captain Sayward for a good price. Born with the ethics of a weasel, it always delighted Fargo when he could rook somebody. Having been a knockabout for much of his life, usually only a short step ahead of the law, he had finally found a home here in the Northwest. At thirty-five, he was riding high, wide, and handsome, his pockets full of money enough to feed his gargantuan appetites for liquor and women. He was a greatly feared man in the Territory. After his reputation as a killer grew, it took a foolhardy man to challenge him. In this country, a man could do pretty much as he pleased without fear of the law. If you had the guts and the money, you could get away with just about anything.

During his five years around Puget Sound, Fargo had gathered around him a rare collection of rogues, all with a lack of ethics to match Fargo's own. He ruled them by a combination of fear and good pay, and they would follow him into Hell, if so ordered. In addition, they were all good loggers.

Fargo much preferred stealing logs that others had worked hard to gather. It gave him great satisfaction, and stealing the collection of logs from the Jorgensons and the Irishers was a feat he'd chortle over for weeks to come. It would teach the goddamned scandies to desert him! No man ever left Jake Fargo's crew who didn't live to regret it.

At the moment Fargo was seated at a rough table in a Port Ludlow saloon, bent on getting roaring drunk in celebration. He was also casting a speculative eye on the bar girl, a buxom wench who called herself Fancy. She was new to Port Ludlow, and

Fargo hadn't bedded her yet. It was a matter of pride with him that he tumbled any new woman, including the married ones. The first few times he had made free with married women, there had been trouble with their husbands; but after Fargo had split a few heads, there had been no more of that. Nowadays, when he took a liking to a man's wife, the husband usually found it expedient to look the other way.

As Fancy came toward Fargo's table with a fresh mug of whiskey, she got an extra swing to her hips. Fargo had known he could go to bed with her from the moment she'd first clapped her green eyes on him. Since that bastard four years ago had snuck up behind him and taken away a part of his nose with one chop of an axe—the last lick he lived to get in—Fargo had learned to expect two reactions from women when they first glimpsed his mutilated face. Some of them were fascinated, immediately sexually aroused. All he had to say was the word and their skirts went flying up. The others, after a first look, turned away in revulsion. These took a little longer. But Fargo usually had his way with them. If all else failed, he would bide his time, corner them in some isolated spot, hold the pickaroon high with one hand, and unfasten his breeches with the other. It hadn't failed yet, and it was all the same to Jake Fargo if they were willing or not.

Fancy set the whiskey down, and started to turn away with a flirty roll of her eyes.

Fargo reached out and tweaked her rump between thumb and forefinger. Fancy jumped, squealing, and slapped at his hand.

Fargo winked. "You and me later, huh, Fancy?"

She tossed her head. "I don't know what you mean, Jake Fargo."

"Oh, you get my meaning, right enough." He leered. "And that ain't all you're going to get before tonight is over and done."

She gave another toss of her head, and strutted away without answering. Fargo bellowed with laughter and drank whiskey. As he set the mug down, he saw Snake enter the tavern and look around. Seeing Fargo, he started in his direction.

Fargo leaned back, waiting. Snake was his bull-of-the-woods, and the men were almost as afraid of him as they were of Fargo. No man knew Snake's real name. He had acquired the sobriquet for two reasons. First, he was a Southerner by birth, and spoke in a soft voice, and men who'd been in the South said he was as quiet and deadly as a cotton-mouth moccasin. Secondly, his cold black eyes had a slight Oriental slant, and were little more than slits.

Snake reached Fargo's table and sat down across from him. In his soft voice, he said, "That Swede, Jorgenson, is in town, Jake."

"So what's the Scandie doing here? Bitching about his logs being stolen right from under his red beak?"

"Not that I heard. He's been doing some supply buying, and he's been over at the blacksmith shop for some time. Now he's headed for the mill."

"Probably going to bellyache to Captain Sayward, claiming those logs the captain bought this morning belong to that Irish bitch he works for."

"What are yu-all going to do, Jake?"

Fargo shrugged. "I ain't worried about what he says to Sayward. What can he prove?" He finished off his whiskey, and got to his feet. "But I guess I'll amble over to the mill and see what's on the Scandie's mind." He shouldered the pickaroon which had been leaning against the table all the while and strode out, his footsteps so heavy the floor shook.

Outside the saloon, he paused to take several gulps of sobering fresh air, shook himself like a wet dog, then shouldered the pickaroon again and started down the slope toward Sayward's sawmill.

The sound of the big saws was a piercing whine in his ears as Fargo neared the buildings. He ignored it, and asked a millhand for Sayward's whereabouts. Informed that the captain was around back, Fargo went in that direction.

He found Sayward and Olaf Jorgenson in conversation. Olaf was showing Sayward a strange looking object, at least something Fargo had never seen the likes of.

"Well, what brings you out of the bushes, Scandie?" he said in his usual bellow.

The two men turned. Olaf said blandly, "We needed supplies, and some more men."

Fargo blinked at the mention of more men. He had been sure that the Donnevans had put together a shoestring outfit, and that the theft of their logs last night would be a finishing blow. He said, "Doing that well, are you, that you need more men?"

"Yah, doing yust fine, Jake," Olaf said, still in that bland voice. "Had a little setback last night, but we can scrape through. Maggie Donnevan is a determined woman, and don't give up easy."

"What setback was that?"

141

"Woke up this morning to find all our logs stolen. . . ."

Fargo bristled. "You're here accusing me of stealing your logs, Jorgenson?"

"Now did I say that, Jake? Strikes me you're pretty dad-damned touchy, for some gent that ain't been accused of anything."

Fargo said belligerently, "Anything happens around the Sound, Jake Fargo is the first one they look to."

"Yah, that's true. But I ain't accusing you, since we got no proof. But anyways, Maggie has figured out a way to put a stop to anyone stealing her logs. This. . . ." He held out the object.

Fargo peered at it suspiciously. It was metal, with a long handle like a pipe, and one end had been bent into the shape of a letter. "What's that?"

"It's an iron to make brands. Maggie's idea," Olaf said cheerfully. "She says down in the cattle country ranchers brand their cattle, to stop thieves from taking them. With this, we heat it and put her brand right on each and every log. See?" Olaf pointed to the letter. "A big D, her brand."

Captain Sayward said admiringly, "It's a brilliant idea. I can only wonder that somebody hasn't thought of it before this. It should put a stop to log stealing. There's far too much of it around the Sound."

Jake Fargo stared at the iron, at a loss for words. What Sayward said was true. No respectable saw-mill operator would buy logs with a brand on them, except from the legal owner. Black rage welled up in Fargo. He managed a casual shrug.

"Don't matter to me, one way or another. I don't go around stealing another man's logs."

"Yah, that's right, Jake," Olaf said, smiling. "You'd never do a thing like that now, would you?"

Fargo scowled at him. "Are you making sport of me, Scandie?"

Olaf assumed a look of innocence. "Now why would I do that, Jake? Everbody knows you're as honest as a minister of the Gospel."

"Go to hell, Jorgenson, and take that object with you," Fargo muttered, and spun on his heel.

He was boiling mad. To think that a silly little Irish bitch had thought of a way to thwart him! He knew that Jorgenson and Captain Sayward were right. That big D spotted on any logs he tried to peddle would immediately queer the sale. That Irish bitch was going to rue the day! Nobody made a fool of Jake Fargo. Wait until he managed to get her alone some place!

When he was out of sight of the mill, Fargo stopped at a pine tree and drove the pickaroon deep into the trunk, venting his great rage. The pickaroon was driven so deep into the wood that it took all his strength to wrench it free.

With the four buckers Olaf had brought back from Port Ludlow, production soon doubled at the Donneven logging camp. Patrick and Dan were now fallers. It didn't take them long to catch on. Olaf watched over them carefully at first to make sure they didn't take too many risks until they got the hang of it.

Maggie also watched, with apprehension in the

143

beginning, but she soon saw that they were doing fine.

Olaf said admiringly, "They might have been born to it, them brothers of yours."

Naturally, at the start, they weren't able to keep up with Lars and Tom Reese. One thing Maggie was fearful of—Patrick's fierce, competitive spirit. She knew he would never be satisfied until he and Dan could fall as many trees as the other pair. For this reason, she was afraid he might become unduly reckless.

However, watching as unobtrusively as possible, she soon realized that Patrick had developed a vast respect for logging, and proceeded with care. She was proud of him. Hopefully he was maturing, learning to curb his impulsive nature.

The small cove began to fill with logs again. Maggie took over the branding herself. She kept a small fire going near where the four buckers worked. Each time they had a section of tree ready to slide down the slope and into the water, she took the branding iron from where it was kept hot in a bed of coals, and planted her brand on it. She felt a small throb of pride every time she burned the big D onto the end of a log.

Most of her money was gone, and this worry nagged at her from time to time. She could always sell more of her remaining hoard of diamonds, yet she was determined to do that only as a last, desperate resort.

Her worries were eased somewhat when Olaf assured her that the money she received from the sale of the batch of logs to William Sayward would be considerable, enough to pay the back wages of the

144

men, buy fresh supplies, and still leave a substantial profit. If nothing dire happened before the logs were sold, her money worries would be over.

Within three weeks, working seven days a week, from sunup until sundown, the small bay had all the logs it could hold. Olaf told Maggie one evening that he would be leaving for Port Ludlow in morning, and return in Sayward's tugboat for the logs. "Should be back with the boat afore noon."

On Olaf's first visit to Port Ludlow, Maggie had instructed him to purchase two complete logger's outfits—flannel shirts, trousers, and boots, in boys' sizes—for her.

Olaf had been scandalized, as had been her brothers, when she started wearing them. The first morning, as Olaf and her brothers expressed their displeasure, Maggie had faced them across the cookfire, hands on hips.

"Whisht! I'm not much concerned about how *you* think I look! I'm just being practical. . . ."

"It ain't fitting, Maggie," Patrick had muttered.

"Fitting or not, get used to it. I can't go around out here wearing dresses. Almost every time I get near underbrush, the dress gets ripped." She had glared at them. "Now I'll hear no more about it, is that understood?"

They had turned away, muttering. Lars, who had listened with a slight smile on his lips, came around the fire to whisper, "I'm not shocked, Maggie. I think you look pretty in those breeches and boots. Of course, I'll have to admit that I'd think you pretty in anything."

Maggie had been glad her face was already

flushed from the fire, for she knew she was blushing. Her feelings about Lars were ambivalent. In the beginning she had thought him a bumbling, timid lout. Now she knew that to be far from the truth, and daily she grew more aware of his thoughtfulness, his high regard for her; but most of all, she became uncomfortably conscious of his maleness in a way that embarrassed her. Her experience with Andrew Kane had made Maggie aware of feelings in herself that she had previously been unaware of, or had chosen to ignore. It was as if that night on the beach had opened a door for her; a door into a different, adult world, a world that on the one hand tantalized, and on the other, frightened her.

For just a moment the memory of Andrew Kane's body against hers was more real than the cookfire and the men around it. Then she tightened her lips and pushed the memory away. At least she was not with child; she had been spared that much. The Saints had been kind.

On the morning Olaf left for his second trip to Port Ludlow, Maggie, instead of trudging up the slope to where the loggers were working as she usually did, sent Kevin along by himself with instructions to stay out of the way. Then she took a bath and put on her best dress and shawl. When the little tugboat came chugging down the channel shortly before the noon hour, Maggie was waiting on the water's edge. Knowing they would have to walk home back up the coastline, she had her heavy shoes in her reticule.

Olaf came ashore in a small rowboat. He gave her a surprised glance, but made no comment on her attire. He faced the tugboat and gave a wave of his hand. The boat sounded two short toots on its whistle.

In a few minutes the men came hurrying down the slope. Under Olaf's instructions, each man took a cant hook and clambered nimbly out onto the floating logs. Two men on the tugboat threw out thick, heavy ropes and chains. The loggers danced about on the logs, lashing them together with the ropes. Once, Patrick lost his balance and tumbled into the water. He came up spluttering, his face turning red as the others hoorahed him.

Within a surprisingly short time, the logs were all lashed together and tied off to the stern of the boat by the chains. The whistle tooted twice, and Olaf untied the rowboat and climbed in.

"Wait, Olaf," Maggie said. "I'm going into Port Ludlow with you."

He looked at her dubiously. "I don't know as that's a good idea, Maggie. I'm going to be busy with Bill Sayward when we get in and . . ."

"Whisht! Don't concern yourself about me bothering you two men in your bargaining," she said tartly, "although the time will soon come when *I* will handle the sale of our logs. Don't be forgetting, Olaf Jorgenson, that this is *my* company!"

His face flushed. "I'm not forgetting, girl. If I ever do, I'm sure you'll be fast enough at reminding me."

"However, I have enough wit to know it's not time for me to do the bargaining yet. Your Captain Sayward would probably swoon away should he have to bargain with a woman. . . . But I've been out here nigh onto two months, Olaf, and not a sniff of civilization have I had!"

Olaf laughed. "Port Ludlow, that's civilization?"

"As close to it as there is around here. Olaf . . ." She resorted to guile. "Don't be balking me. I want to ride in with my first shipment of logs, and I want to shop at the general store. Is that too much to ask?"

"Of course not, Maggie." He made an awkward bow, almost capsizing the tiny rowboat. "You're more than welcome to come along. I was yust caught by surprise, is all. Yust remember, once we get to Port Ludlow, you'll be on your own until we're ready to depart. As it is, we'll have to walk back by dark."

"I'll try to manage on my own," she said in a dry voice.

He helped her into the rowboat, and rowed it out to the tug. The moment they were on board, the boat's pilot got the steam up and started the tugboat forward. The chains tautened, and for a few moments Maggie was positive the tiny boat didn't have the power to tow all the logs. But slowly, almost imperceptibly, it began to inch forward. It cleared the cove and turned south, moving at about two miles an hour. Of course, Maggie thought, the logs were buoyant, and once set in motion, they floated like a huge log raft. It took them almost two hours to reach Port Ludlow. Maggie reflected wryly that they could probably have walked faster.

She experienced an overwhelming surge of pride when the logs were finally towed into the pond by the sawmill, and men came out and danced across the logs to remove the chains and ropes.

She and Olaf went ashore. Olaf said, "I'll go dicker with the captain now." He smiled, touching her shoulder. "He's a fair man, Bill Sayward. You'll get a dad-damned good price for your logs, Maggie girl."

Reluctantly, she left the mill yard, and wandered up the single street, picking her way daintily in the mud. It rained almost every day now, usually in the mornings, clearing by afternoon. It was clear now, and sunny, dispelling the morning chill.

Maggie browsed for a time in the general store, buying several necessities, and finally purchasing a few luxuries she wouldn't have dreamed of buying before. She bought shirts for her brothers, then hesitated a long time debating whether or not to buy something for Lars. In the end she decided against it. If she bought something just for him, and not Olaf and the other loggers, not only would it place their relationship on a different level, but the others, especially her brothers, would view it askance. Although the signs from Lars were unmistakable, Maggie was far from ready to become romantically involved with him.

It was still early, and she knew Olaf would not be finished yet. She left the purchases she had made with the storekeeper, told him that if Olaf Jorgenson came looking for her she would be back before long, and wandered outside.

Undecided, she looked both ways along the short street—two saloons, a blacksmith shop, a small sign over an office advertising both "doctoring and teeth

149

pulled," and a small restaurant that looked about as appetizing as a pigsty.

Then her gaze was drawn to the two-story house on the bluff south of town. The sun glinted off the white paint, and the house seemed a beacon, summoning her. Without further thought, she struck out toward it.

It was about a half hour's walk. The land around the town had been logged off, with nothing left but thick, high stumps and new underbrush growing. But about a hundred yards up the steep slope, Maggie came to a line of trees, a forest so thick that the house was lost from view. Looking in both directions, she saw that the line between the forest and the logged-over land was ruler-straight. She assumed that the unlogged forest was Jonas Kirk's property, and he had refused to have it logged.

After a moment's hesitation, Maggie stepped into the trees, stepped from sunlight into coolness and shadow. The underbrush was so thick she soon questioned her wisdom in venturing in here. Surely the man in the house up there must have some kind of path down to the village. If so, she didn't see it anywhere. Undaunted, she plowed ahead.

Jake Fargo had just stepped out of a saloon and looked up the street in time to see the Irish bitch proceeding toward the line of trees south of town. He glanced around, but he couldn't see her big brothers or Olaf Jorgenson anywhere.

Fargo couldn't believe his good fortune. Smiling evilly, he shouldered the pickaroon and started after her. Hoping she wouldn't look behind her, he stayed some distance back. His good luck held; Maggie Donnevan never looked back once. When she ventured into the trees, Fargo quickened his step. He couldn't see her when he entered the forest, but it wasn't necessary. He could hear her moving through the heavy underbrush.

He began to hurry, anticipation of what he was going to do firing his blood. She was going to pay for thwarting him; oh, was she going to pay!

He caught up to her just as she stepped into the clearing Jonas Kirk had made around his house. She stopped there, gazing up at the house. Jake Fargo reached her in three quick steps.

She heard him then, and twisted her head around. Fear flooded her eyes at the sight of him, and she screamed. Then Fargo was on her. With his free arm he seized her around the waist, and carried her kicking and screaming back into the trees. A few yards in, he dumped her onto the ground on her back.

She started to scramble away, but he came down hard on his knees, one on each side of her, pinning her firmly to the ground.

Fargo raised the pickaroon over his head. He growled, "You scream once more, bitch, and I'll split your skull like a coconut!"

Maggie stared at him out of frightened eyes. She said in a tense whisper, "What do you want of me?"

Fargo laughed raucously. "You're supposed to be so damned smart, you can figure out what I'm going to do." Still holding the pickaroon high in one hand, he began unfastening his breeches with the other.

151

Chapter Seven

Maggie was terrified of this ugly beast of a man, but at the same time a great anger was welling up in her, overcoming her fear. Her thoughts darted frantically, seeking a way out of this predicament. Fargo was having trouble undoing his breeches, and was muttering curses. He took his eyes from Maggie momentarily, and she seized the chance. Just above her head was a young pine tree. Maggie reached up quickly, grabbing at the branches. Using her grip as leverage, she tried to pull herself from beneath Jake Fargo.

Instantly, Fargo clamped his knees together. His legs were hard as oaken planks, and Maggie felt as if she was being squeezed in a vise.

With a snarl Fargo struck her across the face with his open hand. "Try that once more, and I'll

153

use this, bitch." He raised the pickaroon, holding it poised threateningly.

With shocking suddenness the wooden handle splintered apart in his hand, the metal end falling harmlessly to the ground. The sound of a gunshot rang out in the woods. Startled birds flew up from the trees with a great rush of wings.

As the echoes of the gunshot died away, Jake Fargo was still staring stupidly at the short piece of pickaroon in his hand. Then he erupted with a great roar of rage and sprang to his feet, whirling around. Maggie sat up, staring.

A few yards away stood a tall, lean man, dressed immaculately in a ruffled shirt under a scarlet satin jacket, and dove-colored breeches stuffed into hunting boots. He had sandy hair lightly sprinkled with gray, a handsome face with a long, aristocratic nose, and piercing hazel eyes. In one hand he held a Colt, smoke still eddying up from the barrel.

"What right you got butting in here?" Fargo snarled.

"It seems to me that I have every right, old chap." The man's lips were curved in a slight smile. "This is my property. And from my house I saw you seize the lady and drag her into the trees. It occurred to me that she was in dire need of assistance. And from what I just observed, I was correct in my judgment."

It belatedly struck Maggie that he spoke with a British accent as strong as Lord Ramage's.

"Do you know who I am?" Fargo demanded.

"I do indeed know who you are, chappie. You are the infamous Jake Fargo."

"Then you know that nobody balks Jake Fargo without living to regret it."

"As to that, I fear I will have to take my chances."

"You're the loony lives in that big house, Jonas Kirk, ain't you?" Fargo said with a sneer.

"I am that Jonas Kirk, yes." The man's smile turned sardonic. "As to the charge of lunacy . . . well, one is reluctant to admit to having scrambled wits, isn't one? Of course I do know that I am so looked upon by the residents of Port Ludlow."

Fargo said viciously, "When I get my chance at you, without that there pistol, you'll have mush for brains!"

Jonas Kirk shrugged. "To retain one's self-respect in this world, certain risks must be taken. Perhaps I shall have to sleep with my weapon, as I understand you do with yours, Fargo."

As though suddenly reminded, Fargo glanced down at the shattered pickaroon. He nudged it with his boot, and said in a plaintive voice, "By damn, look at that! A perfectly good pickaroon ruined!"

"I'm sure you have others in your possession. Now I suggest," Jonas Kirk motioned with the Colt, "that you take your leave, chappie. Rather promptly, I might add."

Fargo scowled. "Nobody tells . . ."

Without warning, Jonas Kirk fired again, the bullet kicking up dirt between Fargo's feet. "Begone, I said! The third bullet, should it be required, shall not be wasted, I promise you that."

Fargo gave the man a murderous glare, but he turned on his heel and moved off, the sounds of his progress like the crashing passage of a bear through the underbrush.

Maggie spoke for the first time. "We call it fey."

Jonas Kirk, who had been looking after Jake Fargo, gave a start, and snapped his head around. "I beg your pardon, madam?"

"In Ireland, we don't call it loony, but a wee bit fey."

Jonas Kirk burst into laughter. "Ah, you're Irish! It has been so long since I've heard that delightful lilt." He made a courtly bow. "We haven't been properly introduced, madam. I am Jonas Kirk."

"And I am Maggie Donnevan."

"I am delighted to make your acquaintance, Mistress Donnevan." He moved toward her, hand extended. "Here, allow me to help you up."

Maggie's first impulse was to refuse—she could get up without assistance. But something inside told her to keep still. She accepted his hand, and allowed him to help her up.

"Thank you, sir. And I am most grateful for your coming to my aid. That awful man!" She shivered. "He should be caged like a wild animal!"

"Very true, madam. Unfortunately, most people hereabouts are frightened of him. Now, to soothe your nerves, may I offer you a spot of tea, and some cakes?"

She hesitated only momentarily before saying, "I would be grateful for that. A good cup of tea is a powerful restorative." Then she smiled, dimpling. "And I must confess that I am dying to see your house. Such a fine place it is."

"That, I fear, isn't saying a great deal, considering the other houses." He gave her his arm, and they started up the hill. "But I must say that I am inordinately proud of my house on the hill. And glad of a guest, I might add." His smile was wry. "I fear that I do not suffer from a surfeit of visitors."

It was on the tip of her tongue to ask the reason, but again she curbed herself. After all, she knew the reason—Olaf had told her.

But Olaf had also told her that Jonas Kirk was old, as old as Olaf himself. In that he had to be mistaken. Although Jonas Kirk had an air . . . no, an aura, of sadness about him, he looked at least fifteen years younger than Olaf. His step was firm, his body moved with grace and vigor, and there were no lines of age in his face, only the faint streaking of gray in his hair.

In only one respect did he resemble Olaf—that aura of indefinable sorrow about him, as if a great tragedy had descended on him at one time, or was impending. That, Maggie, thought, could be the fact that his wife, to all intents and purposes, had left him.

As they neared the house, something else struck Maggie forcibly. Here she was, arm in arm with an Englishman, about to have tea with him, and back in Ireland all Englishmen were sworn enemies of the Irish. If Patrick knew of this . . . whisht!

Up close, the big house looked even more imposing. It was immaculate outside, with neatly trimmed hedges, and beds of brilliant flowers. As close as she was now, Maggie could see that it had a pitched roof, carved cornices, cupolas, leaded glass windows in front, and an octagonal-shaped tower extending up three stories high.

157

Jonas led her up steep steps to a small porch, and through double doors.

Inside, Maggie stopped with a gasp of awe, looking straight up. There was a remarkable stairway spiraling up to the top of the tower, but what caught her attention was the ceiling, with frescoes representing the four seasons, represented by four classic female figures draped with scarves of blue and rose.

Neck still craned, she said, "That's absolutely beautiful! I've never seen anything to equal it!"

Beside her, Jonas laughed softly. "It also caused shock waves to go through what few ladies have been guests here. The one representing winter, as you can see, is rather scantily clad. Some of the more proper ladies have called it indecently nude, and refused to ever step foot inside here again." His voice changed, became diffident. "The frescoes were Constance's idea. Constance is my wife."

Questions about the missing Constance tumbled through Maggie's mind, but she sensed that it would be imprudent to ask them.

Instead, she said, "The stairway goes up three floors, yet from the outside your house appears to be only two stories."

"That is true. It is an extra extravagance, the stairway. It goes that high for only one purpose, for a closer look at the frescoes, and for a better view of the town and the harbor of Port Ludlow." He laughed softly again. "I grant you that the view is not all that grand. But the founders of Port Ludlow believed their village would become thriving and vigorous with time. Unfortunately, I believed them. Yet . . ." Now his voice became musing and somewhat distant. "I am just as content. I have become accustomed to being somewhat isolated, and now that Constance is not with me, I feel no inclination toward entertaining guests."

It was the last time he made mention of his wife's name during Maggie's visit.

Now she took time to look around her. Off to the right was a sitting room, elegantly furnished; to the left, on another side of the octagonal entryway, was a lovely dining room. An open door in yet a third side showed a library, with an easy chair, a heating stove, and shelves on shelves on shelves of books. The angled arches to the rooms, the walls covered with paper showing a profusion of pink roses—it was all very impressive.

Jonas said, "I fear that only these rooms you see are fully furnished, so it would serve no purpose to show you the rest of the house. Only one room upstairs is furnished as yet, the master bedroom. If you will be so kind as to have a seat in there," he motioned to the sitting room, "I will prepare the tea and cakes. I have no need of servants, since I live here alone. So if you will excuse me for a little, Mistress Donnevan. . . ."

"Maggie, please," she said. "I'd much prefer it. Being called Mistress gives me a feeling of putting on airs."

He looked deep into her eyes, then inclined his head. "Maggie, it is then. I do have a feeling we are to become friends."

Maggie had to look away from his direct gaze. She murmured, "I'd be after liking that, Mr. Kirk."

"In exchange, of course," he said lightly, "you must call me Jonas."

Fearing that she had already been too forward, Maggie went into the sitting room without answering. The furniture here looked unused, although everything was clean as a pin. Now she saw there was an open, connecting doorway between this room and the library. She peeked in. It was obvious that this was the room Jonas used for his own. The easy chair showed signs of much use, and a book lay open on a table beside it. Ashes were visible through the grating of the small heating stove, and wood was stacked high in a log cradle alongside it.

Maggie itched to get her hands on some of the books. She forced herself to turn away. She sat on a cushion on a window seat. The view *was* magnificent, disregarding the ugly sprawl of Port Ludlow. Beyond the town stretched the channel, the water sparkling like blue glass in the lowering sun. She could see both ways along the shoreline, the forests green and towering.

She spun about with a start at the sound of Jonas' footsteps. He was coming toward her with a tray holding delicate china cups, a steaming pot of tea, and a plate of small cakes. Maggie made a move to get up, and Jonas motioned her back down.

"No reason you can't have your tea there, my dear. That is the purpose of the window seat. Unfortunately, it has not been . . ." He broke off and began pouring her tea.

In a rush Maggie said, "All those books! How I would love to have a chance to read them!"

"You love books, my dear? How delightful!" His smile was pleased. "Then you shall borrow any you wish to take with you."

160

"Oh, I couldn't do that!"

"And why not, pray? Books are printed to be read. Without a reader a book is a dead thing. Besides . . ." His smile somehow seemed bolder. "It will give you a reason to return, and provide an excuse for me to see you again. Provided, of course," his smile left him, "you desire to do so."

"Oh, yes! I would like to come back!" She clapped her hands. Feeling heat flood to her face, Maggie looked away.

Sensitive to her discomfiture, Jonas busied himself with the tea, giving her a cup and offering her a choice of cakes. Then he sat down on a straight chair, cup and saucer balanced on one knee, a small cake on the other.

Maggie stole a glance at him. He looked so elegant, so at ease, that she knew he would have been at home in the grandest manor house in England. She took a nibble of the cake and a sip of tea.

"The cakes and tea are delicious!" She wanted to say that he would make some woman a good husband, but again she curbed her tongue, chiding herself. Of late, she had grown accustomed to blurting out her thoughts. It was a habit she would have to watch around this man.

After a few moments they became more at ease with one another, and out of her curiosity Maggie asked, "How on earth did you ever join the gold hunters? It would seem . . . well, so out of place for a man like yourself."

"Not so out of place, Maggie. Fortune hunters come from all countries and all strata of life. Gold has a magnetic attraction for an odd mixture of men. In the gold fields of California I encountered people of all races and creeds. As for myself . . ." His short laugh was self-deprecating, "I had little to lose. Back in London my family was not of the peerage, and while not destitute, they were far from affluent. They were able to provide me with an education, and that was the extent of it. You know what I was in London town? A schoolmaster."

"A schoolmaster?" Maggie echoed. "Whisht! Now a schoolmaster does seem a wee strange out on a search for gold."

"I would have thought so at one time. But I met not only other schoolmasters in the gold fields, but ministers of God as well. Oh, do not misunderstand me, my dear. It took some doing on my part—a man past forty and knowing nothing but teaching—to wrench myself from that life and enter into a frantic search of fortune in a strange, raw country, which, I assure you, was far less civilized than Port Ludlow."

"I should think it would take much fortitude." Maggie took a sip of tea.

"Not any more so than it took you, Maggie, and your brothers."

"There is a wee difference. We had nothing to lose and *all* to gain—" She broke off with a look of surprise. "You know about the Donnevans?"

He laughed outright. "You, an Irish lass and her brothers, entering the logging business? Ah yes, you are the talk of Port Ludlow. While I do not associate overmuch with the residents of the town, I could hardly fail to learn of you and your daring venture."

They chattered easily now, as they finished the

tea and cakes. Maggie told him a little of the hardships the Donnevans had endured, but mostly she just listened. It occurred to her that Jonas was starved for someone to converse with, for someone who would listen with lively interest. He was a witty conversationalist, telling her many droll anecdotes of his years in the gold fields and his finally, literally, stumbling onto a fortune. After many months of hard labor, he told her, he had been about to give up when, one Sunday, he had decided to laze away an afternoon, and went in search of a stream undisturbed by gold seekers in the hope of catching a few trout. He had found such a stream, a shallow, swift-running brook tumbling down out of the mountains. Unable to resist, he had removed his boots and waded into the icy water. He had stubbed a toe on one foot. Stooping, he had groped in the water for what he had stumbled over, and picked up a sizable nugget of pure gold.

". . . whole stream bed was strewn with gold nuggets. I managed to keep the location a secret long enough to actually pick up a fortune from that stream. . . ."

Maggie's attention had strayed; for some time she had been growing aware of a strange, rather disturbing thing happening. In the beginning there had been a tension between them, but a familiar tension—that between two people meeting for the first time. Now there was a new tension, and Maggie was starting to realize what it was.

This man desired her sexually. She knew it as clearly as if he had put it into words. This knowledge both excited and frightened her. Not that she was afraid of the man himself; she knew instinctively that Jonas Kirk would never offer her harm, never force himself on her. She was frightened by the powerful and sudden sensual response of her own body. In that moment, Maggie knew that she would offer little resistance if Jonas took her by the hand and led her upstairs to the one furnished bedroom.

Jonas was still talking, but Maggie's thoughts were yet inside herself, and his voice was a mere murmur. She was wondering why she was feeling the force of his desire. She made herself look at him closely. The tea finished and set aside, he lounged in the chair, long legs stretched out, hands resting on his thighs.

They were long, strong-fingered hands, and the sight of them evoked the memory of Andrew Kane's hands, hot against her breasts. That thought was followed by another even more unprecedented and embarrassing. How would Jonas Kirk's hands feel against her flesh; how would he touch her? Where? . . .

Maggie concealed a shiver, and had to look away from him. What had Andrew done to her that night on the beach at Port Townsend? Was she to be plagued by such feelings whenever she met an attractive man? Suddenly, Maggie was swept by an intense longing for her lost innocence.

Jonas' voice, suddenly concerned, penetrated through the dizzying swirl of her senses. "Are you all right, my dear? You suddenly look pale. . . ."

Maggie's gaze had focused on the outside through the window. It was after sundown. Olaf must be long finished with his business and concerned as to her whereabouts. Seizing this as an excuse, almost weak with relief, she jumped to her feet. "Jonas, I must go."

His features took on a look of dismay as he got to his feet. "So soon?"

She gestured. "It will soon be dark. Olaf, my bull-of-the-woods, will be worrying about me."

"If you must, you must." Then he said eagerly, "But you will return? I cannot recall when I have so enjoyed the pleasure of someone's company."

"So have I enjoyed it, Jonas. Not since I came here . . ."

He was already moving toward the library. "Come along and select some books to take with you." As she murmured a protest, he held up his hand. "No, I insist. That way I will be assured of your returning."

Without further protest, she went along with him and, following his suggestions, she picked three books to take along with her. Whisht! Now how would she explain the books to Olaf? She had already decided it wouldn't be prudent to tell Olaf where she had been. Then she gave a mental shrug. Olaf wasn't her keeper; she owed him no explanation.

"There is a path along the bluff that I use. It leads down to the village. I will accompany you."

"No, I'd rather you didn't, Jonas, although I do appreciate your kindness."

Again, his face showed dismay. "But my dear Maggie, no gentleman would allow a lady to walk alone, especially now that it is growing dark!"

"Please no. I will manage quite well."

Jonas Kirk, looking upon her flushed beauty, felt a great thrust of desire for her. It had been a long while since he had so wanted a woman. He had not lain with a woman since Constance's departure, and had thought that he had resigned himself to being celibate, but it had taken all his will power this afternoon for him not to make his desire known to Maggie Donnevan. It was in his mind to mention the fact that she had not managed so well earlier when Jake Fargo had assaulted her, but a look at the determined set of her chin told him that any argument would be fruitless. This was a proud, self-reliant woman.

He smiled ruefully, "If that is your wish, I concede."

In a rush Maggie said, "I will confess to you, Jonas, that I have a reason, one you might think a wee shabby. If Olaf learns where I have been, he will no doubt inform my brothers, and I would have to endure a great uproar from them. My older brother, especially, still thinks of me as a child, much in need of protecting."

Jonas nodded, still smiling. "I understand. But I *will* see you again?"

"You have my promise. We have been working seven days a week, but now that my first raft of logs has been sold, I believe I will give the crew a day of rest every week, on the Lord's day. I will be after seeing you on a Sunday. If that is all right with you?"

He said gravely, "I will look forward to it with pleasure."

Jonas accompanied her outside and pointed out the path along the edge of the cliff. Maggie hurried along, determinedly not looking back, certain his gaze was on her. She found herself again thinking of Andrew Kane, and the thoughts that rushed through her mind brought a flush to her cheeks.

At the moment that Maggie was returning to Port Ludlow, Andrew Kane was warm and snug in the soft bed of a buxom widow in Seattle. Amy Winslow was a few years younger than Andrew, was without child, and had been a widow for two years. She had not had carnal knowledge of a man in all that time.

Andrew, after a week's acquaintance with the widow, had just provided her with that long-denied pleasure, and both were well content.

There was, however, a slight prodding of Andrew's conscience, as he lay wide-awake beside the sleeping woman. It was not a prodding that disturbed him too deeply, but he did have a motive aside from mere physical satisfaction.

Amy's husband, who had drowned up the Sound during a squall, which had struck his brig and tumbled him overboard, had left her quite well off. Seattle, while far from a metropolis, had begun to grow after Henry Yesler had built his sawmill, and several fine houses had been constructed on what became known as Seattle's First Hill. One of those fine houses had been built by Carter Winslow for his bride. In addition to the house and the brig, Carter Winslow had also left a sizable amount of cash and many acres of timberland, land that would become valuable with time.

All Andrew wanted was the sturdy teakwood brig. It didn't seem too much to ask.

He was no longer Lieutenant Andrew Kane. His association with the Navy and the Customs Service had terminated abruptly two weeks ago in Port Townsend when he had finally decked the customs agent with one punch. After Andrew's intervention in the street fracas, the agent's animosity had grown daily, and his sly, cutting remarks had gotten under Andrew's skin.

Andrew didn't regret it. He had long known that his career was doomed. Better now than later. But he was left without the means to earn a living. With his superb seamanship he could always find a job, of course, yet he wanted more than just a job. Too independent by nature to follow another man's orders for long, he wanted a vessel of his very own, and that took funds he didn't possess. He had some money, but not nearly enough. Casting his eye about, he realized that tugboats were soon going to be as numerous as gulls on the waters of the Sound. The few already in operation were doing very well. Tugboats were needed to tow sailing vessels up to the Strait, and they were being used more and more to herd logs from logging locations to the sawmills. The smaller sawmill operators could not as yet afford their own, and would be happy to employ the services of independent tugboat owners. Now was the time to get into the business, at the beginning.

The problem, of course, was how to get his hands on a boat.

Andrew had drifted down the Sound from Port Townsend, from town to town, hoping for a miracle, hoping to find some boat he could pick up for practically nothing. He knew he couldn't buy a tugboat; they were all too costly. The tugboat had originated in the East and around the Great Lakes, and none had been imported out here. The few tugs on the Sound at present were small sailing vessels converted to steam, and that was what Andrew had in mind.

He hoped he had found his miracle in Amy Winslow. Her husband's teakwood brig would be ideal for his purpose. . . .

As if feeling the force of his thoughts, Amy stirred, throwing an arm across his chest. She gave a startled yelp and sat up, her heavy breasts swinging. Faint moonlight coming through the window gave a pale gleam to her voluptuous figure.

She sighed with relief, relaxing. "For a moment there I was frightened out of my wits. It's been so long since a man's been in my bed, and to wake up and find one . . ." Her hand caressed his chest. "I'm sorry I woke you up, honey."

"That's all right, Amy. I wasn't asleep yet."

"Still awake, were you? My goodness, I would have thought that after . . ." A sensuous smile curved her mouth. "We'll have to do something about that, won't we?"

She dipped her head and gently nipped at his nipple, her stroking hand moving down to his groin.

It was in Andrew's mind to tell her that *that* wasn't the reason he was still awake. But what the hell, he thought.

Taking her by the shoulders, he pulled her face up to his and kissed her. Her flesh was warm from sleep, and her mouth was sweet and hot. Andrew wondered fleetingly if he was up to it again so soon. Amy was a demanding woman, as he'd found out not too many minutes back.

"You just lie still, honey, and let Amy do all the work," she said with a soft laugh. "I've had a nap, I'm all rested up."

After only a token murmur of protest, Andrew sighed and settled back.

Amy might not have known a man sexually for two years, but she knew about all there was to know about sex, and she had forgotten none of it.

It wasn't long before Andrew realized that he was indeed capable of performing again. Amy discovered this with a crow of delight. She rose and straddled his hips, guiding him inside her. She was an energetic, enthusiastic, and a rather noisy lover. Certainly, she left no doubt that she thoroughly enjoyed it.

When their passion culminated, Amy gave a keening cry and collapsed atop him, breathing strenuously. She nuzzled his neck, her breath hot as steam. "Sweet, sweet Andrew! Am I ever glad you happened into my life. No, no!" As he started to speak, she clamped a hand over his mouth. "I don't require any declarations of love, or proposals of marriage. In fact, I'm not even sure I ever want to get married again."

Andrew, who had not been about to mention either love or marriage, deemed it prudent to say nothing for a moment.

She rolled off and stretched out beside him, still breathing heavily.

Sensing that she was about to fall asleep, Andrew thought that now was the opportune moment. He said, "That brig of your husband's . . . what are you going to do with it, Amy?"

170

"What?" she said in a muzzly voice. She raised her head. "Oh, Carter's boat. Sell it, I suppose."

"I . . ." Andrew cleared his throat. "I think I could make us some money with it, if you'd like to go partners. You furnish the brig, I'll do the rest."

"You can have the boat, honey, if you want it. I don't even know what, if anything, I could get for it." Her hand rested heavily on his thigh. "Let's don't talk business now. Amy is sleepy. . . ."

Her voice trailed off, and she was asleep. Content, Andrew settled down beside her. He knew he could sleep now. But even as he drifted into slumber, he well knew that he would never be completely satisfied until the teakwood brig was wholly his. He was confident he could figure out a way to manage it.

For the first time since they had started logging, Maggie slept late the next morning, following the sale of her logs. She was awakened by Olaf's bellow; she muttered to Kevin to go ahead, and fell back into a comfortable doze. They could get along without her for one morning.

Olaf was cross with her anyway. He had been cross as the Devil himself last night when she had come hurrying to the general store long after dark.

"Dad-damnit, where have you been, girl? I been worried to death, waiting here nigh onto two hours!"

"I'm sorry, Olaf," she'd said breathlessly. "I just wandered about exploring, and forgot all about the time."

Olaf had glared at her. "You have any i-*dee* what

171

could happen to a lone female, a pretty one to boot, wandering around here at night?"

Maggie had spread her hands in a helpless gesture. "I'm sorry, Olaf. But I am all right, as you can see."

"By Thor, you're just lucky, you can bet your wad on that! Now we got to hoof it, and that shoreline ain't too safe at night."

He had started off without another word, and Maggie had hurried meekly after him. She could have pointed out that they would have had to make the trek most of the distance in darkness anyway, but she had said nothing. Delighted with her afternoon with Jonas and hugging it to her breast like a secret, she trudged along behind him. Olaf's being cross as a bear delighted her as well, since she knew it was because he had been concerned for her welfare.

Olaf did tell her shortly before they reached camp that he had received a very good price for the logs, adding gruffly, "You're over the hump now, girl, if nothing else dire happens."

Maggie's morning doze was shattered as she was awakened by Kevin screaming somewhere nearby. "Maggie, come see! Come quick!"

Hurriedly, she threw on her clothes and ran from the tent. Confused, she stood looking about for a moment.

"Down here, Maggie! Hurry!"

She saw Kevin's small figure down at the water's edge, waving both hands at her. She wondered what had excited him, and started for him at a run. At least he seemed to be in no danger.

Breathless when she reached him, Maggie gasped out, "What is it, Kevin? What's wrong?"

He turned, pointing out into the channel. "Look!"

Maggie followed his pointing finger. Coming toward the cove, about fifty yards out, was an Indian canoe. There were two Indians in it. One was a man, naked from the waist up, and the other was an enormous woman, wearing voluminous clothing. She sat in the stern, with her arms folded, and the man was paddling, his thin arms straining at the paddle.

"Indians, ain't they, Maggie?" Kevin was jumping up and down in his excitement. "You 'spose they're coming to shoot us with bows and arrows?"

Before Maggie could answer, Olaf spoke from behind them. "Nah, youngster. From here I'd say they're the local Dwamish Indians. They're a peaceable bunch. The only hostiles hereabouts are the Yakimas and Klikitats."

"But what do you suppose they want here?" Maggie asked.

"Don't know." Olaf shrugged and spat. "Guess we'll soon find out. But don't be worrying. It's only a buck and his squaw. Ain't likely they'll offer us any harm. Probably come begging for food."

They all stood silently as the canoe neared the shore. Now they were close enough for the woman's voice to be heard. Clearly she was haranguing the man, who just hunched his shoulders and paddled faster. Shortly he drove the canoe up onto the beach, where it came to rest half out of the water. The big woman climbed ponderously out of the canoe, and waded through the few inches of water. On the beach she turned and motioned imperiously to the man, rattling off several guttural Indian phrases. Instead of answering, he suddenly braced the paddle in the sand and started to push the canoe back into the water. The Indian woman grabbed the prow of the canoe and, with seeming ease, pulled it all the way out of the water. Then she reached in with both hands, lifted the man out, and stood him on the beach.

Again, she spoke in her harsh-sounding language, and pointed a finger north. This time the man spoke back. She cuffed him across the face, and pointed again. Finally the man turned away dejectedly, and started north along the shore. The woman folded her arms and watched him walk away.

Maggie had been watching with amusement, not fully understanding what was going on, but since the Indian woman was twice the size of the man, it *was* humorous.

When the man had disappeared around the headland, the Indian woman snorted triumphantly, and turned to them. "He no be-damn good. No good at hunt. No be-damn good in blankets. Me . . ." She pointed to herself, beaming. "Me called Mother Be-Damn. I come cook for you, lady. Best be-damn cook you find." She spread her arms wide to encompass the whole territory.

Olaf was laughing quietly. Turning to him, Maggie said dubiously, "I don't know, Olaf. We could use a cook, I suppose. What do you think? The thing is, she isn't . . . well, she's not too clean."

"Mother Be-Damn mebbe not look clean." She

grinned. "But cook clean. You see. Not cost much. Food to eat, place to sleep. Little money."

Maggie's glance had strayed to the canoe. An idea came to her.

Dimly she heard Olaf say, "Why not give her a chance, Maggie? Our crew's going to grow. I'm tired of cooking, and I'm sure you are. Yah, what's to lose? She can't cook, I'll boot her Indian ass out." He laughed. "Big as it is."

Maggie gestured to the canoe. "Is that yours, Mother Be-Damn?"

Mother Be-Damn scowled. "Sure, mine. How Mother Be-Damn go to village? Not swim." She laughed uproariously, showing strong, white teeth, and thumping her chest. "Too much squaw. Sink in water."

"Is it hard to use? The canoe, I mean?"

Now Mother Be-Damn looked puzzled. "Not hard. All do is paddle."

"I'll strike a bargain," Maggie said decisively. "You teach me how to use the canoe, and let me borrow it once a week, and I'll hire you. And if you're the best be-damn cook," she smiled, "like you say, you'll be paid a fair wage."

"Is bargain." Mother Be-Damn beamed, and held out a large hand. "What you Bostons say? We shake on bargain?"

Maggie's hand was swallowed up in Mother Be-Damn's huge, brown paw.

In a low voice, Maggie said to Olaf, "Bostons? Why does she call us that?"

Olaf laughed. "That's what the Indians up here call the white man, since most of the first settlers came from Boston, or thereabouts. . . . Maggie, what in thunder are you going to do with the canoe?"

Maggie smiled secretively. "Why, I'm going to use it to go calling," she said.

Chapter Eight

Maggie paddled the canoe briskly along the shore-line on her way to Port Ludlow. She had found that she needed only two lessons from Mother Be-Damn to get the hang of it. The most difficult thing she'd had to learn was how to guide it with the paddle. After several days of paddling it around the cove, she became very skillful at it.

This was her second trip in the canoe to Port Ludlow. She had gone to the village in the middle of last week, to test her skill and to purchase a complete new outfit, which she was wearing now on her way to visit Jonas Kirk. No more would she have to carry the heavy walking shoes in her reticule, and make the arduous trip on foot both ways along the rugged shore.

It had been ten days since her afternoon with Jonas. True to her promise, she had declared that they would only work six days a week henceforth, resting on the Lord's day. Their logging operation was going well; they were falling a goodly amount of trees during six days.

In the canoe were the books Jonas had loaned her. Maggie had read and enjoyed them thoroughly. She was using the return of the books as an excuse to visit with him on this bright, clear Sunday.

Olaf had made no comment when she had emerged from her tent at noon dressed in her new clothing. Patrick, of course, had demanded to know where she was going, off by herself.

Hands on hips, Maggie had snapped at him, "None of your business, Patrick Donnevan! It's time you learned that I do not have to account to you!"

"It's my job to be looking after you, lass."

"No longer it's not. I'm well able to take care of myself. Whisht! You'd think I was a wee child to listen to you!"

Still grumbling, Patrick turned away.

Lars, who had been standing by quietly, gave Maggie a rather ambiguous look, then also walked away. Maggie knew that Olaf had sneaked off to Port Ludlow when he learned they would not be working on Sundays, and she was sure he'd brought back bottles of liquor. They'd all be drunk by nightfall. She had learned that this was the usual custom in logging camps on off days. Still, she'd rather it happen here than in Port Ludlow, where they'd likely get involved in a brawl. They had been working hard and long, and deserved some relaxation.

"Dan," she said, "I'm expecting you to see to Kevin while I'm gone. I'll be back before dark."

"I'll watch after him, Maggie." With a twinkle in his eye, he added, "Have a good time, big sister."

Maggie sniffed, and got into the canoe.

Now, as she rounded the last headland and paddled into the harbor of Port Ludlow, she recalled her words to Patrick. What if Jake Fargo was loafing about in the village and saw her? Would she be able to defend herself better than before? But for Jonas, there was no telling what might have happened to her. She wondered if she should start carrying some sort of weapon with her when she went out alone. She would talk to Olaf about it.

After Maggie had tied the canoe to a piling under the wharf and climbed up the bank, she could see that there was little activity along Port Ludlow's single street. She saw only a few men about, and no one paid her any heed. As she looked around, Maggie was puzzled by a feeling that something was wrong. In a moment it came to her. It was the first time she had been in Port Ludlow that she hadn't heard the noise of the saws, that piercing whine coming from the mill.

Then she heard the sounds of distant singing. Head cocked, she listened intently—hymns.

Intrigued, she walked around the sawmill and looked up toward a small grove of trees to the west. She saw a small, white building—the only painted structure she'd seen in the village itself—almost hidden in the grove of pines. A church, of course! Strange, she hadn't noticed it before. But then she had never walked in that direction. She remembered, then, Olaf telling her that many of the people on the Sound were from that part of the United States called New England, and most New Englanders were pious, church-going folk.

Maggie thought again of Jake Fargo. In Olaf's words, she would have bet her wad that *he* wasn't attending church.

She found the path leading up the bluff to Jonas' house, and struck out resolutely. All the while her nerves sang like taut harp strings as she kept waiting for Jake Fargo to appear. She glanced back often as she toiled up the steep path, but no sign of him did she see.

Somehow she wasn't surprised to find Jonas waiting on the porch of the house. When he saw her, he bounded down the steps and hurried toward her.

"I had a feeling you might come today, and I saw you start up the path from the village." He caught her hands, raised one to his mouth, and kissed it. Then he stood back, still holding onto her hands. "Let me look at you. A new gown, I see, and you look magnificent in it. Truly breathtaking."

Maggie blushed. "Whisht! Jonas, you're after flattering me."

"No," he said seriously, then smiled. "Not even a wee bit. But come along, I have the teapot on." Taking her arm, he led her toward the house. "A strange thing happened after your visit, Maggie. I seemed to look at my house with new eyes. Before, I had been content with it, at least reasonably so, but it dimmed after you took your leave. Since that day, it has been gray and drab." He squeezed her hand.

Inside the house, Maggie dug the books out of her reticule. "I read them all, and I do thank you, Jonas. You have a fine feeling for good books, and I loved them. My days are busy, but the nights can be dull. The books brightened them considerably. I especially liked two of them. *Ivanhoe*, by Sir Walter Scott . . ."

He smiled. "That is considered by most critics the finest of the chivalric novels."

"And this one, *Wuthering Heights*, by Ellis Bell. Such grand passion consumed the characters!"

"I thought you might like that one. Actually, Ellis Bell is a pseudonym. The author was a woman, Emily Brontë." He took the books from her. "You shall take more books back with you. Now, into the sitting room with you. I'll bring the tea and cakes in shortly, my dear."

She watched him walk away. Jonas was dressed casually today, wearing only a ruffled shirt, wine-colored breeches, and a pair of tan boots. Even so, he managed to look elegant and attractive.

Maggie went into the sitting room, choosing the window seat again. She was nervous, quivering inside, but she tried to compose herself as best she could, sitting with her feet close together, long skirts folded over them, and her hands in her lap. But even so, she jumped slightly when Jonas came striding into the room with the tea tray.

He served her, and sat down himself. "Now, tell

me what has transpired with you, Maggie. Nothing has happened here . . ." He spread his hands. "My existence from day to day is dreadfully dull, I fear. I assume that, when you rushed out of here the other day," he smiled, "that someone was waiting for you? Perhaps with impatience?"

"Oh, yes! Olaf . . . he's my bull-of-the-woods, as I told you. He had sold my logs and I was long overdue. He gave me a great scolding, that he did."

Jonas leaned forward. "And did you tell him where you had been?"

"No, I . . ." She lowered her eyes. "I'm afraid I told a great lie. I told him that I had been exploring and forgot the time."

"Not such a great lie, Maggie. A necessary one, perhaps," he said gravely. "He might have been upset had you told him you had been having tea with the loony on the hill."

"I don't think you're loony, Jonas, not at all." Her eyes came up. "Whisht! If I was after thinking that, would I be here then?"

He inclined his head. "Thank you, my dear."

"I just thought it better he not know. Olaf is a wee bit of a gossip, and I'm sure you wouldn't want it bruited about that you had a . . ." She floundered, suddenly at a loss for words.

His smile was tinged with irony. "That Jonas Kirk, a married man, had entertained a lovely woman in his grand house?"

Maggie could only nod.

"I appreciate your concern, and your delicacy, my dear. But actually any gossip would harm you far more than me. It concerns me not a whit. I will tell you this, and if you will be so kind, we will not discuss it again. In a sense, my dear, I am not a married man. It has been over a year since I have seen my wife, and I doubt I ever will again. At least not here. Oh, we both keep up the fiction that she will return some day, when the house is completely furnished. That is the excuse she uses, claiming that she will remain in San Francisco until she has selected and shipped all the furnishings. But I am convinced that she will never return here. Marrying Constance and bringing her up here was a mistake on my part. She is a girl who loves the social whirl, the theater, the gay life. She considers this a barbarous country."

To her surprise, Maggie felt her eyes fill with tears. "I am so sorry, Jonas," she whispered.

"Sorry?" He raised an eyebrow. "No need for you to be. Constance would undoubtedly welcome me in San Francisco. But you see, it would not be because she loves, or longs, for me. It would be because I am wealthy." His voice was musing now. "I fear that I do not love her, either, and for that reason I have no intention of going to her. If I am in error, and she does decide to return here," he spread his hands, "she will be made welcome."

Jonas set his teacup aside and got to his feet, coming to stand before her. "One other fact I wish you to know, Maggie. I have not known another woman, in the physical sense, during my time alone here."

Maggie found her mouth so dry she couldn't speak, and she was so nervous inside she feared she would be sick. Her heart was beating wildly.

Jonas held out his hands. He said quietly, "Come

along, my love. I will now show you the bedroom upstairs."

Her hands, reaching out to take his, didn't seem to Maggie to be a part of her. Certainly she didn't do it of her own volition; she felt she was possessed by a will other than her own.

And yet, the instant her hands touched his, everything was all right. She became calm and . . . yes, in a way resigned, as if fate had ordained this.

Taking her hands in a firm grip, Jonas drew Maggie to her feet. To Maggie, she seemed to be floating on his arm all the way upstairs. There, they turned to the right down a short hallway, and Jonas opened the door to a large bedroom, with a profusion of colors and an elaborate, four-poster bed.

Although the room was flooded with light from outside, Maggie was only peripherally aware of the furnishings of the bedroom. All her being was focused on Jonas' deft hands as he began to remove her clothing. As the back of one hand touched her bare flesh, she trembled.

Jonas cupped her face between his hands and kissed her. The sweet touch of his mouth aroused a riot of feeling in her body, which felt heavy and languorous. She gave way to the sensations his kiss aroused, and clung to him, returning the kiss ardently.

His hands were inside her open bodice now, stroking her breasts. Her tender nipples throbbed in response to his skilled touch, and Maggie could feel the throbbing spread along her nerves until it reached a spot in the secret region between her legs.

"Yes, my love, yes," Jonas murmured. "Don't be frightened, it will be all right."

"I'm not frightened," Maggie said in a small voice.

"Yes, you are. You're all a-tremble. You remind me of a startled doe I came across once in the forest, poised on the verge of flight."

His words, although Maggie heard only the murmur of his voice, calmed her, stilled the fluttering inside her.

And then she was on the bed, her body naked to his gaze, to his knowing hands. It was pleasant, almost lulling, yet at the same time, there was a growing need in her that she dimly sensed would soon demand release. It was a feeling she had begun to experience with Andrew Kane, only to have it die unappeased. Would it die this time?

Maggie felt Jonas' weight leave the bed, and she made a grumbling sound of protest. While he undressed, she lay in a sort of limbo—a time of waiting that seemed to stretch into infinity.

Again his hands and lips touched her, and Maggie reached eagerly for him, speaking words, pleading words, that came from her lips in an unintelligible mumble.

"Yes, my love. Soon."

But Maggie was not to be denied. The urgings of her body were too powerful. She pulled him against her. With a soft sigh, Jonas complied. He rose above her.

At the moment of entry, Maggie felt an intense throb of pleasure and pain, and her hips moved until she and Jonas were locked together.

She heard Jonas' voice, "Gently, my love." But

every nerve in her body cried out for surcease from this torment of the senses, and she rose and fell, moving ever faster. The gathering of ecstasy in her was like a building pressure, like something begging for release from the confinement of her body.

Then it happened, a soft, warm explosion of pleasure, and Maggie cried out, her pelvis pushing against Jonas, lifting him clear of the bed. Finally, she moaned softly, and went lax.

She was aware that Jonas continued moving for a few moments, before a moan, almost of pain, came from his open mouth. She felt him shudder violently twice, three times, and then he was still.

In a little while a chuckle came from Jonas, now lying beside her. "I must say, my dear, that you are a greedy wench for love. . . ."

"I am not!" Maggie said heatedly, feeling a blush stain her cheeks.

"Easy now, my sweet Irish lass." He stroked a finger along her arm. "I did not mean it as an insult. I was greedy myself. It's just that it is unusual to find such enjoyment in things sensual in a woman." A dryly bitter note was in his voice.

Was he referring to his wife, to Constance? Maggie wondered.

Jonas was going on, "To enjoy love-making to its fullest, Maggie, one should savor it, make it last. It should be enjoyed as a gourmet enjoys excellent food . . . if you will forgive the metaphor."

"Food, is it? Whisht!" Maggie sat up, indignant. "I don't find that flattering!"

"Again, no insult intended." He placed a hand on her shoulder, and gently forced her back down

186

onto the bed. "You will learn, in time. I will see to it. I will endeavor to teach you."

A new and rather disturbing thought intruded into Maggie's mind. He spoke as if it was already settled that she would return again, more than once. Was he seeking a commitment from her? He had already spoke slightingly of his absent wife, if in a gentlemanly manner; but he had seemed certain that he would never see Constance again. The idea that Jonas might be considering a permanent relationship frightened Maggie. She'd had no such thought in mind. She had no intention of giving up her independence, of giving herself up body and soul to a man, any man!

She started to sit up, ready to leap out of bed and get into her clothes.

Again, with that ability he seemed to have to almost read her mind, Jonas placed a restraining hand on her shoulder.

"Do not misunderstand me, Maggie. I am not demanding anything of you. You may come and go as you choose. If you decide that this will be your last visit, I will acept your decision. Unhappily, but I will accede to it." He laughed abruptly. "Can you visualize me marching up to you at your logging camp, a man completely out of his element, demanding that you return to my arms? All the while confronting those Paul Bunyan brothers of yours?" He sobered. "On the other hand, my Irish lass, do not make demands of me either . . . beyond what has happened here this afternoon. I cannot meet them. In the first place, I am married. In the second place, and far more importantly, I am too old—"

"Oh, Jonas, darling Jonas! How can you be talk-

ing of being too old after what has just happened?"
Laughing, Maggie flung herself against him, raining
kisses on his face. Yet she knew, in her secret heart,
that she was immensely relieved.

And in truth, Jonas gave no indication of being
too old, as they frolicked on the bed, laughing together, and tumbling about. In a short while both
were aroused again, and this second time Maggie
let Jonas lead the way. He caressed and fondled
and kissed her body until she was in a sweet agony
of torment. When he finally took her, Maggie's
passion consumed her, and she was mindless for a
few blind moments of ecstasy.

The hour was late when Maggie finally took her
leave of Jonas; she calculated she had just enough
time to paddle the canoe back to the logging camp
before dark. She took three more books along with
her, and promised Jonas that she would return the
following Sunday.

Hurrying down the path, she looked back once.
Jonas stood tall on the small porch, watching her.
She waved, and he returned the gesture.

As she hastened on, Maggie heard the clink of
glass in her reticule, and quickly reached inside to
check the bottles Mother Be-Damn had given her.
Finding the bottles unbroken, she continued on her
way.

The business with the bottles had brought the
hot blood surging to her face, despite the cool of
the afternoon air. The fact that she had them with
her was an admission that what had happened this
afternoon between her and Jonas was premeditated
on her part; for the bottles contained two sub-

stances concocted by the Indian woman, the purpose of which was to prevent conception.

The subject had come up unexpectedly, when Maggie had asked the woman if she had any children.

Mother Be-Damn had snorted. "No babies! Babies much be-damn bother; much crying; much pain. No babies!"

Maggie had smiled to herself at the woman's vehemence. She liked the ponderous Indian woman despite her rough ways and uncouth talk. She had the feeling that nothing she could say would shock the older woman, and that Mother Be-Damn was, in her rough manner, honest. And she was, as she had promised, a be-damn fine cook.

So Maggie had asked the question that was in her mind. "But how do you keep from it? I mean, you had a . . . a husband, a man anyway. How do you keep from having babies?"

Mother Be-Damn had smiled slyly. "Why you want know? Pretty little Boston got lover?"

Maggie, now accustomed to the big woman's teasing ways, had laughed the question away. "I may have, some day, who knows? Right now, it's just curious I am."

Mother Be-Damn had leaned close. Her breath had the sharp scent of the leaves she chewed to clean her teeth. "Indian women know many secrets. Know herbs and roots. Make medicine to stop babies."

It had been as simple as that. Upon Maggie's request, Mother Be-Damn had given her two stoppered, glass bottles containing a mixture to prevent pregnancy. Just to be on the safe side, Maggie had used both.

There was no denying, Maggie thought as she rushed down the path, that she had gone to Jonas knowing full well what would happen.

The village of Port Ludlow still drowsed in silence when she reached it. She could hear no singing now from the small church, and there were few people about.

She went down the steep rise to the beach and toward the spot where she had tied off the canoe. Before she reached it, she noticed a puzzling thing—it had been turned over, bottom up. She hadn't left it that way.

Reaching it, she gave a cry of dismay. The bottom of the canoe had been split open by several chops of an axe blade—or a pickaroon. It was completely useless now.

Maggie sank to her knees in the sand, tears of rage welling up into her eyes. Who could have done such a wretched thing? Then she knew. Jake Fargo, of course. Who else? He must have noticed her arrival. She glanced fearfully back over her shoulder, but saw no one. Yet her instinct told her that he was somewhere about, waiting for her next move.

And what was that next move to be? It would be extremely foolish to walk back alone along the shoreline; he would most surely be lying in wait for her somewhere along the way. Jonas would, of course, escort her if asked, but that was out of the question. The only other person she knew in Port Ludlow was Captain Sayward. But it would be humiliating to go to him for assistance. How could she possibly explain her presence here?

Rage filled her as she rocked back and forth on her knees. Curses well worthy of Olaf spilled from her, as she reviled Jake Fargo and all men of his ilk.

Suddenly she heard heavy footsteps on the wooden wharf above her head. She froze, holding her breath.

Andrew Kane had taken the teakwood brig out for a trial run, sailing up the east side of the Kitsap Peninsula from Seattle and into the channel on the other side. He had been gone for several days, stopping at sawmills and various logging camps along the way, inquiring as to who might be interested in employing the services of a tugboat when he had made the necessary changes. The only change he had made so far had been the name. The name now painted on the side of the brig was the *Carolina Belle*.

The responses he had received from most people he had contacted had been encouraging. Having heard of Captain Sayward and his thriving sawmill at Port Ludlow, Andrew had decided to stop in to see the captain.

It had been the wrong day to do so. Captain Sayward had said sternly, "I am a man of God, sir, and a man of God does not discuss business matters on the Sabbath."

With a shrug Andrew had left the man to his Sunday worship. One look at the village had told Andrew that there was nothing here to attract him, to hold him for the night. Although the hour was late, he had decided to sail on until dark. He had as yet no crew to the *Belle*, but he was a good enough seaman to handle her by himself.

Striding along the wharf to where the brig was tied off, Andrew suddenly heard a woman's voice raised in a torrent of angry profanity. The curses spilled out pell-mell, in no discernible order, as if the person speaking was a child, with no real understanding of the words. It took Andrew a moment to realize that the voice was coming from below. He stepped to the edge of the wharf and glanced down.

There on her knees, face turned up to him, was Maggie Donnevan. He felt the jolt of shock in his vitals, but managed to keep his voice calm. "Well, Mistress Donnevan! What a remarkable coincidence coming across you out here!"

"Oh, it's you!" Where before her face had worn a look of fear, it now took on an expression of relief.

By God, she was glad to see him! Vividly recalling their last meeting, Andrew was surprised at this. Yet, despite himself, the thought pleased him exceedingly.

He jumped the short distance to the ground beside her. He said lightly, "You are glad to see me. That delights me, Maggie."

"Oh, I'm not glad to see you, Mr. Kane," she said crossly. "It's just glad I am that you're not someone else."

"Who might that someone else be?"

"Someone you do not know, Mr. Kane. And happy it is you should be for that fact."

A little angry now, Andrew said, "I see that you are as sharp-tongued a shrew as ever."

"Shrew, is it?" Her own troubles momentarily forgotten, Maggie got to her feet and faced him, hands on hips. She took note of the fact that he was wearing rough seaman's clothing instead of a uniform. "Well, I can't say there has been no change in you. I see that you no longer look so fancy, without the uniform. They found out your true nature, did they, and dispensed with your services?"

Andrew turned a dark red. "That is rather unfair, ma'am, and not quite the truth of the matter. Considering that my coming to your rescue in Port Townsend is part of the reason I am no longer a Naval officer, it strikes me you have no cause to speak ill of my character!"

"Now it's the Donnevans you're after blaming, is it?"

"Not exactly." He sighed. "The truth is, I finally decided that my true calling is not the U.S. Navy—"

"Whisht! Of course not! Your true calling is the despoiling of virgins!"

"Maggie . . ." Andrew took a steadying breath. "This is not getting us anywhere. I'm not going to question why you are in Port Ludlow, and without your brothers. I reckon that's your own affair. But a few moments ago I heard you cursing like a common sailor. Evidently something aroused your ire. What caused it?"

"As any great dolt can see," she motioned to the ruined canoe, "my canoe has been destroyed by Jake Fargo, and I have no way to get back to the logging camp. . . ."

"*Your* canoe?" Andrew said incredulously. "You came here in that canoe?"

"And what is wrong with that, pray?"

Andrew stared at the canoe, trying to imagine Maggie in it. "You did go into the logging business then?"

"Yes, and doing very well at it, thank you."

Now he transferred his gaze to her. This was indeed an astonishing woman, he was slowly beginning to realize. "All right, so you came here in the canoe. I'm beginning to believe anything of you. But why alone, for the love of God?"

Maggie hesitated, then threw caution to the wind. In that moment she cared for nothing but to wound this hateful man. "I came here to visit with a man."

"A man?" Andrew felt a stab of jealousy, but he was careful to conceal it. "A tryst?"

Her head went back. "A tryst, yes, Mr. Kane."

Her flushed face and glowing eyes told him that she was telling the truth. With an edge of sarcasm in his voice, he said, "It seems you have progressed a long way, ma'am, from the despoiled virgin. I am sorry, that was ungentlemanly of me. My apologies, Maggie. I have my brig here. I was about to get underway. I would be happy to see you safely back to your camp."

Again, Maggie hesitated. She hated to accept any favors from him, but what alternatives did she have?

As if sensing some of what she was thinking, Andrew smiled wryly, and said, "Do not worry, Maggie. I won't lay a finger on you. You need have no fear on that score. Besides, I have no crew, and it's difficult enough to handle a brig all alone, without dallying with a woman."

"All right, Mr. Kane. I accept your generous offer."

With a nod he extended his arm, and helped her up the bank. Once on top, Maggie took her arm away, and walked with a distance between them until they reached the brig. Andrew handed her on board, and untied the hawser rope, then hurried inside the wheelhouse.

Maggie stood looking about. She knew little of ships, except for those on the long and unpleasant voyage from distant Ireland. This was a tiny thing in comparison, of course. But it was immaculate, the brass fittings glowing softly in the setting sun. There was no clutter on deck, everything tidy and in its place. The brig began to heel about, moving sluggishly with the tide. Andrew came out of the wheelhouse, unfurled and hoisted the sail. The slight breeze filled it out.

Returning to the wheel, he tacked the brig out of the harbor. He called back over his shoulder. "Maggie? Where is this logging camp of yours?"

She started toward the wheelhouse. "It's north, about three miles."

Andrew nodded, and spun the wheel over, taking a northerly course. He filled and lit his pipe. "Who is this Jake Fargo you claim scuttled your canoe?"

In an angry voice Maggie told him what she knew of Jake Fargo, including the attempted rape.

"He sounds like a proper villain," Andrew commented.

"He is all of that, and more."

Andrew fell silent, peering ahead into the gathering darkness, and puffing on his pipe.

Maggie stood alongside him as the brig moved slowly along. In a little while she said, "This is yours, you say?"

"Half mine," he replied. "I intend to see it wholly mine before long."

"What do you intend to do with it? Fish? I seem to detect an odor of fish about it."

"I know. That's the purpose it was once used for. I have scrubbed my knuckles raw trying to rid it of the fish stink. No, I don't intend to fish, Maggie. I'm going to convert it to steam, and turn it into a tugboat. A tugboat, in my opinion, can do well here on the Sound."

Her estimation of him rose a notch. Perhaps there was more substance to Andrew Kane than she had thought. At least he was industrious, and possessed ambition. She said, "A tugboat should do well, I agree. I will have use of one myself from time to time. You say it's half yours? Where is your partner? Why isn't he with you?"

"That would hardly do," he replied with a grin, "since my partner is a woman, a widow woman in Seattle."

"Whisht! I should have known. Just when I was thinking better of you! In exchange for bedding this widow, she gave you a partnership in this boat."

Andrew stiffened. "That, Mistress Donnevan, is none of your affair."

"I should imagine not," she said dryly. "But since you do not deny it, it must be true."

196

She turned and went out of the wheelhouse, traveling the rest of the way leaning on the rail.

What a hateful man! How she despised him! Any man who would make love to a woman to the benefit of his financial welfare was beneath contempt.

The wind off the water was cold, now that it was dark. Obstinately refusing to seek shelter from the wind in the wheelhouse, Maggie huddled against the railing, her shawl pulled closely around her.

Familiar with the shoreline now, she recognized the headland as the boat approached the cove, and almost at the same moment, she saw the pinpoint of flickering light that was the campfire.

She straightened up, calling out, "There, Mr. Kane! To the right is our cove."

At once Andrew spun the wheel over, and the brig sailed into the cove. About fifty yards from shore, he dropped anchor and took in the sail.

"I'll lower the gig and row you in."

"You don't have to bother—"

"Damnation, Maggie, you are a stubborn bitch!" he said explosively. "How are you going to get to shore, shuck your clothes, undergarments and all, and swim?"

"I see no need to use vulgar talk, Mr. Kane."

"Vulgar talk! May the gods forgive me, but I am sorely tempted to toss you overboard right here and sail away!"

"Such behavior on your part would not surprise me, not even a wee bit."

But she made no further protest. Andrew lowered the gig, they climbed down into it, and he rowed them toward the shore.

Simple hospitality prompted Maggie to say, "You probably haven't had supper yet. Since you *have* brought me home, I am prepared to offer you supper."

He gave a grunt of surprise. "Well now, I reckon I never expected that." Then he added suspiciously, "I wonder what ulterior motive you have in mind? You told your brothers what happened at Port Townsend, and you'd like to see them get their hands on me?"

She said stiffly, "I told them nothing. I felt too much shame."

He was silent for a few moments. "I thank you for your offer of hospitality, Maggie, but I believe I will pass up the opportunity. Even if you have told them nothing, I doubt they would look with favor upon me bringing you back after dark. I am no coward, ma'am, but I *am* prudent."

"Suit yourself, sir. It matters little to me, of that you can be sure."

As they neared the shore, Andrew said, "The wind is from the north, so I can't strike sail until it shifts. Likely it will by morning. I'll spend the night anchored in your cove, but will endeavor to be gone by morning."

He ran the gig up onto the beach and stepped out to give Maggie a hand. She started to walk away without a word, but stopped herself, turning back. "My gratitude, Mr. Kane, for your kindness."

"You are most welcome, I am sure," he said ironically.

In the faint light Maggie saw his mocking half-bow. With a sniff she turned and started up the slope. Yet her ears were attuned for the sound of his oars in the water. In a minute she heard them, and was angry at herself for feeling a pang of regret.

She detoured around the fire, where the loggers were gathered—drinking, talking in loud voices, some singing raucously. She went into her tent. A quick glance told her that Kevin was sleeping. Maggie quietly undressed and crawled between the blankets.

It was awhile before she went to sleep, however. Her mind was on Jonas and the delicious afternoon in his bed, but thoughts of Andrew Kane kept intruding rudely; thoughts that she just as rudely thrust from her mind.

As she slowly sank into sleep, Maggie remembered the canoe. The first thing in the morning she would have to talk with Mother Be-Damn or Olaf about having a new one made. There was the problem, of course, of how she would explain its loss to her brothers and Olaf. She decided that the best thing would be the truth—that some vandal had destroyed it, and she had been conveyed back to camp by a kind man in his boat.

But the first thing Maggie did in the morning, when she stepped from her tent, was to look toward the cove. The *Carolina Belle* was no longer at anchor. Andrew Kane was gone.

Chapter Nine

Maggie and her brothers had been in the logging business for over five months now, and they were prospering. Their logging crew had increased to an even dozen men, besides her brothers and the Jorgensons. They had moved camp several times, and Olaf was talking of building a wooden bunkhouse for the loggers. He had also told her they would soon be needing a team of oxen, since they would have to start logging at a distance from the water, adding with a grin, "Which means I'll return to bullwhacking."

To ease her conscience over falling trees on government land, Maggie had bought the logging rights to three hundred acres of good timber in the area north of Port Ludlow, and now there was no question of the Donnevans having a legitimate right to the trees.

She was still spending most Sunday afternoons with Jonas Kirk. She never tired of his wit, his intelligent conversation, his gentleness, and most of all, his love-making. It was certain that the Jorgensons and her brothers knew of the affair by this time. But except for hurt looks from Lars, and a strange quietness in her presence, there were no other indications that they knew.

Everything considered, Maggie knew she should be well content. Yet she wasn't. They should be falling more logs, in her opinion. But short of hiring more men, according to Olaf, there was not much they could do in the way of increasing production.

Maggie believed differently. She was constantly looking for ways to speed things up, looking for shortcuts.

One afternoon, while watching the buckers using their one-man saws on a felled tree, she had an idea. She went to Olaf with it. "Has anybody ever thought of using the crosscut saws the buckers use to make the backcuts?"

Olaf stared at her thoughtfully, then spat a brown stream. "Nah. Not that I ever heard." He took out a voluminous red kerchief and wiped the sweat from his brow. "What you got in mind, girl?"

"Well, I was thinking. Here the buckers are using crosscuts to saw the felled trees into logs. Why can't they also be used on the trees? Not the front undercut," she added hastily. "I know that, being a notch, it has to be chopped out with axes or it would pinch. But the straight backcut could be sawed."

Olaf cocked his head at her, eyes squinted. His glance moved to the buckers, then switched to the towering Douglas fir where Lars and Tom Reese were now making a backcut on their springboards. "One thing against it I can think of is that them crosscuts are too dad-damned short, and since only one man would be working the saw, it would take longer."

"That's easy enough to solve. Why can't the saws be made longer, with a handle on both ends? Then it would become a two-man saw. It seems to me it would not only be faster, much faster, but safer. You know how sometimes, when a tree is chopped through at the backcut, it twists as it falls? I think we've been a wee bit lucky so far. From what you've told me a tree has been known to twist and kill a faller before he can get out of the way."

Olaf was nodding. "Yah, that's true." His faded blue eyes brightened. "By Thor, it yust might work. You know something, Maggie girl, you've got a head on your shoulders!"

"It seems to me somebody has to come up with some new ideas in this business. To get ahead, new ways have to be found to increase production. All the logging outfits seem determined to stick to the old ways."

"So what do you want done, boss lady?" Olaf grinned, taking the sting out of the words.

"Go to the blacksmith shop in Port Ludlow and see if the blacksmith can make the saws we want. If he can't, try somewhere else."

Olaf spat. "Yah, I'll have a talk with him when I go in with the next shipment of logs."

203

Maggie shook her head. "No. Today. There's no need to delay."

"But girl . . ." Olaf motioned around. "We're busy as all hell. I can't yust go off and leave them on their own."

"Yes, you can. I'm here," Maggie said crisply. "I told you in the beginning that I would slowly take over. I will see to it that they don't slow down. Depend on it."

Olaf stared at her. Maggie returned his gaze steadily. After a moment Olaf shrugged, threw up his hands, and turned away.

The blacksmith had a long, two-handled saw ready for them within the week, and Olaf put the two most experienced buckers to work with the saw making a backcut on the first tree ready for it. Since it was a new procedure for them, the buckers proceeded slowly and cautiously. Even so, they finished the backcut in half the time it would have taken a pair of fallers with their axes. And Maggie knew that the time would be shortened even further when they became more proficient at it.

Olaf approached Maggie. "Much as I hate to admit it, girl, you're right again."

"Why do you hate to admit it, Olaf?" Maggie retorted. "Because I'm a woman? Whisht!"

Lars, standing within hearing distance, called over, "Come on, Pa. Own up she's right."

Olaf grinned sheepishly, and spat. "All right, Maggie. I'll own up. Nothing else I *can* do, dad-damnit!"

Impulsively Maggie stood on tiptoe to kiss his

cheek. Olaf went red as fire, and the loggers guffawed.

Maggie said, "I know it's a wee bit hard to accept, but you'll get used to a woman having a good idea from time to time." She added, "Order another saw made just like that one, when you go into Port Ludlow the next time. And Olaf, don't go bragging around about this. We'll just keep it our own wee secret. Let the other loggers wrack their brains for the reason we're cutting more trees than they are."

Maggie had learned that loggers needed little reason for celebration—any excuse to relieve the tedium—and that night they had ample cause for celebration. They had felled two more trees than usual that day.

It wasn't Maggie's habit to join the loggers as they gathered around the campfire after supper to yarn and sometimes pass the bottle, but on this night she made an exception. After all, it had been *her* idea. She slipped quietly into the circle around the fire, and even accepted a tin cup of whiskey from Olaf, later diluting it with water.

The loggers were yarning about somebody they called Paul Bunyan. Maggie recalled Jonas mentioning the name in reference to her brothers. Seating herself beside Lars, she leaned over to whisper to him, "Who's Paul Bunyan?"

"The greatest logger who ever lived." Then he grinned. "He's a legend, Maggie. He never really existed, although many loggers will swear that he did."

"Oh, you mean he's a myth?" Lars nodded. "Whisht! Back in Ireland, we had many such myths."

"None such as Paul Bunyan, I'll wager."

Maggie leaned forward, listening.

A middle-aged man, one of the buckers, was talking. "A lot of people allus asking where old Paul was born. Now anybody knows anything a-tall knows he was born back in Maine, Paul Bunyan was. Why, he was such a size when he was only three weeks old, he wallered around so much in his sleep he rolled down a hill and knocked over a whole four hundred square miles of standing timber. Now, the people there couldn't stand still for that, so they up and built a floating cradle for him to snooze in, and anchored it out of Eastport, Maine. Ever time he rocked that cradle, he brought on a seventy-five foot tide in the Bay of Fundy.

"And when Paul went to sleep in that there cradle, they couldn't waken him, so they called out the British Navy, and that there Navy fired broadsides over the cradle for nigh onto six hours. That finally popped Paul's eyes open, and then he was so excited, he tumbled out of the cradle into the ocean. That made the water rise so high it sunk seven British ships. They couldn't stand still for that, o'course, so they captured his cradle, out'n of which they made seven ships to take the place of the ones sunk. But that there seventy-five foot tide in the Bay of Fundy, she is going yet. Leastways, that's the way I hear it."

Another man picked up the story. "You fellers ever hear about how he come by Babe, his great blue ox? The way I hear it, one winter when Paul was a young man, he lived in a great cave. One night he was woke up by a loud crash. The lake outside was frozen over, and something had fallen through the ice, breaking it up into seven-foot-thick chunks. Far out, Paul Bunyan spied two ears a-sticking up.

"Well sir, Paul waded a mile out, the water coming only up to his chest, and grabbed them ears, which belonged to a baby calf, and drug it ashore. That was the winter they called the Winter of the Blue Snow, which had turned everything blue. That baby ox had been turned blue, and it stayed blue even after Paul nursed it back to health and it had growed to its full size. Paul named it Babe and it was by his side forever afterwards." The speaker had a chew of tobacco in his mouth, and he spat a brown stream into the fire, making a sizzling sound. "Nobody seems to agree about the exact size of old Babe, but he was a big'un, that's for sure. Some fellers say the width between his eyes measured seven axe handles. But I've heard others say it was nearer to forty axe handles. Whatsomever, Babe was big enough to pull anything with two ends on it. That's why Paul Bunyan and his crew was able to log the country from one end to the other."

"Some loggers argue about Paul's own size," said another logger. "I've heard tell that when he was back East and ordered a new pair of boots they had to be delivered lashed down on two railroad cars. He had a fine head of curly black hair, did Paul, and ever morning his wife combed it out with a crosscut saw, after first parting it with an axe. Paul was also proud of his beard. Several times a day he pulled a pine tree out by the roots and combed the beard with the branches, which kept it soft and shiny."

"Whisht!" Maggie laughed. "I don't believe any of this! Such a great lot of lies I'm hearing!"

"It's true, Miss Donnevan," a logger assured her solemnly. "Speaking of his ox Babe, for instance. Once Paul and his crew was driving a bunch of logs down the Wisconsin River back East when the logs suddenly jammed up in the dells. At the head, they were piled two hundred feet high, and backed a mile up the river. Paul, he was back at the rear with Babe. Wondering what had happened, he took Babe and went up front. He found his crew working their asses off . . . 'Scuse me, Miss Donnevan. But he found them working hard trying to break that log jam. Nothing they did would work. Paul told them to stand back. He put Babe at the head of the jam. Standing on the bank, Paul shot the ox in the butt with his rifle. Old Babe thought it was flies after him. He began to switch his tail. And you know that ox switching his tail made the river flow backward, taking the log jam with it? Paul called Babe out'n the water, and when the river flowed back its natural way, the logs went with it."

Yet another man joined in. "Paul Bunyan came out West, you know. Part of the way he drug his pickaroon behind him. Now, you all have heard tell of that big ditch down in the Southwest they call the Grand Canyon. That's what caused it, Paul dragging his pickaroon behind him."

Olaf, who had been listening quietly, spat into the fire, and said, "You dad-damned fellers don't know the half of it. The way I heard tell, Paul Bunyan came on up here. That blue ox of his took sick. Paul and his loggers dug a grave for it, thinking Babe was going to die. But the ox recovered.

Then the grave they dug for him became Puget Sound, and the dad-damned dirt they took out digging the grave became what folks hereabouts now call the Cascade Range over behind us."

"So if this greatest logger of all really existed," Maggie said scornfully, "what happened to him? Where is he now? Did he die?"

"Nah, Paul Bunyan never died, girl," Olaf said. "He figured he'd done all he could around here, so he yust up and walked north with Babe. I hear tell he's retired and taking his ease in some green Alaskan valley. Since he was so famous, he didn't want folks bothering him, so he's kept his abiding place a secret."

"Whisht! Such great lies I have never heard." But she was smiling. Now she got to her feet and stepped out of the firelight. There she stopped, calling out, "Olaf, could I speak with you, please?"

Olaf approached her with a wary look.

Maggie said, "I've been thinking . . . and hearing those lies about this Paul Bunyan and his great ox reminded me. I think it is about time you were after getting your team of oxen, so we can start falling trees farther up the slope. If these saws worked as well on the backcuts as they seemed to have, we will be increasing production considerably."

"Yah, we need oxen. But ain't it too soon, girl?" he said doubtfully. "Can you afford it yust now?"

"I can afford it," she said without hesitation. "You leave that worry to me. The next trip you make into Port Ludlow, Olaf, buy your oxen. Now you may return to the fire and exchange your great lies. I would suggest you keep the crew reasonably sober, since tomorrow is a working day."

Yet, as Maggie crawled into her blankets in the tent, she wasn't as sure as she had sounded to Olaf. Although they had been doing well and making a good profit, there had been expenses, and she didn't have a great deal of spare money. The price of a team of oxen would take just about all the extra cash she had.

They could manage, however, if nothing untoward happened; if, for instance, Jake Fargo didn't try any of his tricks. Maggie had been expecting trouble from Fargo, and was puzzled as to why he had attempted nothing. Many weeks had passed since he had ruined the canoe, and he had made no further moves toward her.

Almost every Sunday, Maggie had made the trip to Port Ludlow in the new canoe Olaf had made for her, and not a glimpse had she seen of Fargo.

Although it was comforting to think that he was no longer a threat to her, it was also mystifying. Jake Fargo had struck her as a vindictive man, one who never forgot a humiliation, and certainly a man who did not give up so readily.

There was an explanation for Jake Fargo's behavior. Had Maggie learned of it, she would have found it astounding.

Andrew Kane had awakened early the morning after he had taken Maggie to her camp, awakened to the creaking of the brig. The night before he had sprawled across his bunk fully clothed, except for his boots. Upon awakening, he had quickly pulled on his boots and stepped on deck. It was just dawn, and a brisk wind was blowing from the south, causing the brig to rock, tugging at the anchor.

Quickly, he pulled up the anchor, unfurled the sail, and set a course north. It was long after sunrise when he rounded the headland and Port Ludlow came into view. Acting on a sudden impulse, he sailed into the harbor and tied up at the wharf. Since he was here, he might as well try once more to attain future business from Captain Sayward.

In the tiny galley, Andrew made his breakfast, performed his toilet, and brushed his clothes. In mid-morning, freshly shaven and his boots polished to a high gloss, he stepped onto the wharf and headed at a brisk walk toward the sawmill.

He found Captain Sayward in his small office, going over his account book.

The captain acted as if yesterday's meeting had not taken place. Andrew introduced himself again, and Captain Sayward rose to shake hands.

"Now, what can I do for ye, Mr. Kane?"

Andrew told him about the *Belle*, his plans to convert her to steam, and turn her into a tugboat. "Right now I'm lining up future business for myself."

Captain Sayward nodded, stroking his chin. "Ye're a bright lad, with an eye for the future. Aye, I have a tug of my own, but it is small and slow, and cannot keep up with my needs. Since most of my profits are being plowed back into the sawmill at present, to make it more efficient, I could use another tug from time to time."

"That's good, Captain," Andrew said. "Within the month, I shall have my brig converted to steam and ready to do business. I will be back to see you. Good day to you, sir."

"And a good day to ye, Mr. Kane."

Outside, Andrew paused to light his pipe, looking along the village's single street. The wind was still strong from the south, and he knew it would continue from that direction for some time. It wouldn't do any harm to have a drink at a local tavern and get a feel for the place. But first, he returned to the brig and stuck the Navy Colt in his belt. Even though it was not yet noon, Andrew knew from experience that he might encounter some rough types.

The tavern was dim, smelling of spilled whiskey, rum, and ale, and it was almost empty of patrons. One lone man sat at a table nursing a drink. Behind the bar, a bartender and a blowsy barmaid with a lowcut bodice were talking idly.

They both broke off their conversation and put on false smiles for Andrew. He selected a table midway down the short room and sat with his back to the wall.

The barmaid swished toward him, smiling brightly. "How do, stranger? I'm called Fancy."

"That has a nice ring to it," Andrew said with a straight face. "I'll have a mug of whiskey, Fancy. And tell the barkeep I want good stuff, not something he's brewed up in the back room."

Fancy tossed her head and walked back to the bar, her rump swaying. From force of habit, Andrew watched her, but his mind was on someone else—Maggie Donnevan, to be specific.

Damnation, but she was an impossible woman! Granted, he had taken advantage of her, forcing himself on her in his urgent need, yet she didn't seem to have suffered a great deal from it, virgin or not. In fact, he thought with a meager grin, it could be said he had done her a favor, since she admitted, and proudly, to being tumbled by some gent here in Port Ludlow. Andrew was still speculating on what kind of a man might strike her fancy, when Fancy returned with his whiskey. Struck by the juxtaposition of the two words, Andrew laughed aloud.

Slamming the whiskey mug down, Fancy drew back, looking offended. "What's so funny, Mister?"

"Oh . . ." Andrew waved his hand. "Sorry, Fancy. I wasn't laughing at you. Something else entirely." He tossed a few coins onto the table. "Take the price of the drink out of that. The rest is yours."

Appeased by the gratuity, Fancy snatched up the coins. "Thank you, kind sir," she said, simpering.

Andrew took a strong pull on the drink, and sat back as the liquor burned its way down. He was still musing on Maggie a few minutes later when the sound of loud footsteps caused him to look up. Just coming in the door was a big man in logger's clothing, carrying a pickaroon on his shoulder. His eyes were bloodshot and puffy, and his face had a day's growth of beard. But it was the scarred face that drew Andrew's attention. He was without a doubt the ugliest man he had ever seen.

A glad cry came from Fancy. "Jake! Good morning, darling!" She rushed at him.

"What's good about it?" the big man growled, pushing her away. "By damn, don't know when

213

I've felt so terrible. Bring me a large whiskey, woman, and be quick about it."

The big man moved unsteadily to a table against the wall, and fell rather than sat in a chair. He leaned the wicked-looking pickaroon against the table. When the whiskey came, he swallowed it at one gulp and shoved the mug at the barmaid. "Another one, Fancy."

"You ain't paid for the first."

The man's huge fist struck the table a thundering blow. "By damn, woman! Just serve me and hop to it. Nobody questions Jake Fargo's ability to pay what's due!"

Bobbing her head, Fancy scurried away with the mug.

Andrew studied the man. So this was the infamous Jake Fargo. After Maggie had related her experiences with Fargo, Andrew had recalled other tales he'd heard about the man. Apparently Jake Fargo was a law unto himself; he had killed countless men, and his was a name used to frighten little children into obedience.

Andrew also remembered what Maggie had told him about Fargo's attempt to rape her, and a slow anger stirred in him. He finished off his own drink, waited until Fancy had hastily served Fargo his second potion, then got to his feet and started toward the front of the saloon.

What happened next, what he *did* next, would puzzle Andrew for some time to come.

Instead of heading directly to the door, he veered right, and planted himself before Fargo's table. As Fargo reached for the mug of whiskey with a trembling hand, Andrew said quietly, "I understand you're Jake Fargo?"

Fargo's hand, clasped around the mug, jumped, and half of the whiskey spilled out onto the table. "Now look what you've done, sneaking up on a man like that!" Fargo snarled. His small, bloodshot eyes looked up. "Yeah, I'm Jake Fargo. Who's asking?"

"My name is Andrew Kane. I want to give you a word of warning about Maggie Donnevan. . . ."

"That bitch!" Fargo slapped his hand down on the table, then leered. "What's she to you? You putting it to her?"

Andrew's anger surfaced, and it took an effort to keep it under control. He said icily, "You take care what you say, sir, when you talk of a lady!"

"A lady?" Fargo said. He leaned back, sneering. "First I knew she was a lady. But saying she is, I'm still asking what claim you got on her?"

"I have no claim, friend, beyond her welfare. If I hear even so much as a whisper of you offering her the slightest harm, you will answer to me."

Fargo's red face reddened even more. "Nobody threatens Jake Fargo! By damn, I do as I please!" One hand made a move toward the pickaroon.

With lightning speed Andrew snatched the Colt from his belt. "You touch that, friend, and I'll blow your hand apart."

Looking into Andrew's blazing eyes, Fargo blanched slightly, and carefully, very carefully, drew his hand back. "Well now, if she's your woman, I won't chase after her." He added virtuously, "Jake Fargo don't go after another man's woman."

"She is not my woman, as you put it. And from the rumors I hear, you go after all females, with or without their permission. But I'm not merely talking about a sexual assault on her person. If you try to harm her logging operation in any way, you will suffer for it."

"We're in the same business. It's a tooth and nail business," Fargo blustered. "All's fair in the logging game."

"Not in my view, it isn't." Andrew pointed the pistol at the other man's head. He cocked it, the sound shockingly loud in the barroom. "If I learn you've offered her personal harm, or have interfered with her logging business, I'll come looking for you. Your infamous pickaroon will do you no good. I'll blow your head off on sight. Be warned, sir, I am deadly serious."

Without another word, Andrew stuck the Colt in his belt, turned his back on Fargo, and strode out of the saloon. He went without looking back, knowing it was a foolish gesture of bravado. His back was tense, as he was expecting the pickaroon to be buried between his shoulders any instant. It was only when he was outside that he breathed a sigh of relief.

It was then that he began to ponder on what he had done, as he would ponder on it for a long time. Damnation, why should he risk his neck for the likes of Maggie Donnevan? She probably would not appreciate it even if she knew. More likely, she would laugh, that lilting Irish laughter that always sent a tingle down his spine.

Back in the saloon, Jake Fargo did close his hand around the pickaroon and half-start to his feet.

216

Then he thought better of it, and slowly sat back down. Besides the fact that he would be killing a man before witnesses, Fargo didn't know who this Andrew Kane was. Always before he had been careful to kill men of little importance, so no great hue and cry would ensue. But there was an air about Andrew Kane, a manner of being accustomed to command. If he happened to kill some government official, Fargo knew he could be in trouble.

He looked down into the whiskey mug and saw that it was empty. He glanced up to find Fancy and the barkeep staring at him in awed silence. "What the hell are you two gawking at? Bring me a whiskey, woman, and be damned quick about it!"

He sat glowering in his black rage. Twice now, he had been humiliated, and before witnesses. He was unaccustomed to being stood up to. It made him feel lessened. He had . . . what did the Chinks call it? Loss of face, that was it. When rumors of this encounter got around, he would be held in less fear. Well, the cracking of a few heads would put a stop to that in a hurry, by damn it would!

It was all the fault of that Irish bitch. He was more determined than ever to pay her back for it. But now he would have to be more crafty about it. Fargo valued his own neck, and he knew men—this Andrew Kane meant every word he had said. There had to be some cunning way he could harm Maggie Donnevan, some indirect means that only she would know about, and yet have no way of being able to connect him with directly.

That Jonas Kirk in his fine house . . . maybe that was the way. Fargo had watched the Don-

217

nevan woman's comings and goings, and knew what was going on between the pair of them. Yes, maybe that was it. He owed Jonas Kirk one, anyway, and he could kill two birds with one whack of his pickaroon, in a manner of speaking. He drank, smacking his lips, an evil smile spreading across his face.

In Jonas' house on the hill, Maggie ran her hands lovingly over Jonas' slender, naked body. An apt learner, she knew now how to kiss and caress him, until he was at a fever pitch of desire. She took great delight and pride in being able to so arouse a man. She was astute enough to realize that it gave her a feeling of power. Yet it was all in love, so what was wrong with that?

"A-ah, my love!" His body arched off the bed, as a long groan of pleasure came from him.

Then he placed his hands on her shoulders, and pushed her down on the bed, his head dipping down to seek her mouth at the same instant he entered her.

Maggie cried out, and pulled him hard against her. His thrustings became faster, rougher, than was his wont. Maggie reveled in the pleasure she felt, and she escaped again into those few mindless moments of ecstasy, during which nothing else in the world existed but the bed, this man, this moment.

When Maggie's small cry of completion rang out in the bedroom, Jonas rolled aside to stretch out beside her. With heaving breath, he said, "You do make a man feel young again, my love."

"And you, darling Jonas," she kissed him ten-

218

derly, "have a dear way of making me feel a woman, all woman."

"You have no need to be *made* to feel that way, my Irish lass. You *are* a woman. I suspect that you were born with all the passion and feelings of a fully mature woman."

"You do flatter me, Jonas Kirk." She kissed him again.

For a time they lay side by side, talking idly. Maggie had developed a habit of relating to Jonas the past week's happenings at the logging camp. He was fascinated by the stories of life around the camp, and was especially delighted when Maggie told him of some new scheme she had devised to increase production, or when she got the best of Olaf or her brothers.

"Olaf is going to buy a team of oxen," she said now. "We're soon going to have all the land near the water logged off, and will have to move uphill. That means it will be too far to slide the logs down to the cove. So a skidroad will have to be built, and oxen used to tow the logs down."

"Skidroad?" Jonas said. "I've heard the expression, but I'm not sure what it means."

"I'm not too sure either, having never seen one. From what Olaf tells me, I gather it's made out of split logs laid a certain distance apart. Then the oxen are chained to the logs, and they pull them down to the water. I'll be able to tell you more about it soon. I'm curious myself. Olaf was a little stubborn, afraid that it was a wee bit early."

"Why too early, if you do indeed need them?"

"Oh . . ." Maggie hesitated, then went ahead. "A team of oxen will cost a great deal, and Olaf is fearful that I can't afford them yet." She laughed softly. "Wait until he learns what I have in mind next!"

"And what might that be, my dear?"

"I've been thinking about it. Logging is fine, we're doing grand. But a sawmill!" She raised up on one elbow in her excitement. "If the Donnevans are to really make their fortune, it would take forever in the logging business alone. But with our own sawmill, we can do it quicker."

Jonas sighed, smiling. "Such ambition, Maggie. Sometimes, I think you're consumed by it."

"You do not know what it's like to be poor, Jonas," she said passionately. "Oh, I know, you told me about your life in England as a schoolteacher. But you have no conception of what it is like to exist on the edge of starvation, to live in a hut not much better than a pigsty. Or to have your very existence depend on an English landlord, who might, on nothing more than a whim, decide to evict whole families. . . ."

"You do have a hatred for the English, don't you, my dear? Of course I understand that we English *are* hated with a passion in Ireland."

"With good reason, Jonas," she said bitterly. "With very good reason!"

"And yet," he said musingly, "here you are in my bed."

"Ah, Jonas darling, I didn't mean you!" She placed a hand over his mouth. "You're different. Seldom it is do I ever think of you as English now."

"For that I suppose I should be grateful." He laughed. "Although I would hazard a guess that my

English relations would be horrified to hear me say so, being a traitor to my heritage, in a manner of speaking."

"But you see how it is with me, do you not? I have determined that the Donnevans shall pull themselves up from dire poverty and make their way in the world. That is why I came to this country. That is why I must have my own sawmill."

"Then what is stopping you, my love? With your determination, intelligence and drive, you will have it, I am sure."

Maggie lay back down, staring up at the ceiling. "Not for a long while, I'm after thinking. It will be very dear, building a sawmill. A permanent building, the equipment necessary . . . whisht! I despair even thinking about it. You see, if I build one, I will want a finer one than Captain Sayward's, for instance. I will want one like Pope and Talbot have built in Port Gamble. I have yet to see it, but Olaf has told me of it."

Jonas was silent for a little, thinking. "There is a way around that, Maggie."

Again she raised her head to look at him. "I must be dense, Jonas. I can't see a way. Not now. And I have wracked my poor brain."

"I am a wealthy man, Maggie, as you know. I have great sums of money lying idle. Why should you not make good use of it?"

"No, no," she said vehemently. "I will not be taking money from you. It would make me feel a kept woman!"

"I don't believe I said anything about *giving* it to you," he said dryly. "I may be infatuated with you, my Irish love, but I am not that much of a dolt about money."

"You mean, you'd make me a loan?"

"A loan, yes, secured by the proper notes, and with the proper interest."

"Ah, Jonas!" She threw her arms around him. "You are a sweet, dear, generous man but . . ." The memory of her father hanging gale, deep in debt to Lord Ramage, flooded into her mind, and she shuddered. "As much as I appreciate it, I am not inclined to go into debt. I fear debt as much as poverty."

"I know what's in your thoughts. But I assure you that I would not be as coldhearted as many of my countrymen in your native Ireland are. However, the decision is yours. The offer will stand. If you, in the future, choose to accept it, I will immediately hand over to you a draft on my bank in San Francisco for whatever amount you need."

Jonas began to make love to her again. Even as Maggie was swept up in a surge of passion, a small part of her mind was considering his proposition. Despite her horror of being in debt to anyone, even Jonas, the thought was very, very tempting.

Lars Jorgenson fell in love with Maggie on sight that first day in Port Townsend, and his love had grown daily since. Although he was not quite as shy around women as he appeared to be, it wasn't his nature to push his suit unless there were some small indications that the woman in question would be receptive to his advances. So it had been with Maggie. In the beginning they had been fully occupied with starting the logging operation, and Lars had decided to bide his time.

And then, almost overnight, he realized that he had made a mistake—his time had passed. A perceptive young man, Lars knew that Maggie was deep into an affair with someone else. He had sensed this even before she began taking the canoe into Port Ludlow every Sunday. He had no hint as to the identity of the man, but knowing Maggie well by this time, Lars was sure it wasn't just some common logger. More than once, he had been tempted to follow her and learn the whole truth. That, however, would be a shabby thing to do, and he curbed the impulse. He had no hold on her. Insofar as he knew, Maggie had never looked upon him as anything more than a member of the logging crew.

But being young and healthy, Lars had the normal lusty urges, and it wasn't long before he began looking around for a woman of his own. He didn't find the release most of the loggers did in drinking, and he was too fastidious by nature to patronize the sleazy whores in Port Ludlow, and the other logging towns.

Surprisingly enough, he found the woman he was looking for in Port Ludlow. Nancy Woods was the twenty-three-year-old daughter of the town blacksmith, Ira Woods. Lars had met her one afternoon when he brought some tools in from camp to be repaired.

The repairs were minor, and since Ira Woods had been receiving quite a lot of business from the Donnevan Logging Company, he said, "I'll get on it right away, Lars. Shouldn't take over a couple of hours. That way you won't have to come back for them. Why don't you go up to the house, and tell Nancy I said to give you a mug of tea? Or something to eat, if you like."

Lars had never met the blacksmith's daughter, but he knew that she was an only child, and that her mother was dead.

So it was with some trepidation that he knocked on the back door to the Woods house, a small, unpainted structure set apart some thirty yards from the smithy.

At his knock the door was opened by a tall young woman with long, dark hair and hazel eyes. A full figure was evident even though it was covered by a loose-fitting housedress, which hung all the way to the floor.

Her eyes widened at the sight of him. "My goodness, you *are* a big one!"

"Ma'am . . ." Fumbling for words, Lars doffed his cap. "I'm Lars Jorgenson, Miss Woods. I brought some things in for your pa to fix. He said I should come and ask you for some tea while I'm waiting. But it it's too much trouble . . ."

"No trouble at all, Mr. Jorgenson. In fact, I'm happy to have the company." She stepped back, opening the door wide.

Cap between his hands, Lars stepped into a small kitchen, in which a wood stove was burning. Aside from the stove, there was a plain wooden table with four chairs. Underneath the window was a zinc sink, with a long-handled water pump. The room was redolent with cooking odors.

"Sit down, Mr. Jorgenson." She motioned to the table. "I'm baking apple pies, and was about to take them out of the oven. Soon as they cool, you may have a wedge if you like."

"If I'm not imposing, ma'am." Lars lowered his bulk gingerly into a straightback chair at the table.

"No imposition, Mr. Jorgenson."

Nancy Woods turned away to open the oven door. Watching the outline of her buttocks against the fabric of the dress as she bent over, Lars became acutely aware of how he looked. He was in his workday clothing, his boots were caked with mud, and he had failed to shave that morning. If he had known he would come across such a pretty girl, he would have slicked up.

She was taking the pies out of the oven, placing them on the windowsill over the sink to cool. Facing around, she untied the apron and wiped the sweat from her face. The fact that she seemed completely unself-conscious about being seen in a housedress put Lars more at ease.

She said, "I can offer you fresh milk with your pie, if you'd prefer that instead of tea." She added proudly, "We have the only cow in Port Ludlow."

"I'd like that, Miss Woods. We don't get fresh milk at the logging camp."

"Why don't we call each other by our first names? I'm Nancy, and you're Lars."

Lars smiled. "That would be fine with me, Nancy."

"The pies will be cool shortly." She came to sit across the table from him. "You work for that new logging outfit, the one run by the Irish girl, Maggie Donnevan?" At Lars' nod, she said, a sly twinkle in her eyes, "So how do you like working for a woman?"

A little uncomfortable under her scrutiny, Lars squirmed. "Why, it don't . . . doesn't bother me all that much. Fact is, my pa is bull-of-the-woods. He gives the orders."

"Still, *his* orders come from a woman, am I right?" She was watching him closely.

Lars shrugged. "You're right there, but no, it doesn't bother me. She pays my wages, she has a right to give the orders." He tried to keep his true feelings for Maggie from showing, and could only hope he was succeeding.

All at once Nancy smiled, a warm, flashing smile. "I think I like you, Lars Jorgenson."

Lars stared at her, thrown into confusion by her straightforwardness.

"Don't worry, Lars, you'll get used to me," she said. She got to her feet. "I think the pies should be cool enough to eat by now."

Suddenly emboldened, Lars spoke to her back, "Why isn't a pretty girl like you married, Nancy?"

She didn't answer at once. She cut a wedge of pie, poured a glass of milk from a pitcher, and served him. She resumed her seat across the table. Chin propped on one hand, she said, "Why am I unmarried at my age? Pa gets around to asking the same question about once a week. I'll give you the same answer I give him . . . who to? The single men around here fall into three categories. Loggers, sawmill hands, and drunken louts. Sometimes it's hard to tell one from the other."

Lars felt color rise to his face.

"Oh, there's nothing wrong with being a logger, don't misunderstand me, except they spend six days

226

a week out in the tules. If they're married, they see their wives on Sundays. *Maybe*. I have no hankering to be a widow six days a week." She drew a deep breath. "Aside from all that, I haven't yet found a man I'd care to marry. Does that answer your question, sir?"

"Yes, ma'am, I guess it does," Lars mumbled. He directed his attention to the pie and milk, both of which were delicious.

"However, if you have in mind to court me, Lars, I would not be averse to it."

Startled, he glanced up. She was smiling at him. Flustered again by her frankness, he could find nothing to say.

"Well, it does get lonely here," she said, defensive now. "I have little in common with the neighbor women. If that makes me sound a snob, so be it." Her head went back. "And Pa, he's no company. He spends twelve hours a day in that blacksmith shop of his, has every day since we've come here, which is going on two years now. We came out here after Mother died back East and he, poor man, works until he's ready to drop, goes to bed, and gets up to lose himself in work again. He even works on Sundays, which is considered a sin by most folks here."

Lars washed down another bite of pie with a swallow of milk, and said, "Well, you *do* bake a good apple pie."

Nancy began to laugh, and soon Lars joined her.

That was the beginning. Before long Lars was inventing excuses to go into Port Ludlow. Olaf, who hated the long walk into the village, was just as

227

happy to let Lars take the broken tools in for mending. Olaf had mentioned buying or constructing a rowboat to use for the necessary trips into Port Ludlow, but Lars told him there was no rush. He didn't mind the walks back and forth. Of course, he admitted to himself, the real reason was that, in a boat, there was always the possibility that he would encounter Maggie in her canoe.

By now he was going into the village on Sundays also, to visit Nancy. On these excursions, he usually had Sunday supper with the Woods, father and daughter, and these were the only times he saw Ira Woods inside the house. During those long, delightful afternoons conversing with Nancy in the small parlor, or listening to her play the small spinet, the sounds of hammer on anvil from the smithy was a counterpoint to Nancy's light music.

She played well, and he loved to listen to her. Nancy had told him, "I'd be willing to give music lessons if I could find any pupils. When we first came here, I spread the word around, but I have yet to get a single pupil. The only one of my talents that seems useful is my talent as a seamstress. I do fine sewing occasionally for the few town ladies who are too grand to do their own." She wrinkled her nose. "Oh, well, it does get me into the better homes in Port Ludlow, not that that means very much."

Although Lars had been visiting Nancy for well over a month, he had yet to do so much as kiss her. Even though she was unusually candid for a woman, she was still a lady, and Lars was at a loss as to how to take proper advantage of these afternoons.

Then, one Sunday afternoon, Lars was standing behind Nancy at the spinet, when the smell of something burning came from the kitchen.

"Oh, I forgot the pie in the oven!"

She jumped up, and in facing about, turned right into his arms before Lars could step back. Her face was very close, her breath warm on his cheek. Without even thinking about it, Lars put his arms around her and pulled her close.

Nancy came willingly, even eagerly, and she returned his kiss with ardor. After a long moment she arched her neck back to gaze into his eyes. "Well! I was beginning to think you would never do that!"

He blinked. "I wasn't sure you wanted me to. . . ."

"For a bright man, you are extraordinarily dense when it comes to women, Lars. Now . . ." She took his hand and started to lead him down the hall. "I've been anticipating this moment for a long while."

"But . . . but," Lars stuttered, "what about the pie?"

"Let it burn. I can always bake another."

Lars was following her now, still slightly dazed by the suddenness of it all. "What about your father?"

"You know he never comes into the house until it's time to eat or sleep. Listen." She stopped, head cocked.

The sound of hammering from the smithy rang

229

out like the pealing of a bell. In the days to come, Lars would listen with some watchful part of himself for the sound of hammering. If it stopped, no matter how involved he and Nancy were in amorous play, he would never feel at ease until it started up again.

But now all he could think about was this warm and vibrant girl as she led him down the short hall, and into her bedroom. They undressed in clumsy haste, and tumbled onto the bed, clutching at each other.

Nancy had a fine figure: broadshouldered and full-breasted, with a small waist and strong hips and thighs.

"One thing, Lars . . . I am not a virgin," she said. "I just wanted you to know."

"Well . . . neither am I."

At that she broke into laughter. One thing he had liked about Nancy in the beginning was her sense of humor. Now he was to learn that it could occasionally take a turn for the ribald.

Lars also discovered that she had few inhibitions, and took a robust enjoyment in love-making. At first, being such a big man, Lars was inclined to be unduly gentle with her.

"None of that, Lars Jorgenson. I'm not an egg. You'll find that I don't break easily."

It was a rousing, joyous session of love, and for a few moments at the very height of his passion, Lars even forgot to listen for the sound of the hammer from the smithy.

When it was over, and they lay side by side, waiting for their heartbeats to return to normal,

Nancy said, "What I said about not being a virgin is true, but I want you to know that I do not tumble into bed with just any man. In fact, this is the first time it has happened since we moved to this godforsaken place. . . ."

Lars silenced her with a finger across her lips. "You owe me no explanations, Nancy. Now or at any time."

Their Sunday afternoon trysts, with the sound of hammering like music in Lars' ears, became a regular thing. Although he was still in love with Maggie and was sure that he always would be, Lars was a happy man. There was a small, nagging worry of what would happen should Maggie ever turn to him and he would have to stop seeing Nancy. Not only was her physical attraction strong, he was very fond of her, and would hate to have to hurt her. Although she laid claim to being a self-sufficient woman, Lars knew that she was becoming more attached to him every day.

The Sunday afternoons in her bedroom continued unbroken for over two months.

Then one day, when Nancy let him in the kitchen door, she had a long face. "Pa is in bed today, Lars. He's got chills and fever. I'm sorry."

Lars tried to conceal his disappointment. "That means we won't be . . ."

She was nodding. "I'm afraid so. Pa in the smithy and us in the bedroom is fine, but Pa across the hall in his own room is a different matter." She stood on tiptoe to kiss him. "I *am* sorry, dear. I'm sure he'll be much better in a few days and back to work next Sunday. But knowing you'd be here, I just took an apple pie out of the oven."

231

So, Lars had to be content with a wedge of pie and a cold glass of milk from the wellhouse, and a few words of idle conversation with Nancy.

As he prepared to leave, Nancy stepped into his arms. They kissed long and hard. In a moment Lars felt his passion begin to rise.

Sensing this, Nancy said, "I *am* sorry, lover." She got that impish glint in her eyes. "We could go for a walk in the woods."

Lars was strongly tempted. But he shook his head. "No, that wouldn't be right. I respect you too much for that, Nancy."

"Respect is not what I want right now." She sighed. "But you're right. Be sure and come next Sunday now."

"You can be sure of that."

She kissed him, and pushed him out the door. It was so much earlier than he usually left that he felt somewhat at a loss. He ambled along, taking his time. As he neared the wharf, his glance was caught by a movement along the path coming down the bluff south of town.

Some instinct prompted him to step back behind the sawmill. In a moment he peered around the corner of the building. The person hurrying down the path was Maggie. Somehow, Lars had known in his heart that it would be.

He watched until she went down the path to the beach and her canoe, disappearing from view. Then he stepped out into the open, his gaze drawn to the big white house on the hill.

He finally knew the identity of Maggie's lover— Jonas Kirk.

For a long moment he was in the grip of a jealous rage. If Kirk was within reach right now, Lars knew he would gladly wrap his big hands around the man's throat and squeeze. . . .

Chapter Ten

Since there were no oxen available locally, and Olaf had to order them from Oregon, it was a month before they were delivered. Maggie was grateful for the reprieve. In the meantime, they had sold another shipment of logs to Captain Sayward, and the profits of that sale gave her sufficient funds to pay for the animals with something left over.

Before Olaf could start using the team, the skidroad had to be constructed. All the loggers were put to work building it; beginning a mile up the slope at the spot where they were now logging, and continuing all the way down to the cove.

Olaf was everywhere at once—supervising, bellowing orders. The way had to be cleared first of stumps and underbrush. In some cases, they had to use dynamite to blast the huge stumps out of the ground.

When the route was cleared, the buckers prepared the skids—foot-thick timbers about twelve feet long. They were laid across the cleared pathway and half-buried in the ground at about seven-foot intervals, so that a moving sixteen-foot log, which was the shortest standard length, would always be resting on at least two of them. A scallop was cut out of the top surface of each skid to act as a cradle for the passing logs. To reinforce the skid, Olaf had the buckers fit a four-inch lining of oak wood precisely into the scallops.

Olaf, as bull-of-the-woods and bullwhacker, was the man who made it all go. Maggie watched him working with the oxen every afternoon while the skidroad was being completed. She was a little surprised at his patience, but also pleased, since the 1,800-pound Durham oxen had cost her three hundred dollars each.

Olaf told her, "Most times, it takes a month to train a new animal. They have to learn to pull hard or easy, turn right or left, when to move ahead and when to stop. I hope to have them ready much sooner than that."

He worked them for several hours every day. He fed them hay and bran; groomed and occasionally washed them; rubbed arnica into their chafed necks; nursed them when they came up lame; fitted brass caps on the sharp ends of their horns; and after they started to work in earnest, he helped Ira Woods, who came in from Port Ludlow every other Sunday, to shoe them.

The day finally came when Olaf pronounced the oxen ready to move the first two logs down the hill to the cove. Maggie watched closely as the first logs were prepared. The forward end of the log was, in Olaf's words "sniped"—rounded and smoothed with an axe so that it wouldn't tear up the roadway as it hit the skids.

The coupling between the two logs were metal chains, held fast by bent metal spikes called dogs. A longer chain ran forward from the first dog, passing between the pairs of oxen, and then attaching to the heavy wood-and-leather yokes that hung around the animals' necks. Olaf had explained that the wood used to make the yokes was very important. "I use Bishop pine, when I can get it. The pitch oozing from Bishop pine somehow seems to toughen the necks of the beasts and stops them from getting gall sores."

When the first logs were ready, Olaf in his floppy hat, red galluses and calked boots, positioned himself beside them.

He roared, "Move, dad-damn you! Move out, Buck!"

He had given each animal a name, and Buck was the name of the front leader. The oxen strained forward, but this was the first time they had been hitched to such a heavy load, and at first Maggie was afraid they couldn't budge it.

Now curses such as Maggie had never heard poured from Olaf. She covered her ears. She had noticed that he had been carrying around a short stick, but hadn't known the reason why. Now she saw its purpose. He used the stick as a goad, jabbing at the oxen on the rumps and shoulders. Maggie saw dots of blood appear. The stick had a sharp nail implanted in the end!

Maggie started toward Olaf to voice a protest,

then stopped as the oxen began to move the huge logs. Slowly the two five-feet-thick logs picked up momentum, as the oxen, straining and grunting, moved faster. Their hooves pawed for the skidroad timbers, sometimes plopping heavily into the mud between each one.

The combined sounds of the chains clanking, Olaf's curses, the oxen grunting, and the jolting noise of the logs bumping along the skidroad, created a great din.

To escape the sound, Maggie started to hurry on ahead, but alongside the rear oxen she paused to watch the skid greaser work. For the job Olaf had hired a young Indian boy in his teens. His was a dirty, thankless task. Carrying a bucket of fish oil and a burlap swab on a stick, he had to scamper along behind the rearmost pair of oxen and just ahead of the front log, and grease the skids. This was done to reduce the friction and help keep the logs moving along as smoothly as possible. Also, when the downgrade steepened, he threw dirt onto the skids to slow down the logs and prevent them from ramming into the rear oxen.

Olaf had explained, "I've tried to keep the downgrade as gentle as possible, yah. But sometimes they get to moving too fast. When that happens, the skid greaser will throw on his dirt, and I will loop heavy chains around them logs to act as a brake, dragging into the dirt."

An aggrieved voice said behind Maggie, "I could have done that job just as easy as that Indian boy."

Maggie turned. Kevin was standing beside her, staring in resentment at the skid greaser. Absently, she ruffled Kevin's hair. "It's too dangerous, Kevin.

I told you that. Wait until you grow up a little. Then we'll be after finding a task for you to perform."

As Olaf had explained, the skid greaser had an additional chore to do. At the end of each trip to the cove, he had to collect the chains and the dogs and often extra equipment, and pile them onto the "boat" for the return trip up the slope. The boat was a hollowed-out log used as a sort of sled, chained to the team and dragged back to the logging location. The chains and the other items were quite heavy, too heavy for Kevin's tender years. Maggie had tried to explain this to her little brother, but he had still clamored for the job, until she was forced to be firm with him.

Patrick, overhearing the argument, had said, "You're spoiling the lad, Maggie, I'm thinking. If he won't listen to you, come to me. I'll give him a clout. *Then* he'll listen."

Maggie had started to snap back, but realizing there was some truth to Patrick's charge, she had refrained. Yet she was grimly determined that Kevin should grow up to be something of a gentleman.

When they finally reached the cove, with the logs unchained and safely in the water, Maggie said to a sweating Olaf, "Those poor oxen! Whisht! That's brutal treatment, Olaf. That nail draws blood."

"You sorry for these dad-damned dumb beasts, girl?" Olaf spat. "Don't be wasting your sympathy. What I do to them ain't nothing to what I've seen other bullwhackers do. I've seen some use pitchforks, bullwhips, whatever's handy. Besides, it's their lot in life, it's what they're for. If not, why else would God have created the beasts? They don't feel pain, anyways, not like humans do."

Maggie doubted this very much, but she did grasp the fact that they wouldn't do the work they were supposed to do without the abuse Olaf gave them.

She sighed, reflecting on the ways her thinking had changed. Back in Ireland, she would have been outraged at such treatment of animals. Then she reminded herself that she had paid a goodly sum for the eight oxen to perform the function they were now engaged in. And she couldn't deny the thrill she felt now that Olaf had successfully completed the first trip down the skidroad, the logs floating in the water. It struck Maggie that this was another giant step on the way to the Donnevans becoming "lumber barons", a phrase just coming into popular usage. It was a phrase that pleased her greatly. "Baron" had a connotation of nobility, and in its own way could make the Donnevans equal to Lord Ramage.

That reminded Maggie of Kathleen's plight. She decided to dispatch another letter. Kathleen should have the first one by now; it had been on its way for eight months.

In her tent that evening, she penned the second letter to her sister:

My Dearest Kathleen,

We are all well and thriving. I pray that you are also well. I also pray that you have received my first letter, knowing that it takes a long time for letters to cross the great sea.

The Donnevan Logging Company is doing grand, Kathleen! We are earning good profits, and today I saw our team of oxen towing the first logs down into the cove. I will not endeavor to explain this operation, since it is highly technical, and you would have to witness it to fully comprehend.

I am expecting a reply to my first letter soon, and pray that you will have good news to pass on about yourself. The best news of all would be for you to write me that you are ready and willing to rejoin your family. Although Patrick has not mentioned your name, I am confident that he would be delighted to have you with us once again. Patrick has changed a great deal. He has now matured mentally and emotionally to match his great size, and once I tell him all the truth, I am sure he will welcome you. He fought against me all the way across the great ocean and all the way up here, wanting to rush off to the gold fields of California. Now he is happy we came here. Such is the change in him now that I am beginning to allow him to give orders to our logging crew. He makes a good bull-of-the-woods, when neither Olaf nor I are present.

To prove to you, dear Kathleen, how well we are doing, I am strongly considering building our own sawmill. If I do so decide, then we will indeed prosper. In this country they use the words "lumber barons" to denote people who are prominent in the logging business, people who log over thousands of acres. They are all men, of course, but Kathleen, I intend to be the very first woman lumber baron! To become so, I *must*

241

have my own sawmill. But to build it, I must do something that I would never have dreamed of doing back home in Ireland. Yet I have learned one thing here in this great, new country. If you have a daring dream, you must be prepared to take daring measures to accomplish it!

All our love, dearest Kathleen, and it is my fondest hope to be reunited with you ere long. You should see our wee brother, Kevin! He is growing apace, and soon you will not recognize him!

Your Loving Sister, Maggie.

Back in Ireland, Kathleen had received Maggie's first letter. She had been fortunate in that it had arrived during one of Lord Ramage's frequent absences, and she had been able to keep it a secret from him.

She had read the letter so many times it had become creased and torn. The contents of Maggie's letter had pleased Kathleen to the depths. It was proof that her own sacrifice had not been in vain. Her family was well and happy and thriving! She could not have envisioned a better answer to her prayers.

Again and again, she had read Maggie's plea that she come to them, and how she yearned to do so. But how? The only way open to her was to steal more of Lord Ramage's jewels, and that was repugnant to her. She had felt no qualms about stealing the first time, since that had been toward the benefit of Maggie and her brothers, but stealing for her own advantage was a different matter.

However, as time passed, it became more and more attractive.

Lord Ramage's abuse of her was growing unbearable. He had, of course, discovered the theft of the jewels soon after the deed was done, but fortunately not until the Donnevans had escaped the country.

Suspecting the reason behind the theft, Lord Ramage had ridden immediately to the Donnevan cottage, and had returned to the castle in a towering rage.

Kathleen awaited him in the library, resigned to whatever fate was in store for her.

He walked directly to her and struck her across the face, with enough force to drive her back against the wall. His ring cut into her cheek, and started a flow of blood.

He stood over her, handsome face frozen in a mask of fury. His blue eyes glittered with the coldness of his diamonds. "It is bad enough for you to steal from me to adorn yourself, or even to sell the jewels for money of your own. But to steal to help that miserable family of yours I find unforgivable!" He drew back his foot and sank the toe of his boot into her side. The pain was terrible, and Kathleen felt something tear loose inside.

In a snarling voice, he said, "Where did they flee to, madam? I will have them fetched back and punished. Damme, if you don't tell me, I will kick you until there isn't an unbroken bone left in your body!"

"I do not know where they are. They have gone to America, but where I know not." Kathleen's voice was weak but triumphant. "There is no way,

Your Lordship, that you will ever find them. You may kill me, if that is your wish, but I can tell you nothing more."

"Oh, I will find them. Be sure of that, madam."

In his raging fury, Lord Ramage did almost kill her. He punished her savagely, with both fists and boots, until she finally lapsed into unconsciousness.

Kathleen was alone in the cold library when she regained consciousness, and managed to hobble to her room, part of the time forced to crawl upon her hands and knees.

Lord Ramage had stormed from the castle, leaving orders with the servants that Kathleen was not to be allowed a doctor. He was gone for a full week. Fortunately, no bones were broken, although Kathleen suspected that one rib was cracked. She healed slowly, except for her side, which still bothered her even now, nine months after the beating.

As she had surmised, Lord Ramage's pride would not allow him to broadcast the knowledge that property of his had been stolen by his mistress, and so he did not call the constables to arrest her. For a time Kathleen thought that he would throw her out of the castle. This didn't concern her, even though she would have no place to go and no money to live on. But he did not. He allowed her to remain, and still came to her bed from time to time, abusing her body in his lust. Kathleen thought several times of leaving on her own accord, but somehow she seemed to lack the will. She existed in a sort of gray limbo. She ate when necessary, slept when necessary, and felt dead in mind and body. She ceased to care about her personal appearance, and would go for days without changing her clothing or combing her hair.

One night Lord Ramage strode into her bedchamber in his nightshirt, carrying a candle in one hand. With the other he stripped the coverlet from her naked body, and stopped, staring down at her with an expression of disgust. "On my oath, madam, you look a fearsome sight! I have seen farmers with better looking scarecrows in their fields! Damme, I am sorely tempted to rid myself of you."

Kathleen asked curiously, "Why don't you do that, Your Lordship?"

"I do not know, madam, I honestly do not know. I will think on it."

He turned on his heel and went out of the room without throwing himself on her, and Kathleen was too dispirited to even experience relief.

The weeks and months dragged by, and she was still at Ramage Castle. True, Lord Ramage ceased to come to her bed, and was often gone for days on end. Kathleen suspected that the reason he hadn't evicted her from the castle was because he still hoped to somehow get a hint from her as to the whereabouts of the rest of the Donnevans.

And then Maggie's letter arrived.

Before Kathleen had considered herself among the living dead, but slowly, even as she fought against it, life began to stir in her. More, she started to hope that possibly, just possibly, she could escape from Lord Ramage, and join Maggie and her brothers. In the beginning she derided herself for such a fancy, yet it grew, taking on a life of its own, like a child gestating inside her. It was in her thoughts constantly, until it became an obsession.

Her appetite returned, and she began to eat, and even gained a little weight. She was careful to act the same in Lord Ramage's presence, and continued to neglect her personal appearance. It would never do for him to suspect anything.

By now Kathleen knew that when Lord Ramage became quite restless, roaming around the castle for hours, or drinking himself into a stupor in the library, he was about to absent himself from the castle for several days. During these absences, he would usually stay away at least four days, often longer.

So, she was prepared when he rode off early one morning, with extra clothing in his saddle bags. Less than an hour after his departure, Kathleen was in the black coach, headed for Galway. This was the only touchy part of her plan. If Lord Ramage had given the coachman orders not to take her anywhere, Kathleen would be thwarted before she even began.

But the sullen coachman hitched the horses to the coach, and drove her into Galway. Kathleen knew that he would inform Lord Ramage of her actions, and His Lordship would fly into a great rage, demanding to know her purpose and where she had been. She would handle that when the time came.

In Galway she directed the coachman to wait for her at a stable, and Kathleen performed her errands on foot. She made three stops. First, she visited a shipping office and booked passage on a ship sailing for America two weeks hence. There were more ships departing from Limerick, but that city was too far from Ramage Castle. Next, she stopped at a jeweler's shop and made arrangements for the sale of several jewels on the morning of the day the ship sailed. Kathleen had already picked out the pieces she intended to steal. She described the pieces to the jeweler and was quoted a tentative price. Her last stop was at a ladies' shop. She was known there, as Lord Ramage's mistress, and had no trouble charging her purchases to his account.

Lord Ramage was gone five days, returning on the afternoon of the fifth day. As Kathleen had surmised, the coachman made haste to inform His Lordship of Kathleen's journey into Galway.

In her bedchamber Kathleen was prepared. Lord Ramage slammed the door open without knocking, and strode into the room. His handsome face showed clear signs of his debauchery.

Face dark with rage, he stopped before her, hands on hips. "Tim, the coachman, tells me that you took the coach into Galway the moment I left. I demand to know for what purpose, madam! And why did you not inform me beforehand?"

Kathleen stood up, a vapid simper on her face. "I wanted it to be a surprise, Your Lordship. I only sought to please you. I know you have been considering me a drab of late."

He peered at her suspiciously. "Please me how, madam? Pray tell me."

"Why, with my new dress," she said, simpering again. She made a full turn, giving him a good look at the expensive new garment she had purchased in Galway. She had purposely bought a garment much too large for her; it hung on her like a sack. She had made no attempt to do anything to her face, and her haid was a tangle, uncombed for days. Kathleen knew she looked a dreadful sight, and she could scarcely keep from smiling.

Lord Ramage fell back a step, and swept her with an incredulous look. "You believe that new garment will make you attractive to me? Do you take me for a blind man, madam? I have seen bawds more attractive lying in the gutters in Galway!"

Kathleen made herself look as disappointed as possible. "I'm sorry, Your Lordship. I thought . . ."

He gave her another suspicious look. "Damme, I do not understand this sudden desire of yours to appeal to my manhood. In bed you have been like a lump of ice! Why this sudden change of attitude?"

"Well, we do have a bargain, and I thought perhaps I should make more of an effort to keep my part of it."

"My dear Kathleen, dispel any thought that I will *ever* approach you in passion again. You have as much appeal to me as the potatoes rotting in the fields of Ireland. The only reason I have not evicted you from my castle is because you belong to me, body and soul, and I do not easily rid myself of a possession. Especially not one that has cost me so dearly. Perhaps I shall find some use for you yet, although I must admit that I have wracked my poor brain to no avail." He started to turn away, then swung back. "But there will be no more trips, is that quite clear, madam? I have given the servants orders that you are not to be transported again from this castle. I will not have you spending my good money on fancy clothes. Please me indeed!" He snorted contemptuously.

He stormed out of the room. As the door closed, Kathleen sank to the floor, immensely pleased that her deception had worked. His order confining her to the castle troubled her not at all. She had already foreseen that, and did not intend to flee in the coach.

But how she had duped him, oh how she had duped His Lordship!

A giggle escaped her, and in a moment hysterical laughter spilled from her in a torrent. She clapped both hands over her mouth to muffle the sound, and rocked back and forth in a seizure of glee that verged on madness.

Kathleen took full advantage of the two weeks before her ship sailed, plotting her every move carefully. She did not plan to take many belongings with her: only a few changes of clothing, the bare necessities for travel, and several of Lord Ramage's jewels. When her conscience started to prick her, she reminded herself of how badly he had mistreated her, and told herself that the jewels would only repay part of the debt she was due!

Since coming to Ramage Castle, Kathleen had learned to ride, as Lord Ramage had a great love of horses and owned a stable of a dozen fine riding animals. Now Kathleen familiarized herself more thoroughly with the stable, and the horses. She had already gained the confidence of the animal that was usually her mount, a great, broad-chested gray stallion, and during the two weeks, she would creep into the stable long after midnight. Each time she found all the stablehands asleep in the tack room; none awoke as she approached the gray stallion's stall, crooning to him in low tones. The chief problem she would have would be saddling him.

On the days when Lord Ramage was out riding to the hunt, the stablehands usually accompanied him to care for his mount, and those of his hunting companions. On those occasions, Kathleen went into the stable and practiced saddling the stallion. It was difficult, and she knew it would have been even more difficult to manage at night without arousing the stablehands, but that was something she had to risk.

Lord Ramage completely ignored Kathleen now. She had stopped joining him in the dining room for supper; her meals were brought up to her room on a tray. His disregard of her gave Kathleen the freedom she needed to make her plans and preparations.

The night before her ship was due to sail, Kathleen was ready. She didn't sleep at all that night, but kept a close watch on the hall. It was late when Lord Ramage finally stumbled upstairs and to his bedchamber. He was quite drunk, and this gave her great encouragement. He would sleep like the dead, and likely would not awaken until mid-morning. She waited another hour, until the castle was quiet, before she stole down the stairs and into the library. There, she went directly to the hidden chest where Lord Ramage kept his hoard of jewels, and quickly selected the pieces she wanted.

She still had some time to wait before she could leave. Having calculated the time it would take her to ride to Galway, Kathleen wanted to arrive just as the jeweler's shop opened, so she could sell the jewels and go directly to the ship. It was unlikely that she would be missed until morning, but in the event her absence was discovered earlier, she wanted to cut the time as fine as possible.

As she waited, Kathleen read Maggie's letter again and again. By now she had the letter committed to memory, yet each reading somehow made her feel much closer to Maggie and her brothers. There was a long voyage ahead of her, she knew, but each league put behind her would bring her closer and closer to her beloved family.

Finally it was time to go. She folded the letter and put it into her pocket, picked up the saddlebags into which she had packed her belongings, and crept silently from the room without a glance behind her.

Had she looked back, Kathleen would have seen the envelope Maggie's letter had come in lying on the floor where she had dropped it.

There was not a sound behind her as she tiptoed out of the castle. In the stable all the men were asleep on their pallets in the tack room at the front. A single candle lantern burned in the stable, casting a dim light.

The gray stallion nickered softly as Kathleen opened his stall door. She had filched an apple from the kitchen. Now she held it in her hand, and let the animal crunch on it, all the while caressing his great neck and murmuring to him.

Moving about as quietly as she could, she put the heavy saddle on him, and fastened the saddle bags. She paused several times with bated breath when she made a clatter, but there was no sound from the tack room. Finally, she mounted up, and guided the stallion at a walk down the lane between the stalls and outside. She kept him at a walk until they had reached the main road and had turned in the direction of Galway.

There, Kathleen sighed with relief. She had made it without being discovered! Happily, there was enough moonlight so she wouldn't be riding in darkness.

She loosened the reins, and drummed her heels into the stallion's sides. "Now! Go!"

The great stallion gave a startled leap forward, and within seconds had settled down into a ground-devouring gallop carrying Kathleen toward Galway —and freedom from Lord Ramage.

Lord Ramage was awakened from his drunken stupor by a loud pounding on his door. He rolled over, opening his eyes. It was past daylight. But even so . . .

"Damme, who is it?" he shouted. "Who dares to wake me at this ungodly hour?"

"It's Tim, Your Lordship. The coachman. I have dire news."

"Come in, come in," Lord Ramage grumbled.

He sat up, propping his back against the headboard. His mouth had the taste of gall, and his head throbbed.

The coachman came hurrying in. Cap in hand, he dipped a knee. "Sorry to rouse Your Lordship."

"What is it, man?" Lord Ramage said irritably. "Spit it out."

"The gray stallion, sire, the gray stallion has been stolen!"

"How could that be? No damned Irish peasant would *dare* steal from me!" He shook his head, the needles of pain pierced his skull. "Damme, I do believe my brains have shaken loose from their moorings. . . ." But the pain eased somewhat, and he became more attentive. "When did you discover the animal missing?"

"When I went to the stable this morning, Your Lordship."

"The beast was there last night?"

"On my word, sire, it was."

Lord Ramage knew then, at least was reasonably sure; but he would not deign to reveal this to a mere servant, so he said, "There is a possibility that the animal has escaped. You and the stablehands search the estate and make sure that is not the case. Be off with you now."

Tim dipped a knee in obsequiousness, and backed out of the room. Lord Ramage waited until the door closed behind the man, then got carefully out of bed, cursing the pounding in his head. He hurried down the hall and into Kathleen's room.

There was no sign of her, as he had expected, and her bed had not been slept in. A quick search of the room disclosed that a few of her clothes were missing. All of a sudden, a horrible thought struck him.

No, it could not be! She would not dare do it a second time!

He started to hasten from the room when something white before the fireplace caught his eye. He picked it up. An envelope, creased from much handling. It was addressed to Kathleen Donnevan of Ramage Castle and the return address was: *Maggie Donnevan, Port Ludlow, Washington Territory, United States of America.*

253

Would Kathleen have dared to so defy him? Had the cowed, mouse-like creature he'd seen these past months summoned up the courage to steal from him again, and to hie herself across the ocean to join her renegade family?

He would have sworn that he had beaten all the spirit out of the damned woman, and it had never crossed his mind that she would steal from him again. He could have hidden the diamonds in another place, but to be forced to do that in his own castle was demeaning. He should have followed his first instincts and thrown her out, bag and baggage!

Realizing that he was already accepting her perfidy as fact, he began to curse, vile oaths that even he had never used before. Some way, somehow, he would repay the Donnevans for the pain and trouble they had caused him!

No longer in a hurry, Lord Ramage went downstairs and into the library. He had been right—some of the diamonds were missing. How ironic! It was so like Kathleen that she hadn't taken them all. That coach trip to Galway, of course. She had inquired about the cost of a ship's passage to this Washington Territory, prepared in advance for the sale of the diamonds, and then stolen just enough for her needs.

Ignoring the fact that he was still in his nightshirt, Lord Ramage strode through the drafty halls to the front door. On the steps outside, he directed his glance toward the stable and saw that the coachman had gathered the stablehands around him, and was giving them instructions for the search for the missing stallion.

"Coachman," Lord Ramage called. "Forget the search. Come here immediately."

The coachman hurried to him.

"I have new instructions for you," Lord Ramage said. "I believe that you will find the missing stallion in Galway. I want you to go there. The Irish wench is also missing. In Galway, you will inquire about her, especially at the shipping offices. It is my belief that she has fled on board a ship bound for America. But be discreet about this, you understand? Under no circumstances do I wish this to become public knowledge. Whatever you learn, report it only to me. Do you comprehend my meaning?"

"Yes, Your Lordship." The coachman touched his cap. "I understand."

"To insure that you do, you stand in peril of your life if one whisper of this gets out. Should it, the blame will be on your shoulders, and I will shoot you down like a cur!"

Tim backed a step, fear leaping into his eyes. "On my oath, sire, I will not breathe a word."

"Excellent." Lord Ramage nodded, dismissing the man with a gesture. "On your way. With all haste, man!"

The coachman ran toward the stable and Lord Ramage turned back inside.

He returned to the library. He brooded over the hoard of jewels, so sorely depleted by the thievery of Kathleen Donnevan, and once again vowed vengeance. Early as it was, he poured a large brandy and sat down to gulp at it. The liquor only added fuel to his anger. Once again, he pored over the envelope and the address for the Donnevans.

Lord Ramage knew then what he was going to do. The minute he could put his affairs in order, he was going to follow Kathleen. He took another drink and laughed aloud. Most people, he knew, would think him addled to chase a woman halfway around the world. But it wasn't only the stolen diamonds and the fact that his mistress had run away. There were other factors involved.

In his early manhood, after his parents died and left the vast Ramage holdings to him, Lord Ramage had traveled extensively. He had enjoyed it. Yet he had never been to America, confining his travels to the European continent. Now he had a valid reason for journeying to a continent he had always considered uncivilized and beneath his notice.

There was also the fact that he was growing bored with his life here. A life of wenching, drinking, and hunting was grand; but at this stage in his life, new places, new excitements, presented a pleasing prospect. And at the end was a worthwhile goal. In America, he would use whatever law there was in Washington Territory to threaten the Donnevans with prison unless they repaid him for the jewels Kathleen had stolen. If no law existed, well and good. He would confront them himself, and get his due. Of a certainty there would be some bully boys he could employ to back up his threat. In his heart, Lord Ramage knew he would never be content now until he saw both female Donnevans dead!

Excitement prodding him now, he finished off the brandy and got up to pour another. Instead of sitting down, he began to pace. The glass of brandy had restored his physical well-being. He had awakened, still feeling the efforts of falling into bed last night in a drunken stupor. That would not happen again, he promised himself. For much too long he had been drifting, with no purpose to his life.

Now he had that purpose. An adventure such as this would put fire back into his blood, sweep his mind clear of cobwebs, the challenge of it putting him on his mettle.

He drank, his thoughts racing ahead. It would take a few weeks to put his affairs in order. He anticipated no difficulty in finding a man capable of managing the estate in his absence. It practically ran itself, anyway. All it took was someone to collect the yearly rentals from the Irish tenants, deal harshly with those slow to pay, and see that order was maintained in Ramage Castle.

In his excitement, he continued to pace back and forth across the library, thinking hard for a way he could hasten his departure for America, and Washington Territory.

"Damme, Kathleen Donnevan, you are going to rue the day you stole from me," he said aloud. "You are going to pay. You are going to pay in blood, madam!"

Chapter Eleven

It had taken Maggie three months to finally overcome her qualms about being in debt to Jonas Kirk. During those months the logging operation proceeded smoothly. Olaf had increased the size of the crew and now housed them in a newly constructed wooden structure—a combination bunkhouse, kitchen and dining hall.

Mother Be-Damn now had two assistants, two Chinese males she bullied like wayward sons, but under her supervision, the Donnevan Logging Company had gained the reputation of serving the best victuals of any logging company in the Northwest. And Maggie was amused to notice that Mother Be-Damn was in romantic pursuit of Olaf. At first Olaf had shied away, but of late they had taken to slipping off into the woods after supper.

Maggie thought that this wasn't so strange as it

might seem. It was summer now, and Mother Be-Damn had undergone a strange metamorphosis. As the weather warmed, she became slimmer and slimmer. Some time passed before Maggie understood the reason for this. Then the explanation finally dawned on her. On their first glimpse of Mother Be-Damn on that chill autumn day, the Indian woman had been wearing all the clothes she possessed. As the weather warmed, she removed them layer by layer. She still was not sylph-like by any means, for even wearing a single garment, she was a large woman; yet the removal of the other garments had reduced her bulk by a third.

Maggie wished them joy in their affair—if such it was. Certainly Olaf deserved it. He had reported to her that while his wife had improved somewhat in health, she would never be able to return to the cold and wet of the Northwest, and since Olaf knew nothing but logging, he could never join her. So why shouldn't he find companionship with Mother Be-Damn? So long as both received some happiness from the liaison, what harm did it do?

Maggie did wonder if she would be so understanding if she wasn't happy in her own secret affair. With those wonderful Sunday afternoons with Jonas to look forward to after a week's hard work, she was quite content—both in her love life and business affairs. According to Captain Sayward, the Donnevans were logging more timber than any other outfit selling to him. In fact, their output had grown so that he was finding it difficult to handle, which was one more reason that Maggie knew it was time she arrived at a decision about building her own sawmill.

One evening after supper, she asked Olaf and Patrick to come to her office, a small wooden building Olaf had constructed at the same time as the bunkhouse. He had offered to build her wooden sleeping quarters as well, but Maggie had declined. She was comfortable in her tent, and saw no reason to go to the extra expense just for her personal comfort.

The office was small, with a table she used for a desk, and only enough room for two chairs. On this table-desk she took care of her accounts, and paid the men in cash every Saturday night, as they formed a single line outside, coming in one by one for their wages.

Olaf and Patrick occupied the chairs, and Maggie sat behind the table. Olaf had a wad of snuff in his cheek, and Patrick was smoking a pipe, a custom he had taken up recently. At least, Maggie thought, it wasn't as filthy a habit as dipping snuff.

She began abruptly, "We're doing very well, aren't we?"

"Yah." Olaf nodded. "We're doing yust fine."

His look was wary, and Maggie suppressed a laugh. She knew that he was wondering what wild scheme she would come up with now. With a straight face, she said, "I think it's time we built our own sawmill. . . ."

"Sawmill!" Olaf exclaimed.

Patrick simply stared.

"Whisht! Olaf, you look as shocked as though I'd just proposed something sinful."

"Girl, do you know how much it's going to cost you to build a sawmill? Everthing, all the parts, has to be shipped in, and it's going to cost dearly."

"I know all that, Olaf," she said calmly. "But if we're going to grow, we need it. You know what Captain Sayward said when we delivered our last raft of logs. If we increase production much more, he's not going to be able to handle it. That would mean we'd have to raft the logs to either Port Gamble or Seattle, and that would cut into our profits."

"Where are you going to get the money?" Olaf asked.

"I'll worry about that," she said crisply.

Olaf shook his head dubiously. "I don't know, Maggie. It yust seems like such a drastic move."

"Olaf," she sighed, "by this time you should know better than to balk me." She leaned across the table. "Wasn't I right about putting our brand on the logs? Wasn't I right about using the saws for the backcuts instead of axes? And you were dubious about buying oxen too soon, yet look what happened."

Olaf turned his head aside to spit a brown stream through the open door. Then he shrugged, spreading his hands wide. "You're the boss lady."

"That I am." She transferred her gaze to Patrick. "Not a word have I heard from you, brother Patrick. What do you think?"

Patrick grinned broadly. "What do I think, lass? I think that you've been right since the day you told me we Donnevans were leaving Ireland. You have been right about everything. Whatever you wish, little sister, I'm with you, that's what I'm after thinking."

Maggie studied him. Patrick had indeed grown up. She smiled suddenly. "Thank you for that, Patrick. Now I feel better about everything, since I'm going to be away for a time, maybe a month or more. You'll be left in charge, Patrick . . . our bull-of-the-woods. Is that all right with you, Olaf?"

"Fine with me, girl," Olaf said, showing no resentment. "Yah, I'm happy being bullwhacker. Being *your* bull-of-the-woods is too much of a load on my shoulders, especially now that you're on your way to becoming a dad-damned timber baron!"

Maggie nodded. "That is exactly what I have in mind, Olaf, and it's what I intend to become, what I intend for the Donnevans to become."

"You said you'd be away a month, Maggie," Patrick said. "Where?"

"Port Gamble first, then Seattle, perhaps with stops along the way to inspect other sawmills."

"Why Port Gamble?" Olaf asked.

"I want to inspect the sawmill Pope and Talbot have built there."

"You're not thinking of trying to build a sawmill like theirs?"

"I've been doing a wee bit of thinking on it, yes."

"But theirs is the best dad-damned sawmill on the Sound!"

"So you've told me, Olaf. That's the reason I wish to see it."

"And the most expensive," Olaf added.

"Olaf, if I'm going to construct my own sawmill, I'll be wanting the best."

"By thunder!" Olaf shook his head in wonder. "You *are* the dad-damnedest woman I ever seen!"

"Maggie," Patrick said in sudden alarm, "you'd not be thinking of going off alone?"

"Let's not get into that, Patrick. Whisht! I thought it had already been decided that I'd come and go as I pleased."

"But this is different, Maggie, that it is. A lass such as yourself sallying forth among strangers on your own. No, I won't allow it!"

"You'll allow what *I* say, brother. Besides, who'd go with me? I'm leaving you in charge. Olaf has his oxen to work. Dan has to stay here to look after wee Kevin. We can't spare a single man. And did it ever enter your brain, brother, that I just might be liking some time on my own, away from the Donnevan clan?"

Patrick stiffened. "Maggie! 'Tis a shocking thing you're saying! You sound like a wanton woman talking!"

"Why? Would it strike *you* that way if you were doing it?"

"That's not the same thing, little sister. I'm a man grown."

"So I was thinking but a moment ago. Now I wonder. But I am also a grown woman, and I'm going alone. Now I'll be hearing no more about it." She got to her feet. "I'll be leaving in a few days."

Patrick, muttering darkly under his breath, made his departure.

As Olaf started to follow him out, Maggie said, "Olaf, just a minute."

He paused, looking at her inquiringly.

"Just a word of caution," she said with a straight face. "Don't be letting your evening jaunts into the woods with Mother Be-Damn interfere with your work whilst I'm away."

Olaf's face flushed a dark red. He stammered, "I . . . I don't know what you mean, girl."

Now Maggie allowed herself to smile. "You know very well what I mean. And forgive me, Olaf. I was doing a wee bit of teasing." She came around the table to take his hand in both of hers. She squeezed. "I'm glad for you, Olaf. If you can find enjoyment with Mother Be-Damn, you deserve it."

"Thunderation, you can come up with the daddamnedest things, girl," he mumbled, still embarrassed. "How did you know? Do any of the men know?"

Maggie patted his bristly cheek. "A woman has a way of figuring out these things, dear Olaf. And no, I don't think any of the men know. If they do, what does it matter? It's none of their affair, and you're your own man. Now, go along with you."

She returned to her chair behind the table after Olaf had left, and propped her chin on her hands. It was working out fine. Soon, she would have her own sawmill!

Now there was only one thing left to do. This Sunday, she would tell Jonas that she agreed to his proposal, and would accept the bank draft from him for the money she needed.

That ever-present doubt, her inherent dread of debt, nagged at her, but she dismissed it impatiently from her thoughts.

Three weeks later, Maggie was on board a small inland schooner as it sailed into the sheltered

Gamble Bay, on the east bank of the Hood Canal, and she had her first glimpse of Port Gamble. Olaf had informed her that the village's original name, given to it by the Indians, had been "Teekalet," meaning brightness of the noon-day sun.

There was a flat, sandy spit of land projecting out into the bay, and there Pope and Talbot had built their sawmill. It was comprised of two buildings, and the sawmills and the yard were bustling with activity. At each end of the buildings loomed tall, brick chimneys, from which smoke poured. A great number of logs floated alongside the mills, and the mill yard was stacked high with sawed lumber.

This sawmill operation put Captain Sayward's small mill to shame, but what impressed Maggie the most was the neatness of the village itself. Streets had been laid out, and there were many grand houses in sight, all very neat and freshly painted and gleaming white. Maggie understood that the village and the houses were close to exact replicas of a New England coastal town, since Pope, Talbot, and Cyrus Walker—the enterprising individual that everyone predicted would soon become manager of the Pope and Talbot mill—were all from New England. Pope and Talbot, she also understood, resided in San Francisco, where the company's main offices were located.

Maggie disembarked from the schooner, and carrying her small bag, she walked along the wooden wharf toward the town. As she stepped ashore, she was approached by a balding man wearing a dark suit, a starched white collar, and a black string tie.

"I am Cyrus Walker, madam," he said in a deep voice. "Welcome to Port Gamble."

"And I am Maggie Donnevan."

His eyes brightened. "Aye, I've heard of you, Miss Donnevan. You and your brothers have a logging company over north of Port Ludlow. And doing very well, I understand. Have you come to interest us in buying logs from you? We would be happy to oblige, and you will receive top price."

"Well . . . not exactly," Maggie hedged. "I'm here to inspect your sawmill, if you do not object. I understand it is the wonder of the Sound."

"Why should I object? We are always happy to show our mill to interested visitors, because we are indeed proud of it."

"That is very kind of you, Mr. Walker," Maggie said. "But first I must find lodgings for the night. I believe you have a hotel here?"

"We do, Miss Donnevan, but it is a low place—not fitting for a lady such as yourself—catering to loggers, millhands, and loose women." Cyrus Walker grimaced. "Most of Port Gamble is a company town, and is maintained as neat as a pin, and policed to be kept free of vice, but the hotel is not within the province of the company. I would be delighted to offer you hospitality for the length of your stay in Port Gamble. I have recently built a fine house of my own. It is close to the sawmill, true, and since we work the clock around, the mill noises might disturb your rest. I have become accustomed to the noises. Aye, you might say," his smile was prideful, "it is music to my ears."

"But Mr. Walker," Maggie said innocently, "I understand that you are not married. Would it be

267

proper for me to spend the night in the domicile of an unmarried man?"

Cyrus Walker flushed. "Oh, entirely proper, madam, I assure you. Although it is true I am a bachelor, I have household help, a housekeeper and a maid, both on the premises at all times. It will not be considered improper by our citizens, and no gossip will attach to you."

"Then I accept your kind offer, sir, and with gratitude," Maggie said, smiling.

As they walked along, Cyrus Walker pointed out many features of Port Gamble, with obvious pride.

"See those maples?" He pointed to the half-grown trees lining the immaculately clean streets. "As you probably know, the maple is not native to the West Coast. They come from seedlings that Mrs. J. P. Keller, the spouse of the present mill manager, lovingly imported from Maine. When they attain full growth, they will spread across the streets, almost meeting. And up there . . ." He pointed up to the end of the street to a small white church, with a steeple as sharp as a needle. "That house of worship is an exact replica of ours back home in East Machias, Maine."

"From what I have been told, all of Port Gamble looks very much like the villages of your New England," Maggie commented.

"That is true, Miss Donnevan. We New Englanders are quite proud of our heritage, and have tried to bring it with us. Do you find that strange?"

Maggie did find it exceedingly strange, reflecting that she certainly had no inclination to reproduce anything of her *own* native land. But she supposed the heritage of these people was something they could be proud of, while hers was the exact opposite, so she merely said, "If *you* don't find it strange, why should I, a stranger here?"

Cyrus Walker's house, while not as grand as Jonas' house on the hill, was comfortable, and Maggie was made to feel at home. Her host insisted that she postpone her tour of the mill until the morning, and Maggie consented. The supper was ample enough but simple fare: boiled meat, potatoes, and vegetables, accompanied by strong, hot tea.

Weary from her long day, she retired early, and found Cyrus Walker's warning to be true. Despite her weariness, her sleep was uneasy, disturbed often by the shrill whine of the saws from the mill, the steam whistle, and the thumping sounds of sawed lumber being stacked in the yard.

Cyrus Walker had informed her that it was his custom to rise early in the morning to make his first tour of the mill. "If you wish, Miss Donnevan, you may sleep late, and I will take you through the mill later in the day."

"No, I have much to do and see in the brief time I have, so please wake me when you are up."

When the maid rapped on the bedroom door shortly after dawn, Maggie wished she had accepted her host's suggestion that she sleep late. But she got out of bed, hastily washed her hands and face in the wash basin, and got dressed. Instead of the dress she had worn yesterday, she put on the trousers and man's shirt she wore around the logging camp.

Cyrus Walker reared back in surprise when she entered the dining room.

Maggie said, "I hope my garments do not shock you, sir, nor the other good folks of Port Gamble."

"Well, madam, I must say it is . . . uh, a trifle unusual to see a woman wearing a man's clothing." He coughed behind his hand, maintaining a stern countenance. "The good folks hereabouts have rather fixed ideas about how a woman should consort herself. And there are the millhands . . ."

"Whisht! This is what I wear while working with the loggers. It's the only practical thing to wear in the woods, and I would think the same would be true around a sawmill. As for the millhands . . ." she smiled, "I should think they would be less likely to . . . well, less likely to be disturbed by viewing the female form in men's clothing than in a dress."

"Your logic is strong, madam. So . . ." He nodded. "If you can bear up under possible disapproval from our more proper ladies, I will not refuse you."

"I am on a business trip, Mr. Walker, and will have no time to be after consorting with your proper ladies."

After another New England meal, Maggie was escorted to the mill by Cyrus Walker. As they approached the first building, she saw two huge piles of sawdust. Men were busily dousing the sawdust down with water.

She halted. "Why are they doing that?"

"By dampening them down, we hope to prevent fires. Dry sawdust is highly inflammable. We live in deadly fear of a sawmill fire. Almost every month a mill burns to the ground somewhere along the Sound. So far, we have been most fortunate.

We have not as yet had a fire. With all the expensive equipment, it could be disastrous for us."

They resumed walking. Maggie noticed that several of the sawmill workers gave her curious glances, but most of them ignored her, probably assuming that she was a man. The two mill buildings—long, wooden structures—were set some distance apart.

Cyrus Walker stopped before one building. "This is our newest mill. It began operating only a month back. Pope and Talbot were among the first mill operators on the Sound to use steam-driven saws. From the very first day, with just the one mill, we were cutting two thousand feet of lumber a day. Within only a few months that production was doubled, then redoubled as we added more saws. Now, with the new mill operating we will probably cut close to eight million feet a year." He wore a proud smile. "For your information, Miss Donnevan, that is enough lumber to fill a ship a week, to be shipped down to San Francisco. On Andrew Pope's last visit, two months back, he informed me that the company is aggressively seeking foreign markets for our lumber, ranging as far across the world as China and Australia."

"That is most impressive," Maggie murmured. She *was* impressed, but the strongest feeling she experienced just then was envy. What this man was telling her also filled her with excitement, and served to strengthen her resolve. If she could build a mill and attain *half* their production, the Donnevans would indeed soon be lumber barons to be reckoned with!

Cyrus Walker lent her his arm, and they entered

the building. The din of the whining saws was tremendous, and Maggie fought back an impulse to cover her ears. If she was to have a sawmill of her own, she would have to become accustomed to the noise. It would have to become, in Cyrus Walker's words, music to her ears.

At a touch of her elbow from Cyrus Walker, she stopped, looking in the direction he was pointing. She saw a number of strange-looking contraptions lined up in rows, machines with long, narrow blades flashing up and down in a reciprocating action. The six vertical blades on each machine were set a fixed distance apart.

"Those are gang saws," Cyrus Walker shouted in her ear. "We now have thirty-eight of them in operation."

There was a sort of carriage on iron rails that moved slowly through the saws, carrying logs. When the saw blades bit into the wood, there was a high-pitched scream, like that of some animal in agony.

Cyrus Walker said in her ear, "When each log runs its course through the gang saw, it will be sawed up into planks."

At the far end of the building was an opening as wide as a barn, and the logs were propelled through it, dripping with water from the log pond outside. Maggie could catch just a glimpse of the pond, the water shining like silver, and the pine logs shone like gold as the rays of the morning sun struck them.

The air inside the mill was rich with the scent of pine and pitch.

Suddenly, Maggie sensed something of what

Cyrus Walker felt. The uproar was music. The saws sang, she thought; it must be wonderful music to a sawmill owner's ears.

Cyrus Walker showed Maggie the boilers, which were fed chunks of wood by the sweating boiler tenders, to keep the steam up to drive the saws. She studied everything carefully, trying to commit to memory every phase of the mill's operation.

Finally, she returned outside with Cyrus Walker. He said, "Those gang saws are woefully inefficient. For one thing, they slice every log identically, regardless of flaws. And the engine wastes energy, overcoming inertia on every stroke and return. Mr. Pope told me, when he was here, that the circular saw is coming into use, and is far more efficient. It takes less power to operate, and cuts more logs per day, although it does require more men to operate. But with circular saws, we could cut just as many feet of lumber with far less saws than we use now. He intends to install them soon."

"Are there any circular saws in operation on the Sound, so I could observe them?"

"I believe Henry Yesler, in Seattle, is now using one." He looked at her curiously. "Pardon my prying, Miss Donnevan, but why should you, a woman, show so much interest in the operation of a sawmill? I do believe you are the first woman, outside of our own women here, to express such curiosity; and the *only* woman I know who has not been repelled by the dust and the noise."

"I will be honest with you, Mr. Walker." She faced him squarely. "I am considering building a sawmill of my own."

273

"You, madam?" His face went blank with astonishment. "*You* are building a sawmill?"

"Afraid of the competition, Mr. Walker?" she said teasingly.

He was shaking his head. "Not of the competition, madam. It would take a vast investment of funds to compete with Pope and Talbot. No, we do not fear competition."

"Oh, I understand. Whisht! You're surprised that a woman should be so brazen as to compete with your grand sawmill. Is that the way of it, Mr. Walker?"

"Perhaps, Miss Donnevan." He relaxed, smiling slightly. "You must admit that it is unusual, and will take some getting used to."

"Then you and your employers should be after getting used to the idea, because I am determined to do it."

"Well, that at least explains your interest in our mill."

"And you believe that was underhanded of me?"

Again, he shook his head. "Not at all. We have no secrets to conceal. To show that I harbor you no ill will, it was in my mind to invite several of my friends to supper tonight to meet you."

Maggie relented. "I am sorry, Mr. Walker. It was small of me. I do admit that I'm a wee bit touchy, having been greeted with much laughter and derision since the day I started the Donnevan Logging Company. As for your hospitality, I must regretfully decline. I sail with the schooner at high noon. If I remained over, there is no telling when I would find transportation on to Seattle."

"Then I wish you good fortune, Miss Donnevan," Cyrus Walker said stiffly, dipping his head.

On the way to Seattle, Maggie stopped to inspect two other, smaller sawmills. She learned nothing of any value to her. They were not on the scale of the Port Gamble mill, but more resembled Captain Sayward's sawmill. In addition, she was greeted with thinly veiled hostility in both instances.

The schooner continued on to Seattle. The town, at first glance, was not impressive. The only attractive feature was the hill rising steeply to the east, with a small cluster of fine houses atop it. The rest of the village, mostly waterfront, was mostly taken up by what she assumed to be Yesler's sawmill, and a long wharf. A large number of ships, of all sizes, was docked at the wharf.

"That's what they call 'The Sag' where Henry has his sawmill," said a voice by her side. Maggie glanced around at Captain Potter, a rotund man of fifty-odd years; he owned the schooner and earned his living transporting passengers, mail, and small items up and down the Sound.

"His sawmill's built practically on the water. In fact, at high tide the streets there are often flooded." The captain laughed, jolly laughter that caused him to quiver all over. "Henry Yesler is an ambitious coot, but he ain't always too practical. Much lumber as he saws and sells, he's broke often as not. I hear tell that just last month he had to borrow two hundred dollars from the town's minister to meet his payroll."

Now they were close enough for Maggie to see better. Remembering the mill yard in Port Gamble, she said, "I don't see any sawdust piles. Isn't this Henry Yesler operating his mill now?"

"That, again, is a brainstorm of Henry's." Captain Potter laughed heartily. "You see, the waterfront section, where Henry's mill is, as I have said, is so low it is often covered with water. In fact, some have called it Ballast Island. Ships coming up empty of cargo from San Francisco are loaded with ballast. They have to dump it somewheres before the trip back downcoast with a load of lumber. So somebody got the idea of charging each ship five dollars every time they dumped their ballast on shore. That's helped build it up somewhat, but she still floods with a good storm. So Henry got himself an idea. He hired a man with a wheelbarrow to load it down with sawdust and trundle it along, dumping the sawdust on the streets and into the bay. All day you can see that galoot trundling back and forth with his wheelbarrow of sawdust. I don't know how much it really helps, but it sure keeps Henry's mill yard cleared of sawdust, lessening his chances of fire. Oh, that Henry Yesler is a real pistol, he is!"

They were nearing the wharf area now, and Maggie looked up at the steep hill as she heard a rumbling sound. A strip of land had been cleared going straight up the hill. And down it tumbled logs, sped along by the force of gravity, rumbling and smoking from the friction.

Beside her Captain Potter said, "Another money-saving idea of Henry's. He, and other loggers, are logging off the top of Seattle's First Hill, as that there hill is called, and they let the logs slide right down the hill, to Henry's mill."

276

"Why doesn't he build a skidroad?"

"Oh, he's thinking on it. He and the city fathers have been at it tooth and nail. That First Hill, as you can see, is where what fine houses Seattle has is located. They want him to stop sliding logs down that strip, stirring up dust and noise. Sometimes one of them logs goes haywire and goes whomping off by itself and lands in somebody's yard. Last month one went right through a window and there was a great hurrah about *that*, you can bet your boots! Henry says if they'll let him build a skidroad, he'll stop sliding the logs down thataway. I suspect old Henry will get his way. His mill is about the onliest thing keeping this town alive. Well, Miss Donnevan, we're about to dock. I have to get back to the wheel. The lad at the wheel now is likely to run us right up onto land, high and dry. . . ."

"Captain, wait! Is there a hotel in Seattle?"

"Yep. Some of the first lumber Yesler turned out was used to build the Felker House. It's run by a woman named Mary Ann Conklin. She's a salty wench, the widow of a whaling captain, and she runs an orderly place, allowing no shenanigans. She keeps order with profanity such as a lady like yourself never heard. If that doesn't work, she uses sticks of kindling wood, and her aim is good." Captain Potter chuckled. "Some call her Madame Damnable. But it's a clean hotel, serves good food, and she'll see to it that you're not bothered by ruffians."

Mrs. Conklin was a large woman, with a rough tongue, but she took to Maggie at once, and showed her to a small, but very clean room. "Now if any of these roughnecks bother you, missy," the big woman said in a gravelly voice, "you just come to me, and I'll dampen their fires. 'Course I cater to high class here, but some of the gents do tank up on liquor and get out of hand. A stick of kindling laid alongside their heads usually calms them down."

Maggie was smiling as Madame Damnable left the room. She was the white counterpart of Mother Be-Damn, Maggie thought.

It was still early in the day, and Maggie left the hotel after freshening up, strolling along the muddy streets. Aside from the houses on First Hill, it resembled Port Ludlow more than the neat and orderly Port Gamble. Yet there was an air of excitement about it, a bustle and a feeling of activity that she liked. This gave her pause to wonder, realizing for the first time that she liked this rough-and-ready village, and Port Ludlow, more than Port Gamble. *Whisht*, she thought wryly, *I have indeed changed.*

She continued on toward Yesler's sawmill. Inquiring after Henry Yesler, she finally found him in a long, log building behind the sawmill. He was a burly, gruff individual, with wild hair and a full beard, beginning to gray.

Yet he was friendly enough, and seemed to find nothing strange in her request to inspect his sawmill. "Glad to show it to you, Miss Donnevan. My mill is what keeps Seattle afloat." His laughter was startling, a deep, rumbling sound. "In more ways than one. You've probably heard that the streets here below the hill are prone to flooding. Well, I'm doing my best to stop that, spreading the streets with sawdust." Again, he roared with laughter, his eyes unnaturally bright.

Maggie stared at him apprehensively. She had heard the expression people often used here—pouring water down a rathole—and now she knew what it meant. For this man to think that he could build up the streets of Seattle, a wheelbarrow of sawdust at a time . . .

Whisht! He was not only an eccentric, but a wee bit fey, in her opinion.

Without noticing her uneasiness, Yesler had turned aside. He waved a hand around the long building. "In a way, this is the social as well as the commercial center of Seattle. It not only serves as a cookhouse for my hands, but is Seattle's church, tavern, meeting house, and jail. I also have living quarters here. I'm staying here until I can bring my wife out from Massillon. And now, Miss Donnevan, come see my sawmill."

After her experience with Cyrus Walker, Maggie had decided to wear a dress this time. As long as she was careful, she should be all right.

Yesler's sawmill was crude in comparison to the one in Port Gamble. It was small, sloppily run, and filthy, with sawdust and wood shavings ankle-deep on the floor.

Henry Yesler ignored all this as he led Maggie toward his circular saw. He nodded at it with pride. "The only circular saw on Puget Sound." He had to raise his voice to a shout to be heard over the shrill whine of the spinning circular saw blade, which spewed sawdust and wood chips helter-skelter as it sliced into the log inching along the carriage. Although Yesler's was a badly run operation, Maggie at once grasped the advantage of circular saws over the gang saws Cyrus Walker had showed her. If she could purchase a couple of these . . .

She flinched, jumping back, as a wood chip struck her a glancing blow on the cheek. She touched Yesler's arm and motioned outside. Reluctantly, he ushered her out.

Maggie brushed at the sawdust clinging to her dress.

Yesler said, "Sorry, Miss Donnevan. I suppose that ain't the best place for a lady. I'm so used to it I didn't think."

"Are those circular saws expensive?"

"They don't come cheap, I can tell you! But they're worth it." He squinted at her. "Why you asking?"

"I'm going to build a sawmill of my own."

"Ah, *now* I know where I've heard your name. You're the Irish woman running her own logging outfit. And you're thinking of building a sawmill?"

"Not only thinking, but I'm going to do it."

Yesler threw back his head and roared with laughter.

Maggie bridled, taking offense. "Sir, I do not find it humorous!"

"Beg pardon." Yesler batted a hand at her, getting his laughter under control. "I ain't laughing at you. I'm just thinking of how the other millers are going to take to a woman competing with them. Me, the more competition the better. There's more logs in the territory than we could all log and saw in a hundred years. I say, good fortune to you, Miss Donnevan."

280

Maggie peered at him suspiciously. "You'd not be laughing because I'm a woman?"

"Not at all, Miss Donnevan. I hope you do well at it, and I suspect you will."

Maggie had seen all she needed to see. She knew now what machinery she needed for her sawmill. The mill building, of course, could be constructed from her own logs. After leaving Henry Yesler, she proceeded directly to the offices of a mill supply company on the waterfront, and ordered two circular saws, boilers, and the other pieces of equipment she would need, paying for everything with Jonas' bank draft. The machinery would have to be shipped up from San Francisco, and she was given a vague promise of delivery at Seattle in about two months time.

It was mid-afternoon when she returned to the Felker House. And the first person she saw as she swept into the small lobby was Andrew Kane.

Maggie stopped short in surprise. This time he was wearing neither the Naval uniform, nor rough seaman's clothing. He was resplendent in a black suit, white silk shirt, highly polished black boots, and a wide-brimmed, black hat. "Well! Mr. Kane, we do seem to encounter one another from time to time, do we not?"

"I like to think of it as fate bringing us together, Maggie," he said, smiling. He removed his hat, and gave her a small bow.

"Fate, is it? Whisht!" As much as she hated to admit it to herself, Maggie was uncommonly glad to see him. Her heart was beating wildly.

"Of course, I suppose it shouldn't be considered

unusual, since I do reside here at present. How about you, Maggie? What are you doing in Seattle?"

"I'm here on business. I'm building my own sawmill, and have just placed an order for the machinery I will need."

"Well, now, you *are* doing well. Knowing you, I must say I'm not in the least surprised. You are an enterprising young woman, Maggie Donnevan."

"And you, Mr. Kane? Is your tugboat in operation now?"

Andrew smiled broadly. "I have just finished converting the *Carolina Belle* to steam this week. It was an onerous chore, but now it's done, and I will be working with her soon now."

"Then perhaps I could employ your services, Mr. Kane. The machinery I have ordered will be unloaded here. They refuse to drop it off at Port Ludlow. Would you transport the equipment to my logging location when it arrives?"

"I would be most happy to oblige, Maggie." Now his smile turned mocking. "But I must confess to being somewhat baffled, well knowing your feelings toward me."

"Personal feelings have nothing to do with business," she retorted.

"Spoken like a true businesswoman, madam."

"Besides, you performed a favor for me when last we met. Now I will return the favor, and no longer be in your debt. I will, naturally, expect to pay the proper shipping fees."

"Naturally." His eyes reflected his amusement. He added gravely, "I will charge the going rate. I will not rook you, Miss Donnevan."

"I think you are an honest man, Mr. Kane, in your business dealings."

"But not with women, is that your meaning?" There was a teasing note in his voice. "It strikes me you're looking well and healthy, so what happened that night could not have harmed you overmuch."

Refusing to lose her temper, Maggie said coldly, "There are things that hurt, inside a person, that do not show."

He looked deep into her eyes. "Are you happy with your lover, Maggie?"

"That, sir, is none of your business! You are a cad to dare ask such a question!"

"You see, I know more about women than you seem to believe," he said, smiling again.

Why must he always be so hateful? Seething, Maggie said, "Good day to you, Mr. Kane," and started to sail past him.

Andrew placed his hand on her arm, restraining her. "I apologize, Maggie. I have no right to pry into your private life. Somehow, we always seem at cross purposes whenever we chance to meet. You know what popped into my mind at the sight of you? I thought of asking you on board the *Belle* this evening for a champagne supper. I am a good cook. A seafaring man must learn how. I would be delighted should you accept. And I promise," he held up both hands, palms out, "that I will not molest you, madam."

She looked directly into his eyes. "What about your widow, why not invite her?"

Maggie expected him to show anger, but instead he smiled lazily, and said, "Amy is terrified of boats and the water. She refused to board the *Belle*, even tied up at the wharf."

"But won't she be a wee bit resentful of your having another woman on board?"

"It matters not." He gestured carelessly. "Understand one thing, Maggie. I am my own man. I belong to no one."

"Whisht! It's independent you are, is it?"

"That I am, and in like company, it seems." He smiled. "But will you come, Maggie? Or perhaps you are fearful of being alone with me?"

"I am fearful of no man, sir!" she said indignantly.

"Well then?"

Maggie realized that she had been dense, and had allowed him to maneuver her into a trap. If she spurned his invitation now, he would indeed think she was afraid of him. "It's devious you are, Andrew Kane."

"Devious?" he said innocently. "I don't take your meaning."

"I accept your invitation, Mr. Kane. And if you do make improper advances, you will regret it, that I promise *you*."

She started off, and he called after her, "Seven o'clock, Maggie. The *Belle* is tied up at the wharf not far from Yesler's mill. You can't miss it."

She continued on, and Andrew stood staring after her until she disappeared toward the rear. Absently, he took out his pipe, filled, and lit it. Amy would find out, of course, and she would be furious with him. Perhaps this was the way to rid himself of her. He had long since become bored with Amy. She had good looks, true, but she was as emptyheaded as a gourd, and her endless, pointless prattle had begun to wear on his nerves. It wouldn't take him long, now that the *Belle* was ready to put to work, to earn enough money to buy out her interest in the boat, and he would be rid of her for good.

That, however, had not been the reason for the invitation to Maggie. It had been an impromptu thing, the invitation given without any forethought whatsoever.

Now Andrew had to wonder if it was a mistake. His desire for Maggie Donnevan was powerful, and many times over the past months he had had erotic visions of how it would be with her, how it would be to lie with her with her full consent. She was a passionate woman, he was positive of that. Clearly she had not realized that about herself that night on the beach at Port Townsend, but she undoubtedly knew by this time. She was a mature woman now, deeply involved in a love affair.

Yet, if he didn't stick to his promise tonight, if he tried to seduce her, it was entirely possible that he would alienate her for good. Well aware of his own passionate nature, Andrew wasn't sure that he could restrain himself.

Well, what the hell! Let matters take their natural course. He shrugged all such concerns from his mind, and left the hotel to shop for food and champagne for tonight's supper.

Maggie's only prior experience with tugboats had been with Captain Sayward's, and it was disgracefully filthy, with black grease all over everything, and the deck littered with soot belched from the stubby smokestack. Consequently, it was with some trepidation that she put on her best dress—a silken garment that was a light peach in color—and dainty slippers. If the dress and slippers were ruined by Andrew's tugboat, so be it. But she absolutely would not go to supper with Andrew Kane wearing less than her best.

There were no carriages for hire in Seattle, so she had to pick her way daintily along the waterfront street, with her skirts held up off the ground by one hand, avoiding the worst of the mud, until she reached the wooden wharf.

The *Carolina Belle* was docked about halfway down the long line of ships. Andrew saw her coming and helped her on board. Once on deck, she shook down her skirts, and stood with hands on hips, looking about. The deck was still as immaculate as it had been on that Sunday afternoon in Port Ludlow. The only change she could see was the absence of the mast and the sail, and a short smokestack just forward of the wheelhouse. The smokestack was painted black.

Set up on the deck were a small table and folding chairs.

Andrew, noticing the direction of her glance, said, "My galley is small, and it's steaming hot in there, so I thought we'd be more comfortable out here. I'm baking quail, Maggie. I hope you like them."

"I must say this looks cleaner than the other tugboat I've been on."

"And it will stay that way, I'll see to it. Most tugboat owners consider their boats nothing but working craft. I intend to live on board the *Belle*, and it's going to remain clean and livable. Come along," he took her arm, "and have a glass of champagne."

He seated her with a flourish. On the table were two stemmed glasses and a bucket, with a bottle of champagne nestled in cracked ice.

"It's pretty fancy you are, Mr. Kane. Ice, in the summer? Where did you find it?"

"It wasn't easy, and cost dearly," he said with a lazy grin. "But I wanted only the best for you, my dear."

He poured champagne into the glasses, and offered her one.

"Thank you, Mr. Kane," she said primly.

"Maggie . . ." He sighed. "Can't you bring yourself to call me Andrew? At least for this evening. You sound so damned formal."

"I'll think on it." She sipped at the champagne. She had partaken of champagne before. On occasion Jonas had provided it for their enjoyment. "This is delicious . . . Andrew."

"There, you see? That didn't hurt, did it?" He raised his glass. "A toast to friendship, Maggie."

"Whisht! About that, I don't know." But she drank the toast with him.

By the time the bottle was empty and another put into the ice bucket, Andrew had shown her through the boat. The galley was an extension of the captain's cabin, which was rather richly furnished, with a comfortable sofa along one wall.

"That's my own innovation," Andrew said with a straight face. "Instead of a regulation bunk, I had the old one taken out, and this built in. It can be converted into a bunk, easily enough. Shall I show you?"

"No need for that," she retorted. "I'll take your word for it."

It *was* warm in the cabin, with the heat coming in waves from the small wood cookstove in the galley, and Maggie used it as an excuse to return abovedecks.

The second bottle of champagne was soon consumed, and yet a third put into the ice bucket to chill. Maggie was more relaxed than she could remember being, and certainly more at ease with Andrew than ever before. She dimly realized that she was lightheaded from the champagne; but the chief reason for her ease with him was Andrew's own attitude. He was on his best behavior, charming and witty, entertaining her with stories of his youth back in North Carolina and of his abortive naval career.

The quail, when finally served, was deliciously brown and crisp. The potatoes, baked in hot coals, were white and crumbly inside, and the carrots and peas Andrew had cooked were equally tasty.

Finally, she leaned back. "Whisht! Such grand food I have never eaten. Yours was not an idle boast, Andrew. You are a fine cook."

"Wait." Andrew held up his hand. "You're not finished yet. I have a special treat for you."

"No, nothing more, please! I couldn't take another bite."

"Of this you will, I promise."

Quickly he cleared the small table of dishes, and carried them below. He returned carrying a bowl of fresh, ripe strawberries. He dished them out into small bowls, then took the champagne bottle from its bed of ice, and poured the remains of the champagne over the strawberries.

Tempted despite herself, Maggie spooned up a bite. He was right, it was ambrosia!

Andrew grinned. "Was I lying to you, Maggie?"

"No, you were not. I have never tasted anything so marvelous!"

She ate all the strawberries and champagne. And that was a mistake. The extra champagne made her giddy, she found as she started to stand up, and lurched sideways. She would have fallen if Andrew hadn't jumped up to catch her.

"My goodness," she said vaguely, "I'm so dizzy. . . ."

At the same time she was acutely conscious of his closeness, of his male odor, and the strength of his hands. Before she was aware of what was happening, he had turned her into his arms, and kissed her lingeringly on the mouth.

The kiss fired her blood, and yet gave her a feeling of deep languor. His hands were roaming gently in tender exploration of her body.

Maggie was only peripherally aware that he was moving her slowly toward the steps leading down to the cabin. She made a halfhearted sound of protest, and tried, feebly, to pull away from him. Andrew grasped her arms, and kissed her again.

Maggie knew she should stop him. She had sworn to herself to stop him, if such an incident occurred, but the pressure of his lips was too compelling, so insistent, the taste of his mouth so sweet, and the touch of his hands stirred such warm currents in her blood. . . .

Somehow, they had reached the inside of the cabin without her halting the ever bolder forays of his hands. Things were pleasantly blurred, and every time Maggie moved, she had the dreamy impression that she was immersed in warm, heavy water, her limbs incapable of sustained movement.

Andrew's fingers were busy with buttons and hooks, and then Maggie was stretched on the sofa, feeling the warm air against her naked flesh. Andrew's hands were stroking her breasts, teasing the nipples, and his lips followed where his fingers touched. Maggie arched to his hand, moaning deep in her throat. She lost all sense of time, only aware of her need for this man.

Her need was a sweet ache in her breasts, and between her thighs, and she was ready for Andrew when he entered her. Moaning, hands clutching at his shoulders, she rose to meet him, savoring the sweet warmth of his flesh against hers, and the hard fullness of him, pressing deep inside her.

It was different than with Jonas. With Jonas, it was a sweet, prolonged, delightful romp, but the sensual hunger she felt now was wild, fierce, consuming her with a wanton fire that was a torment of the senses, a fire that had to be quenched or she would die.

"Ah-h, sweet, sweet Maggie," Andrew murmured. "My fiery Irish wench."

Dimly, Maggie heard her own voice uttering endearments. Then, she was caught in such a seizure of ecstasy that she ceased to think, becoming all sensation, becoming as one with Andrew.

Later, Maggie realized that she must have fallen into a deep sleep, for she awoke, startled to find herself in a strange place and in a strange bed. Slowly, awareness of what she had done flooded in on her. She sat up, and a throbbing pain started up in her head. She cried out.

Beside her, Andrew put out a hand to touch her. "What is it, dearest? What's wrong?"

"You know what's wrong, damn you, Andrew Kane!"

"Oh, Maggie." His soft laughter sounded. "Don't act the outraged maiden again, please!"

"You made me a promise," she said hotly. "When you invited me here, you promised you wouldn't touch me."

"Maggie . . ." He sighed, and sat up. "All right, I made you a promise, but tell me something . . . the truth now. Before you came here tonight, didn't you make a promise to yourself that you wouldn't let it happen?"

It was a long moment before she answered, her voice faint. "Yes."

"You see? We're even. I broke a promise and so did you."

"Oh! You turn everything around. You are a despicable man! I hate you!" Her open hand flashed out and struck him across the cheek.

He grunted in surprise, then reached out for her before she could scramble off the sofa. "Despicable, am I? You didn't seem to think so earlier."

Holding her against him, Andrew found her lips and ground his mouth hard against hers. Despite herself, Maggie felt a leap of response, a moment of weakening.

Then she began to struggle, pushing with all her strength against his broad chest. "No, no! Not again, not ever again! I'm not giddy-headed with your champagne now!"

Andrew let her go, and she began fumbling around on the cabin floor for her clothes.

"Very well, my dear. If that's the way you feel. Never let it be said that Andrew Kane forced a woman against her will."

She settled her dress down over her hips, all the while glaring at the blur of his figure in the dimness. "How about what happened in Port Townsend?"

"I have asked your forgiveness for that."

"I will never forgive you! Never!"

Maggie felt blindly along the deck for her slippers, then balanced herself against the cabin wall to wriggle her feet into them. Andrew had filled his pipe, and was now lighting it. In the flare of light, his face looked wicked, almost satanic.

The match went out, and Maggie started for the cabin steps. Blinded from staring into the match flame, she stumbled on the first step, and righted herself by clutching at the handrail.

"Miss Donnevan?" Andrew asked, his voice formal.

"Haven't you said enough for one night, Mr. Kane?"

"I was simply wondering about our business deal, my transporting your machinery to your logging location. Am I still to do that?"

Maggie stifled an impulse toward laughter. He had a practical turn of mind, did Andrew Kane. After what had just occurred, after she had scalded him with her tongue, he could still think of business. She said coldly, "As I have said before, one thing has nothing to do with the other. Our business deal still stands." She started on up the steps.

His mocking voice followed her. "Ah, that's my practical Maggie Donnevan."

Now Maggie did laugh, helpless laughter, and was still laughing as she stepped off the *Belle* onto the wharf.

Two days later, Maggie stepped off Captain Potter's schooner onto the wharf at Port Ludlow. Since she hadn't known exactly when she would return, there wasn't anyone to meet her. She stood for a moment in indecision, her glance going to Jonas' house on the bluff. She was strongly tempted to make the trip up there to tell him her news, but it wasn't Sunday, and she was anxious to get back to camp after her long absence.

She had bought several presents for her brothers, the Jorgensons, and Mother Be-Damn, and had to make three trips carrying them down to the canoe, which was still tied up to the piling below.

In a little while she was paddling north toward camp. Long accustomed to the canoe now, Maggie could sustain a rapid pace with the paddle without tiring herself, and it wasn't long before she turned into the cove. Logs floated in the water, like sleeping sea creatures. She saw smoke coming from the cookhouse, but no one came to meet her as she beached the canoe.

She loaded her arms with packages and started up the slope toward camp. She was trudging along, head down, when she heard her name called.

She looked up to see Lars hurrying down the

slope with long strides. She said, "Lars, it's glad I am to see you!"

Lars simply nodded. He took the packages from her, placed them on the ground, then took her hands in his. His face was grave. "Maggie, I have bad news. . . ."

She clutched at his hands. "Has something happened to my brothers? To little Kevin?" She waited, heart cold with dread.

"No, your brothers are fine, Maggie," he said slowly. "It's just that . . ." He swallowed, blue eyes stricken. "I'm sorry to be the one to tell you this, Maggie, but Jonas Kirk is dead."

Chapter Twelve

"Jonas dead?" Maggie went rigid. "How? When?"

"He was found at the bottom of the cliff, smashed to death on the rocks. They found him Tuesday of last week."

"Oh, dear God! How awful! Poor Jonas." She swayed, eyes closed, her mind going numb.

Lars caught her before she crumpled, and held her cradled gently against his broad chest. After a little, Maggie's mind began to function again. A wave of sorrow and a great sense of loss swept through her, and she began to weep great, wracking sobs. Lars held her until she was cried out, big hand clumsily smoothing her hair.

Finally she stood back, knuckling the tears out of her eyes.

"Here, use this," Lars said gruffly, handing her a large kerchief.

Maggie wiped at her eyes, blew her nose, and stood back, staring at Lars narrowly. "How long have you known, Lars? About Jonas and me, I mean?"

His face went red, and his glance slid away. He mumbled, "For some months. But Maggie, I didn't sneak around and follow you. I swear. I came by the knowledge by chance. I was in Port Ludlow one Sunday afternoon, and saw you coming down the cliff road from his house. I had suspected something, but I wasn't sure until then. . . ."

Now his eyes met hers, and Maggie was shocked out of her grief momentarily by the misery in his face. Lars was in love with her! It was a discovery that shook her, yet touched her deeply. Impulsively, she stepped to him and touched his face with her fingers. "Dear Lars. You are a nice man."

Then grief for Jonas swept over her again, and she had to turn away, her shoulders heaving. Lars stood quietly until she got herself under control again. He said quietly, "Did you love the man, Maggie?"

She thought for a long moment. "I . . . not love, not true love, but I cared for him very much." Sudden anger overcame her grief. "Who did it, Lars? Who killed him?"

"Nobody knows, Maggie. Besides, how can you be sure he was killed?" He gazed at her in speculation. "It could have been an accident. People are saying he had too much to drink and fell over the cliff to the rocks below. Others are saying he jumped, despondent over the long absence of his wife."

Maggie was shaking her head. "No, he did not

jump, not Jonas. I knew him too well to believe that. He was not despondent in the least. The opposite, in fact. As for it being an accident, too much to drink . . . no, I don't believe that, either."

"But who would wish to kill him, Maggie? I understand that he wasn't robbed. He had money on his person."

"Jake Fargo," she said positively. "I have no way of proving it, but I know in my bones that Jake Fargo pushed poor Jonas off the cliff."

Lars' gaze was intent. "But why? Jake Fargo is a vicious man, but even *he* wouldn't kill without a reason."

"He had a reason." Maggie sighed and told him then of Fargo's attempt to rape her, and how she was rescued by Jonas.

Lars' big hands curled into fists. "That miserable bastard . . . excuse me, Maggie. But Fargo should be made to pay for daring to attack you! I shall see to it myself!"

"No, Lars, please!" Stepping quickly to him, she took his big hand in hers, and pried his fingers apart. "That is all over and past now. I wouldn't want you killed, too." She shuddered. "And for the love of God, don't tell Patrick or Dan, or they'll be rushing off, seeking him out in a great rage."

Calmer now, Lars said thoughtfully, "But Fargo's usual way of killing is with a pickaroon. Why not this time?"

"Because he *is* known for that. This way, no suspicion would attach to him." She fell silent, thinking. "He is everything you say he is, is Jake Fargo, but he has a wild animal's cunning. He *knows* that I know he killed poor Jonas, but can do nothing

297

about it." Her face settled into grim lines. "Don't worry, Lars, I will find a way to avenge Jonas' death, but facing Fargo and his villainous crew is not the way. I will find a better way, I promise. I will see to it that Jonas' death will not go un-avenged."

Towering above her, he gazed down into her eyes. "When the time comes, you'll let me know? You'll not attempt something foolhardy alone?"

"I will let you know, Lars."

He held her with his gaze and Maggie felt a flut-tering inside, in that moment intensely aware of his maleness.

Then the moment was shattered by shouts from up the slope. Looking in that direction, she saw her brothers with Kevin in the lead, hurrying down the hill toward them. Olaf was limping along behind.

"Do my brothers, or Olaf, know about Jonas and me?"

Lars shook his head. "Not to my knowledge. I'm sure they don't even suspect."

"Then we will leave it that way, for now. I would much prefer they not know."

Lars merely nodded, and stepped aside as Kevin charged at Maggie, who kneeled and caught him in a great hug.

"Maggie! Maggie!" he squealed.

"Ah, it's happy I am to see you, little Kevin!"

He pulled back from her embrace, scowling. "I am not so little anymore. See how I have grown!"

He spun around for her inspection. Although she knew it was hardly possible, he did seem to have grown an inch or two in the weeks she had been gone. Tears stung her eyes again, and she said gravely, "You do seem to have sprouted a wee bit, and I promise not to call you little Kevin again."

She stood and bestowed a kiss on both her older brothers.

"Welcome back, Maggie," said Dan. "It seems you have been gone forever."

"I see no harm came to you, Sister," Patrick said gruffly. "'Tis glad I am to see you back."

She stepped back after kissing Olaf on the cheek and looked at them. "How did the logging go in my absence?"

"It went dad-damned fine, little lady," Olaf said, beaming. "We been humming right along. Delivered one raft of logs to the captain, and soon will have another ready."

"And soon we will have our own sawmill, and will no longer have to divide our profits with Captain Sayward!" She clapped her hands.

Olaf turned his head, and spat. "You went and did it then?"

"I did. We can start building a millhouse in our spare time. The machinery for the mill will be delivered in about two months, perhaps less. I ordered two circular saws and the best of everything!"

"Circular saws, you say?" Olaf's eyes brightened. "That must have cost you dear."

"That it did, but it will be worth it."

"Circular saws, is it?" Patrick growled. "Now would you be after telling me what they might be?"

"I will, brother Patrick. But first, let's unload the canoe, and go up to the camp. I have gifts for all of you."

From then until after supper, Maggie kept herself

busy, handing out the gifts, telling of what she had seen, and in return hearing what had happened in her absence. It was only when she looked across the fire and caught Lars' eyes on her that Maggie remembered Jonas and his fate. They had built a bonfire in the yard before her office shack.

There was something strangely disturbing about Lars tonight. It was as if something had subtly changed in their relationship, and Maggie was annoyingly aware of his presence even when she wasn't looking at him. Always before he had been little more than another man around the fire.

Now he was more than that, and Maggie didn't like it. She felt vaguely threatened, which was silly. . . .

With a determined effort, she thrust him out of her mind and turned to Olaf beside her. "I'm thinking it's time we thought of making our permanent headquarters here on the cove. Build the mill here, of course, with an office attached, and living quarters for myself, and my brothers, also you and Lars. I'm going to see if I can't get permanent title to the cove and the land surrounding it. I can't think of a better spot. And I'll see about purchasing stumpage rights to the adjoining timber acreage, so we won't have to move when we log all this. . . ."

"Whoa, girl, hold up!" Olaf said, laughing. "You're chattering away like a magpie!"

"The excitement of being home again, I suppose," Maggie said in a more subdued voice. "Home! You know, in all our lives we Donnevans have never had a place we could truly call home, certainly not that hovel back in Ireland. Now we have! Let me tell you, Olaf Jorgenson, it's a grand feeling, that it is!"

When she was finally in her bed, it was inevitable that Maggie's thoughts should turn to Jonas. Such a kind, gentle, generous man he had been. Rage welled up in her throat, almost choking her. It was unthinkable that such a fine man should be murdered by the likes of Jake Fargo! There was no doubt whatsoever in her mind but that Jonas had been the victim of Fargo's villainy.

For the first time she thought of the loan Jonas had made her, the bank draft for fifteen thousand dollars. In Seattle, she had spent it all but a few dollars for the machinery and mill equipment she needed. They had both signed a note for the money that Sunday afternoon when Maggie had last seen him. Now she recalled his last words to her, "The note, my dear, is open-end, as you can see. That means there is no repayment date. You may repay the loan at your convenience."

What would happen now? Maggie supposed that Constance Kirk would return to Port Ludlow to settle Jonas' affairs. Would she live in the house on the bluff, or sell it? From what Jonas had told her, Maggie felt certain that Constance would not remain in Port Ludlow longer than necessary.

Maggie went to sleep with tears of grief for Jonas drying on her cheeks.

For the next few weeks, Maggie drove herself hard, busy with overseeing the logging. However, something had happened while she was away. Patrick had taken charge and he now ran things with a firm hand. He got on well with the men and could give orders in a strong voice that brooked no disobedience. Maggie, watching him, was a victim of warring feelings—pride, astonishment at the change in him, and a sense of not being needed anymore. She still kept the accounts, of course, and paid the men on Saturdays, but she realized now that she had enjoyed herself more out in the woods, actively participating in the logging.

She wracked her brain for new ideas to improve and speed up their logging, and did find a few small ways to cut corners. On the trip to Seattle, Maggie had witnessed a couple of new methods—at least new to her—to move logs, but it was too soon for that; the skidroad and the oxen were handling the job adequately.

Maggie knew she would be busy again, of course, when the mill machinery arrived, and she could lose herself in that. She already had those men among the crew with carpentry talents working on the building to house the mill.

Meanwhile, she was at loose ends. Sundays were the worst. No longer was there a reason to go into Port Ludlow in the canoe. Several times she was tempted to go in anyway and walk up to the house. It was probably nailed shut, but at least she could look at it. Sternly, she told herself that it would only set her to grieving for Jonas, and she knew that he would not have approved of that.

So, on Sundays, she began taking a picnic basket deep into the woods for a day's solitude. One of her first decisions, when they started logging over the mountain, was that there would be certain areas left as they had been for centuries. One such area was located on the other side of the mountain, about two hours walk from camp. They had a long way to go yet before they began logging the area, but Maggie, having discovered the spot some time back, had already determined that it would remain untouched.

It was a park-like area, with a small meadow, probably created by a burn many years ago. A few trees had been left intact, offering shade on hot days, and a deep, fast-running stream tumbled down the slanting meadow.

One Sunday morning Maggie took her picnic basket and struck out for the meadow, telling no one where she was going. Instead of her logging clothes, she wore a dress, the one she had worn on her visit with Jonas. Since she had to travel over some rough terrain, she wore the heavy working shoes, but she carried along a pair of dainty slippers in the basket.

It was a clear, sunny day, except for some white clouds hovering over the distant Cascades like a nebulous crown. When she reached the meadow, Maggie spread out a cloth and put on her dress shoes. Instead of taking the food out immediately, she sat for a time, folded arms resting on her raised knees, staring dreamily into the distance. A feeling of melancholy stole over her as her thoughts dwelled on Jonas. It had been a mistake to wear the dress, she realized now; it reminded her of too much that was past and would never come again.

Deep in a reverie, her thoughts reliving those long, languorous afternoons with Jonas Kirk, she heard a sound. Looking around, Maggie saw Lars striding across the meadow. Her first feeling was one of annoyance, but then, as she watched him come toward her, she was suddenly glad to see him.

She watched him approach hesitantly, his step slowing, and from the look on his face, Maggie knew that he was afraid he was in for a scolding.

She got to her feet, smiling. "It's all right, Lars. It's not angry with you I am. In fact, I'm glad to see you. You can share my picnic."

She took his hand and drew him down beside her on the grass.

Lars' face took on a look of relief. "I have noticed you going off almost every Sunday of late. But I know how angry you get at your brothers for being so protective, and I was afraid you'd be angry with me. But I was concerned, Maggie. One of the loggers told me he'd seen Jake Fargo skulking about along the coast."

Looking into his face, something came together for Maggie. "Speaking of Sundays, I suddenly remember that, for a number of Sundays past, you have dressed up and gone in the direction of Port Ludlow. You have a girl there, don't you, Lars?"

Lars glanced at her in surprise, then he flushed. He nodded, gulping.

"Then why not today? Why not this Sunday?"

"I . . ." Lars looked away. "Last Sunday I told Nancy that I would not be coming in again to see her."

"But why on earth not?"

"You know, Maggie. You must know."

"Know what? Whisht, man, I'm not a mind reader!"

He said simply, "I care for you, Maggie. Very much."

Maggie wasn't surprised by his declaration, not really, and yet she knew she must look the idiot, gaping at him, and uttering a faint, "Oh."

Instinctively, she drew back slightly, and Lars' face fell.

"I suppose I shouldn't be surprised you're offended, but I waited too long once before, and I swore to myself that I wouldn't do that again."

"Oh, Lars! Saints above, I'm not offended." She moved close to him again, taking his hand. "You said, you waited too long once . . . you mean, with Jonas?"

He nodded. "Yes."

"Then how long have you . . ." She floundered, suddenly at a loss for words.

"Since I first clapped eyes on you in Port Townsend, Maggie."

"And all this time I never knew . . . no, that's not being honest. Looking back, I realize now that I suspected, but I was too involved in my own selfishness to take heed. But even now, Lars, even though I do find your love touching . . ." She lifted the back of his hand to her flushed cheek. "I don't know if I can ever return it."

"It isn't necessary, Maggie."

"Don't talk like that! I don't want a man devoting himself to me like a dog, licking the hand that rejects him!" She drew back. "This Nancy you speak of . . . you spoke to her so cruelly? It must have been a great shock to her."

"It was, I know. She must have thought me unfeeling. . . ."

Lars stared off into the distance, remembering Nancy's stricken look when he had told her, much

305

too abruptly, "Nancy, I won't be coming in to see you again."

"Why not, Lars? I don't understand. . . ."

"There is someone . . ." Lars had swallowed. Telling her this way was extremely painful for him, but being the man he was, he could not in good conscience continue seeing Nancy when now Maggie, he hoped, was free of emotional ties. "There is another woman, Nancy."

"There always was another woman, wasn't there? You think I didn't know that, Lars?" She had turned cold then, her voice cutting, her face an expressionless mask. "It's your Irish boss lady, isn't it? What happened? Did she finally get around to noticing you mooning around her? I was always second choice, wasn't I, Lars? Do you know how cheap that makes a woman feel?" Then she had broken, her face working, sobs coming from her. "I wish to God I had never met you!"

She had slammed the door in his face, and Lars could hear her crying on the other side. . . .

"Lars?" Maggie touched his hand. "Don't look so grim. I know it was painful for you, and I wish you hadn't . . . well, knowing the fine, considerate man you are, I'm sure you thought there was no other way."

Lars looked at her, grateful for her understanding. "I have a deep feeling and respect for Nancy, but I couldn't bring myself to deceive her."

"Whisht!" Maggie said tartly. "Now you're making me feel an obligation and I'm not after liking that!"

'No, Maggie," he said gravely. "No obligations. I will not ask anything of you, against your wishes."

Confused as to her own feelings, and still piqued at him for placing it all on her plate, so to speak, Maggie said briskly, "Well, I'm hungry. Fortunately I brought along enough food for two." She laughed. "When I ask Mother Be-Damn to prepare me a picnic basket, she always puts in enough for two." She mimicked, "Pretty little Boston too skinny to catch man."

And that, of course, was the wrong thing to say under the circumstances. Face pinking, she turned to the basket and began taking out the food.

As they ate, Maggie determinedly turned the conversation to matters other than themselves. She waxed enthusiastic, telling Lars of her grand plans for the future of the Donnevans.

All the while, underneath her chatter, she was acutely aware of Lars—his masculinity and his declared love for her. His closeness made her conscious of the mounting excitement in her own body, and she reached a decision.

The food consumed, she returned the plates and eating implements to the basket, then shook the crumbs from the tablecloth, and spread it out on the grass. She sat, and looked over at Lars, who was standing a few feet away, his back to her, staring off.

"Lars?" When he faced about, she patted the tablecloth beside her. "Come here."

For a second he looked stunned, then his face came alive, the blue eyes beginning to glow. "Maggie!" He lumbered awkwardly toward her, coming down on his knees on the tablecloth. Then he paused, his face going still. "I want no pity from

307

you. I beg you not to do anything just to please me."

"Whisht! Did it ever occur to you that *I* might want to?" she said with asperity. "You are an attractive man, Lars, and I am not made of stone."

"Ah, then it's all right."

"Of course, it is all right," she said.

It was a combination of many things, Maggie thought, as they stretched out side by side on the tablecloth. It was from gratitude for all he'd done for her, for the love he felt for her, and compassion for his needs as a man. Besides, how could offering Lars her body as a gift harm either of them?

She pulled away from his mouth for just a moment. "But I want a promise from you in return. This will be our secret, and it does not mean a commitment from me. It merely means that a man and a woman are gratifying mutual needs. As for love . . . if it comes, for me, Lars, *then* we shall see."

"I ask no more of you," he said readily.

For such a big man, Lars was a gentle, considerate and surprisingly skillful lover. For a brief time Maggie held back, but it wasn't long before all inner resistance left her and she went with the tide of feeling sweeping over her.

His awkward fingers unbuttoned the bodice of her dress with touching tenderness, and the expression upon his open face revealed awe and love, as his rough palms gently smoothed the skin of her exposed body.

"Ah, Maggie, Maggie," he groaned, burying his face in the hollow between her breasts. "It's been

308

so long. I've wanted you so long, and dreamed of this. I never thought . . ."

"Hush now. Hush, my sweet man." Looking up into Lars' face, seeing the clear skin and strong features, seeing the love in his eyes, Maggie was astonished at the depth of affection she felt for him.

He entered her with a gentle reverence that awed her, but soon his need made him urgent, and Maggie met every demand with abandon.

When her small cry of ecstasy had sounded and Lars lay spent beside her, Maggie stroked his damp, blond hair, "Ah, Lars," she said tenderly. "Sweet, gentle Lars."

He turned his head and looked at her with such devotion that she felt a pain touch her heart.

It had been fine for her—a joyous, tender moment—but it meant so much more to him. Again, she wondered at the strangeness of nature that enabled a woman to give a man such happiness by giving him only the gift of her body; a gift that she could give and still keep.

Near the end of the following week, Captain Sayward's tugboat chugged down to the cove to tow the raft of logs back to his mill. Maggie, busy with her accounts, didn't go down to watch the logs being towed away. Hearing a toot from the tug's whistle signaling its departure, she looked up abstractedly, then returned her attention to her bookkeeping.

A short time later, a rap sounded on the door. At her call, the door opened, admitting Lars. His face was unduly sober and he seemed oddly hesitant.

"What is it, Lars?"

"I had a brief conversation with the tugboat men, Maggie. Port Ludlow is agog with the news."

"What news is that, pray?" She smiled. "Almost anything can set tongues to wagging in Port Ludlow, I'm thinking."

"This is not just anything. Constance Kirk has returned, and is in the Kirk house, settling her dead husband's affairs."

"Oh." Maggie's smile died and she sat up, a feeling of foreboding seizing her. "That *is* something to think about." She had not told Lars about the loan from Jonas; she had not told anyone. "I must go in Sunday and pay my respects." She nodded to herself. "Yes, I must do that."

"Maggie . . . Maggie, look at me!"

Maggie gave a start, looking up.

"Do you think that wise? Do you think you will be welcomed with great delight? You just said yourself how the gossip flows in Port Ludlow. Someone has certainly told her by now."

"It doesn't matter. It's still something I have to do."

"But why?" Lars was frowning. "Why not leave it alone? Jonas Kirk is dead and buried. Do you have to dig him up again?"

"Lars! That is a cruel thing to say, not at all like you. . . ."

"Then tell me why you insist on seeing this woman. I have a right to know!"

"A *right*! What right?" She came to her feet, her anger aimed at him like an arrow. "Because I let you make love to me? That gives you the right to question what I do?"

"That's not what I meant."

"Then what did you mean? Tell me!"

"Maggie, I . . ." He raised and lowered his shoulders helplessly. "At least let me go with you."

"No, Lars, I will go alone." She softened her tone. "I do appreciate your concern. I know you're only thinking of my welfare. Besides . . ." She smiled wryly. "Are you after thinking that this Constance Kirk is going to physically attack me? As for what she has to say to me . . ." Her smile went away. "That, I'm sure I can take, and no doubt deserve, to her way of thinking."

So, on Sunday, wearing her best dress, a new garment she had bought in Seattle in the hope of showing it off to Jonas, Maggie was in the canoe on her way to Port Ludlow.

She had brought along a canvas poncho Mother Be-Damn had made for her. The sky was heavy with clouds, threatening rain. A fitting day for such a melancholy errand, Maggie thought, as she paddled along.

As was her habit now, she looked around warily for Jake Fargo after she had tied up the canoe and climbed up the slope. There wasn't a soul in sight. A few fat drops of rain drummed on the poncho as she trudged up the bluff, but the storm held off.

Finally, she stood before the porch to the white house. It had a deserted, almost desolate look about it. The flowers Jonas had been so proud of were untended, choked with weeds. Even the white paint of the house seemed to have taken on a tinge of dirty gray.

Despite her reassurances to Lars, this wasn't a confrontation Maggie was looking forward to with

311

any pleasure and she had to steel herself to walk up those few steps. It was the hardest thing she'd ever had to do.

At the door she removed the poncho, folded it over her arm, and knocked firmly. There was no sound from inside. Perhaps Constance Kirk wasn't home. This thought sent a wave of relief through Maggie that left her weak. This weakness made her furious with herself and she knocked harder.

This time there was a sound of movement inside. In a moment Maggie heard the noise of a latch being thrown back, and the door opened. A tall woman in a long black dress stood in the doorway. Her hair was dark, tied back, accentuating the pale, severe lines of her face. Her eyes were black and as expressionless as stone.

Was this the beautiful young woman Jonas had married, the woman who liked the gay, social whirl? To Maggie, it seemed that this woman had never worn a smile in her life.

Constance Kirk said tonelessly, "I am in mourning for my husband, and am not receiving visitors."

"Yes, I know. That's not the reason I am here, although I do offer my condolences." Maggie found that she had trouble breathing. She looked directly into the woman's eyes, and said, "I am Maggie Donnevan. I knew Jonas . . . I knew your husband."

Almost a full minute passed, and Constance Kirk did not alter her expression a whit. Maggie was about to speak again, thinking the woman, in her private grief, hadn't heard or understood.

"Maggie Donnevan . . . yes, I have heard the name. Several good citizens of Port Ludlow have pointedly made me familiar with it." The black eyes were merciless now. "I must say, Miss Donnevan, that I admire your . . . shall I say gall? It isn't often that a wife is given the opportunity to meet her dead husband's paramour face to face."

Maggie felt her face turn hot, and she hung onto her temper with an effort. She cast about frantically for something to say, and could think of nothing. Hands tightening around her reticule, she finally said lamely, "Well . . . I suppose we have nothing more to say to one another, Mrs. Kirk . . . I bid you good day."

"Oh, in that you are wrong, *Miss* Donnevan. We have a great deal to say to each other. At least *I* have much to say." Constance Kirk stood back. "Would you come in, please?"

Maggie hesitated, then entered the house with as much dignity as she could muster. She followed the woman's rigid back into the sitting room where she had spent so many wonderful afternoons with Jonas.

Constance Kirk gestured. "If you will have a seat, I will be back shortly."

The woman in black left the room. Maggie started to sit in her old place on the window seat, then quickly changed her mind and sat stiffly on the sofa. She waited tensely, back straight, hands folded in her lap.

She had expected Constance to return with a tea tray. Instead, she came back carrying a document in one hand. Maggie's expression must have betrayed her expectations, for Constance smiled tightly and said, "Surely you did not expect me to serve tea to my husband's whore?"

Stung, Maggie started to her feet. "I understand your anger, and your grief, but I will not stay here to be insulted! Your husband and I were friends, yes, and he had few enough friends here to console him while his wife was away, buying furniture for such a long time!" she said with contempt.

Maggie started from the room, and found the tall woman barring her way.

"You will remain here until our conversation is finished." She waved the document, and Maggie recognized it with a sinking heart. "I have here a note signed by my foolish husband, stating that he made a loan to you, Maggie Donnevan, for fifteen thousand dollars. A *personal* loan . . ."

"It was a purely business transaction!"

"Oh?" Constance's lip curled. "A business transaction made in bed, no doubt?"

Never in her life had Maggie felt such scalding humiliation. In a trembling voice, she said, "It *was* a business transaction. Jonas loaned me the money to . . ."

"It is of no concern to me the purpose for which you use the money my husband loaned you." She flicked the document disdainfully. "The point is, I am familiar with legal documents, and this is an open-end agreement, with no date written in for repayment. And in effect, that means that I, my husband's legatee, may call in the loan at my desire. That is exactly what I am doing. The note is due and payable *now*."

"But you can't do that, Mrs. Kirk," Maggie said desperately. "I used that money to buy equipment to build a mill. There is no way I can possibly pay you back now."

Maggie might as well have not spoken, for all the heed Constance paid her words. "I know this is a primitive country and it is very difficult to get action from the courts. But I have also learned something else." Her smile was cold as ice. "The courts do tend to act, and quickly, in favor of widows. And in this instance, I am sure they will move even more quickly, when it is learned that the whore of Jonas Kirk owes a goodly sum of money to his widow."

"But that is so unfair!" Maggie hated herself for the note of pleading that had crept into her voice. "I will need time!"

"Fairness does not concern me. But since you speak of fairness, I do not consider it fair to discover that my husband, shortly before his death, loaned a large sum of money to his whore!" Constance's voice burned with contempt. "You say you cannot repay it. Since learning of the loan, I have made inquiries. You own a prospering logging company, plus the stumpage rights to several hundred acres of timberland. I have no conception of its value, but I will settle for that, if nothing else. I will, if this note is not repaid, move to take over everything you own. In short, *Miss* Donnevan," the smile was pure malice now, "I would thoroughly enjoy seeing you destitute, and forced to whore in the taverns, where you will find your true calling!"

Maggie was rendered speechless by anger, outrage and panic at the thought of what this woman was threatening to take from her.

Constance Kirk continued, "To show you that I am not truly heartless . . . I will wind up my hus-

315

band's affairs within one week. At the end of that week, I shall return to San Francisco. You have until then, Miss Donnevan, to return my money. One week, Miss Donnevan, not one day longer!"

Chapter Thirteen

By the time Maggie left the house on the bluff, the rain was coming down in gray sheets. The raindrops drove at her like hailstones, hard and stinging.

Maggie ran from the house as though her anger and fear were demons pursuing her. Her despair was as gray and depressing as the rain. Whatever was she going to *do*?

It was her own fault. She should have followed her first instincts and never have gone into debt. The fact that this situation would never have occurred if Jonas were still alive was of little consolation. She was deeply in debt, and there was no way she could remedy it.

Plunging headlong down the slope, now slippery with mud, Maggie fell several times, only to get up and run on, ignoring the fact that she was ruining the new dress.

Then, as she reached the bottom of the cliff, with the perverseness of the weather of the northwestern United States, the rain stopped and the sun came out. The poncho steaming, Maggie slowed her step, for with the sun came the solution to her dilemma. *The remaining jewels!* She had carried them in the pouch between her breasts for so long that she had almost forgotten them.

What sixth sense had prompted her to retain the last of Lord Ramage's jewels? In a way the thought of selling them, even now, was repugnant to her. They had become a sort of talisman, what the Americans called a good luck piece. Yet she had saved them for an emergency, and she certainly faced an emergency now. Worse, the Donnevans faced ruin if she could not raise the money needed to repay the loan within the week. Maggie didn't doubt for an instant that Constance Kirk was perfectly capable of carrying out her threat.

Paddling the canoe back to camp, a new fear struck her. Would she be able to sell the jewels for the needed fifteen thousand dollars? And that brought up another, perhaps more pressing question—*where* would she sell them? Back in Ireland, it had presented no problem, but here was a different matter. In a city like San Francisco, she would probably have no trouble, but she didn't have the time to sail downcoast to San Francisco and back. *Who here in this near-wilderness would have the money to buy the jewels, or even the inclination? Surely there was somebody, but who? Where?*

As she rounded the headland and paddled into

the cove, there was the solution before her very eyes. The *Carolina Belle* was anchored in as close to shore as the shallow water of the cove would allow, and the logging crew, under Andrew's and Olaf's supervision, was unloading the heavy equipment onto a raft made of lashed-together logs. As Maggie rowed closer, she noticed that two men were on deck using a hand-operated winch to lower the heavy pieces of mill machinery. Even as she watched, a steam boiler was lowered down to the makeshift raft, almost swamping it.

"Hold it steady, dad-damnit!" Olaf bellowed. "Or we'll end up with our asses in the water, and the boiler will be on the bottom!"

Olaf was on the raft, along with Patrick and Dan, and two other men. They lashed the boiler down, and began to pole the raft toward the beach, where Maggie could see other pieces of machinery scattered about.

No one had as yet taken notice of her presence, and she paddled the canoe around to the opposite side of the tug, so she was hidden from view of both those on the raft and on the shore. The canoe bumped gently against the tugboat, and Maggie grabbed at a dangling rope and held on.

She called softly, "Andrew! Andrew Kane!"

Shortly, Andrew leaned over the rail, peering down at her. "Well, if it isn't Miss Donnevan! No one mentioned you, and I was damned if I'd ask. I thought you were hiding somewhere, refusing to see me."

"Andrew, I must talk to you," she said urgently.

"Well, now, this is a pleasant surprise. Have you forgotten so soon your last words to me?" His eyebrows arched, giving him the wicked, devilish look she'd seen in the cabin.

Maggie felt color stain her cheeks, but she managed to keep her voice steady. "Knowing your lecherous turn of mind, I can well imagine what's in your thoughts, but that is not the way of it. I badly need your help, and you may be sure, sir, that I would not beg this of you had I any alternative."

He sobered. "Maggie, you may ask anything of me. If it is within my power, I will do it."

"When you are finished with your unloading, you will have to come to my office for your money. We will talk then. I'd rather no one knew of our conversation."

He nodded gravely, and watched as she pushed away from the tugboat and paddled toward shore. When she had beached the canoe, everyone crowded around her, excited with the arrival of the mill equipment. There was an air of gaiety about the scene. Maggie agreed to herself that it was an occasion for celebration, and she would gladly have joined in at any other time.

She got through them as quickly as she could without being too rude and headed for her office. She saw Lars frowning at her in question, and she dredged up a smile, gesturing to indicate that everything was all right.

Before she reached the office, Maggie changed her mind and went into her tent, where she packed a small bag and left it on the dirt floor. Inside her office, she couldn't sit still, pacing back and forth, stopping often to peer out the door in the direction of the tugboat. About an hour later she heaved a sigh of relief as she saw Andrew rowing ashore in his dinghy. She hurried to the table-desk and pretended to be busy, glancing up at his knock on the door.

"Come in, please."

His pipe fuming, Andrew took a chair across from her, and stretched his long legs out before him. "Now, Maggie, what is it I may help you with?"

"First, let me pay your due," she said briskly. She had the agreed-upon sum already counted out and she handed it to him across the table. Andrew put the money into his pocket without counting it, his curious gaze never leaving her face. "Well, Maggie?"

"I . . ." Now that it was time, how was she going to tell him? Exactly how much *should* she tell him?

Before she could speak further, Olaf stuck his head in the door. Grinning, he said, "Well, little lady, the pieces are all here. Now all we have to do is yust put her together."

"So put it together," she snapped. "That's your job, isn't it?"

"Yah, I guess it is," he said slowly. He turned his head, and spat. "You expect it put together and going tonight, do you?"

As he started to turn away, she called after him, "Olaf, I'm sorry! I . . ."

Olaf strode on out of sight.

Andrew drawled, "I reckon that whatever's on your mind is bothering you considerable."

"Of that you may be sure." She glanced around nervously. The walls of the shack were thin and anyone standing outside could overhear every word spoken in there. She stood up. "Would you walk with me?"

"I would be delighted." Andrew stood and gallantly offered her his arm.

They walked away from the camp and at a nod from Maggie, they went south toward a stand of timber. Inside the trees, they were soon hidden from camp. Andrew pushed aside the underbrush for her and Maggie indicated a fallen log. "That should do," she said.

They sat down side by side. Maggie said shakily, "I don't wish anyone at camp to even suspect what this is all about."

"Now you have me afire with curiosity, Maggie."

She faced him. "My business affairs have taken a turn for the worse, Andrew . . . as of today. To purchase the mill equipment, I went into debt." She laughed shortly. "Something I swore I would never do, under any circumstances. I have been told that I am too ambitious, in too much of a hurry to make timber barons of the Donnevans, and that could be true. Anyway, I found out a few hours ago that the money I borrowed is due and payable within one week, no longer."

"And just how much money are we talking about?"

"Fifteen thousand dollars."

"Damnation, Maggie!" He whistled softly. "That is a large sum of money." He spread his hands. "I would help you if I could, but I fear but for the money you have just paid me, and a few dollars more for other deliveries made on the way, I am as destitute as you. If I had it, I would gladly loan it to you."

"It's not a loan I'm after asking of you. That's the reason I'm in trouble now. . . ." She broke off as she heard a rustling sound in the underbrush behind her. "What was that?"

Andrew shrugged. "Probably some animal. If not a loan, what then do you want of me?"

"I need your services, Andrew. . . ." She turned away from him to take the pouch from between her breasts. "Hold out your hands."

Andrew held them out, palms up. Maggie loosened the drawstring and spilled the diamonds into his cupper hands. There were five left, including the large stone, glittering like fiery ice.

He whistled again. "My God, Maggie! Where did you get these? They're worth a great deal of money."

"Enough to repay my fifteen-thousand-dollar debt?"

"Of that, I wouldn't even hazard a guess, since I'm not an expert on precious stones." He looked at her levelly. "You're evading my question, Maggie. Where?"

She started to retort that it was none of his business. Instead, she tried to make her voice wheedling. "If I were to beg of you to take me on faith?"

His gaze held steady. "Damn you for a witch, Miss Donnevan! You do ask a lot of a man!" He sighed. "All right, I'll not go into it. I still fail to see what you need of me."

"I need to sell them, as you can see. But . . ." She made a helpless gesture. "But I have no idea of where or to whom. I have no one, but you, to turn to who might know."

"So, thinking that I am familiar with low types, with someone willing to buy stolen jewels, you come to me? They *are* stolen, aren't they?" He laughed shortly. "Now don't tell me they are the family jewels. It is too late, madam, to tell me that. You have told me too much of yourself."

"Why should it matter to you how I came by them? I'm only after asking you to sell them!"

"If the jewels are purloined, my dear Maggie, to sell them for you I would be compounding a crime, committing a criminal offense."

"Whisht! It strikes me, Andrew Kane, that such a wee thing as that would not bother your conscience much!"

He laughed, throwing back his head. "You know me well, don't you? You are right, it would trouble me little."

"Andrew, I will tell you this. . . ." She leaned toward him, serious now. "If the diamonds were stolen, it was in a good cause, and I do not consider it a crime, but as my due, our due, the Donnevan's due."

He looked at her intently, and shook his head with a mock sigh. "What a contradiction you are, Miss Donnevan! But I confess that I am inclined to believe you."

"Then you will help me?" she asked eagerly.

"I do know a man in Seattle, Dexter Horton," he said musingly. "His is a rather amusing story. Once a mill employee of Henry Yesler's, he quit to run the cookhouse over at the Pope and Talbot mill. Then he returned to Seattle, opened a store, and became, in a sense, Seattle's first banker. The only one, so far. What is amusing is the huge safe he placed in his store. He became a trusted man, and began keeping huge sums, belonging to various Seattle citizens, in that safe. Only recently it was discovered that, all the while, his safe was about as secure as a lady's reticule. The damned safe had no back to it, and any thief could have shoved it away from the wall and rifled it. But now he has a real safe, and is doing a brisk business both keeping and loaning money. He always has large sums of ready cash, and I understand that he does occasionally deal in diamonds. . . ."

Jake Fargo could not believe his good fortune. Hidden in the underbrush a few feet behind Andrew Kane and Maggie Donnevan, his eyes had almost bugged out of his head when he saw the Irish bitch spill those diamonds into Kane's hands.

Since the afternoon when he had pushed Jonas Kirk over the cliff, Fargo had been lurking about the Donnevan camp from time to time. He wasn't quite sure why, except that he was gloating over his killing Kirk undetected, and he hoped to catch a glimpse of Maggie Donnevan's face and see there the knowledge of who had killed her lover. He had been frustrated in this. Oh, he had seen her a number of times, but neither her face nor her actions had revealed anything to him.

One Sunday afternoon he had even followed her into the woods and watched from concealment as she sat alone in a mountain meadow. Fargo had been contemplating an assault upon her, but that hulking Swede, the younger Jorgenson, had come upon the scene and Fargo had left in disgust.

Now his vigil was paying dividends. First, he had been surprised when the tugboat had anchored in the cove and started unloading machinery. A glimpse of the tugboat captain had revealed Andrew Kane, the gent who had threatened and humiliated him in the tavern. All this time Fargo had thought the man someone of importance, and now it turned out he was nothing but a damned tugboat captain!

After his anger over being so flummoxed had cooled, Fargo began to scheme of ways to kill this Andrew Kane. He had skulked about the rest of the day, not really expecting to get his chance so soon.

But now here they both were, only a few feet distant. Fargo had been fondling the pistol in his belt, a pistol he had taken to carrying of late, debating whether or not to risk two gunshots this close to the logging camp, when the Irish woman had dumped the diamonds into Kane's hand. A small fortune, and his for the taking!

But to kill them now and get away unscathed was still a risk. Fargo had been paying little heed to their talk. Now he perked up his ears and listened.

Andrew Kane was saying, ". . . I will help you, Maggie. I can see your predicament, and will try to sell the diamonds for you."

"It must be done so I can have the money before Constance Kirk leaves."

Andrew Kane shrugged. "If it can be done, if Dexter Horton will buy your jewels, the transaction can be completed the day I return to Seattle. . . ."

"Not you, us. I am going with you!"

Andrew Kane laughed shortly. "I still don't have your complete trust, I see."

"It is not that, Andrew." She placed a hand on his. "But I would be frantic with worry here, not knowing what is happening. No, I *must* go with you."

"Very well," Maggie, if you insist." He laughed again. "In fact, you will be of help to me, at least on the way back to Port Ludlow. I stopped there first, having a delivery to make to Captain Sayward. There, I made a grievous mistake. The idiot I have hired as a deckhand, and to stoke the boiler, asked to go to the village while I transacted my business with the captain. And idiot that *I* am, I gave permission. He had not returned when I was ready to depart. I went looking for him, and found him drunk and passed out before a tavern. It is a difficult task indeed for a man alone to stoke a boiler and handle the wheel. Do you think you are capable of feeding wood into a boiler to keep the steam up?"

"To hasten the solution of my problem, I feel capable of just about anything!"

"Then shall we prepare to depart, Miss Donnevan?" Andrew Kane stood and offered his arm to her.

Jake Fargo remained where he was. He saw a safer way to get his revenge on this pair and his hands on the diamonds at the same time. He remained still until they had passed from his sight; then he got to his feet and started toward the cove

327

by a circuitous route, the ever-present pickaroon slung over his shoulder.

Maggie had anticipated resistance from her brothers, and Lars as well, when the time came to inform them that she was leaving for Seattle in Andrew's tugboat, but she was not quite prepared for Patrick's rage.

Lars, on hearing of her intentions, gave her a bitter, wounded look and stalked away.

Patrick roared, "I will not have it, my sister going off alone with a stranger!"

"He's not a stranger, brother," she said patiently. "Andrew Kane came to our rescue in Port Townsend, and he has just delivered our sawmill equipment." She started to add that Andrew was an honorable man, but knowing his perverse sense of humor, he just might burst out laughing at that.

"He is a man, and he is a stranger. If you're going on that boat, I'm going! Aye, or Brother Dan. I will not allow it, otherwise."

Her own temper rising, Maggie stormed at him. "Must we go through this every time I have something in mind you do not approve of, Patrick? I thought it was settled the last time. I came back safely from Seattle, did I not? I'm a grown woman, Patrick Donnevan, and don't you be forgetting it! You may be bull-of-the-woods, but I am the one who has placed us in this position, and I am the one who gives the orders. I have listened to you about this for the last time. Now, is that clearly understood?"

Patrick stared at her flushed face and flashing eyes, as though he had never seen her before. Finally he said sullenly, "Why is it you're going away? It's just getting back you are."

"Why I am going is not your affair." She picked up the small bag. "Shall we go, Andrew?"

Andrew gave her his arm and they started down toward the dinghy. In a low voice he said, "Seeing you cow that big lout of a brother of yours . . . I almost burst out laughing."

Maggie pulled away from his arm. "Patrick is *not* a lout! In Ireland men are brought up to be looking after their women-folk!"

"Now Maggie," he said amusedly, "the truth. From the things I've heard they treat their women like cattle over there."

"From what I've heard men in your South treat *their* women like delicate china, afraid they'll be breaking into wee bits should misfortune occur!"

"There is some truth in what you say. However . . ." He gave her a sidelong glance. "Wouldn't you prefer being placed on a pedestal to being treated like a lower species than the male?"

"I prefer neither," she retorted hotly. "All I ask of a man, any man, is to be treated like a person, treated like an equal."

"I'm afraid, my dear, that you're asking a great deal. The way you look . . ." his gaze roamed insolently over her body and he gave her a mock leer, "it would be difficult for any normal man to treat you like anything but the desirable creature that you are."

"Oh! You're an impossible man!"

She hurried on ahead, spurred by his mocking laughter. Without waiting for him she got into the dinghy. Andrew was still smiling when he got in

329

with her and started rowing them toward the tug-boat.

Reaching the tug, Andrew held the Jacob's ladder while Maggie climbed up. Halfway up, it occurred to her that he was probably looking up and could see under her skirts. She resisted an urge to glance down at him and climbed on.

She stood at the railing while Andrew quickly climbed the ladder. On deck, he straightened up and looked at her without expression.

Hands on hips, face hot as fire, she glared at him. "A gentleman, sir, would have come up the ladder *first!* You did that deliberately, so you could see my limbs."

"Now why should I do that?" he asked innocently. "If you will think back, Miss Donnevan, you will recall that I've seen your limbs before."

She stared at him, speechless.

"Besides, being a gentleman has nothing to do with it. It's not easy, climbing a Jacob's ladder, without someone holding it steady, and I couldn't very well do that from up here, now could I?"

"Andrew Kane, I want something understood. This is a business trip. There will be no shenanigans. If necessary, I will sleep on deck. You are not luring me to that cabin of yours again, sir!"

"As you wish, madam." He made a mock bow. "Now, if you have had your say, shall we get under way?"

Without waiting for an answer, he stalked past her. He fed wood chunks into the boiler until he had steam up. Then he pulled up the dinghy and the anchor, and took the wheel.

"If you would tend the boiler, Miss Donnevan,"

330

he said formally, "I will endeavor to get under way. All that's necessary is to toss in a chunk of wood now and then. We'll put into Port Ludlow and hopefully that damned deckhand of mine will be sober by now."

The tugboat moved slowly out of the cove and Andrew turned it south. It was late afternoon now and the clouds that had brought rain earlier in the day had thickened again. The wind off the channel was cold and Maggie was grateful for the heat given off by the boiler. With the possible solution to her problem in sight now, she was less apprehensive. Lulled by the warmth of the boiler and the motion of the tug, she was almost asleep on her feet when a sudden, loud crash jarred her fully awake.

She looked in the direction of the sound. There, at the top of the cabin steps, stood Jake Fargo, like some monstrous, leering figure out of a nightmare. Buried in the wood of the deck was the source of the noise—the pickaroon, the handle still quivering. In Fargo's hand was a pistol, aimed at the shadowy figure of Andrew in the wheelhouse.

A harsh chuckle came from Fargo. "Come on out of there, Mr. Kane." He motioned with the pistol. "Get out here where I can see you better."

In the wheelhouse, Andrew glanced back over his shoulder and saw Jake Fargo. Andrew cursed under his breath. When he had gone ashore to talk to Maggie, he had left his Colt in the cabin below, not thinking he would need it.

"Did you hear me, *Mister* Kane?" Fargo bellowed. "Get your ass out here!"

"If I leave the wheel, we'll run aground."

"You take me for a fool? Tie it off."

Andrew sighed, then set the wheel in a position to keep them moving down the coast and lashed it off. He went outside the wheelhouse.

Fargo motioned again with the pistol. "Over beside him, you Irish bitch, so I can keep an eye on both of you."

Trembling, Maggie moved to stand beside Andrew. He took her hand and squeezed it reassuringly.

"So, Kane, you're nothing but a tugboat tramp," Fargo said in a sneering voice. "Here I was thinking you somebody important that day."

Andrew shrugged contemptuously. "I'm not responsible for whatever you might think, Fargo."

"You, missy, that there bag of diamonds between your tits . . . throw it to me."

Maggie gasped. "How did you know about the diamonds?"

"Jake Fargo knows many things. Now throw it here or I'll blow your brains out," Fargo snarled. He cocked the pistol.

"You'd better do as he says, Maggie," Andrew said in a quiet voice.

Maggie was seized by a despair such as she had never before experienced. She said, "No, I won't do it! You'll have to kill me first!"

"Don't think I won't, missy, if I have to. But first, how about I kill Mr. Kane here? How'd you like to watch him die, hey? I've been told that a gutshot man dies a slow and horrible death. . . ."

"All right," she said dully. She sensed that Fargo was going to kill them anyway, but if she could postpone it for a few precious minutes . . .

She half-turned away to take the diamond pouch

from between her breasts. Turning back, she flung it toward Fargo. The pouch landed on the deck a few feet in front of him.

Fargo's eyes flared wide with greed and he moved forward eagerly, bending down to scoop up the pouch.

Andrew, who had been tensely waiting for just such an opportunity, sprang at Fargo, taking two quick steps, then launching himself into the air. Fargo was still half-bent over when Andrew's shoulder struck him in the back. At the same time Andrew wrapped his arms around the man and the two men careened back against the railing.

The pistol clattered to the deck and slid off into the water. The pouch still lay untouched where it had fallen. Heart in her throat, Maggie darted forward, snatched it up, and stepped back out of the way. Her gaze fastened on the men struggling along the deck, she placed the diamond pouch again between her breasts.

Although the two men were the same height, Fargo outweighed Andrew by at least twenty pounds, but Andrew was agile and quicker. They rolled over and over, grappling, with Fargo grunting and spewing curses. Abruptly, Fargo reared to his feet by sheer brute strength and shaking himself like a great bear, jarred Andrew loose from his back. Andrew came to his feet, facing the other.

"Now I've got you, Mr. Kane!" Fargo shouted. He lumbered toward Andrew, hands reaching for him.

"Don't be too sure of that, friend," Andrew said with a smile on his face, and Maggie realized that he was enjoying this.

Whisht, she thought, *the man's as bad as Brother Patrick*. But even so, she had to admit that she felt a secret delight at the thought of Andrew Kane doing battle for her.

Moving in and out, Andrew flicked rights and lefts into Fargo's face. Fargo grunted at the impact of each blow, and blood appeared on his face. Yet he never stopped coming and Maggie knew that if he ever wrapped his arms around Andrew, he would squeeze the life from him.

Andrew had another advantage—he was more accustomed to the roll of the deck. Several times Fargo almost had him in his grasp when the deck would tilt slightly, throwing Fargo just enough off-balance. The fight raged back and forth across the tiny deck. Then suddenly Fargo had Andrew cornered between the wheelhouse and the railing. He moved in cautiously. Andrew danced aside, and seemed about to elude the big man's grasp once more.

Maggie gasped as she saw a coil of rope directly behind him. She opened her mouth to scream a warning, but she was too late. In backing, Andrew's right foot struck the coil of rope, and he lost his balance, falling back against the rail.

Jake Fargo was on him before Andrew could recover. Wrapping his arms around him, Fargo roared, "Now I've got you, bastard! I'm gonna break you like an egg!"

Andrew struggled with all his strength, beating on the big man's neck and shoulders with his fists. He might as well have been pounding on a tree trunk. Fargo squeezed and squeezed. Andrew's breath left him in an explosive grunt and Maggie could see his eyes bulging.

Frantically, she looked around for something she could use to help. Her gaze lit on the pickaroon. Even in her present frame of mind, could she bury that in Fargo's back? She shuddered at the thought, but if she didn't do something, she would soon be at the man's mercy.

She ran to the pickaroon and grasped the wooden handle. She tugged with all her strength, but it was buried deep in the deck and wouldn't budge. She took a deep breath and tried again. It still wouldn't come free of the wood.

A yowl of pain came from Fargo and Maggie glanced around. Fargo had let go his bear hug of Andrew and was backed up against the wheelhouse, half-bent over, hands covering his groin, still yelling in agony.

Against the railing, Andrew was trying to regain his breath. He had been near the point of blacking out when he had gathered his waning strength and brought his knee up into Fargo's groin.

Again, he called on his reserve of strength and propelled himself away from the rail at Fargo. He didn't bother to use his fists. He seized the big man by one arm and shoulder, turned with him, and went at a run for the railing. Just short of it, he levered the man's bulk from the deck and sent him flying over the rail. He leaned forward, watching Fargo hit the water with a mighty splash. The man sank out of sight, but in a moment he came to the surface, sputtering and flailing his arms.

With a final tug at the pickaroon, Maggie had

freed it and now ran with it to where Andrew was. She peered down at the water.

She asked, "Is he dead?"

"Not if he can swim, he isn't," Andrew said.

Just then Fargo looked at the tugboat, slowly moving away from him, shook his fist, shouted something unintelligible, and then started to swim toward the distant shore.

Andrew turned to Maggie. "Good Lord, woman, what were you going to do with that thing?"

Maggie looked at the pickaroon in her hand as if she had forgotten it. "I was going to use it, bury it in his back if I had to."

"Would you really have done that?"

She said stoutly, "I would have . . ." She broke off, adding in a weak voice, "at least I think I would have, if it came to that."

Shaking his head, Andrew said, "Give me that." He took it from her and sent it after Fargo. After they had watched it splash out of sight into the water, Andrew rubbed his hands together. "Now I reckon we can be on our way . . . damnation! The diamonds, where are the diamonds?"

"Right here," Maggie said complacently, patting the spot between her breasts.

Andrew gave a shout of laughter. "That's my practical Maggie! Here I thought you were coming to my defense with that pickaroon!" His eyes mocked her. "And all the while you were protecting your precious diamonds."

In truth, Maggie had forgotten the diamonds and *was* ready to come to his defense. But she wasn't about to give him the satisfaction of admitting it.

336

Without replying she turned away to the boiler and began feeding it chunks of wood.

Andrew was back at the wheel a few minutes later, when she remembered something that had been said between the two men. She went into the wheelhouse. "Andrew, Jake Fargo said something that puzzles me. I didn't know you had ever met the man, yet he talked as if you had."

He glanced at her, his face unreadable. "It was nothing, Maggie. Just a chance meeting in a tavern. Call it a drunken argument, if you like."

"Oh," she said. The answer didn't quite satisfy her, yet she didn't question him further. Something about his attitude warned her off. Besides, it was probably true. He had a wild, devil-may-care streak in him, did Andrew Kane, and tavern brawling was probably not an uncommon thing with him.

Three days later, Maggie stood at the rail on board the *Belle* as it neared the cove. In her reticule was the fifteen thousand dollars she needed to pay off the note, and well within the deadline Constance Kirk had set.

She should have been content, yet she was not, not entirely. She had, in a manner of speaking, made the trip to Seattle and back with her virtue intact. In fact, it had never been in the slightest danger that she could see. Andrew Kane had been the perfect gentleman at all times. Not by so much as a word or gesture had he done anything to offend. He had slept on deck and let Maggie have the cabin all to herself.

It had been what she wanted, of course, and she

337

would have rebuffed him cruelly had he so much as quirked an eyebrow at her.

But it was so much unlike the Andrew Kane she had come to know! It was mystifying, it was aggravating, it was maddening! Damn him, anyway!

Didn't he desire her any more?

The very least he could have done was to make an improper advance, so she could have spurned him, thus salvaging her pride.

The tugboat chugged around the last headland, and they entered the cove. Maggie was glad to see a goodly number of logs floating in the water and she saw that the mill building was nearing completion. Most of the machinery that had littered the beach was gone, so she assumed that much of it had been installed already.

Andrew brought the tugboat around and Tod Dorsey, his deckhand, lowered the anchor.

Andrew came to stand beside Maggie at the railing. "Well, Mistress Donnevan, I trust you are content with your business transaction?"

"I am, Andrew, and you have my gratitude," she said warmly. She placed her hand on his on the rail. "If I can ever do anything to repay you, you'll be after asking, I suppose?"

His gaze was level, but glints of that mocking amusement showed in the depths of his eyes. "I thought we *were* even, Maggie. So you were careful to inform me."

"No, I was wrong. I am still in your debt. I fear that I would never have carried off the transaction without your help."

"Had I realized you felt so, perhaps I would not have been so careful to keep my distance these past three days."

"Why did you, sir?" she said without thinking.

"You mean I have disillusioned you, Maggie?" he said with a grave face. "You find it hard to believe I could be on my best behavior? Or could it be . . ." Now his handsome face got that devilish look. "Could it possibly be that you are disappointed?"

"Oh!" She snatched her hand from his, flushing. "You are a *most* exasperating man, Andrew Kane! It's impossible for a person to speak frankly to you, without you twisting the words around!"

He made a negligent gesture and said dryly, "I should think you would be content with my being a gentleman, Maggie. If you only knew what a strain it was on my baser nature, a nature that you seem to have a great talent for bringing to the fore." He turned, calling, "Tod, will you lower the dinghy and row Miss Donnevan ashore?" He glanced at Maggie. "I assume you will be happier rowing in with him than with me, and I do not feel up to facing the prospect of undergoing extensive questioning by your big brother. So, I wish you good day, madam."

"Whisht!" Maggie refused to look at him. "Good day to you, too, Andrew Kane."

She heard his footsteps going away toward the wheelhouse, and she did not look toward him again. In the dinghy she rode facing toward shore, and did not spare a single look back at the *Belle*.

Dorsey beached the dinghy. Lars was coming toward them with bounding strides, arriving in time to help Maggie out of the boat. He lifted her out bodily, a huge grin on his face.

"I'm glad to see you safe and sound, Maggie!"

"Did you think I wouldn't be?"

339

"I didn't know." Grave-faced now, he searched her face with his eyes. "Did everything go all right?"

"Everything went fine. But I appreciate your concern." She stood on tiptoe, skidding a kiss off his cheek. "Dear Lars, I promise to tell you what it was about, most of it anyway." The memory of Jake Fargo and his attempt to take the diamonds returned to her, and she barely suppressed a shudder. She could not risk going alone to see Constance Kirk carrying fifteen thousand dollars on her person. She said, "Lars, I have an errand in Port Ludlow on the morrow. I shall want you to go with me, and I will explain then . . ."

She was interrupted by a bellow. "Maggie girl!"

Looking past Lars, she saw Patrick approaching. She was surprised to see him grinning from ear to ear, thinking he would still be angry at her for going off alone. Then she frowned, squinting against the glare of the setting sun.

There was someone behind him, hidden by his great size. Someone smaller . . . Kevin? Could it be Kevin?

Then Patrick stopped, stepping to one side. Beaming, he said, "Look who's here, come all that great way to be with us again!"

Maggie took an uncertain step forward. It was a woman, small, emaciated, with a gray, bruised look . . .

"Kathleen!" Maggie began to run, arms outstretched. "Oh, dear God! Kathleen! Kathleen!"

Chapter Fourteen

As Lord Ramage saw Port Ludlow from the deck of the small inland schooner, his first thought was that it was the most primitive village he had slapped eyes on yet; and he had certainly seen some sorry villages since coming to Puget Sound two weeks before.

He had quickly learned that he could expect little or no help from the local authorities in regard to his diamonds, either recovering their value or seeing that the Donnevans paid the penalty. Upon his arrival, he had stopped off at Port Townsend to see the customs agent there, an officious ass who had told him that stolen diamonds were not within his jurisdiction. Later, Lord Ramage's discussions with law officers in Port Townsend and Seattle had yielded the same results. The gist of the matter was that they all had enough to do in their efforts to enforce the laws broken within their own domain and that an alleged crime, committed in a distant country, was not their concern, even though the criminals might now reside in Washington Territory.

Now, knowing where he stood, Lord Ramage realized that he would have to fall back on his own resources. He was weary from the long, uncomfortable journey from Ireland—transferring from one ship to another, each one worse than the one before—and a cold fury simmered just underneath his calm exterior.

Now this huddle of huts calling itself a town offended his sensibilities; and he was greeted by such a combination of foul odors as he stepped off the schooner that he felt close to vomiting. Lord Ramage had never taken to the custom of carrying a perfumed handkerchief tucked into his sleeve to wave before his nostrils to fend off offending odors, as did many lords in the British Isles. He had always believed that a man should smell like a man and even the stench of the pigstyes inhabited by his Irish tenant farmers had never bothered him overmuch.

Now he had to admit that a perfumed handkerchief held to his nostrils would be handy here. As best he could, he ignored the stench and directed the retinue of servants that had accompanied him in the unloading of his luggage.

As his belongings were being unloaded, Lord Ramage looked along the wharf. There were several natives, brown-skinned men with long hair and broad cheekbones, fishing off the wharf.

Lord Ramage approached one and nudged his

thigh with his boot. "I say, fellow, who is in charge of the miserable place?"

The Indian looked up at him, grunted, and slid along the wharf a few feet. Angered, Lord Ramage considered booting him into the water. But just then he saw a white man shambling toward him. At least he seemed to be white under a layer of dirt and straggly whiskers.

"My dear fellow, I am Lord Ramage."

The man stared at him stupidly. "Ya don't say? Now ain't that something?"

Keeping his irritation under control, Lord Ramage said coldly, "Come, man! Who is in charge of your village? Who is your Lord Mayor?"

"Ain't got one that I know of."

"Your constable then?"

"Ain't got one of them, neither."

"Damme, fellow!" Lord Ramage exploded. "There must be *somebody* to administer the law!"

"A U.S. Marshal drops in once in a while. That's it. I guess if anybody has much to say about running Port Ludlow, it'd be Captain Sayward." The man jerked his thumb. "Owns the sawmill over there."

The man strode on down the wharf, studying the piles of luggage with elaborate interest. Fuming, Lord Ramage pondered his next move.

Suddenly, his mood changed. Perhaps it was for the best. If there was no law, he would be his own law. In fact, a whole new concept opened up for him—a man with some initiative, capital, and few scruples could become a wealthy, important man here. From what he had observed so far, the business of logging timber and turning it into lumber was a pretty haphazard business, with the possible exception of the Pope and Talbot operation at Port Gamble. He had long been bored by his life in Ireland. If he could gain a foothold in this raw, new land, there was a fortune to be made, plus the excitement of the game!

Spirits buoyed by the exciting prospects suddenly before him, Lord Ramage called over to his servants, "Remain here and guard my belongings. I will return shortly."

He strode along the wharf toward the sawmill. On the way his gaze was drawn to a fine white house set on a bluff some distance south of the town. He was struck by its appearance, so much more handsome than the other unpainted shacks he could see. Curious, he thought: such a grand house in primitive surroundings such as this. Mayhap it belonged to this Captain Sayward, evidently a man of some importance here.

This judgment Lord Ramage found doubtful, when he finally met the fellow, a rather taciturn individual in workman's clothing, who spoke with a strange twang. In Lord Ramage's opinion, it was not befitting a gentleman to wear clothing similar to that worn by his employees, even though he might be supervising their activities.

The introductions over, he said, "Captain, I am inquiring after an Irish family by the name of Donnevan. Do you know of them?"

"Aye, I know them all," Captain Sayward said with the first enthusiasm he had shown. "They are logging north of Port Ludlow. They have been doing business at my sawmill. But now they are building a mill of their very own."

Ah, Lord Ramage thought, fortune smiles! He said, "Prospering are they, sir?"

"Doing quite well indeed."

"Perchance did a Kathleen Donnevan arrive here within the month?"

"That she did, sir. Arrived some weeks back." For the first time Captain Sayward showed some curiosity. "For what reason might ye be inquiring after the Donnevans, Lord Ramage?"

Lord Ramage shrugged negligently. "I am from Ireland, as are they. I know the Donnevans. Being in the country, I had it in mind to visit with them . . . especially since they seem to be prospering so well."

Curiosity seemingly satisfied, Captain Sayward nodded. "They are a fine family, thrifty and hard-working, are the Donnevans."

"Tell me, sir, I have need of some bully boys. Could you perhaps recommend some to me?"

Captain Sayward's face took on a grim look. "We have rough types aplenty hereabouts. The worst two ruffians in the Territory are Jake Fargo and his sidekick, Snake." Again, the captain's eyes brightened with curiosity and some disapproval. "For what reason might ye be asking?"

"I am a wealthy man, Captain, and have found that travel can be dangerous. I have need of body-guards while here."

"Then ye wouldn't be interested in that pair." Captain Sayward gestured contemptuously. "Hiring that pair of fine bastards to guard ye and yours would be like hiring thieves to guard a treasure."

"Thank you, Captain. You have been most kind, and helpful." Lord Ramage started to turn away, then paused to ask, "That house on the bluff . . . does that happen to belong to you?"

"Oh, no. It's too fine for the likes of me." The captain grinned. "That house belonged to Jonas Kirk. He died some time back, and his widow settled his affairs, and put the house up for sale. So happens, she left it in my hands to sell. She's gone down to San Francisco."

Lord Ramage debated with himself for a moment. "Have you sold it yet, Captain?"

"Not yet. I'm afraid there ain't much of a market for such a fine house."

"I might be interested," Lord Ramage said cautiously. "Would you by any chance be authorized to rent it to me until I make my decision?"

"No reason why not." Captain Sayward shrugged. "It is scantily furnished, but there are beds and such like, enough for you to manage until you can purchase the things you need."

They haggled a bit on terms, but within a half-hour Lord Ramage was walking back to the wharf with the keys to the house in his hands.

The following day, after he had settled his servants into the house on the bluff, Lord Ramage made his way down to the village and inquired as to the whereabouts of Jake Fargo. As it turned out, Fargo wasn't difficult to find.

He was in one of Port Ludlow's two taverns, guzzling whiskey and jollying a blowsy-looking serving girl.

The few patrons in the tavern fell silent and eyed Lord Ramage and his finery with thunderstruck eyes. He strolled over to Fargo's table. Lord

Ramage thought that Fargo was one of the most evil-looking men he had ever seen—exactly the man to fit his needs!

Now Fargo glanced up. His small eyes glinted with derision as he leaned back and surveyed Lord Ramage. "Well, what do we have here? I don't recall when I ever clapped eyes on such a dandy!"

"I may look the dandy, Mr. Fargo," Lord Ramage said in his coldest voice, "but I assure you that I am not what I appear to be."

"Is that so?" Fargo said, his eyes turning hard as flint. "You know my name, now what's yours?"

"I am Lord Ramage, newly arrived from Ireland."

"Lord Ramage, is it? Fancy clothes, fancy name. What do you want with me?"

"If you will send the bawd on her way, I will tell you."

"Bawd, is it?" the serving girl said angrily. "You can't talk to me that way, fancy man or not. Tell him, Jake!"

"On your way, Fancy." Fargo clapped her on the rear and leered. "We'll continue our chat later."

Fancy flounced off, her nose in the air.

Fargo waved a hand expansively. "Sit yourself down, Your Lordship. What's your pleasure from the bar?"

Lord Ramage sat down. "I do not indulge in spirits while discussing business, Fargo."

"Then what's the business?" Fargo absently fondled the handle of a wicked-looking object leaning against the table.

"Do you know of the Donnevan family?"

347

Fargo growled, "Yeah, I know the Donnevans. Especially that bitch, Maggie." His huge hands opened and closed on the table top. "Nothing would give me more joy than to have her neck between my hands. I would see to it that the sassiness was squeezed out of her, that I would!"

Lord Ramage nodded. "Then you are indeed the man I am looking for."

Fargo looked at him curiously. "What's your interest in the Donnevans?"

"They are the reason I came all the way from Ireland. The Donnevans were tenants on my estate. In gratitude, they repaid me in sorry coin. They stole a small fortune in diamonds from me."

"You're the gent she stole the jewels from!"

Lord Ramage's gaze sharpened. "What do you know of my jewels?"

"I know that Maggie Donnevan has some jewels she stole, that much I know."

"Not Maggie. Her sister, Kathleen, is the thief." Lord Ramage was gratified to learn that the Donnevans still had some of his gems. "Maggie has some left in her possession, you say? Damme, I may get some of my own back yet!"

Fargo was shaking his head. "I doubt that, Your Lordship. She *had* some left, but I believe she has disposed of them by now."

"Tell me what you know, Fargo."

Fargo hesitated, his eyes showing uneasiness.

"You tried to steal them from her, is that not right?"

Fargo reared back in astonishment. "How did you come to know that?"

I know a thief and a murderer when I see one,

Lord Ramage thought. Aloud, he said, "A surmise on my part, but accurate I am sure. Tell me the details. Do not worry about offending or shocking me. If we are to work together for mutual profit, and I am certain we shall, I need the truth from you at all times."

Fargo launched into the tale of his attempt to rob Andrew Kane and Maggie Donnevan of the diamonds. "Fate was against me," he finished. "Just as I had the pouch of jewels in my grasp, that damned tugboat skittered, one side tilting up. I lost my footing and slid right under the rail and into the channel."

Lord Ramage said thoughtfully, "You say she was on her way to sell the jewels?"

"From the talk I overheard between her and this man Kane, it would appear so."

Lord Ramage sighed. "Damme, I have not come all this distance to be thwarted! I understand you have a logging crew? Men loyal to you, and not averse to violence?"

"They are true to me, and do what I say." Fargo wore an evil grin. "They love nothing better than a little rough stuff, should it put money in their pockets."

"I shall make it worth their while, and yours, Fargo. Now here is what I have in mind . . ." He leaned forward, lowering his voice, and told Fargo of his plan.

At the end, Fargo grinned hugely and slapped his palm on the table. "By damn, I am with you, Your Lordship! 'Twill delight my soul to see Maggie Donnevan get her comeuppance!"

Maggie was appalled at the change in Kathleen. She could accept the emaciation; she could even accept the awful scars left by Lord Ramage's "punishments"; what she could not deal with was the mental change in her sister.

There seemed to be nothing left of the bright, spirited girl that Maggie had known. The sister she loved and to whom they all owed so much was now only the shell of a woman, empty of feeling and almost unable to communicate.

Maggie was grateful for one thing. Her brothers were clearly happy to have Kathleen with them. Even Patrick had surprised her; he had accepted Kathleen's appearance not only with good grace, but he had welcomed her with open arms.

"Aye, 'tis good to be having the Donnevans all together again," he had told Maggie the evening of her return from Seattle with Andrew. "We are a family once more, that we are."

Maggie had told Patrick and Dan that night how she had gotten the money to bring them to America. Again, Patrick had surprised her, accepting it with maturity. "It's sorry I am for the harsh things I said of her before, and now I see that the Donnevans owe her a debt that we can never repay."

After Kathleen had been with them for a week, Patrick sought out Maggie. "What ails our sister? She seems so different . . . I'm not after meaning this the wrong way, but it strikes me she's acting a bit strange!"

"I know, Patrick. I am as concerned as you. Mother Be-Damn will soon put meat on her bones, and some color in her cheeks, but how do we heal the hurt in her mind? She seems so joyless, so beaten down. Sometimes I think she doesn't care whether she lives or dies. We can only hope that she will return to her old self with the passage of time."

But the days and weeks passed, and there was little change in Kathleen's condition. She did put on weight, and her body rounded out again. However, she remained listless, showing little interest in anything around her, and Maggie had to badger her into bathing and combing her hair. She would sit for hours at a time on a rock on the shore, staring out at the water. Also, she developed a distressing habit of wandering off into the forest, and would be gone for hours.

Maggie at last began to lose patience with her sister. The sawmill was in operation now and Maggie was busier than at any time since they began logging. She simply could not spare the time to look after Kathleen every minute of the day.

Finally, in exasperation, she got Kathleen alone in their sleeping tent one evening, intending to remonstrate with her. It was difficult to start, they all owed Kathleen so much, but this could not go on! It was hurtful to them all, and to Kathleen in particular. She was only living a half life and seemed to be drifting further away from them every day. The words must be said, firmly, but in love.

Maggie looked down at Kathleen sitting passively on the edge of the cot, and hardened her will. "Kathleen, I know how you have suffered in our behalf. I think I know how badly you have fared at Lord Ramage's hands, but . . ."

At this Kathleen stirred, showing a brief spark of her former spirit. "Maggie, you don't know, you

351

can't even possibly guess the degradation and humiliation I have endured at that man's hands! There are no words to tell of such foul abuse, or if there are, I do not know them!"

Maggie reached out and touched her sister's hand. "But if you could try to tell me, try to talk out the hurt and the pain, then . . . why then perhaps you can begin to heal inside. And when you've done that, why then you'll be our Kathleen again, the sister we remember."

Kathleen turned her head aside. "And what am I now, then? What am I now, if not the sister you knew?"

Maggie, tears swimming in her eyes, shook her head angrily. "Ah, Kathleen, Kathleen, can't you see yourself as you are now? It's as if you're adrift in some awful, lonely world of your own, and you won't let any of us in to help you. Whisht! The past has been terrible, I know, but it *is* past, and must be forgotten, if you are ever to get on with the business of living."

"I'll never forget, and it's not over. Don't you see, sister? It'll never be over!"

"No, I don't see. You sacrificed yourself for the Donnevans. It was a terrible price you paid. Don't you think I know that? But through your sacrifice, the Donnevans have survived and are prospering. I've told Patrick and Dan what you did for us, and they're grateful. Before, they would not have understood. But now they do, and they love you, Kathleen. We all love you."

Kathleen shook her head and her eyes went empty. "I have sinned grievously, Maggie. I went to Lord Ramage's bed without the sanction of a priest, and I have stolen! Twice, I have stolen! I will never be forgiven. I will never forgive myself!"

Angry now, Maggie made her voice harsh. "I will not listen to such talk! You sinned, if you must call it that, for a good cause, and now you are safe in the arms of your own dear ones."

Kathleen said starkly, "He will come after me, Maggie."

"Who? Lord Ramage? Whisht! You are talking foolishness, sister! The man would have to be daft to come all this great distance just because a few jewels were stolen from him. He probably spends sums equal to their value in a week's wenching and drinking!"

"He will come. I know it. You do not know this man, Maggie."

Kathleen began to weep, silent tears coursing down her cheeks. Heart softening, Maggie reached out for her, and held her in her arms, rocking back and forth, comforting her as best she could.

It was the first time Kathleen had wept since her arrival. Not even at the moment when they embraced on the beach had she shed any tears. Now the dam had broken. Perhaps the tears would take away some of the hurt.

In that thought Maggie was mistaken. In the following days, Kathleen became more distant and withdrawn than ever. When Maggie tried to talk to her again, Kathleen answered only in monosyllables, and then walked away.

Lars and Maggie were still going to their meadow every Sunday. On the first Sunday after Kathleen appeared, Maggie had taken her along, with Lars' approval, but Kathleen's presence had been so depressing that Maggie had not asked her again. It wasn't fair to Lars to spoil the few hours that they had alone.

Emotionally, Maggie was more dependent on Lars now than she would have liked. She was very fond of him, but with her independence in the balance, she had not told him the depth of her affection, fearful that he would demand a commitment from her.

On a nice Sunday afternoon, six weeks after Kathleen's arrival, Maggie and Lars walked over the mountain to their meadow, Lars carrying the picnic basket.

When they sat down on the grass, Maggie sighed and said, "It's worried I am about Kathleen, Lars. It made me happy, my life seemed full, when she came to us. But now I don't know what is going to happen. At times I think she is going mad. Not that she hasn't ample cause. Dear God, how she has suffered!"

His big hand cupped her shoulder. "I'm sorry, Maggie. I know you love your sister dearly, and it hurts me to see you in such pain."

Something broke inside Maggie at his touch, and she turned into his arms, clutching at him. "Hold me, Lars!"

He held her gently as she cried. When her sobs subsided, he tilted her face up with a forefinger, and kissed her. Maggie responded eagerly, seeking forgetfulness in passion.

Lars made fierce yet gentle love to her, as if he hoped his hands and lips could caress away her pain; and Maggie gave herself up to the sensations of her body, all else forgotten, burned away for the moment by the hungry fire in her body. When it was finally over and they lay side by side, clothing still in disarray, Maggie felt content and drowsy.

"Dear Lars." She stroked a hand down his bare chest. "You're so good to me. With you, I can forget my troubles. I can be myself with you."

"I love you, Maggie."

"I know, Lars, I know," she said sleepily. She turned on her side, and went to sleep with her face nestled in the cradle of his shoulder.

When Maggie and Lars returned to camp, Patrick came striding toward them. He was frowning, and his voice was troubled as he said, "Maggie, I have to talk with you, with you and Sister Kathleen."

"What is it, Patrick? What's wrong?"

"No, it's to the pair of you together I'm talking." He motioned with his head. "Kathleen is mooning down by the water again."

"Excuse me, Lars," Maggie said, and hurried after Patrick, who was heading toward the water's edge in long strides. Maggie didn't catch up to him until he had reached the rock where Kathleen sat, staring vacantly out at the channel.

"Whisht, Patrick! What is all the mystery?" Maggie demanded, slightly out of breath. She stepped up to take Kathleen's cold hand.

Patrick faced them, hands on hips. "Captain Sayward came down to camp today. He had some bad news for the Donnevans, I'm thinking. There is someone in Port Ludlow asking after us."

Maggie felt her heart begin to pound. She

squeezed Kathleen's hand. "What someone? Who was it?"

"Lord Ramage."

Maggie was struck speechless, but Kathleen uttered a strangled cry and tore her hand from Maggie's grasp.

"He's come for me! I knew he would!"

Before Maggie could move, Kathleen was running toward the woods, black hair streaming out behind her.

Maggie glared at her brother. "Such a great dolt you are, Patrick Donnevan, blurting that out to her like that!"

She whirled and ran after Kathleen, calling her name. Kathleen ran on, disappearing into the trees.

Chapter Fifteen

Lord Ramage chose to make his foray against the Donnevans in the early afternoon of a weekday. He calculated that the men would all be at work in the woods and he would find the two Donnevan women alone in the camp.

He had twenty men in all, with Jake Fargo and the man called Snake in command. A more villainous crew he had never seen. Fargo and Snake alone were enough to strike fear into the hearts of all but the bravest of men.

Fargo had managed to scrounge up three longboats. Lord Ramage was in command of the lead boat, Fargo the second, and Snake was in charge of the third. All of the men, except Lord Ramage himself, were armed with pistols.

Lord Ramage was impressed as they rowed into the cove, and he had his first glimpse of the Donnevan logging camp. There were several buildings, the largest of them a long, wooden building obviously the sawmill. Smoke poured from a tall chimney at one end, and the whine of the saws could be heard long before they reached the beach. Lord Ramage was pleased. If the Donnevans refused to cough up a sum equal to the value of the stolen diamonds, he would simply take over the logging operation by force.

During the two days he had been in Port Ludlow, Lord Ramage had reached a firm decision. He was going to stay in this country and go into the logging business. He had already dispatched a letter to Ireland, instructing the man he had left in charge of his affairs to arrange for the sale of his estate. In addition, he had sent another letter to his bank in Galway, directing that his bank drafts be honored immediately.

His first instinct had been correct, Lord Ramage was certain. There was a fortune to be made here. With a crew of bully boys like Fargo's working for him, he figured that the possibilities were limitless. Jake Fargo had an animal's cunning and a savage nature, but he badly needed direction by a man of Lord Ramage's superior intelligence.

He would be off to a good start if he could, on this day, take over an already thriving logging operation, along with a sawmill. Already he was dreaming of becoming a more powerful timber baron than Pope and Talbot.

Lord Ramage anticipated no strong resistance from the Donnevans. True, it was likely that they knew of his arrival here, but the Irish, in his opinion, were a carefree and arrogant race, confident that they could handle themselves in any brawl. They would not dream that he would come up against them with armed men.

This opinion was borne out as he directed the longboats to be beached. The scene was peaceful, and except for the activity around the sawmill, he could see no forces awaiting them. Even their arrival seemed to have gone unnoticed.

Lord Ramage stepped confidently out of the boat. When the others were beached, he said, "Fargo, you accompany me. Snake, you are in charge of the men. Deploy them in a long line, pistols drawn. As I move up the slope toward the Donnevan camp, remain about thirty yards behind me. I expect no trouble, as I believe we are catching them completely unprepared. But keep alert, in any case. If we do encounter resistance, do not fire until I give this signal . . ." He raised his right hand and brought it down in a chopping motion. Then he turned to Fargo. "Come along, Fargo."

Lord Ramage moved forward with a firm step. Fargo, a pickaroon in one hand and a pistol in the other, matched him stride for stride. Breathing heavily with excitement, Fargo said in a thick voice, "I hope they do put up a fight. It would do my heart good to shoot that Donnevan woman down like the bitch she is!"

"You will do nothing until I give the signal," Lord Ramage said sharply. He broke off, his step slowing as he saw three people coming toward him. Maggie Donnevan he recognized easily, although she had blossomed since that night in the castle. His blood thickened at the sight of her. By God, she was a desirable wench! The two big men bracketing her he had never seen before, but from their appearance he knew they must be Patrick and Daniel Donnevan. He breathed easier when he saw that they were unarmed.

He paused now, motioning Fargo to a stop. The Donnevans came on, finally halting a few feet away.

Maggie advanced a step. "What is your purpose here, Your Lordship? This is private property, and you are not welcome."

"I have come for Kathleen Donnevan," Lord Fargo said formally.

"This is not Ireland, Your Lordship." Maggie's voice was acid and contemptuous. "Here, you do not own people like cattle. Kathleen is back with the Donnevans now, and here she remains."

"I bought her. Damme, the woman is mine! She is my property, and no one takes my property from me!"

Patrick growled deep in his throat, and stepped up with his fists raised. "You are a foul-mouthed bucko! I will not be after listening to you befoul Kathleen with your filthy tongue!"

"Patience, Patrick." Maggie motioned him silent. "Let His Lordship spill his venom before we have him tossed into the channel."

"You Donnevans are all thieves. My diamonds were stolen by your precious sister. Now I demand their return."

"Your diamonds are not available," Maggie said with a toss of her head. "The theft, as you call it, was committed in Ireland, not here, and I do not consider it a crime. I consider it as our due for the treatment you gave the Donnevans. Most of all, for the manner in which you degraded and humiliated poor Kathleen."

Lord Ramage was seething with a cold rage at this woman who so dared to stand up to him. In a voice as hard as steel, he said, "If I do not receive full value for my stolen property, I will take over your sawmill and everything here as recompense."

"I defy you to try, Your Lordship," Maggie said steadily.

Lord Ramage was baffled as to the reason this woman could so defy him. "Are you blind, wench?" he said with his cold smile. "I have twenty men backing me, armed to the teeth."

"I see your men, sir."

"Well, then?"

"Patrick?"

Patrick put two fingers in his mouth and whistled shrilly, twice.

Maggie laughed. "If you will look around, Your Lordship?"

Lord Ramage looked to his left, then to his right. As if by magic, men had appeared at the edge of the trees to the north, and others had popped out of the sawmill building. All were armed, with either rifles or shotguns. At another whistle all the men raised their weapons to their shoulders and sighted down the barrels. At a rough count, Lord Ramage saw that his own men were outnumbered, almost two to one.

Again Maggie laughed, laughter that curled at Lord Ramage like the lash of a whip. "Do you take us for fools, Lord Ramage? We were told that you had arrived in Port Ludlow. Knowing that you were up to no good, we armed ourselves and were waiting. We have had a man down the coast watching for your approach day and night. Now, if one of your men so much as fires a single shot, you shall all die. Perhaps some of us will die as well, but we Donnevans are prepared to die defending what is ours!"

Almost strangling on his anger and frustration, Lord Ramage choked out, "You will rue this day, woman. You and all your sorry tribe!"

Maggie said calmly, "From now on, Your Lordship, we shall be on our guard, and you will have hell's own time sneaking up on us."

Fargo said in a hoarse whisper, "Let me give the signal, and have the boys start shooting! They ain't afraid of this here bunch!"

Lord Ramage gestured him quiet.

But Maggie had heard. She stared at Fargo with bitter hatred. "The first man to die will be you, Jake Fargo. You have plagued me enough. To see you dead would delight me, may God forgive me but it would!"

Regaining his composure, Lord Ramage said, "Very well, madam. You have carried the day. But believe this . . . I shall never give up until I have my just due. From this day forward you will wake up at night at every little sound, fearful that it is your last moment on earth."

"I can live with that, Lord Ramage," Maggie said, her stare unyielding. "And you should believe this . . . we are not the same Donnevans who were your virtual slaves back in Ireland. We are free and unafraid, and you will find us resourceful."

With a curt gesture to Fargo, Lord Ramage

turned away and strode down to the longboats, maintaining an even pace and as much of his tattered dignity as he could. He didn't speak as Fargo's men got into the boats and pushed them off the beach. Jake Fargo rode with him this time.

Fargo said bitterly, "That Donnevan woman must be a witch or something. She sure as hell has a charmed life."

"She will be nothing when I am finished with her!" Lord Ramage said in his cold voice. He took a deep breath. "Fargo, I am a wealthy man, and I am going into the logging business. I want you and your bully boys to work for me."

"Well now, I don't know." Fargo hefted the pickaroon thoughtfully. "I ain't never taken much to working for somebody else."

"I will make it worth your while. You are operating what is known as a gypo logging crew. With my resources behind you, you will earn more money than you ever dreamed possible. In addition, you will see Maggie Donnevan broken. That I promise you."

Fargo looked at him curiously. "You mean you're just going into the logging business to best her?"

"That is my prime motive, I will admit. I do not accept defeat easily. But in the doing, I also intend to become the most powerful timber baron in this territory. But first, everything will be directed toward humbling that damned female. Damme, I have never hated any person so much as Maggie Donnevan. *All* the Donnevans!"

"We could sneak in there late at night and wipe them out," Fargo said.

"No, they will be on their guard now. I wish to see them suffer first. I want to bring them to their knees, no matter how much time it requires. I want to see them destitute, in rags and begging. I will spend every pound I possess to bring this about." He looked squarely at the scar-faced man. "Are you with me, Jake Fargo?"

"I'll try her for awhile. It could be fine sport."

"I pledge my word that it shall be," Lord Ramage said grimly. "Maggie Donnevan wishes to play at being a timber baron, I will defeat her on her own ground. I will harass and plague them unto their doom. Maggie Donnevan will indeed rue this day!"

As the longboats pulled slowly out of the cove, Patrick erupted with a whoop. "We stood those boyos off, that we did! Although I would dearly love to have laid a shillelagh alongside the heads of that fine pair, Fargo and Lord Ramage!"

The other men were gathering around now, all grinning with great glee.

Maggie, who had been smiling in triumph, now frowned around at them. "Don't be after celebrating yet, Brother Patrick. We have not seen the last of Lord Ramage, nor Jake Fargo, I'd hazard, since they seemed to have joined forces. We will have to keep a watchful eye out every minute of the day and night."

Olaf groaned. "Dad-damnit, that's going to cut back on our logging, we have to spare men to stand watch."

"Then we'll hire more." She faced him squarely. "I'm not after letting that awful man frighten me,

Olaf. You didn't hear what he threatened. He intends to take over our logging, and the sawmill by force."

Olaf studied her carefully. "Now why should he want to do that, little girl? From the looks of him, he's a wealthy man. If'n he wants to go into the logging business, why try to take over yours?"

"Because he's a vindictive, evil man. He was the Donnevans' landlord back in Ireland. He's the one who so abused our poor sister. She ran away from him, fled to us here. I think that Lord Ramage is a wee bit touched in the head. To come all this distance, to go to such lengths to gain vengeance. . . . Whisht, it's mad he is, I'm thinking!"

"Seems to me the best thing for you would be to go to the law."

"What law, Olaf?" she said challengingly. "You have told me yourself that little law exists here. He intends to take the law into his own hands, and who will gainsay him, except us? We're foreigners, Olaf. If I were to go to what law there is and ask for protection, they'd be after laughing at me, you can be sure." She shook her head. "No, we Donnevans do not give up so easily. If he wants to take out his venom on us, we will fight him. We'll fight him if I have to hire an army!"

She slapped her hands together. "Now we'd better get back to work. We've lost enough time for one day!"

The men scattered, some returning to the sawmill, the others going back up the mountain to the spot where they were logging.

Maggie went at a brisk walk to the new, small building behind the bunkhouse, recently erected

365

for living quarters, that she shared with Kathleen. From the moment that Maggie had fetched her back from the woods after learning of Lord Ramage's arrival, Kathleen had not left the cabin. Maggie had to scold her in the morning to get her out of bed and into her clothes.

Now Maggie pushed the door open and went in. A whimper came from Kathleen, and she cowered back against the wall. Physically, she seemed in perfect health now. Her beauty had returned with the gained weight, and color had come back to her cheeks.

Maggie said gently, "No need to be afraid, Kathleen dear. Lord Ramage has come and gone. We were prepared for him, and ran him off. We will protect you until our dying breath. You need not fear him any longer."

Kathleen stared at her with round, blank eyes. Maggie sighed .She doubted that Kathleen even knew she was in the room, or heard a word she had said.

Kathleen did know that her sister was in the cabin, and she was dimly aware of what Maggie was telling her. She tried to take heart from Maggie's reassuring words, but it seemed too much of an effort to stir from her apathy. She watched Maggie turn away, shoulders drooping in disappointment, and wanted desperately to call out to her, but the words would not come. Maggie left the cabin, closing the door gently behind her.

Kathleen sat on. There had been many times, more than Maggie realized, when Kathleen had been completely lucid, and she had ached to put her arms around her sister, express her love, and tell her how very much she appreciated the manner in which she had been welcomed by the Donnevans. But somehow she had never managed to summon up the energy, for always in the back of her mind, crouching there like a beast about to attack her, was the thought of Lord Ramage.

When the presence of that cruel entity in her mind began to grow in size, Kathleen would retreat into those gray, mindless periods when she did not have to think. During those periods, the days and nights had no color, no sounds, and she experienced only a dim awareness of the people around her. She lived in a world of her own, a world she had created to wall herself off. It took a great effort to break through the shell of that world, and when she did, Kathleen was too exhausted to make the effort to communicate.

With the passing of time, with all that distance separating her from Lord Ramage, the gray spells became less frequent and Kathleen had begun to yearn toward her loved ones. She grew more and more determined to make the effort necessary to respond to their devotion and gentle care.

All the while, of course, there was that grinding burden of guilt for all the sins she had committed. But even that she was learning to live with. The guilt did not lessen, but it was in the past. If her brothers could forgive her, Kathleen knew she had to come to terms with her sins and forgive herself.

In time, she might have. And then had come the news that Lord Ramage was not far across the great sea. He was here, he was in Port Ludlow!

The crouching beast in her mind grew apace like some devouring tumor. Kathleen lived in terror, a scream she could not utter always on her lips.

After the passage of three days and Maggie's continued reassurances that Lord Ramage would not be taking her away, Kathleen finally ventured out of the cabin. The sun striking her eyes sent splinters of pain into her skull and she moved carefully, as though her limbs might give way at any moment.

It was midday and the men were all busy. Even Maggie was not around to notice her emerging from the cabin. Kathleen started to walk down to the water's edge, to the rock where she often sat for hours staring blankly at the channel. Something told her that would be a mistake. The water would be gray, and would remind her of the ocean she had fled across to reach here.

Instead, she turned toward the trees, welcoming their concealment when she walked among them. She had discovered a secret place of her own, a half hour's walk from the logging camp. She headed there now.

The place was on the slope of the mountain, where a deep, swift-running stream tumbled down the slant of ground. Here, she didn't need the gray shell around her. Here, she could sit on the grassy bank with her shoes off, dangling her feet in the icy rush of water. It wasn't soundless or colorless here. Summer flowers bloomed, a riot of color, and the music of bird-song and bee-hum filled the glade with pleasant and comforting sound.

The air was rich with the scent of pine and the fragrance of wildflowers, and Kathleen closed her mind to everything, greedily absorbing the sights and sounds and scents. She dreamed, at peace with herself and the world.

She surfaced slowly to the sound of feet crunching pine needles and turned her head like a startled doe.

"Well, my lady," said Lord Ramage, "what an unexpected pleasure. We meet again, do we not? Are you happy to see me, Kathleen?"

From his great height, he smiled lazily down at her. By his side was a wide, enormous man, with a fearsome face like something out of one of Kathleen's nightmares.

Kathleen drew herself up into a knot. Her mouth opened, and from it came the long-bottled-up scream, a shrill, piercing sound that sent birds flapping up in fright.

"Shut her up, Fargo," Lord Ramage said crossly.

The scar-faced man bent down and struck Kathleen a stunning blow on the face with his fist. She was knocked flat, her skirts flying up. The hurt was terrible, and waves of blackness washed over her.

Dimly, she saw Fargo's face assume a lewd look. He said thickly, "Damn but she's a luscious wench, Your Lordship!"

"You want her, Fargo? Take her," Lord Ramage said with a languid flip of his hand. "I've had my fill of her long ago. Methinks you'll find her a cold fish."

"They all warm up when Jake Fargo has at them."

Kathleen felt her skirts being pushed up above her waist. Hands fumbled with her undergarments, brutally ripping them away.

As she became fully aware of the imminent violation, she screamed and attempted to rise. A boot landed on her shoulder, slamming her back to the ground.

"Make haste, man," Lord Ramage said in that same cross voice. "Someone may stumble upon us."

Then the man Fargo was upon her. He plunged into her with enough force to drive the breath from her lungs. His organ was enormous, and the cruel entry into her was very painful. The reek of whiskey was on Fargo's breath, and Kathleen could smell the rest of him—the sour, rank odor of a rutting animal.

She fought with fists and knees, screaming until her throat was raw. But Lord Ramage's foot was on her shoulder and Fargo's great weight pinned her to the ground. And all the while Fargo's body pounded at her like hammer blows. His breath whistled like steam escaping a teakettle. Then suddenly, a long, drawn-out grunt came from him and he lay still.

Kathleen was on the verge of fainting from terror, pain, and humiliation. Fargo, broad chest heaving for breath, rested his weight on his elbow propped on the ground alongside Kathleen's face, an inch from her mouth. In a last burst of defiance, she sank her teeth into the flesh of his arm and bit down hard.

Fargo yowled and jerked his arm away, blood spurting. "You bitch!" he snarled.

He drew back his fist and hit her high on the cheek. Pain burst in her skull and Kathleen welcomed the darkness that enclosed her like a refuge.

As Fargo got to his feet, Lord Ramage gazed

370

down at the unconscious Kathleen dispassionately. He prodded her with his boot toe. She didn't move.

"She bit me, bitch that she is," Fargo whined. "She drew blood."

Lord Ramage looked at him. He gestured. "Get rid of her, Fargo."

Fargo grinned savagely. He plucked the pickaroon from where he'd driven it into the ground, hefting it in his hand. "I'll split her skull like a melon, hey, Your Lordship?"

"No, you dolt. No need to leave her marked like that. 'Twill be known she was slain. We must make it appear she met her death by happenstance." His gaze moved around, finally lighting on the swift-running stream. He motioned. "There, toss her in the stream. She will drown before she regains consciousness."

Fargo picked up Kathleen in his arms as easily as he would a doll, strode to the bank of the stream, and threw her into the swift water.

The strong current caught her, sweeping her limp body against the rocks, then washing her away down the mountain, her long, dark hair streaming behind her in the water.

"There's one debt paid," Lord Ramage said softly. "Now for the rest of the Donnevan clan!"

Chapter Sixteen

Hearing a knock on the office door, Maggie glanced up. Olaf stood in the doorway, peering in. "Busy, little lady?"

"Never too busy for you, Olaf." She leaned back, stretching. "Come in."

Olaf spat into the dust outside the office and came in, sprawling his length before the desk, which had replaced the table.

"What's on your mind, Olaf?"

"Well, Maggie, I've been meaning to talk to you about this for some time, but after all that's happened . . ." He gestured, his long face melancholy.

"It's all right, Olaf. Poor Kathleen's been dead and gone these past eight months now. Grieving time is long past." She blinked back a tear. "I keep trying to convince myself that her death was a blessing, an end to her suffering. But dear God, I do miss her so, Olaf! I keep telling myself that it's partly my fault. If I hadn't been so selfish and impatient with her, she might have eventually become the old Kathleen that we all once knew and loved."

"Shouldn't go blaming yourself, girl. I thought the same thing when my Helga died last month down south. I kept thinking if'n I'd yust been with her it wouldn't have happened. But good sense finally told me it did no good me fretting away like that. Same thing with you."

"You're right, Olaf. I know you are, but . . . anyway," she said briskly, "enough of that. What did you want to see me about?"

"It's about the oxen and the skidroad, Maggie. We're logging so far up the mountain that it's getting too much for them beasts to work right. The distance is too dad-damned great even for them. Aside from that, you know what happened yust last week. That load of logs got away from them and tore loose. By Thor, it's fortunate them logs didn't kill one of the oxen. The mountain's getting too steep."

Maggie nodded. "I know. I've realized that myself."

"So, the way I figure it, we're going to have to do one of two things . . . we're going to have to move our whole operation, kit and caboodle, to another location nearer the water. Or we're going to have to start logging the low land either north or south."

"No, neither one," Maggie said decisively. "I don't wish to start on either side yet, and I certainly have no intention of moving camp. We'd be too far from the sawmill. Besides, the trees up

374

where we are now are the best timber we've struck yet. I want to clear it off before someone else gets at it." Her mouth got a bitter twist. "Like Lord Ramage and Jake Fargo, for instance. They get a chance at that fine stand of timber, they'll log it clean as a whistle. You know how little they care for stumpage rights. They're land pirates, a disgrace to the Territory!"

"Well, they ain't given us much trouble so far."

"No? How about the two loggers we found under that felled tree? How about the axe blade buried in that log a month back, ruining a circular saw? That cost a pretty penny to replace. And the fire halfway up the mountain a month before that? If it hadn't rained at the right time, the fire could have burned every tree on our mountain!"

"They all could have been by chance, girl. Loggers do get careless and let trees fall and kill them. And I've seen some strange objects buried in tree trunks. The axe blade could have been broken off in that tree trunk years back by some logger who gave up in disgust. Trees do grow around such things, yust like a person's wound heals. And the fire . . . well, dad-damnit, a fire is something we all have to watch out for. Sun boring through a sliver of glass can start it, a bolt of lightning, a careless hunter dumping out his pipe, anything like that."

"All true, I know. But I don't believe it for a wee minute. I feel it in my bones. Lord Ramage was behind it all. Whisht! Do *you* believe it was all pure chance?"

Olaf sighed. "Nah, I guess I don't, Maggie girl. But that ain't solving our problem here. You've always got a scheme in mind. How do we manage to

375

keep logging up on that there mountain and still get the logs down to the sawmill?"

Maggie leaned back. "We're going to build a log chute."

"A chute?" Olaf scratched his chin. "Yah, I've heard of such, but I ain't never seen one. All logging I've done has been close to the water."

"I've seen a couple of log chutes in operation on my trips. Both were quite primitive and I can think of several ways to improve them."

Olaf was grinning. "Yah, I'm sure."

"One I saw was little more than a trough gouged out of the hillside, and I'm sure it didn't work well, or for very long. Gravity, Olaf, is the key to it. This one I saw had a team of horses on a towpath alongside it, pulling the logs, and it was actually only a different version of the skidroad. What we're going to do is make our trough with peeled logs, or something better, and keep it well-greased with fish oil, lard, or something of that nature. We've got a pretty steep slope, so the logs should whiz right down to the cove and the log pond with no trouble. . . ."

"Whoa, Maggie!" Olaf held up his hand. "There you go, running ahead of me again. 'Spose I yust start some of the boys peeling the logs, and when they're ready, you can take it from there."

Maggie smiled sheepishly. "All right, Olaf. You get started, and I'll tell you the rest later."

Olaf got to his feet, still grinning. "I'm dad-damned happy to see you taking an interest again. By Thor, I am!"

Maggie's smile lingered on after he had left. He

was right; it was the first time she had showed her usual enthusiasm since Kathleen's death.

Her smile faded. *Poor Kathleen! To suffer as she had, to travel all those thousands of miles to reach her family and then to drown in a stream!* Maggie would never forget that awful night when Kathleen was discovered missing. Frantic with fear, she had turned all the men out in a night-long search of the forest. Shortly after dawn, Kathleen's body had been discovered wedged between two rocks in the stream. Her clothes had been torn, and her poor body battered and bruised from tumbling over and over down the mountain stream. They never did find the spot where she had fallen in.

Maggie was perceptive enough to realize that much of her overwhelming grief came from the thought that Kathleen might have drowned herself. Taking into consideration her frame of mind at the time, it was not impossible, and the thought that it might have happened that way tore Maggie apart. She had never voiced this suspicion to her brothers and apparently no such thought had ever entered their minds.

Maggie sighed now, trying to put the sad memories out of her mind. It was over and past and Kathleen would never be with them again. Maggie looked down at herself. She had worn black since that dreadful day. It was long past the time to stop grieving and return to living. Poor Lars! She had given him a bad time of it. He had respected her mourning without protest for months, but eventually he had lost patience, and asked her to resume their Sunday outings. The first few times he had pressed her, Maggie had flared up, accusing him of being unfeeling. Only two months ago had she finally agreed to go with him to their meadow and they had returned several times since.

Each time had been dismal. The stream running through their meadow, while not the one in which Kathleen had drowned, reminded Maggie of her sister's shocking death. She could not bring herself to respond to Lars' lovemaking—it seemed a sacrilege!

The last time they had gone had been three Sundays back. Again, it hadn't gone well. Finally, Lars had reared up in disgust. Standing tall over her prone figure, he spoke to her in the angriest voice he had ever used. "This is the last time I come here with you, Maggie, until you are yourself again! I'm sorry about your sister, but you're letting your grief ruin your *own* life!"

Sitting up, Maggie snapped, "Maybe you'd better go back to your Nancy Woods . . . if she'll have you!"

"I have thought about it and I may. I damned well may!"

With that, he stalked off across the meadow, leaving Maggie to get back to camp alone. He hadn't spoken directly to her since. Of course he was right. The words he had spoken to her that day in the meadow were almost the same words she had used to Kathleen and they were still true. Excessive grieving helped no one and served only to prolong pain.

She got to her feet and left the office for her living quarters. There, she quickly changed from the black dress, selecting the brightest colored garment she possessed to put on. Then she started toward the cookhouse with the black dress under her arm.

Just before she reached the cookhouse, Lars came out the door chewing on a slice of meat between two pieces of bread. At the sight of her, his step slowed; his face turning hard as granite and he started to detour around her. Then he stopped, a pleased grin spreading across his face.

"Maggie! You're not wearing black!"

"Whisht! It's sharp eyes you have, Lars Jorgenson." His face darkened, and he started to whirl away. Quickly, Maggie reached out and touched his cheek. "I'm sorry, Lars. I was teasing. To prove my good intentions, I'm going to burn this in Mother Be-Damn's cookstove." She shook the black dress at him. "No more black."

His smile came back. "I'm glad, Maggie."

"Will you forgive me for the way I've been acting of late?"

"Of course."

"Dear Lars." She stood on tiptoe and kissed him. His big hands caught and held her to him for just a moment. Then he stepped back, face reddening, his gaze darting around.

Maggie laughed. "Don't fret, no one saw. Even if they did, let them gawk. Lars . . . have you been in to see your Nancy?"

His face reddened even more and he looked down. He mumbled. "No, I thought on it, but I kept hoping . . ."

"Then, sir, would you share a picnic basket with me this Sunday?"

"I would, I certainly would!" he said fervently.

379

"This time I promise to be . . . 'the old Maggie.' "

She started on into the cookhouse.

"Maggie . . . "

"Yes, Lars?"

"Have you heard about Lord Ramage and the Jonas Kirk house?"

Maggie said tightly, "I've heard about His Lordship living there, yes."

"More than that. He has bought it. Captain Sayward, who was handling it for Mrs. Kirk, told me last week."

"Dear God, how ironic!" she said grimly. "One of the most villainous men who ever lived owning the house where Jonas once lived, the gentlest man I ever knew."

The work on the log chute went quickly, even with the improvements Maggie thought of. For instance, instead of peeled logs, she decided to construct the deep trough out of smoothly hewn timbers—a wide one at the bottom and narrower ones on each side set at a slight slant.

The log chute had to extend up the mountain two miles to the spot where they were logging. To complete it, they had to use dynamite to blast a cut in an intervening hill, and it was necessary to build a rather rickety trestle across a deep depression in the mountainside.

Maggie supervised the building of the trestle personally. She realized that when the logs came whistling down the chute, a great deal of vibration would be set up, so she devised a system of elaborate cross braces made of thick timbers from the bottom of the gully all the way up to the top, where the chute rested on V-shaped supports.

When it was completed, Olaf shook his head gloomily, and spat. "It looks dad-damned shaky to me. I wouldn't be at all surprised if it collapses and dumps all the logs into that gully!"

"It will stand more vibration than you think, Olaf," Maggie said. "Before you go throwing buckets of cold water on my idea, why don't you wait and see if it works? Haven't most of my ideas worked?"

"Yah, you're right there, Maggie," Olaf said lugubriously. "Yust call me Gloomy Gus. We scandies are known for looking on the dark side of things."

"It's all right, Olaf." Maggie smiled. "I need someone like you to dampen down my enthusiasms from time to time. I'm glad you're working for me." She slid a kiss off his whiskery cheek.

"How about the younger Jorgenson, yah?" His grin was sly. "You're not glad about him?"

Maggie knew she was blushing, but she said quietly, "Yes, Olaf. I'm glad about Lars. He's a dear man, and has helped me over some rough spots."

Finally the log chute was completed. Maggie, wearing her working clothes, walked the full length of it, from the logging location all the way down to the cove. It looked sturdy enough, and she was confident it would work. Despite her confidence, however, she had a few nagging doubts. Many things could go wrong. She could have miscalculated on the strength of the cross struts supporting the chute over the gully, for instance. Or any number of a hundred other things could go amiss.

Behind her as she walked down the mountain came the grease dauber, the same Indian lad they had hired to grease the skidroad. Instead of a bucket and a swab, he now toted a can of lubricant. Each gallon can had a hook so it could be hung on branches at calculated distances along the chute. When one can was empty, there was a full one waiting on a pine branch. Maggie had decided to use a combination of fish oil and bear grease as lubricants. The grease dauber walked along, aiming a thin stream of the lubricant from the narrow spout of the can along the sides and bottom of the log chute.

Maggie smiled to herself. Again, Kevin had set up a howl, demanding that *he* do the chute greasing. Maggie had stood firm against it. True, he had grown like a weed the past year, but she didn't wish to see him becoming a grease dauber, although she knew the Indian boy couldn't do it by himself when the chute was operating full time and she would have to provide him with a helper. It was too much for one person to handle.

Among the mill hands she hired recently was a man who had once been a schoolteacher back East. He was a toper, and apt to go on a spree from time to time, yet he was a fine teacher when sober. Out here there was little need of a schoolteacher, and a drunken one at that. Maggie had offered him a few dollars extra a week if he would teach Kevin how to read and write and do his figures. Kevin had balked, sulked and done everything possible to avoid it, but she had been adamant. He was in the office right now, having his daily lesson.

Reaching the log pond alongside the sawmill, Maggie stopped, looking back up the mountain. Then she glanced at the pocket watch she had borrowed from Lars. It was two minutes short of twelve o'clock and Olaf had told her that he would send the first logs on their way at twelve sharp. Maggie had made some rough calculations, taking into consideration the steepness of the slope, and figured that the first log should arrive at approximately two minutes after twelve, sliding down the chute at sixty miles an hour after it had built up momentum.

She waited, glancing impatiently from the watch face up to the chute. It was nearing the two-minute mark . . .

She looked up again at a rumbling, clattering sound. She saw the first log coming and others strung out behind it. She let out a yell of sheer exuberance. It was working!

The first log arrived smoking from the friction of the long glide and flew out of the mouth of the chute, which was about ten feet high and projected out over the log pond. The log hit the water with a tremendous, sizzling splash and others followed right on the heels of it.

Maggie started up the slope, just as Mother Be-Damn came hurrying out of the cookhouse. "Pretty little Boston scare Mother Be-Damn." She flapped her voluminous apron. "Yell like being wrestled to the ground by bad man!"

"It's working, Mother Be-Damn," Maggie yelled as she hurried past. "It's working!"

She went on up the mountain, staying close to the chute, watching with delight as the logs slid past, often in bunches, the ones behind bumping against the front log.

A thought came to her. If there was some way water could be made to flow down the chute, it would speed up the operation considerably. There *was* water available up the mountain, a swift stream not far from where they were logging. It could be diverted. The log chute would have to be bigger, much bigger, to accommodate both water and the logs. But it was something to think about, something for the future.

Maggie plodded on alongside the chute.

Maggie was wrong about Kevin being at his lessons. He had sneaked off and made his way up the mountain; he wasn't about to miss seeing the first logs go down the chute. He loved Maggie dearly—she was a Donnevan and his sister—but she was too bossy by far and didn't give him credit for having the brains of a goose. Couldn't she see that he was grown up? Or near enough to it? Kevin considered himself close to being a man now and figured he should be treated like one. A boy grew into a man in a hurry in this country; everybody said so.

Although he knew that Maggie was adamantly opposed, Kevin was bound and determined to grow up to be a faller. How he loved to watch Lars and Patrick and the other fallers on their platforms, axes flashing in the sun. Watching them in action, they reminded Kevin of the legends he'd heard of the knights of old doing battle with dragons. He should be out there with them all the time, learning as much as he could. Maggie kept talking of the danger to a boy his age. Kevin scoffed at danger.

She wouldn't buy him logger's clothes. How many times had he asked for calked boots, for instance? In the end he had made his own. Taking an old pair, telling Maggie that they were worn out so she would buy him a new pair, he had laboriously fastened hobnails in the soles, and thus made a passable pair of calked boots. He had tried them in secret several times on the logs floating in the log pond, and they bit into the logs just fine. He had become quite expert at log rolling, able to keep a log spinning under his boots for minutes at a time without falling off.

After sneaking away from camp, wearing the calked boots, Kevin toiled halfway up the mountain, well above the trestle, and found a good vantage point—a small knoll covered with thick underbrush. He concealed himself just in time, before Maggie came down on her inspection trip, followed by the grease dauber.

Kevin worked his lips, turned his head aside, and spat in a fair imitation of Olaf Jorgenson. He could have done that job, Maggie to the contrary. But come to think of it, maybe it was for the best. Who had ever heard of a faller starting out as a grease dauber?

A short time later, Kevin was alerted by a rumbling sound. He stood up, looking east along the chute. A chill coursed down his spine—logs were moving down the chute, like enormous, disjointed reptiles. Even as Kevin watched, they picked up speed, until they were a blur before his eyes.

In his excitement he moved over to the chute. Here, it was laid right on the ground. If he wanted to, he could reach right out and touch the passing logs. Now he noticed that they would occasionally slow almost to a stop before picking up speed again. Looking downslope, he saw the reason. About fifty yards distant there was a slight hump in the slope, just enough to act as a momentary brake on the flow of logs and cause them to jam together.

As one great section of log stopped right in front of him, Kevin, without even thinking about it, climbed over the side of the chute and straddled the log. He heard a shout from up the mountain, but he didn't look around. Just then the logs began to move again. The one he straddled moved over the slight hump, then began to pick up speed. He was careful to keep his legs and feet drawn up out of the way, so they wouldn't get caught between the log and the sides of the chute.

Soon, the log was moving at great speed. It was the most exhilarating experience of Kevin's young life. He had a moment of fear as the log sped across the trestle. It seemed to him that the gully below was deep as a yawning chasm. Then he was safely past the trestle, moving faster and faster.

Remembering the times he had ridden logs in the pond alongside the sawmill, Kevin couldn't resist. He stood upright. For a heart-stopping moment, he almost lost his balance. Then the hobnails bit into the log, and he rode easily, regaining his balance. He felt ten feet tall. The stumps and the trees too small for logging flashed past him on both sides with blinding speed.

Then, ahead of him, Kevin saw that the logs had clogged again and he was fast approaching the butt end of a slower moving log. Panic struck at Kevin and he frantically tried to think of a way out of his predicament.

It was too late. The log he was riding struck the one ahead with a grinding thump, and Kevin was thrown high and far. A yell of fright erupted from him, as he saw the ground coming up to meet him.

Maggie was toiling up the slope, her head down, her eyes on the logs speeding down the chute, when she heard a shout. She looked up to see a body flying through the air about thirty yards in front of her. It took her a moment to recognize the figure.

Dear God, it was Kevin! She stood for a frozen instant, unable to believe her eyes. How *could* it be Kevin? He was down at camp having his lessons!

Then Kevin hit the ground, tumbling over and over. He fetched up hard against a pine stump and lay without moving.

Crying out his name, Maggie began to run toward him.

Chapter Seventeen

Kevin lay unmoving as Maggie raced up the slope toward him. As she fell to her knees beside him, she could not see his chest moving and she gave a harsh cry as she bent to put her ear to his chest. Hearing the faint beat, she murmured, "Thank God!"

Taking both his hands in hers, she began to chafe them. His small hands were cold as ice. "Kevin dear, speak to me!"

At the pound of footsteps behind her, she looked around to see Patrick bounding down the slope. Behind him came Lars and Dan.

"Patrick! It's wee Kevin. He's bad hurt!"

"Let me see." Patrick shoved her roughly aside, and cupped the back of Kevin's head in his hand, raising it.

Maggie clapped her hands over her mouth at the sight of the blood streaming from a wound in

Kevin's forehead. He moaned, then cried out in pain as Patrick raised him higher. His eyes fluttered open.

"Easy now, little brother, easy," Patrick said in a gentle voice. "Let me be after seeing where you're hurt."

His big hands probed gingerly over the boy's body. As he lifted Kevin's left arm, the lad cried out, his face going white.

"You're hurting him, Patrick!" Maggie started to kneel, and again Patrick pushed her aside.

"The lad has a broken arm, Maggie. That's all that ails him."

"All?" she echoed. "Poor, wee Kevin!"

Patrick turned an angry face to her. "Wee Kevin, is it? Maggie, you . . ."

Maggie wasn't listening. She had spied the hobnails on Kevin's boots. "Where did you get those calked boots?"

"I made them myself, Maggie," Kevin said weakly.

"*You* made them! Kevin, you deliberately disobeyed me! You have no business wearing such things!"

"And why not, pray?" Patrick said sternly. "It's time he was learning the logging business."

Maggie gasped. "What are you saying. Patrick? He's but a tad, and has no business being out in the woods at the risk of hurting himself. Just look at what has happened here! Doing an idiot thing like riding a log down the chute! He could have been killed. Now look at his poor arm, and all because he disobeyed me!"

"The blame is yours, Maggie."

Now Maggie's temper flared. "How can you say that? How can I be blamed?"

"Because you've been mollycoddling him. Kevin is no longer the lad he was back home. Look at him, sister. Look at him with open eyes. He's sprouting, coming into manhood. You have spoiled him, kept him away from learning the business. It's his right, the same as yours, or mine, or Dan's. He is a Donnevan, not some prissy city lad. I've watched you coddling him like a babe, and no longer will I stand still for it!"

"*You* won't stand still for it! Don't be forgetting, Patrick Donnevan, that *I* am in charge of the Donnevan Logging company!"

"I'm not forgetting, sister, and I'm not after disputing that fact. It's Kevin I'm talking about. And in this I'm having my way. When he is well, he goes to the trees with us, to learn."

Maggie stared at him with her mouth agape. This was a different Patrick than she had ever seen before. True, back in Ireland, during their voyage across the sea, and in San Francisco, he had resisted her stubbornly, but always he had given way. But now, looking at his set face and hard eyes, she realized that this time he would not give.

Patrick stooped and picked Kevin up in his arms. Without looking again at Maggie he started down the mountain with the boy.

Still dumbfounded, Maggie simply stood, staring after them.

At her side Dan said gently, "He's right, Maggie, is our Patrick. It's time you were facing up to the truth. Our little brother is growing up. You cannot

391

keep him tied to your skirts forever. Let loose of him."

"But he's still a boy! He might get hurt."

"It's all a part of growing up. If he's to learn the business, he has to take that chance." Dan's hand came to rest on her shoulder. "Let him go, Maggie."

As Dan went down the hill after Patrick, Maggie still didn't move. In her heart she knew that her brothers were right. In sheltering Kevin from harm, she was doing the lad an injustice. He was a Donnevan and it was his right to follow in the footsteps of his older brothers. But knowing the rightness of it didn't ease the feeling of loss that swept over her. She had lost Kathleen, and now Kevin . . .

Whisht! She shook herself. *Such foolishness!* She hadn't lost Kevin. She realized now that she *might* have lost him if she had continued overprotecting him. Given his nature, he likely would have rebelled in the end, and left his family, if there was no other way left open to him.

"Maggie?" Lars said gently.

Maggie gave a start. She had forgotten him. She said in a tart voice, "I suppose you agree with my brothers?"

He nodded. "I'm afraid I do, but since it was none of my affair, I said nothing."

She smiled with an effort. "You're right, you are *all* right. I see that now."

"Then shall we go down and see to Kevin?"

He held out his hand. Maggie took it, and they went down the mountain together.

Patrick had also been right about the extent of Kevin's injuries. When Kevin's arm was set, he was soon up and about. Reluctantly, Maggie loosened the reins on him, promising that he could go to the woods with the men as soon as his arm was completely healed—*provided* he would sit still for at least an hour's tutoring every day. On this point, she would not yield.

But the breaking of her younger brother's arm soon struck Maggie as a bad omen, the beginning of a sorry time for the Donnevans.

Things began going wrong all at once. There were several accidents, accidents for which there was no ready explanation. The sawmill boiler exploded early one morning. Although the boiler tender swore that he had dampened the fires down when the sawmill closed the night before, it had built up an overload of steam and exploded like a stick of dynamite. Another small fire broke out, and they were fortunate that it was spotted in time and put out. A section of the log chute was destroyed, and logs spilled out in great numbers, ending up in a pile of kindling at the bottom of the gully.

Maggie knew that it was all done deliberately, and by Lord Ramage's crew, yet she had no way of proving it.

It was expensive, time-consuming, and slowed their production, but Maggie doggedly doled out the money for a new boiler and the repair of the chute.

There was worse to come. She had been hiring a schooner to haul the lumber turned out by the sawmill into Seattle for sale and shipment on down to San Francisco.

One afternoon the schooner captain came to her office. Captain Coxe, a scrawny individual in his fifties, wore a hangdog look and stood before her twisting his cap between his hands. "I'm sorry, Miss Donnevan, but I can no longer haul your lumber for you."

Concealing a lurch of dismay, Maggie stared up at him. "Why not, Captain? I'm paying you the regular freight charges. Is it more money you're asking?"

"Naw, it ain't that, Miss Donnevan." Captain Coxe would not meet her eyes. "It's just that . . . well, I got all the business I can handle over along the Hood Canal without coming way over here."

There was something evasive about the man's manner, and Maggie knew instinctively that he wasn't telling the truth. She said in a hard voice, "I can sense when I'm being lied to, Captain Coxe, and I know you're lying to me. The truth now, I want the truth from you, and you'll not be leaving here until I have it!"

Captain Coxe heaved a weighty sigh. "All right, I'll tell you, but you ain't going to like it," he said in a rush. "I was warned off, told that if I continue to haul your lumber, I'd come to harm. Either that or my vessel would be scuttled and sunk to the bottom of the channel." He added defensively, "I'm a poor man, Miss Donnevan, and I got obligations, a family and such like. I can't take the risk."

"Who gave you this warning? Was it Lord Ramage, or his animal henchman, Jake Fargo?"

His gaze shifted away again. "I ain't saying.

Anyways, it don't matter who. Just take it from me that I believe the threat and deem it prudent to take heed."

Maggie stared at him, her thoughts a turmoil. She tapped a finger angrily on the desk. "Of course it was Lord Ramage, damn his black soul to perdition! Who else would bother?" She leaned forward. "I can see how you might be fearful of the man, and I will not press you, Captain Coxe. Can you recommend another boat to transport my lumber to Seattle?"

"I'm afraid not. You see . . ." His voice trailed off.

"He warned you not to send anyone else my way?" she said shrewdly. "Didn't he? Or else he said the same fate would be in store for any who dared?"

Captain Coxe sighed again. "I'm afraid that's about the gist of it. I'm sorry," he said wretchedly. "I feel bad about this. So if you'll excuse me, I'll be on my way."

"Wait!" Maggie rapped the desk with a knuckle. "Hold just a minute, Captain. Let me think."

The captain waited, fidgeting, while Maggie pondered her alternatives. She simply had to have means of transporting the lumber to Seattle or cease operations. Within a very short time the lumber would stack up on them, and without the money from the sale of the lumber, she couldn't meet the payroll. A schooner of her own? She dismissed that at once. She had no money to purchase a boat, and the very thought of going into debt again was inconceivable.

Another possibility occurred to her and she sat

up. "Would you carry me as a passenger to Seattle? Or did Lord Ramage," she made her voice biting, "warn you away from that, too?"

"Nothing was said about that." He squared his shoulders. "Yes, Miss Donnevan, I will take you back to Seattle with me. And without charging you passage. I owe you that much."

Andrew Kane was polishing the brass on the *Belle*, tied off at the Seattle wharf, when he heard the tapping of heels on the planks. He glanced up, rearing back in astonishment at the sight of Maggie Donnevan tripping toward the tug, a vision in pink and white, all ribbons and furbelows, twirling a dainty, pink parasol. She looked up at him, and said, "It's glad I am to see you at anchor here, Andrew. I feared you might be busy and out on the Sound somewhere."

Taking the cold pipe from his mouth, Andrew stepped to the rail. He said in mimicry, "And it's glad I am to see you, Miss Donnevan."

Maggie sighed. "Whisht! Must you always mock me?" She added tartly, "If you're really glad to see me, why don't you help me on board?"

"My apologies, Maggie. You caught me by surprise." With alacrity he hooked the short steps to the deck, then went halfway down to take her hand and help her up. On deck, he gestured to his rough, not-too-clean clothes. "Like I said, Maggie, I wasn't expecting you."

"And why should you be?"

Andrew relaxed, aplomb restored. "To what do I owe the pleasure, madam?"

She looked at him thoughtfully. "I've come to ask your help again, Andrew."

"I'm at your service, Maggie." He spread his hands. "As always."

"You may change your mind when you hear what I have to tell you."

"I doubt that. Wait, I'll fetch chairs."

He went below and returned with two chairs. He placed them on the deck in a spot of sun. "Maggie, I heard about your sister. My condolences. It must have been a great shock."

"It was that, and Kathleen is a part of the story I must tell you."

"Then tell away." He motioned to a chair, waited until she was seated, and sat down himself. He began filling his pipe.

"Have you heard of Lord Ramage, Andrew?"

"I have heard rumors of some English Lord now in the logging business at Port Ludlow, but I have not had the pleasure of meeting him." He grinned. "I have little in common with nobility."

"It would not be a pleasure, I assure you," she said grimly. "Lord Ramage was the Donnevans' landlord back in Ireland."

His pipe going now, his gaze was intent. "It was from him you stole the diamonds, wasn't it?"

"Whisht! Sometimes, Andrew Kane, I think you must be fey! You seem to read my mind." She took a deep breath. "But it was not myself, it was my sister, Kathleen, and for a good cause."

"I'm listening, Maggie," he said quietly.

She told him then, beginning with the death of John Donnevan, holding nothing back. By the time she was finished, his pipe had gone out. He hadn't interrupted her once.

Chewing on the pipe stem, Andrew looked at her gravely. "I certainly cannot find it in me to blame you, or your sister, for what you did. I don't look upon her theft as a crime, either. This Lord Ramage sounds like a proper blackguard, and quite mad as well. For a man to go to such lengths to gain vengeance is difficult to believe."

"Should you meet him, you would believe. He is a horrible man, the devil's own spawn!"

"His henchman, Fargo, I have met twice and I find it hard to believe a more dastardly man exists."

"Lord Ramage is all of that, but he is intelligent as well. Jake Fargo is nothing but an animal, with little more wit than one."

"Now this English Lord has stopped your shipping, frightening off all the boat owners?"

"He has that." She leaned forward. "Don't you see, without the means to transport my lumber, it will rot in the yard, and I cannot continue to pay my men."

Andrew sighed. "Of course, you've come to ask of me the use of the *Belle*."

"I have Andrew, well knowing it is asking a great deal." She added, "If you are also frightened, I will understand."

His eyes flashed. "It is not necessary to goad me, Maggie."

Instantly contrite, she said, "I'm sorry. That was spiteful of me. But I am in desperate straits."

"I can realize that." Now his eyes took on a shine of excitement. "I am not afraid of them. In fact, I sometimes find the life of a tugboat captain

398

boring in the extreme. A little excitement and danger should spice it up a little. Yet there are a few problems I can foresee." He tapped the pipe stem against his cheek. "A tugboat, as you may know, wasn't designed to transport lumber. I have precious little cargo space below. Much of your lumber will have to be carried on deck, lashed down. The *Belle's* capacity will probably be half that of a schooner, or even less."

"I realize that, but the schooner I have been using only made perhaps two, never more than three, trips a month."

He was nodding. "I would be going back and forth constantly. What I am saying is, I would have to be employed full time."

"That I know as well, but I will see that you are compensated. I am willing to pay more than the usual freight rates. If I have to suffer some loss of profit, I am willing to do so," she said vehemently. "Anything to best Lord Ramage."

"And I would likely have to carry an armed guard, perhaps two."

"I am willing to pay their wages, too."

"It seems we have a bargain then." He cocked his head, his eyes dancing with that satanic amusement. He drawled, "We poker players have a saying . . . sweeten the pot. Would you be willing to sweeten the pot, Miss Donnevan? I am not talking about money now."

Her head went back, and she looked directly into his laughing eyes. "That too, if need be."

"But not so willingly as paying additional money?"

Her heart began to pound and her lips went dry.

"I give myself willingly to no man under such terms. But if it takes that, sir, to strike your bargain, I will agree."

"And I take no woman against her will." He held up a hand, palm out. "And pray do not mention Port Townsend to me again." He smiled lazily. "I am a patient man. I'll wait until you're willing."

"Then you shall have a long wait," she said. "I will never come to you willingly, Andrew Kane!"

"We shall see," he said enigmatically.

"Now what does that mean? Whisht! Are you after saying? . . ."

"I'm after saying nothing, my dear Maggie. But there is another old saying . . . all comes to him who waits."

"Patience is a virtue I have never observed in you, sir."

"Perhaps I have learned." He got to his feet. "When will you be ready to depart?" He extended a hand to help her up.

"Within the hour. No longer than it will take to pick up my belongings at the hotel."

Early in the afternoon, the *Belle* chugged across the channel directly toward the harbor of Port Ludlow.

When she saw where they were heading, Maggie hurried to Andrew in the wheelhouse. "Why are you heading into Port Ludlow?"

"I have a few things Captain Sayward ordered on board, Maggie. I want to deliver them before I take on a load of lumber. Then, on the way back, I can bypass Port Ludlow entirely."

"But what if Lord Ramage and Fargo are waiting?"

He shot her an incredulous look. "Come, my dear Maggie! This Englishman really has you spooked. Why should he bother us now? I have no lumber. He doesn't even know *you* are on board."

"I'm sorry, Andrew," she said shakily. "But I don't wish to even go near Port Ludlow so long as that terrible man lives here."

"I can understand your apprehensions, Maggie, but it'll be all right," he said. "You remain on board with Tod Dorsey and I'll attend to my errand. I'll only be gone fifteen minutes, no longer."

"That could be too long," she said, but inaudibly, turning away. Instead of standing at the rail as they entered the harbor, she went below to the cabin. There was no way to lock the cabin door, or she would have done so. She realized that Andrew was undoubtedly right. But then he had never encountered the icy evil of Lord Ramage and Maggie had a feeling deep in her bones that she was in peril any time she came close to the man.

The tugboat bumped against the wharf. In a few minutes Andrew opened the cabin door, peering in. "There you are! I was wondering . . . " He shook his head. "This man really does frighten you, doesn't he?"

"To the very marrow of my bones. This near him, I seem to feel a deep chill. Maybe it's just a fancy, I don't know."

Andrew had gone to the trunk against one wall. He opened it, took out his Colt, and rammed it into his belt.

"I am sorry, Maggie. I wish I'd had time to scout

up a couple of armed men before we left Seattle. I'll tell Tod to keep a sharp eye out and I'll be back before you know it." He cupped her face and kissed her on the cheek. "You are dear to me, Maggie, whether you realize it or not, and I promise that I will let nothing happen to you."

He was gone then, and Maggie sat tense and apprehensive on the sofa-bunk. After the passage of several minutes, she heard the sound of angry voices above, followed by something that sounded like a heavy weight hitting the deck. Footsteps come toward the cabin. In a flash Maggie was off the bunk and through the cabin door. If either Lord Ramage or Jake Fargo were out there, she certainly didn't intend for them to corner her in the small cabin.

They were there, both of the evil pair. A flashing glance showed her Tod Dorsey sprawled unconscious on the deck by the steps down to the wharf.

Lord Ramage motioned to Fargo and they stopped their progress toward the cabin. "Well, Mistress Donnevan, this is indeed a pleasure. I did not expect you."

"Indeed it is, damned if it ain't!" Fargo trumpeted. His eyes were alight and seemed to Maggie to harbor small, leaping flames. He licked his thick lips. "Can I have her, Your Lordship?"

"You would like that, would you, Fargo?" Lord Ramage asked casually.

"That I would. She's a juicy piece, she is."

"That assessment I cannot dispute, but this one is not yours, Fargo." Lord Ramage's thin lips peeled back in a wolfish smile. "This one is mine. She will be the replacement for poor, mad Kathleen, who drowned herself."

"How dare you say that about Kathleen? If she was mad, it was you made her so!"

"What matter?" Lord Ramage gave a careless shrug. "She is gone and can no longer cater to my needs. You will take her place, Maggie Donnevan."

He moved toward her languidly, and Maggie slid along the side of the wheelhouse. He reminded her of a reptile slithering across the deck.

Still backing up, Maggie said, "You wouldn't dare touch me, not right here on the wharf!"

"Who's to say me nay, Mistress Donnevan? In a manner of speaking, I *own* Port Ludlow now. I provide employment for a great number of people, and they look upon me with awe, having never before encountered a member of the nobility. . .'."

"Nobility!" Maggie spat the word at him. "You, sir, are cow dung! In this country, no man is better than another because of his birth!"

"Tut, tut, it is not befitting a lady to use such language. But then methinks you are far from being a lady. One who consorts with thieves, uses the proceeds of their thievery for her own advantage, and wears men's clothing, scarcely appears the lady. But since this primitive country is sadly lacking in ladies of the gentry, you will have to do. Besides," his voice trickened, "I have wanted you since that long ago evening when I saw you naked in Ramage Castle. Damme, if I haven't!"

He took another sliding step and Maggie said, "If you so much as touch me, I'll kill you!"

His mouth shaped that cold smile. "I think not. Together with Fargo here, we can subdue you. I like my women with fire and spirit. Poor Kathleen had all the fire of a barnyard fowl!"

He reached out a hand for her. Just before he touched her a shot rang out and a bullet buried itself in the wood of the wheelhouse, scant inches from his hand. Lord Ramage froze, his head turning.

Andrew stood on the boat steps, just his head and shoulders showing. Smoke eddied up from the Colt gripped in both hands. His voice was cold. "I would strongly advise you gents to back off. Slow and easy now." He looked directly at Lord Ramage. "The next bullet lodges in your skull, friend. I assume you are the English Lord of whom I have heard so much, none of it good." Andrew's eyes danced. "I have never killed a member of the nobility before. I do believe it would pleasure me."

Lord Ramage backed up a few steps. "I am Lord Ramage, yes. Who are you, sir?"

"Andrew Kane, commoner, Your Lordship." Andrew was smiling sardonically. He came on up the steps and onto the deck. His eyes flicked at Fargo, whose hand was inching toward the pistol in his belt. "Touch that weapon, Fargo, and you'll be missing a hand!"

Jake Fargo muttered a curse and let his hand fall away from the pistol.

"That's better," Andrew said cheerfully. "You look lost without your pickaroon, Jake. What happened? Did someone break it over your head . . . I hope?" His voice hardened. "What did I tell you would happen if you ever offered harm to Maggie Donnevan, Jake? You don't listen well, do you?"

"Now that you know who I am, fellow," Lord

Ramage said arrogantly, "you would deem it wise to not interfere. I do not easily brook being balked."

"So I have been told. But then neither do I." Andrew moved down the deck to where Tod Dorsey lay sprawled. He never once removed his gaze from Lord Ramage and Fargo. He prodded Dorsey with his toe. "Tod, are you all right?"

Tod Dorsey groaned and sat up. His liquor-reddened face was the color of ashes. "I reckon so . . ." He felt the back of his head and winced. "Except'n the back of my skull feels as squishy as an over-ripe peach." His voice took on a whine. "I'm sorry, Mister Kane, but that pair snuck up on me and bashed me on the noggin."

"Never mind that now," Andrew said sharply. He gestured with the Colt. "Suppose the fine pair of you leave my boat. Right now!"

"We will leave, Kane," Lord Ramage said in a choked voice. "But heed my warning . . . you will rue this day!"

"Perhaps. But in my philosophy, I believe in letting tomorrow take care of itself."

Lord Ramage motioned to Fargo with a jerk of his head, and the two men started for the steps. There, Lord Ramage faced about. In a frigid voice he said, "If it is in your mind to help this wretched female, I would strongly advise you to reconsider, Kane. If you do come to her assistance, some fine day you will discover this miserable tugboat of yours on the bottom of the channel!"

"Scat, both of you!" Andrew fired, the bullet kicking up splinters from the deck between Lord Ramage's feet.

Without flinching, Lord Ramage looked down at the deck, then directed his menacing glare at Andrew. "You will regret this, sir. You have the word of Lord Ramage on it!"

"Good day to you, *Lord* Ramage."

With Lord Ramage proceeding first, the pair went down the steps. Once safely on the wharf, Fargo looked back at the *Belle*, and shook his fist. Lord Ramage walked on without once looking back.

"He's a cool one, your English Lord. I'll have to say that for him," Andrew said in grudging admiration.

Maggie shivered, and moved close to him. "I think he has blood of ice, like a snake. He frightens me, that man!"

"My apologies, Maggie." He put a comforting arm around her shoulders. "You were right, I should never have left you alone. It seems I underestimated His Lordship." He raised his voice. "Tod, you able to feed the boiler?"

"I . . . I think so, Mister Kane."

"Then get up a head of steam, and let's get the hell out of here!"

Although it was a warm day, Maggie huddled inside the wheelhouse, shivering as though from the ague. It wasn't until their cove was in sight that she felt safe again.

Andrew anchored as close in as he could to the sawmill. Before going ashore in the dinghy, Maggie said, "It's grateful to you I am, Andrew Kane. Once again, you have saved me from ruin."

"Ruin?" His eyebrows elevated. "I thought I had accomplished your ruination in Port Townsend?"

406

"Nothing you can say at this moment can get my ire up. I'm too beholden to you."

"Again, it was my pleasure, Maggie." His eyes dancing, he kissed her on the cheek. "I think I'm going to enjoy balking our Lord Blackguard. He, I do believe, is a man I could truly come to hate. Expect to see me every two or three days, Maggie. Don't worry about your lumber, I'll see to it."

"You *will* be careful?" she said anxiously. "He will stop at nothing."

"Why, I didn't think you . . ." He broke off, turning serious. "I will be careful, Maggie, you can be sure. In Seattle I will hire a pair of armed men. Hopefully, I can find a couple as snake-mean as Jake Fargo. Now, get yourself ashore and start sending your lumber out to me."

It took a little over two hours to load the tugboat down with lumber. At a farewell toot from the *Belle*'s whistle, Maggie hurried down to the beach to watch Andrew's departure. She was astounded to see lumber stacked so high on both sides of the wheelhouse that it was impossible to see it.

She turned to Olaf, who had been supervising the loading of the lumber. "How can he even see where he's going? Why did he stack the lumber so high around the wheelhouse?"

Olaf laughed, turned his head aside, and spat a brown stream. "He . . ."

At that moment a fusillade of rifle fire broke out. Maggie looked toward the sound of the shots. South of the cove, she could see several tiny figures lined up on the cliff above the channel. It was too far to recognize any of them, or even see their rifles, but even as she watched, shots rang out again, and Maggie could see puffs of smoke.

In alarm she looked in the direction of the *Belle*. The tugboat was chugging straight ahead, and seemed undeterred by the rifle fire. Already it was moving out of range. Just then Andrew gave a derisive toot-toot of the tug's whistle.

Olaf laughed again. "Your Andrew Kane's no dolt. He told me of the possibility of being fired on from shore. But they'll have a dad-damned hard time of it getting a bullet in to him behind all that there lumber!"

Relieved at Andrew's escaping unharmed, Maggie looked at Olaf and saw that Lars had walked up in time to hear his father's remark. His face reddened and he gave her a scowling look.

Maggie said quickly, "Olaf, he's not *my* Andrew Kane..."

Lars had already turned away, and was walking off with angry, lunging strides.

Chapter Eighteen

After Maggie's and Andrew's confrontation with Lord Ramage, life went smoothly for the Donnevans. There were no more "accidents," nothing to slow down their lumber production. Andrew made at least two trips a week, two men armed with rifles on board. But the *Belle* was not bothered again by Lord Ramage's crew.

Three weeks after that confrontation, Andrew came ashore while the tugboat was being loaded and sought out Maggie.

"I'm beginning to think that the guards are an unnecessary expense, Maggie. The Englishman seems to have given up. Perhaps he thinks it isn't worth the trouble and expense to harass you further."

"No, Andrew," she said quickly. "I don't trust him. He's sly and devious, is Lord Ramage. It could be he's hoping we'll think he's given up, hoping we'll lower our guard; then he'll strike. We'll keep the guards. It's naught out of your pockets, sir. I'm paying their wages."

"True." He gave her that lazy grin. "Besides, if he really has given up, there'd be no more use for my services, would there? You could go back to using schooners, saving yourself money; and well knowing your thrifty nature, I'm sure you'd do just that, casting me aside like an old shoe."

"You can hardly be considered an old shoe, Andrew," she retorted, then was sorry she'd said it. She had determined to keep their relationship on a strictly business level; she would not play the coquette with him again. She'd had enough grumblings from Lars about Andrew Kane and had finally succeeded in convincing Lars that there was nothing between them.

Andrew just grinned. "I hope not, Miss Donnevan. An old shoe is considered comfortable and I would never want you to think me that." He tipped his hat and said gravely, "Good day to you, Maggie. I'll see you next trip."

Despite the peace they were enjoying, Maggie still felt an occasional quiver of apprehension along her nerve-ends. It often seemed like the lull before a great and violent storm that might come at any time.

Kevin's arm had knitted cleanly and he was out in the woods every day now, after faithfully having his lessons. *Maybe*, Maggie thought, *his healing is a good omen, as I thought the breaking of his poor arm was a bad one!*

She scoffed at herself for harboring such a fancy and plunged into work. There was enough of that;

410

with the chute speeding the logs to the mill, the sawmill whining along merrily, and the fallers' axes flashing, bringing great trees crashing down—it was a fine and busy time.

The lazy, summer Sunday afternoons with Lars in the meadow were fine, too. They were easy with one another now—when Lars wasn't fretting about Andrew Kane.

The Sunday following her talk with Andrew, Maggie went with Lars to the meadow. It was a hot, cloudless day, the sky a brilliant blue. The stream meandering through the meadow had dwindled down to a trickle.

Lars frowned as he stood gazing down at it. He said gravely, "I have been logging around the Sound for some years now, Maggie, and this is the driest year I have ever witnessed. Even the old-timers are concerned. They can't remember when the rainfall has been so little. If it continues without rain, the forests are going to become as dry as tinder and we could have terrible fires."

From the spread blanket, Maggie said, "I do believe what your father says is true, dear. He told me that the Swedes tend toward gloominess. It's such a nice day and everything is going so well, I do not wish to trouble my mind with possible dire happenings." She held out her arms. "Come here, Lars, and love me. I will make you forget all thoughts of doom."

His face brightened with a smile. "You always do, Maggie darling." He came to the blanket, kneeling beside her. "You are like a tonic to me."

"Whisht! It's medicine I am now, is it?" she said impishly.

411

"Not medicine, Maggie. It's like . . . " He searched for the right word. "It's all mixed up in my head. It's love, and uplifting, almost reverence. From you I get a feeling like many men must get from strong drink."

"Don't revere me, Lars!" she said crossly. "I'm human, sometimes too much so, I fear."

She unbuttoned his shirt and ran her hands inside, her palms gliding across his broad chest. The silken wiriness of the mat of hairs there tickled her hands, sending a shiver over her body. She leaned to him with parted lips.

The familiar heaviness stole over her as his kiss stirred her blood. One big hand cupped her head, holding her mouth firm against his. The other stroked her back and shoulders. Gently, he stretched her out on the blanket.

"Sweet Maggie."

She murmured deep in her throat and arched her body off the ground as he began to remove her clothes. In the beginning Lars had been awkward about that, but now he knew just where to unbutton and what to undo, and Maggie was sure he could have undressed her in the darkest night.

It occurred to her for the first time that they had never made love at night. Somehow that seemed fitting. Their loving was an openness, a thing best done in light and spill of sunshine, nothing secret or furtive, nothing held back.

The warm breeze caressed her nakedness and Maggie lay back with her eyes closed, waiting with pounding heart as Lars stood and removed his own clothes. Then he was back, hands gentle on her shoulders, his lips demanding.

He was ready, she could feel the hardness of him. She shifted slightly to accommodate his entry into her.

At his first thrust ecstasy swept through her like a warm pour of honey. She looped her arms around his neck and held his mouth fast to hers while their bodies moved in unison.

Maggie rode the crest of sensation as she would a tumultuous sea, uttering little cries of delight, stroking the hard muscles of Lars' back. Lars took his mouth from hers, a groan coming from him. Maggie rose to meet him a final time, and they were one for a timeless moment.

After it was over, Maggie lay motionless, her heart still thundering in her rib cage. She lay with her face turned aside, resting in a nest of tumbled hair.

Lars' face loomed over hers. With unusual gravity, he said, "Maggie, it has been many months now and I have not spoken of it again, as you wished. Now I think it's time we discussed it . . . I want you for my wife."

"Oh, Lars!" She sat up, pushing him back with her hands flat on his chest. "Why do you always have to spoil things?"

"How can my asking you to be my wife spoil things?" he said aggrievedly. "It's the normal thing, when two people love each other as we do."

"When I asked you not to speak of it, didn't I say that I wasn't ready to commit myself completely?"

"But when will you be?"

"I don't know, Lars!" she said explosively. "Perhaps never. My life is full. I have this dream of making the Donnevans timber barons to be reckoned with. I told you that!"

"Ambition such as that can destroy a person. It is not right for a woman to . . . "

"Don't say it, Lars." She placed a hand over his mouth. "You're after making me angry, and I don't want . . . "

Maggie was interrupted by a strange sound, two thumps one after the other, muffled by distance. She felt a tremor pass over the earth beneath her.

"What was that?"

"I don't know," Lars said worriedly. "It sounded like dynamite, and not too far from the camp . . . "

Maggie was on her feet. "Let's go!"

They scrambled into their clothes, Lars scooped up the blanket and picnic basket and they began to run toward the camp. Before too long, Maggie's lungs were on fire and she had a stitch in her side. Her step slowed. Lars turned back in question. She waved him on, gasping out, "Hurry, Lars, find out what's amiss! Don't wait for me!"

Lars nodded and headed out at a lope, soon disappearing in the trees.

Maggie saw smoke rising long before she reached camp. At first she thought it was the camp itself. She breathed a heart-felt sigh of relief when she broke through the edge of the trees and saw the camp and sawmill intact. Slowing, she looked up the slope and saw not only smoke but flames on the mountain, in the general location of the trestle. She started that way, staggering with exhaustion now.

The camp seemed deserted as she hurried through it. Soon, she saw that Lars' surmise had been correct—the trestle was gone, and several small fires

414

raged in the gully. Patrick, smoke-blackened, his hair singed, came plunging up the side of the gully toward her, as Maggie halted on the edge.

"Praise be to the Saints, Patrick, you're all right! Is anyone harmed?"

"Nothing but a few burns and too much smoke from fighting the fire," Patrick said.

"Thank God for that." Maggie gazed down into the gully where Olaf and Lars were directing the men in fighting the fires. Since there was no water available here, all they could do was start a number of backfires. Fortunately, Maggie saw, there was plenty of dry brush in the gully and the backfires seemed to be blocking the spread of the flames; but the trestle was a total loss.

She sighed and looked at Patrick. "What happened, brother?"

Patrick swiped a sweaty hand down across his sooty face. "I'm not after knowing for certain, Maggie. We were all in camp when we heard the explosions. By the time we got up here, the trestle was gone and several small fires burning. I'd be guessing a few dynamite sticks were touched off under the trestle."

"By Lord Ramage's ruffians, you may be sure." She added sharply, "Why wasn't someone patrolling along the chute? You know my instructions about that!"

"It was Sunday, Maggie, and naught has happened these past weeks," Patrick said somewhat sheepishly. "It was my thought we could let the boys rest on the Lord's day. They work hard all week."

"The ones guarding our property are paid extra

to work on Sundays! I told you Lord Ramage was trying to lull us offguard. Now look at what has happened! The trestle will have to be rebuilt and it's fortunate we'll be if the whole mountain isn't burned off!"

"It's sorry I am, Maggie." His eyes began to burn with anger. "After the fires are out, I'll lead the boys into Port Ludlow and we'll thrash Lord Ramage and his buckos for this day's deed!"

"You will not, Patrick Donnevan! That would be breaking the law, and I will not stoop to his level. The Donnevans will fight for what's ours, but only on our own property."

"What law, sister? You have been telling me there is no law in these parts."

"Even so, a pitched battle in town will accomplish little except to get a few heads broken, ours as well as theirs! Now, let's go down and help the others fight the fires. . . ."

Before she took more than two steps, Patrick seized her arm. He raked her with his glance. "Maggie, you shouldn't go down there in a dress. It's dangerous, I'm thinking. Fighting fires is men's . . ."

"Men's work, I know," she finished. "Whisht! I will listen to no more of that nonsense. And if it's speaking of dresses you are, I can recall the many times you've scorned me for wearing men's clothes. I haven't time to go to camp to change clothes."

She pulled her arm out of his grip, and started down the steep bank, half-sliding most of the way.

By the time she reached Olaf where he stood supervising the fire-fighting, a number of men arrived from camp, where Olaf had sent them for croker sacks and strips of burlap wetted down in the cove. They were also toting buckets of water. Olaf directed them to use the dampened material to beat at tongues of flame shooting out along the ground from the bigger blazes.

Maggie seized one of the sacks and waded in with the men, beating along the ground where the flames raced. Already exhausted, she called upon her reserves of strength and doggedly worked as fast as she could, forgetting everything else. If they didn't contain the fire, if it got out of hand and into the trees, there would not *be* anything else.

She lost all track of time, working in a sort of mindless frenzy. Later, she learned that they fought the fires for over two hours.

At a touch on her shoulder, she started and looked up. Olaf was standing beside her, a tired smile on his blackened features. "She's under control, Maggie girl. We can stop now."

Maggie looked around dazedly. The fires were all out. The flames had burned the underbrush from the bottom of the gully and partway up the sides, but it had not escaped into the trees.

"You look a sight, girl," Olaf said.

Maggie wiped a hand across her face and stared numbly at the soot on her hand. She dredged up a wan smile. "You don't look so dad-damned fine yourself, Olaf Jorgenson."

" 'Spose not," he said. He worked his mouth and spat, a look of surprise spreading across his face. "I've been so dad-damned busy I forgot to take a dip of snoose in I don't know how long."

The weary men were climbing up the sides of the gully now. Lars, as blackened as the rest, came to lend her his arm and to help her up out of the gully.

"We were fortunate, Lars," Maggie said. "And I'm after thinking that your dire predictions earlier were on the mark."

Lars said soberly, "I can only hope that today was the extent of it."

Maggie found another shock awaiting her at camp. Patrick, Dan and Olaf were gathered before the cookhouse talking to Mother Be-Damn.

The big woman broke away when she saw Maggie and stepped forward, holding a folded paper between thumb and forefinger as if fearful of contamination. "Be-damn pickaroon man bring this during fire. Only for little Boston, he say."

Maggie took the paper. It was an envelope, with a seal imprinted in wax. There were letters curving across the top of the seal—RAMAGE.

Patrick said, "It's from His Lordship, I'm thinking."

"It would seem so," Maggie said.

"Then don't open it, sister. Burn it in Mother Be-Damn's cookstove."

"That would serve no useful purpose, Patrick. At least I'll see what he has to say."

She broke the seal and read the contents of the letter aloud:

Mistress Maggie Donnevan:
I desire an audience with you. It would be advantageous to both of us. I shall expect you at Ramage Hall at four sharp on the morrow, for tea.

418

Come alone. I have no business with your brothers. If you arrive alone, you will come to no harm. You have my word of honor on that, Madam.

Lord Ramage.

Maggie let the hand holding the letter fall to her side. With a wry smile she said, "Whatever else might be said of him, it appears that His Lordship observes protocol."

Patrick struck the palm of one hand with the fist of the other. "The nerve of that blackguard! After doing every foul thing he can against us, he has the gall to send such a letter. As if, after all that's happened, all he has to do is be proper, and polite, and you will come running to see what he has in mind! You were right, Maggie. The man's daft!"

Thinking hard, Maggie passed a hand distractedly through her mussed hair. "Wait now, Patrick. Let me think on this a wee bit. If there is a way of settling things with His Lordship, other than more destruction and bloodshed, I am about ready to take it. Perhaps it would do no harm to hear what the man has to say."

Patrick took a step toward her. "It's a trick, I'm thinking. Once he has you, there's no telling what fate might be yours. He could hold you and use you against us. We would have to do his bidding if he threatened to harm you. I say no, Maggie!"

Maggie was shaking her head. "No, I don't think any harm will come to me. Much as I detest the man, I'm thinking that he does have his own strange code of honor. I do believe he values his word. If he says no harm will come to me, I believe him."

"It's foolish you are, Maggie Donnevan," Patrick exclaimed. "If the man was behind what happened today, we could all be dead at this moment; and here you're walking, bold as brass, right into his spider's web!"

"Patrick, I'm weary to the bone, and filthy as a pig, and not in the mood to debate with you. I will accept His Lordship's invitation. I have to admit," she smiled slightly, "that I *am* somewhat curious."

"Let it be on your head then, sister," Patrick growled, and stalked away.

Lars said slowly, "You can't go alone, Maggie."

"Lars, I appreciate your concern, but you heard what the letter said. If I come alone, I will come to no harm. By that, I'm thinking he means that the same will not apply should someone accompany me."

"At least let me go to the village with you in the canoe," he pleaded. "I will wait there for you." He added grimly, "One hour I will wait. If you are not back by that time, I will come after you. And I will be armed, of that you may be sure."

Maggie hesitated, then gave him an affectionate smile. She patted his cheek. "If you insist, dear. I can see no harm in your waiting there for me. I must confess it will be reassuring."

Maggie appeared at the door of Lord Ramage's new abode in her working clothes—man's shirt and trousers and scuffed boots. She refused to call it

Ramage Hall, even in her thoughts; to her, it would always be the Jonas Kirk house. It was a gesture of defiance, the wearing of rough clothing; she would not give Lord Ramage the satisfaction of appearing in finery.

She paused a moment before going up the steps, a sadness welling up inside her as she remembered the times she had visited Jonas there. To Lord Ramage's credit, the house and grounds appeared in good repair.

Finally, she squared her shoulders, went up the steps, and knocked on the door. A liveried manservant answered her knock. He elevated his nose disdainfully at her. "His Lordship does not favor beggars at his door. . . ."

"Beggar, is it?" Maggie said in as haughty a tone as his own. "I'm not accustomed to being so spoken to by lackeys. Suppose you inform your master that Maggie Donnevan is here, at *his* request. I would be most happy to just walk away!"

"If you will wait," the manservant said frostily, "I will inform His Lordship."

Maggie waited, her anger growing apace. She was coldly furious when the man returned and ushered her into the sitting room where Lord Ramage lounged at ease, one booted leg crossed over the other. He was elegantly turned-out in tight, russet-colored breeches and a white silk shirt; and the gloss on his boots had a mirror-shine.

The manservant said, "Maggie Donnevan, Your Lordship," and bowed himself out.

Lord Ramage got to his feet, his cold face as arrogant as a hawk's. He wrinkled his nostrils as though he had detected a bad odor. "Madam, did

421

you find it necessary to dress in such a fashion? I am not accustomed to receiving ladies in my parlor in such sorry attire."

Maggie met his eyes with a hauteur of her own. "The last time we met, sir, you made quite a point of stating that I was no lady, so I saw no cause to disillusion you. I am a working woman and have come directly from work."

"Pray be seated, madam." He motioned languidly and Maggie sat on the sofa, perching gingerly on the edge. "The tea cart will be in shortly."

"This is not a social call, sir. I came simply out of curiosity, wondering what is now in your foul mind."

"Do not provoke me, Mistress Donnevan. You are my guest, and one must observe the amenities."

"Whisht! I do not consider myself a guest . . . "

She was interrupted as the tea cart was wheeled in by the manservant. With a sigh she sat back, and let matters take their course. Lars had sworn that he would come for her within the hour, but whatever this man had to say could not possibly take that long, even if they had to dawdle over tea.

Maggie had to admit that the aromatic tea and tiny cakes were delicious. She had been too apprehensive this morning to eat and now found that she was hungry. She would not reveal her hunger, however, and ate and sipped daintily. They were silent until each one had consumed one cup of tea and two small cakes.

Then Maggie sat her cup down with a thump. "Now, sir, your amenities are over and I demand to know the reason behind this meeting."

"Very well, Mistress Donnevan." Lord Ramage

dabbed delicately at his lips with a lace handker-chief. His eyes were hooded as he contemplated her. "I have a proposition that should be of interest to you . . ."

"That I very much doubt, sir," Maggie said with a sniff.

Unruffled, he continued, "I have made no secret of my desire for you, Maggie Donnevan," he paused, "so much so that I am willing to make you my wife."

"Your wife!" Maggie stared, torn between outrage and outright laughter. "I have always con-sidered you mad, Lord Ramage, but now it's sure I am. No power on earth could force me to marry you! Why, I . . ."

He waved a hand in protest against her flow of words. "Methinks you will agree, when you hear me out."

"Dear God! The very thought is repugnant to me! What makes you think . . ." She paused, looking intently at him. "Tell me, Lord Ramage . . . why should you even *consider* marriage with me? A commoner, a thief, of low Irish stock, a Donnevan? And each time we meet you have been careful to point out that I am not your concept of a lady. Nobility such as yourself, I have always thought, never weds below your station."

"That is true, madam. In Ireland, in England." Lord Ramage was smiling, a smile turned inward, as though he was amused at himself. "But I have decided to remain in this country, to make my home here as well as my fortune. I have learned that many men of nobility have come here, married into strong peasant stock and sired fine sons. All

423

too often, in England, nobility marries royalty to the point of incest and blueblood runs thin. I am nearing forty, Mistress Donnevan, and have suddenly discovered that I wish to have a son to carry on the Ramage name. I have decided you would be ideal as a mother to my son." He looked her up and down appraisingly. "Despite your crude ways, your Irish ancestors, you are uncommonly comely. I am also a handsome man. With blood from both our veins commingled, a handsome son should result."

The idea of being responsible for passing on the evil and madness in this man to a younger Ramage was even more abhorrent to Maggie than the thought of letting him touch her in passion.

"I gather I am supposed to feel honored by your offer," she said dryly, "but I must tell you frankly that I am sickened more than honored."

"I would advise you to hear me out, madam." He no longer lounged at ease, but sat up, tense as though straining at a leash. Those cold eyes burned with a wicked flame. "I do not make idle threats. When I have told you what I have in mind, you will agree to wed me. Damme, you will!"

"Threats? What more can you do to the Donnevans? Just yesterday you, or one of your minions, dynamited my chute trestle, setting fires. That *was* your work, was it not?"

"Since we are alone, I readily admit it. Not myself, no, I never find it necessary to stoop to that sort of skullduggery personally. I pay to have it done."

"In that way, your hands remain clean, your

peculiar sense of honor is not stained? Is that not the truth of it, sir?"

"Phrase it any way you wish." He shrugged. "The destruction of your trestle was done to a purpose . . . so you would realize that I am serious about what I intend to do."

"What more can you do?" she asked bitterly. "You have tried in every way to harm us, but so far we have survived."

"I have not even begun, madam. I have not had my full resources at my disposal until this past week. My estate in County Galway has been sold and all my considerable funds transferred to a bank in San Francisco. I tell you now that I will use every last pound of those funds to see you and yours driven to the wall, if you do not consent to be my wife."

"Do your damnedest, Lord Ramage," Maggie said in a steady voice. "I will fight you until my last breath."

"Mayhap you will, madam, but how about your brothers, the young one included? Do you have any conception of how easy it would be for me to take the boy from you? You cannot watch a growing lad all the time. And how about your lover, Lars Jorgenson . . . oh, yes, I know about him. Would you still love him with an arm or a leg gone, or with his face scarred like Jake Fargo's? And this Andrew Kane . . ." His voice was furry with menace now. "Will you fight until *their* last breaths? Would you care to see them dead?"

Maggie's breath caught. "You would not dare!"

"Oh, I would, and I intend to if you balk me. In fact, it would give me a savage pleasure. They have all, at one time or another, thwarted me. Your Andrew Kane, for instance. I have not touched him. The affair with the rifles above your cove was Fargo's idea." His lip curled. "Like most of Fargo's ideas, it came to naught. But when *I* move against him, Andrew Kane will lose both his boat and his life. You may depend on it, madam. I mean every word I say." He spread his hands. "Consider well the alternative. If you become my wife, I will cease to hound the Donnevans. They may go their way without further hindrance from me. You have the word of Lord Ramage on that. Then, I will be free to devote my time to becoming a timber baron and to," his smile grew, "being attentive to my bride."

Maggie could not find words to voice her thoughts. She stared at Lord Ramage in fear and loathing. Her thoughts went back to that dreadful moment in Ireland when she had seen Kathleen leave the Donnevan cottage that last time, driven away in the black coach. In that moment Maggie had sworn to herself that she would never become mistress or wife to a man she despised. What good my promise now, she thought, as she gazed at the man she most detested of all men.

Lord Ramage smiled his cold smile and leaned back, at ease again. "I see from your face, my dear Maggie, that you have finally grasped the situation. I thought you would. I have never underestimated your intelligence, devious though it might be. I treasure that quality in you as much as your beauty."

Maggie said dully, "I do not understand one thing . . . why should you even wish to marry someone who hates you as much as I do?"

He made a slight gesture. "That is of little importance. In fact, I have never bedded a woman who did not hate me, except for the tarts I have paid for the dubious privilege. Hate, I've found, adds a certain . . . spice to the bedchamber. In your case, I do have hopes of eventually taming you. I will bend every effort toward molding you into the lady you should be."

"Never!" she said adamantly. "You will never bend me to your will, sir!"

"We shall see, madam, we shall see," he said with maddening complacency.

Sunk in gloom, Maggie trudged down the cliff path toward the village. She walked along with her head down, thoughts circling inside her head like carrion birds.

"Maggie!"

She looked up to see Lars hurrying toward her. His open face mirrored relief.

"The hour was up, and I was fearful for you. . . ." He skidded to a stop before her. "What is it, Maggie? Your face looks like death! What's wrong? Did he harm you in some way?" Face darkening, he half-turned, glaring up at the white house. "If he has he will suffer for it."

"No, Lars, he didn't touch me," Maggie said listlessly. "I'm all right."

"But something is wrong, I know it. Why don't you tell me?"

"I don't wish to talk about it now, Lars. Let's start back to camp."

Lars looked rebellious for a moment. Then he sighed gustily, and offered his arm.

Maggie was scarcely aware of Lars, or her surroundings, as they walked on down the path, and got into the canoe. While Lars paddled, Maggie rode with her head down, eyes tightly closed. Across her closed eyelids swam Lord Ramage's cruel face, and his cold voice echoed in her ears, ". . . make you my wife . . . make you my wife . . ."

A small cry escaped her, and she sat up, shivering as if from a chill.

Lars looked at her in alarm. He stopped the canoe, resting on the paddle. "Maggie, what is it?"

Maggie sighed, and looked directly into his eyes. In a dead voice, she said, "Lars, I am to be wedded to Lord Ramage, two days hence."

Chapter Nineteen

Lord Ramage had insisted that the wedding be a festive occasion. "I want to show these bumpkins what it means to have nobility in their midst, and in that respect, you will dress to suit the occasion. In anticipation of your acceptance of my proposal, I ordered a wedding gown for you. I have found a woman in the village with some ability as a dressmaker, the daughter of the local blacksmith. If the garment does not fit, she will make the necessary alterations. You may come to Ramage Hall tomorrow, if you like." His lips had curved in amusement. "When you inform your brothers of your intentions, they will undoubtedly cast you out. Do not worry. If you stay here, you will be properly chaperoned. I promise not to touch you until after the wedding ceremony."

In predicting the reaction of her brothers, Lord Ramage was correct. Maggie made no attempt to explain her reasons for marrying the Englishman, either to Lars or her brothers, beyond the flat statement of fact. She well knew that if they learned she was sacrificing herself, they would not permit it. Instead, they would march against Lord Ramage en masse, even if it meant going to their death.

Lars, from the moment Maggie had told him of her intentions, had said very little. In a broken voice, he asked, "Why, Maggie? In God's name, why?"

"It is not your place to question what I do, Lars."

"Not my place to . . ." A light dawned in his eyes. "I do believe you had this in mind all along. It's the reason you refused to marry me, isn't it?"

Maggie, her heart aching at the hurt she was causing him, turned her head aside so he would not see the tears start in her eyes.

Lars picked up the paddle and paddled them on to camp in silence. Her brothers were waiting for her on the shore and the moment they stepped out of the canoe, Lars had disappeared and Maggie had not seen him since.

Patrick, when told of her marriage plans, roared like an enraged bull. "You are going to wed that devil's spawn! I cannot believe my hearing!"

"It's true, Patrick, you might as well accept it."

He stormed back and forth. "It's the same as with Kathleen! I was after believing you when you told me she did it for us. Now I think you lied! There must be something corrupt in the Donnevan women, or this English Lord is indeed a spawn of

430

the devil, drawing the pair of you to his bed by his dark powers!"

In a way, Patrick's raging outburst made it easier for Maggie. Dan remained silent, his puzzled gaze upon her in mute accusation, and Maggie avoided his glance, concentrating on Patrick's rage.

Finally Patrick paused to draw a breath, glaring at her with blazing eyes. "There must be a reason, sister." His voice was almost pleading now. "Tell me there is a reason, Maggie."

"Yes, Brother Patrick, there is a very good reason." It took a great effort of will for Maggie to keep her voice steady. "I am tired of fighting him. I am tired of working like a slave here in the woods. He is a wealthy man, is His Lordship. He has promised me the best of everything; a fine house to live in; fine clothes to wear; anything my heart desires. Anything that a woman might wish will be mine. In addition, as his wife I will be nobility, Lady Ramage. What Donnevan can say that?"

Patrick drew in his breath with a hissing sound. "I can't believe that I would ever be hearing such words from a sister of mine! Himself was right when he disowned Kathleen. I now disown you. You are no longer a Donnevan, *Lady* Ramage!"

He wheeled and stalked away. Maggie glanced at Dan, Olaf and Kevin, standing off to one side. Now Dan gave her a sorrowful look and turned away. Kevin snuffled once, then hurried after his brothers.

"Dad-damned if I understand it, girl. By Thor, I don't," Olaf said. He spat without turning his head aside, the brown snuff juice splattering Maggie's boots. "Never in my whole life have I so misjudged a person. My guess is it'd be best for your brothers if'n they never clapped eyes on you again."

He also turned on his heel and walked off, leaving Maggie all alone.

She stood motionless for a few minutes, her body and mind numb with hurt. She was past tears now, past all feeling. From the moment she had agreed to Lord Ramage's terms, something had died inside her and she felt that she would never be whole again. Yet, what alternative did she have? Lord Ramage had made it very clear what he would do, and she did not doubt it for an instant. If she had not made the bargain with him, the death of her brothers, the death or the crippling of Lars, and likely Andrew's death as well, would all be on her head.

She had thought of fleeing, as they had done in Ireland, but she knew instinctively that there was no way she could possibly talk her brothers into running, leaving behind all they had built up. Running away by herself would solve nothing. She suspected that her flight would only inflame Lord Ramage's madness and he would methodically go about destroying the remaining Donnevans and everyone connected with them.

No matter how repellent it might be to her, Maggie knew that she had made the only possible choice.

Now she heaved a sigh and walked with bent head to her cabin. Inside, she began to pack the few things she intended to take with her tomorrow. The last items she packed were the preparations Mother Be-Damn had given her. Finished, she stretched out on her back on the bed and stared dry-eyed at the ceiling.

A timid knock sounded on the door.

Maggie raised her head. She was not up to going through another stormy scene with Patrick or Lars. She said, "Who is it?"

"It's Kevin, Maggie."

Dear God, she thought, *I can't face him, either!*

Then she scolded herself for being a coward. You've chosen your course, Maggie Donnevan, so don't be afraid to face up to the consequences.

She sat up on the edge of the bed, smoothing down her hair. Finally, hands folded in her lap, she called out, "Come in, Kevin."

Kevin entered the cabin hesitantly. His eyes were red; clearly he had been crying. Maggie's heart went out to him. She managed to keep her face expressionless. "Yes, Kevin?"

"Maggie . . ." He took two steps toward her. "It's not true, what you said, is it now?" He smiled tentatively. "You were after funning with us, weren't you?"

"I'm afraid not, Kevin," she said firmly. "All I said was true."

"But how can you leave us and go to that awful man!" The words were a cry wrung from him.

"There are things between a man and a woman, I know, that are hard for a lad your age to understand. Some day, hopefully, you *will* understand." Maggie ached to reach out her arms to him. She locked her hands together in her lap, holding them still. "Then, when you do understand, perhaps you will . . ."

His face worked. "I will never understand.

433

Never! All I know is that you're deserting us, your own family!"

Maggie deliberately made her voice stern and cold. "You have been prattling to me, Kevin, about how grown up you are. Then act like it! You do not need me any longer. A *man* does not cling to his sister."

Kevin's face crumpled, a muted cry came from him, and he spun away, running out the open door.

Maggie got up and crept across the cabin like an old woman to close the door. She returned to the bed and the tears came. They came in a flood and she fell across the bed, great sobs wracking her body.

She left camp early the next morning, at first light. No one was astir and only a pencil-stream of smoke arose from the cookhouse chimney. Insofar as she could tell, there was no one to take note of her departure as she paddled the canoe out of the cove and turned south.

It was long after sunrise when she beached the canoe under the wharf at Port Ludlow. As she started to tie it off to the usual piling, she paused and laughed, a mirthless bark. She would have no more use for the canoe now. Glancing around, she spotted a large rock. With an effort she lifted it, carried it over to the canoe and, stretching as high as she could reach, she dropped it. The heavy stone struck the bottom of the canoe and went right on through. Water began to bubble up. Maggie stood unmoving until the canoe had sunk out of sight.

She picked up the small bag and made her way slowly up the cliff path. At the top of the bluff she paused, staring at the house. It sparkled in the morning sun. Not for the first time the irony of her coming here to live struck her—in this house where she had known so much joy with Jonas Kirk.

"Forgive me, dear Jonas," she murmured, "for what I am about to do. I had no choice, you see? But I'm sure, wherever you are, you understand, being the kind of man you are."

It seemed to her that the house had taken on a sinister aspect, for all its beauty and neatness. Superimposed over it seemed to shimmer the bleak, gray outlines of Ramage Castle back in Ireland. Maggie blinked her eyes, trying to dispell the disquieting image. It was fanciful, she knew; the house was no different than it had ever been. Could a house absorb evil from its owner? Was this house, which had held naught but joy for her, now tainted? Fanciful or not, Maggie knew that it would always appear so to her, from this day forward.

Resolutely, she started on toward the house. The door was opened by the same manservant. Maggie had a name for him now—Thomas. She didn't know his surname, if he had one.

From his height he looked down his long nose at her. "His Lordship is not in residence and will not be back until the morrow. On his departure he informed me that you are to have the East Bedroom. A Mistress Nancy Woods is coming this afternoon, a seamstress from the village below."

Hysterical laughter formed in Maggie's throat, and it was all she could to keep it from bubbling out. *Nancy Woods, Lars' former lady friend! Was there no end to this day's ironies?* At Lord Ramage's mention of the blacksmith's daughter yesterday, Maggie had been too distraught to make the connection.

She gave a mental shrug, and tossed her head. "Whisht! It was gracious of His Lordship to allow me a bedroom in his fine, new house! I thought perhaps he would consign me to a stall in the barn."

Thomas looked startled, losing his composure for a moment, and in that instant Maggie's course was set. She was here under duress, and she would wed Lord Ramage against her will, but that did not mean that she couldn't fight back in whatever small ways she could. No matter what indignities should be heaped upon her, Maggie resolved that she would not end up the poor, cowed, mad creature Kathleen had become. If she could shake this haughty manservant's composure, perhaps she could do the same to His Lordship.

Maggie was lying on the fourposter bed in the "East Bedroom" that afternoon when Nancy Woods made her appearance. Maggie was wide awake, staring at the wedding gown hanging on hooks on one wall. It was all white, beautifully made, with fine lace and ribbons adorning it. She had not tried it on, caring little whether or not it fitted her.

Thomas' peremptory knock sounded on the door. Maggie sat up. "Yes?"

The door opened, and Thomas stepped in and to one side. In his haughtiest voice, he announced, "Nancy Woods, the seamstress."

A tall, full-bodied young woman with long dark hair and hazel eyes moved past Thomas, who started out, turning his back to Maggie. Maggie, looking at the other woman, felt a sense of recognition; then she realized that it was because Nancy Woods somewhat resembled herself. The coloring, in particular, was almost the same.

Whisht, Maggie thought, coming to her feet. "Thomas!"

The manservant paused, facing about. "Yes?"

Maggie drew herself up. "I do believe you are forgetting something, Thomas."

His long face flushed. Then he dipped a knee, murmuring, "Yes, milady. I am sorry."

He is not a dolt, at least, Maggie thought.

"That's better. Just see that you do not forget your place in the future." She waved a hand in a lordly manner. "You are dismissed."

Thomas backed out of the room, closing the door softly.

Maggie's hand flew to her mouth, smothering a giggle. Her glance darted to Nancy Woods. Nancy's eyes were alive with amusement and they both erupted in quiet laughter.

Why, she's lovely, Maggie thought, *and quick; she caught on right away to the fact that a commoner was putting a noble manservant in his place.*

Then they both sobered, as each recognized the other as a natural opponent.

Maggie said, "Nancy Woods . . . Lars has told me of you."

"And he has told me of you, the Irish woman he worked for, whose lover he has been these past months."

"I'm sorry, Nancy," Maggie said, the apology coming from her with difficulty, "but I did not steal him from you. Please believe that."

"I do believe that, particularly now I've seen you. He was in love with you long before he met me. I was just a replacement, a surrogate for a love he thought he couldn't win! But I cannot find it in me to forgive your breaking the poor man's heart, after he was sure that . . . "

Maggie broke in, "How did you know about that, Nancy? Have you seen Lars?"

"Yes, I have seen him, late last night." Nancy's voice was cool. "Lars came by to tell me what had happened. He has left Port Ludlow, driven away by your cruelty. And I did not give you permission, Miss Donnevan, to call me Nancy. I am not a servant in this house."

Maggie stiffened, her head going back. "My apologies, Miss Woods. I will not make the same mistake again. You have a chore to perform, I believe. Shall we get on with it, so you will no longer have to suffer my presence?"

In reply she received a stiff nod. Nancy took the dress from the wall hooks. Maggie had no choice but to remove the dress she was wearing. She was rosy with embarrassment at having to remove her outer garment under the gaze of another woman who had known Lars Jorgenson intimately. At the same time she felt a measure of sorrow. She had a strong feeling that she could have become close friends with this Nancy Woods, if not for the circumstances.

Nancy worked in silence, gathering cloth, pinning and marking. Maggie endured it all patiently.

Finally it was done. Nancy stood up and said briskly, "The message from your Lord Ramage informed me that there was a sewing room I could use here to make the necessary alterations. If such is the case, I can complete my work this afternoon, and the dress will be ready for your," her lips curled, "wedding tomorrow."

"Ask Thomas," Maggie said curtly. "He will show you."

Nancy nodded and started for the door, the white dress draped over her arm.

Maggie said, "Nancy . . . "

Nancy looked back, frowning.

"I . . ." Maggie gestured impotently. "Never mind, I doubt if you'd care to hear what I have to say."

Maggie was surprised at the number of people who were present for the wedding the next afternoon.

She did not see Lord Ramage until she came downstairs. Apparently he had returned late the evening before, while Maggie had remained in the East Bedroom. A servant girl had spent the night outside her door, and had brought breakfast to her room this morning. The maid, named Flora, was friendly and warm, totally different from Thomas. She had spent the hours after breakfast fussing with Maggie—toting hot water up to the room for Maggie's bath, helping her into and out of the wedding dress a half-dozen times, making minute alterations of her own.

Now Flora came sedately behind Maggie, carrying the long train of the white wedding gown.

Maggie stopped momentarily halfway down the stairs, a gasp coming from her at the sight of the numerous guests. The entryway overflowed, the people spilling into the dining room and the sitting room. A punch bowl had been set up in the entryway and Thomas was serving the punch in crystal glasses. All faces turned, gazing up at her.

The crowd was predominately male, Maggie saw, with only a few women. To her surprise she saw several faces she knew—Captain Sayward, Cyrus Walker from Port Gamble, and Henry Yesler from Seattle.

Then she uttered a small cry as a tall figure came from the sitting room into the entryway, staring up at her. It was Andrew! He raised the glass in his hand in a mocking toast to her, his eyes dancing with amusement.

For a moment Maggie was tempted to run through the crowd and out the front door, away from this place and Andrew. How came he to be here? He must have been invited! Her glance roved frantically over the upturned faces, searching for Lars or her brothers, knowing that she would not have been too surprised if Lord Ramage had invited them, even while she realized that they would not have come.

Then she saw Lord Ramage pushing his way through to the foot of the staircase. He was wearing a tricornered hat, a white coat and shirt, white satin knee breeches, white silk stockings and black shoes with gleaming silver buckles. His handsome features wore a high flush and she knew that he had been drinking. Now he removed the tricornered hat, crossed his arm over his chest, and made a leg.

Maggie came on down the stairs. At the bottom Lord Ramage took her hand and walking apart from her, he led her forward, at least two feet separating them. The crowd pressed back, forming a lane for them.

The wedding was to take place in the room Jonas had used as a study. A minister was already ensconced behind a portable pulpit, a tall, forbidding man with a full black beard.

There were a few murmurs from the spectators, quickly quieting at a scowl from the minister. Maggie knew that she and Lord Ramage must make a striking pair, both in pristine white.

And neither of us a virgin, she thought, concealing a smile. I am not, and God knows His Lordship is not; he probably lost his virginity before he was waist-high to his manservant, Thomas.

Maggie closed her ears to the words of the ceremony and had to be nudged by Lord Ramage so she could make the proper responses.

Then they were pronounced man and wife and it was all over. When the final words were spoken, a gray mantle of despair settled over Maggie. She barely suppressed a shudder as his cool lips touched hers in the wedding kiss. Fortunately, the guests crowded around with congratulations just then, separating them. Maggie mumbled incoherent responses to the congratulations. Suddenly, the despair was too much and the room seemed stifling. She swayed, on the verge of fainting.

"Careful, my dear Maggie," said Andrew's voice in her ear. " 'Twould never do for the virgin bride to swoon at her wedding. The guests might think something amiss. Could I fetch Lady Ramage a restorative glass of punch? It is most potent. His Lordship does not stint on refreshments, I will say that for him."

"Oh, Andrew! Dear God, yes!" She clutched at his arm. "And please get me out of this crush of people."

He guided her into the sitting room, where they found the window seat empty. With elaborate ceremony he helped her to sit, and stood back with a small bow. "If you will excuse me, Your Ladyship, I will fetch the punch."

As he made his way through the crowd, she caught her first full glimpse of him. He was dressed more elegantly than she had ever seen him—a new black suit, exquisitely tailored to fit his tall, muscular body, with a white shirt and starched collar, and a black string tie. She found herself unwillingly noticing how handsome he was.

Maggie closed her eyes, leaning her head back against the window. The window was raised a crack and she was grateful for the rush of fresh air on her face.

"Madam . . ."

She opened her eyes to see Captain Sayward looming over her.

His face grave, he said, "I am leaving now and I wished to say my congratulations. I only put in an appearance out of respect for ye. When Lord Ramage delivered the invitation, he couched it in a vague threat. . . ."

"He threatened you, sir? It's sorry I am about that."

442

The captain made a dismissing gesture. "It's of no importance. His threats bother me little. That is not why I came. As I said, I came out of respect for ye, a woman I have come to admire very much. I must confess that I cannot see any reason on earth why ye should marry this man." His kind face was troubled now. "I find it hard to accept the rumors about, that ye are wedding him for his wealth and the station in life it would provide ye. Ye do not strike me as such a woman. I do not like your . . . husband, madam. I have made no secret of that. Perhaps I am wrong in both instances. Perhaps ye see something in the Englishman that I do not see. . . ."

"I owe you no explanation, sir," she said stiffly. She swiftly relented, impulsively reached for his hand. "I will tell you this . . . your judgment of Lord Ramage is not in error, and be warned to steer clear of him."

He gazed down at her intently, then slowly nodded. "I would do that in any event. Ye have my best wishes, Maggie Donnevan." He laughed shortly. "I'm afraid I will always think of ye as Maggie Donnevan."

"Continue to do so, please, Captain Sayward," she said softly.

Andrew's arrival with two glasses of punch ended the conversation. His bright gaze jumped from one to the other.

"Good day, madam." Captain Sayward inclined his head. "And to ye, Mr. Kane." The captain turned and made his way toward the door.

Andrew sat down beside Maggie on the window

seat, giving her a glass of punch. "Now what did the good captain want, Maggie?"

"To offer his congratulations." She took a hearty drink of the punch. It *was* very strong, and almost choked her in its fiery path down her throat. But it did revive her. She looked at Andrew with a touch of her old spirit. "And when do you congratulate me, Andrew?"

"Never, Maggie," he said with a short laugh. "If I were to offer anything, it would be my condolences. . . ."

She became serious. "Why did you come, Andrew?"

"Out of curiosity, I suppose. I was stunned when I heard the news from your brother, Patrick, quite literally stunned, and would not have believed it coming from anyone else. I had to come, after I received the invitation, thinking perhaps I would detect some signs that you had taken leave of your senses. But I can see no such indications, except that moment of near-swooning back there. And that could have been from the overwhelming happiness of a bride." He looked deep into her eyes. "Tell me, Maggie, was that it?"

She ignored his question. "He *did* invite you then?"

"He did. I would not be here, if he had not. I am sometimes foolhardy, Maggie, but not an utter fool. He even had invitations delivered to your brothers. I'm sure you can imagine the reception such invitations received there."

Maggie shook her head in wonder. "The gall of the man!"

"Maggie, why? In Christ's sweet name, why?"

Andrew's voice was low, tortured, the first real display of emotion Maggie had seen in him. "This strutting peacock, this most dastardly of villains, as you yourself named him more than once . . . why have you done this? If you can offer me even *one* sensible reason, perhaps I can live with that."

"I owe you no explanation, Andrew," she said.

He flinched slightly. "Touché. I suppose I deserve that; but your brothers, the other Donnevans, do not. Can you give me some hint I can use to ease their hurt?"

"I told my brothers all I intend to."

"That cock-and-bull story!" He snorted. "I do not for an instant believe that you married this blackguard for his wealth, his noble status, or anything of the sort. I know you too well to ever believe . . ."

She broke in, "It seems you have suddenly become great friends of my brothers. Whisht! I cannot remember you holding them in such high esteem before!"

"Maggie . . ." He sighed. "Will you for one moment stop skittering around the subject like a bug on ice? *Why?*"

She said distantly, "I have said all I intend to on the subject, Mr. Kane."

"The guests are taking their leave, madam," said a slurred voice.

With a start Maggie glanced up. Lord Ramage, still carrying a glass of punch, stood swaying slightly on widely spaced feet. With astonishment she noted that it had grown dark while she talked with Andrew and the last of the guests were filing out. Inwardly, she shrank away from the man be-

445

fore her. With the night, it would not be long before she had to face the greatest ordeal of all—being closeted alone with him in their nuptial bedchamber.

Lord Ramage was saying, " . . . includes you as well, Kane."

Andrew stood up. "I shall take my leave at once, Your Lordship."

"As for your tugboat . . ." The Englishman sneered. "You are free to come and go, Kane, without harm."

Andrew said dryly, "That is most generous of you, sir."

"I have promised Lady Ramage that you will come to no harm . . ."

Andrew shot a quick glance at Maggie.

Noticing the look, Lord Ramage said, "But you will not approach Lady Ramage again! Is that clearly understood, sir? If you dare to do so, you will regret it."

"There is no need to concern yourself on that score. I will make it a point not to inflict my presence on either of you again." Andrew bowed stiffly. "I bid you good day, Lord and Lady Ramage. Forgive me if I do not wish you future happiness." His voice grated. "It strikes me you deserve each other, and whatever fate awaits you."

Andrew left quickly. Maggie desperately wanted to call out to him, to beg him to take her with him. She willed herself to remain silent.

Lord Ramage glared after Andrew. He muttered, "Insolent chap, that Kane." He shrugged, offering his arm to Maggie.

She stood up and took it. Thomas preceding

them with a kerosene lamp, they moved toward the staircase.

In a low voice Maggie said, "I am surprised that you did not invite Jake Fargo to the wedding, sir."

Lord Ramage lurched, catching at the banister for support. The punch glass fell out of his hand, tumbling down the stairs and shattering on the way. He said, "One does not invite one's hirelings to a social event, madam."

His state of drunkenness seemed far advanced, and Maggie experienced a throb of hope. Men too far gone in their cups were said to have difficulty performing in bed. Was she to be spared his attentions for at least one night?

Thomas awaited them at the top of the stairs, his face a shadow above the lamp globe. He opened a door, bowed them in, then crossed to place the lamp atop a bureau and bowed himself out. It was then that Maggie realized the room they were in was the very same room where she had spent so many lazy, joyous afternoons with Jonas. Her stomach knotted, and for a moment she half-bent over, fearful she would vomit.

"On the bed with you, madam!" Lord Ramage's voice cracked like a whip. "I want you naked as Eve!"

Her hope that he might not be capable of bedding her dwindled as she straightened up.

He glared at her with those cold, emotionless eyes. "Must I remind you of our bargain, Lady Ramage? I have kept my part of it. Now it is your turn."

Maggie half-turned away from him and began

removing her clothing. Finally naked, she hesitated for a moment, then turned to face him fully. One look at him and the last vestige of hope was gone.

Lord Ramage had also divested himself of clothing and stood naked now, the staff of his manhood erect and jutting obscenely. Even in the depths of her despair, a part of Maggie's mind had to marvel at the symmetrical beauty of this man—wide shoulders, broad chest, tapering hips and slender, yet columnar thighs. He had the beauty of a Greek statue and there was the same lack of humanity. His physical beauty was something to be admired from a distance, without hope of human contact.

He gestured arrogantly. "On the bed, madam."

Maggie obeyed automatically. She stretched out on her back, willing herself to feel nothing, not even revulsion. She determined to remain as one dead.

Lord Ramage stood beside the bed, his drunken gaze touching her flesh like flames. Maggie imagined she could even feel the scorching touch of fire.

As he climbed into the bed, she said, "Shouldn't you turn off the lamp, sir?"

"Why? I want to observe you." He laughed coarsely. "I want to *see* what I have bought."

With brutal hands he spread her tense thighs and penetrated her immediately, his body coming down hard on hers. His flesh was cool and clammy, and Maggie instinctively cringed away despite her resolve.

Far gone in his raging lust, her husband did not notice. He plunged into her with an ever-quickening rhythm. Due to the fact that she was not ready for him, his thrusts were dryly painful. His hands fastened onto the flesh of her upper arms, fingers digging in like talons.

Maggie lay with her face turned away from his hot breath. Not until his breath grew rasping, panting, did she look fully into his face. His features were as rigid as a mask, his eyes as opaque and blind as agates.

Dear God, she thought appalled, *in this moment I might as well not exist for him!*

She was merely a means for his physical gratification. It was a horrible, degrading thought. Now she finally realized how Kathleen's spirit had been broken. Physical abuse would be preferable; at least if he was beating her, he would be aware of her as a person, if only as an outlet for his sadistic rage.

Now his mouth opened and his breath left him in a whistling sigh. He shuddered violently twice, then shook his head as though to clear it. He looked at her as though seeing her for the first time since the instant he violated her body.

He shook his head disgustedly, full lips sneering. "Damme, but you are as cold as your sister was! What kind of a bargain have I made?"

"So absorbed were you in your own pleasure, sir . . . if that name can be given to it . . . that I fail to see that it matters little to you."

He merely grunted and moved away from her. He stretched out on his back, without bothering to pull up the bedcovers.

The sight of his blatant nakedness revolted Maggie Driven by a need to goad him, she said calmly,

"It's sorry I am that I was not the virgin you had in mind with the white wedding dress."

"You take me for a fool, madam?" he said. 'I knew you were not virgin. I knew of your Swede lover."

She raised her head to look at him. "But the others, sir . . . do you also know of them?"

He grew still. "What others?"

"A lady does not prattle of her bedchamber secrets," she said with mock severity. "I cannot tell you names, but perhaps I can give you numbers. Would that suffice?" She was thoroughly enjoying herself now. She propped her head on one elbow, and tapped a forefinger against her chin, counting, "Let me see if I can recall them all . . . one, two, three, four . . ."

Without warning he hit her with his fist in the midriff, driving the breath from her. Even in her agony, Maggie managed a coughing laugh and gasped out, "So you see, Your Lordship, it's damaged goods you're after getting for your end of the bargain."

"You Irish slut!" With each name he called her, Lord Ramage slammed his fist into her. "Common whore . . . street strumpet!"

Maggie noticed, through a haze of pain, that he was careful to strike only in places where her clothing would hide the marks and bruises. But even so, the pain was severe. She clamped her lips shut, refusing to scream. She went soft and lax, willing herself into unconsciousness, content with the knowledge that she had bested him once again.

Dimly she heard his voice, "Tart you may be, madam, but you are now Lady Ramage and you will act the part. And you will bear me a son, damme, you will! When that is accomplished, when I have had my fill of you, killing you will give me great pleasure!"

Chapter Twenty

The events of Maggie's wedding night set a pattern for the following days and weeks.

Every time Lord Ramage took her, Maggie made him pay—goading and mocking him until he was in a rage—and he would pummel her body until it was one solid mass of pain. Maggie bore the hurt stoically, considering it a small price to pay for the fact that she had been able to break through the cold complacency of the man and arouse his ire. This she considered a victory of sorts. She concluded wryly that it was probably also a form of penance she felt it necessary to bear for sharing his bed, even though suffering him to possess her body should have been penance enough. Not once during those terrible nights did she feel the slightest response to his love-making, if so self-absorbed an activity could be called that. She developed a facility for walling herself off from his forays on her body, stirring to goad him again when it was over.

He need not have feared that she would show the bruises and marks he left on her to anyone. She felt a strong sense of shame about the signs of punishment, well realizing that this attitude might strike many people as curious; however, it was the way she felt.

Maggie discovered an unexpected ally in Flora Jenkins, the maid who attended her. For a long time she was careful not to disrobe in Flora's presence. This was difficult, since Flora was a faithful lady's maid and often Maggie would have to drive her from the room when she changed clothes or bathed.

But one afternoon, weary in mind and body, she dropped off to sleep in the great, cast-iron bathtub that was brought to her room each time she had a bath, and Flora came bustling in unexpectedly.

Maggie was startled awake and sat up without thinking.

Flora stopped short. "I'm sorry, Your Ladyship. So much time had passed, I thought you'd be out of your bath by . . ." Her eyes widened, hand flying to her mouth. "Oh, sweet Jesus! Your poor body. Did *he* do that to you, Your Ladyship?"

Maggie sighed, knowing that she couldn't hide it any longer. "Yes, *he* did it to me." She added crossly, "And stop calling me Your Ladyship. Whisht! It sounds ridiculous, that it does!"

The buxom Flora drew closer, her blue eyes round with compassion. "Oh, you poor thing!" She made a face. "*He* did that to me, too, you know."

454

Maggie's interest stirred. "He did? You mean . . . in bed?"

Flora blushed and dropped her eyes. "That's what I mean, Your . . . If I can't call you Your Ladyship, what can I call you?" Flora's voice was distressed.

"Maggie, that's my name."

Flora shook her head, red curls bobbing. "He wouldn't like that. It ain't right and proper, he'd say "

"Bother what he would say. All right . . . in front of him it's Your Ladyship. When we're alone, it's Maggie. Now . . . I want to know. Lord Ramage has bedded you *and* beaten you."

"Oh, yes, both. You know something . . . uh, Maggie?" Flora leaned closer, eyes darting fearfully. "With him, I think the two go together."

"That has occurred to me," Maggie said dryly. "Did he force you into his bed?"

Flora bobbed her head. "Yes."

"All the way from Ireland?"

"Oh, no, San Francisco. He hired all us serving people in San Francisco."

"That explains something," Maggie said absently. "The staff of four here . . . I never saw any of them in Ramage Castle back in Ireland."

Flora was going on, her voice bitter. "His Lordship made fine promises. I was in service in San Francisco. He offered me more money and spoke of great opportunities up here in a new country. We were hardly out of the Bay when he threw me across his bunk and raped me. It's been that way since and I was glad when you came along. Oh, was I ever glad to see you, Maggie! I thought to

455

myself, now he'll leave me be. Oh!" She went rosy, hand going to her mouth. "I'm sorry, Maggie. I didn't think . . . "

"It's all right." Maggie smiled. "In your place, I'd feel the same way. If you hate him, as you obviously do, why haven't you left his service?"

"I had it in mind, that I did, and was saving the money for passage back to San Francisco. Then you became his wife, and I thought . . . well, I like you, Maggie, and knowing what would likely happen with him, I thought you might need me."

"I do, Flora dear." She reached out for the girl's hand. "I am badly in need of a friend, that I am."

Maggie stood up in the tub and Flora handed her a towel. Maggie dried herself briskly and put on the dressing gown that Flora handed her.

Flora had brought up a tea cart. Now she went outside the room and pushed it in. As she began to serve, Maggie gestured. "Join me, Flora. I know His Lordship isn't in residence this afternoon, so we needn't fear he'll catch us."

Flora, plainly uneasy, did as she was told, sipping the steaming tea and nibbling on a cake. Finally, her curiosity must have become too much. She blurted out, "Why did you wed His Lordship? Didn't you know the sort of man he was?"

"Oh, I knew," Maggie said. "At least I thought I did. But since then I have learned that he is much more depraved than even I thought." A strong urge to talk swept over her and now the whole story came pouring out. When it was over, she slumped back, relieved at having confided in someone.

"You poor, poor dear!" Flora clucked in sympathy, and so far forgot herself as to pat Maggie's

456

hand. "It's a touching tale, Maggie, and I think you were noble to sacrifice yourself for your brothers."

"I don't know about noble," Maggie said with a wry grimace, "but at the time it was the only thing I could see to do. Now, after these past weeks, I'm after wondering if *anything* is worth this sacrifice. It could be I was being foolish. Flora . . ." She leaned forward. "You come and go to the village, do you not?"

The girl's head bobbed. "Oh, yes. I go down once or twice a week."

"Do you know any people prone to gossip, people who know what is going on hereabouts?"

Flora laughed. "Port Ludlow people love to gossip. It's their only entertainment, I'd guess."

"Then I want you to find out for me if Lord Ramage is keeping his word." Maggie unconsciously lowered her voice. "I doubt I'd be welcome in the village, and would likely be lied to in any case. I wish to know if His Lordship has stopped harassing my family."

"I'd be happy to do anything I can." Flora added wistfully, "I wish I had a family, although I don't think I would have had the courage to do what you have done. I'm an orphan, never knew any family."

Maggie patted her arm. "We'll have to be family to each other, dear. I'm an orphan now too, in a manner of speaking."

The almost nightly ravishment and punishment from Lord Ramage continued. Maggie supposed that, strictly speaking, it wasn't ravishment, since she submitted to him without protest, but she could think of it in no other terms.

Somehow it didn't seem quite so bad now with Flora as a confidante, someone she could talk with and someone to offer sympathy. Maggie did experience disappointment with the news the maid brought back from the village. From all accounts, Lord Ramage was hewing to his word; he had left the Donnevans alone and they were prospering. This news made Maggie realize how very much she hated her life with him. To have learned that he wasn't keeping his promise would have given her an excuse to leave. Facing the prospects of months, of years, in such dreadful bondage was unthinkable; but, again, she shrank back from the alternative. Her leaving him would surely touch off his madness; it would turn him into a bloody executioner.

And so the awful nights dragged on. The days, of course, were not so bad. Lord Ramage was gone all day, even Sundays, and she learned from Flora—not from Lord Ramage himself, who never discussed business matters with her—that His Lordship was becoming the timber baron that he wished to be, and was considering building his own sawmill. Flora told her that he had repeatedly offered to purchase Captain Sayward's sawmill, and had been rebuffed. At least, Maggie thought, there is *someone* with the courage to stand up to him. Not once during all that time had she seen Jake Fargo, and for this she was grateful.

All the while there was a feeling of events building toward a climax. When at the house on the bluff, Lord Ramage was becoming surlier, more irritable than usual. He was drinking heavily and often she caught him eyeing her in speculation.

In his bedroom one night, she learned the reason for those speculative looks.

On this night, his habitual over-indulgence in French brandy finally took its toll and he was impotent. After nearly a half hour's effort he was red in the face and short of breath and Maggie was barely able to contain her amusement. He gave vent to an angry snarl and rolled off her.

He sat on the edge of the bed, and stared accusingly at her flat stomach. "Are you with child yet, madam?"

Maggie went tense. This was the moment she had been waiting for, she knew suddenly. Now she would deliver the telling blow. She said calmly enough, "I am not."

"How long does it take? I thought you Irish bred like cattle in the fields."

"It will take forever, as far as you are concerned, sir."

"What!" He reared back, thunderstruck. "That was a part of our bargain, madam!"

"No, not as far as I was concerned. Our bargain was that I would wed you in exchange for you leaving my brothers in peace. You mentioned your longing for a son, that is true, but I made no promises as to that. If you will think back, Your Lordship, you will remember, I am sure."

"You are provoking me, madam." His glare turned malevolent. "Whatever you may or may not wish has little to do with it. My seed is potent, that I know well. On two occasions back in Ireland I got wenches with child, but in both instances the offspring was a girl. I had no desire for girl children, of what use are they? But my point is . . ." he leaned on his knuckles on the bed, the brandy stench of his breath in her nostrils, "that I have given you my seed enough times to impregnate you. Are you infertile?"

"I'm not after knowing, but to my knowledge I am not. Still, that does not matter. I will not become pregnant."

"And why is that, pray?" he demanded.

"At my logging camp the cook is an Indian woman. She is versed in Indian lore, and the Indians know of ancient ways, of herbal concoctions to prevent pregnancy. She gave me a goodly supply of her herbs. I know what you are thinking, but it will do you no good." She held up her hand "The herbs are well-hidden, where you will never find them. Now will you beat me until I reveal their hiding place? You, of all people, should know how much that will gain you."

His face had gone quite pale. He gritted his teeth in his anger. She had never seen him so furious. "You like to taunt me, madam, that I know. You are taunting me now!"

"I am not, sir. Every word I say is true." She added sarcastically, "You have the word of Lady Ramage on it."

Maggie held herself tense for the first blow. He remained leaning on his knuckles for an endless time, breathing heavily. Then, in a cold whisper, he said, "You will regret this . . . this female deviousness, madam. That I promise you!"

Maggie did not flinch away, although her heart was beating with dread. But Lord Ramage surprised her. He made no move to strike her; instead he got up and strode from the room, slamming the door so hard the house shook. She heard his heavy tread on the stairs going down. She waited until she could no longer hear him before going to her room.

Maggie should have been relieved that he had not retaliated in some way, yet she was not. Still vaguely apprehensive, she finally drifted off to sleep.

Flora tiptoed into her bedroom the next morning with the breakfast tray. "His Lordship spent the night drinking brandy in the book room. He is now snoring away in the big chair, stinking of drink." She smiled. "You get his dander up in some way, Maggie?"

"You might put it that way," Maggie said with an answering smile. She sat up, and Flora put the tray in her lap, then sat on the side of the bed. Maggie ate hungrily, telling Flora the events of the night before, between bites.

At the end they were both giggling uncontrollably. Flora sprang to her feet, finger to her lips. "Sh-h, let's not wake His Lordship. He hear us up here giggling away, he might come up and beat us both."

Maggie deemed it prudent to remain in her bedroom the rest of the day. Flora was in and out, bringing her news of Lord Ramage. He had awakened at noon, roared for his breakfast. But after eating he had resumed drinking and was drunk again before long. Maggie expected him to come slamming into the room at any minute, but as time passed and he didn't appear, she relaxed a little.

Around three Flora came into the room with a curling iron, preparatory to curling Maggie's hair.

"He is still swilling that French brandy. He just sent Thomas out of the house on some errand."

"I'm mystified, Flora. This conduct is so unlike him but . . ." She shrugged. "All I can do is wait, I suppose."

Flora lit the kerosene lamp, then held the curling iron in the flame, turning it slowly until it was hot. She began to work with Maggie's hair and the room soon filled with the smell of singed hair.

Midway through the process, they heard footsteps on the stairs. Flora touched Maggie's shoulder and both women waited with bated breath. The footsteps came on, stopping outside the door. Then the door crashed back against the wall and Lord Ramage strode in. He walked unsteadily and his hair was rumpled, his clothing mussed; a day's stubble of beard was on his face. It was the first time Maggie had ever seen him anything but immaculate.

Maggie's fears heightened when she saw the two grinning men coming in behind him—Jake Fargo and the man called Snake.

Lord Ramage planted himself before Maggie. He jerked a thumb at Flora. "Out, girl!" He sneered. "I wish a private audience with Lady Ramage!"

Flora didn't move, her mouth opening and closing.

"I gave you an order, girl! Obey me, or suffer the consequences."

Maggie closed her hand around Flora's, squeezing. She said quietly, "You'd better do as he says, Flora."

Flora backed out of the room, hands across her mouth.

Lord Ramage said, "Watch the door, Snake. Let no one in." He addressed himself to Maggie. "Your news of last evening has caused me to come to a decision. No longer will you balk me. I erred, I confess, in taking you to wife. The Irish are intractable, insolent, and peasant blood will out. Irish women are sluttish and beneath contempt. I must have been daft to think that I could make a lady out of you. As for the mother of my son . . . methinks a tavern whore would serve to better purpose. You once told me of the number of your lovers . . ." His drunken grin was evil incarnate. "You should not mind adding to that number. Fargo and Snake are going to have you, in turn, until they are sated. It should provide me with an hour or so of entertainment."

Maggie sprang to her feet, the knuckles of one hand pressed to her mouth "No!" She looked in horror at Fargo's leering, scarred face. "God help me, no!"

" . . . after which they will toss you to your death over the bluff to the rocks below, as I now understand Fargo did to another of your lovers, the former owner of this house."

Maggie forgot her own predicament for a moment. She directed a bitter look at Jake Fargo. "You! You unspeakable creature! I knew you had murdered poor Jonas!"

"Your Lordship," Fargo said uneasily, "should you be telling the bitch? That was told to you in secret, it was."

"What does it matter, Fargo?" Lord Ramage

gestured carelessly. "She dies when you are done with her and will be able to tell no one." His voice hardened. "My thought was to allow you to choose who would be first, madam, but then I decided that Fargo was deserving of the honor, since he has been thwarted a number of times, I understand."

"No, no!" Maggie whispered. "This is too much. Some things are too vile to be worth the sacrifice!" She backed up until she was against the bureau.

"You have little choice in the matter, madam. Oh, I am going to enjoy this." His laughter slashed at her like an axe blade. "Take her, Fargo!"

As Fargo moved toward her, Maggie half-turned and snatched up the kerosene lamp. She held it high in both hands. "One step closer and I smash this on the bed!"

"Fargo," Lord Ramage said crossly, "get on with it."

Fargo's step slowed and fear made him uncertain. "You don't know how easily things burn here in dry weather, Your Lordship. That lamp smashed, kerosene and flames spilling all over, and this room, the whole house, could go up like a torch."

"Damme, Fargo, are you a milksop? Will you let a mere woman balk you?"

He started toward Maggie and she held the lamp higher, prepared to fling it at the bed. "What he says is true, Your Lordship. Are you willing to risk your fine house and your life as well?"

"You would not dare, madam. You would die as well."

"Death would be preferable to violation by this pair!"

"I do not believe you, madam. You do not have

the courage. If you had, you would not have agreed to our sorry bargain." He came on.

Fargo seized his arm, staying him.

Lord Ramage glared at him haughtily. "You dare to lay a hand on *me*, Fargo?"

"Your Lordship," Fargo said in a pleading voice, "you must listen to me! You haven't experienced the terrors of fire. I have. Believe me, she's not worth the risk!"

Maggie seized her chance. Still holding the lamp in both hands, she darted around the pair and confronted Snake in the doorway. "Stand aside or I will dash this lamp to the floor!"

Snake looked uncertainly at her, then at Fargo, who said, "Do as she says, Snake. We'll get her, never fear!"

Snake moved to one side. Maggie turned her back to the door. Holding the lamp high in one hand, she fumbled for the doorknob with the other. "I am going down the stairs and out of this house. If I see one of you run after me, I'll use the lamp to set the house afire. I pray you believe me, if you value your property and your life, Lord Ramage!"

She felt the knob turn. Then the door was open and she backed out, slamming it after her.

Flora awaited her in the hall. She was trembling all over. "If you're leaving, Maggie, take me with you. *He* will kill me, if I'm left behind!"

Maggie hesitated only for a moment. "All right, Flora. Go ahead of me down the stairs. If I see them after us and have to throw the lamp, don't wait. Run, run for dear life!"

Halfway down the stairs, Maggie tripped and would have fallen but for Flora catching her from behind. She came dangerously close to dropping the lamp. Finally regaining her equilibrium, she continued backing. She never once took her gaze from the top of the stairs. Then they were through the front door and outside.

"Now run, Flora," she said. "Run as hard as you can!"

Together, they fled down the cliff path. As the path veered close to the edge of the cliff, Maggie tossed the lamp high and far into the channel below.

Even as she ran, Maggie remembered Jake Fargo's last words, "We'll get her, never fear!"

In the bedroom Lord Ramage had taken one step after Maggie as the door closed. Fargo's grip tightened, holding him.

In a cold voice Lord Ramage said, "I have never suffered another man to touch me, Fargo."

"I'm sorry, Your Lordship, but 'twas for your own benefit." Fargo let him go. "Besides, she can't get away. We'll catch her afore she gets far."

Lord Ramage brushed at the sleeve where Fargo had held him. Then he straightened up, drawing a sobering breath. "You're right, Fargo. Perhaps, in my anger, I was being foolhardy." He motioned tiredly. "When the Irish slut is out of the house, go after her. Get rid of her. I do not care how you accomplish it. I do not wish to see her face ever again. When she is dead, report back to me here."

Andrew Kane had never accepted the story Maggie had told her brothers. It had sounded even more dubious after the chance remark Lord Ramage had made concerning his, Andrew's, freedom to come and go as he pleased. Andrew found it hard to grasp that anyone could be so self-sacrificing as to marry that arrogant, self-serving Englishman in return for his calling off his dogs; yet, as the weeks passed following the wedding, he came to believe it could be true. There was no more harassment from Lord Ramage's thugs. The Donnevans were doing very well for themselves and Andrew steamed in and out of the cove at least twice a week, transporting lumber to Seattle. He had not mentioned his growing conviction to the Donnevan brothers, having learned that they froze at the mention of Maggie's name and would not listen to any good word of her.

"Maggie is no longer our sister, Andrew," Patrick had said in that booming voice. "She is dead to us, and I will be after thanking you not to speak her name again in our presence."

Andrew had been amused when Lars Jorgenson returned to work for the Donnevans a week ago. He had come back wearing a hangdog look, in Andrew's opinion. He had long known that the Swede was infatuated with Maggie Donnevan. Hurt by her marriage to the English Lord, Lars had taken his leave, but apparently two months away was all he could bear. Andrew had to wonder why he had come back—hoping for a pat from the hand that had hurt him? Andrew couldn't fathom a man being so infatuated with a woman, any woman, that he would stoop to curry her favor after being rejected.

Damn the woman, anyway!

That a woman of Maggie's fire and spirit would sacrifice herself in such a manner was hard for him to accept. He knew that her feeling for her brothers was strong. Even so, it was a quixotic, damnfool thing to do! He had to admit that what particularly galled him was the possibility that she might, in part, have wed Lord Ramage to protect him—to protect Andrew Kane!

So, as the weeks passed, he vacillated between believing that she had gone to Lord Ramage of her own accord and not believing it. Or, he thought to himself, not *wanting* to believe it.

But what could he do? The damned woman had made her bed, so let her lie in it! She had made it abundantly clear that she wanted no help from him. He certainly couldn't go up there and drag her out—not unless she gave him some sign.

Every time the tugboat steamed along the coast near Port Ludlow, his gaze was drawn irresistibly to that white house on the bluff. He didn't know what he was looking for. A flag of distress flying from one of the cornices? That was good for a chuckle every time he thought it. It was highly unlikely that the Maggie he knew would beg for help. True, she had come to him twice asking for his aid, but both times it concerned what were basically business matters. Even the sale of the stolen jewels had not involved her personal life. Andrew reflected with wry amusement on the greeting he might expect from Maggie if he barged into that house against her wishes, like a knight charging to the rescue of a damsel in distress and belatedly discovering that she did not consider herself in any danger.

Still, every time he steamed past the bluff below Port Ludlow, he nudged the tugboat in dangerously close to shore and kept his gaze pinned on the white house until it was behind him.

He followed the same routine on this warm, sunny afternoon. Running unloaded, he was headed for the cove and another shipment of Donnevan lumber. Since any threat from Lord Ramage seemed past, Andrew had discharged the two guards, considering it an unnecessary expense, and he was alone on the *Belle* except for Tod Dorsey.

As the bluff approached, Andrew lost headway and edged the *Belle* in closer to shore. Puffing on his pipe, he leaned on the wheel, staring up at the house. For all the signs of life, the house could be empty of occupants. For a moment a wild idea nudged at his mind. Rumor had it that Lady Ramage had never once appeared in the village of Port Ludlow. Was it possible that she wasn't even there any more?

Dorsey's excited voice pulled his attention back. "Mr. Kane, look there!"

Andrew craned his neck out the wheelhouse window, and saw Dorsey pointing toward the shore. Andrew followed the direction of his pointing finger.

Along here, the bluff towered above the rocks below. There was a narrow wedge of beach between the water and the rocks and Andrew knew that a path wound along there, leading toward the Donnevan logging camp.

He blinked, then squinted. He saw two figures running hard along the sand. Skirts whipped back in the wind, so they had to be women. He was too far out to recognize them, but a cold premonition seized him, and prompted him to head the *Belle* in even nearer to shore. As he drew closer, he saw sunlight flashing off some object about a hundred yards behind the fleeing women.

Now he saw two other figures in full pursuit. Again, sunlight glinted and with a sinking heart Andrew knew that it could be none else but Jake Fargo. And that had to mean that one of the women was Maggie. How and why this had come about, God only knew!

He couldn't spare the time to ponder it now. Even as he watched, he saw that the men were gaining on the women. Andrew pushed up the steam and aimed the *Belle* directly for a spot on the beach that would bring him roughly between the women and their pursuers.

"Mr. Kane, you're gonna run her aground!" Dorsey bawled.

"That's my intention," Andrew shouted back. "She'll float off at high tide." He added in an undertone, "I hope."

He kept the steam up until the very last moment, then cut off the chugging engine. Even so, the *Belle* still hit the beach with a thump and Andrew heard a grinding sound along the bottom of the hull. He winced, closing his eyes, as though the damage was to his own body.

Then he came racing out of the wheelhouse, pulling the Colt from his belt. At the bow, a quick glance told him that his judgment had been reasonably accurate. The *Belle* had beached about halfway between the men and the fleeing women. Andrew was close enough now that he could see it was indeed Maggie. She had stopped and was staring at him openmouthed.

Andrew didn't take the time to spare her another glance. With one hand on the rail he vaulted over. It was a long drop and he kept his knees drawn up to cushion the shock. He landed feet first and staggered several yards but managed to keep his balance and his grip on the Colt.

He spun about in a half-crouch, leveling the Colt at the two men who were already slowing. The big man in the lead was Jake Fargo; the other one Andrew didn't know. They were about thirty yards distant.

"That's far enough, Fargo!" Andrew shouted. "Halt right there!"

Fargo skidded to a stop in the moist sand. In a paroxysm of rage and frustration he drove the pickaroon to the hilt in the sand. "Damn you to hell and back, Kane! This is none of your affair, stay out of it! That bitch is no longer Maggie Donnevan, she's Lady Ramage and as such belongs to His Lordship!"

"I'm making it my affair, Fargo."

The big man's hand twitched toward the pistol stuck in his trouser band. Andrew fired, the bullet kicking up sand inches in front of Fargo's boots.

"Don't go for the pistol, friend, or you're dead. I'd be most happy to kill you. You're long overdue."

Scarred face contorting in a silent snarl, Fargo let his hand fall away.

"Now turn around and head back to your Lord Ramage. I know not what's happening here, but since Maggie is running, I assume she has good cause."

471

"He'll kill you, Kane. He's a harsh man when stirred up."

"So am I, and I'm stirred up. Damnation, but I am! Now, move! Both of you bastards!"

Shoulders slumped, Fargo motioned to his companion, and turned away.

"Fargo!" As the man looked back in question, Andrew gestured with the pistol. "Your pickaroon. Don't forget it. You'd be lost without it."

Fargo plucked the pickaroon out of the sand, shook it at Andrew in defiance, and plodded on north along the beach.

Andrew took a deep breath and straightened up. He didn't return the Colt to his belt, but watched warily as the two men grew smaller in the distance.

"Thank the saints for you, Andrew Kane!" said Maggie's breathless voice behind him.

A glad smile slashed across Andrew's face, but he was careful to assume a sober expression when he turned, after one last glance to see that the two men were gone. "Lady Ramage! It strikes me as strange to find such a fine lady sporting along the beach with the likes of Jake Fargo."

"Whisht!" Still breathless, Maggie pushed stray wisps of hair back. She was barefoot and generally disheveled, her skirt torn where she had evidently fallen on the rocks. "It's not sporting with them I was and you know it."

"Now how would I know that, Lady Ramage?" Andrew said in mock innocence.

"Don't call me by that name, not ever again!" she said angrily. "It's Maggie Donnevan, and Maggie Donnevan I will remain!"

"But how could that be, my dear?" His eye-

472

brows climbed. "I witnessed you legally wed to the man. I was a wedding guest, if you will recall."

"That was a mistake," she said ruefully, "and it's glad I am it's over."

"You seem positive about that."

"I am positive, Andrew."

"But is Lord Ramage as positive?"

"I would think so. That horrible man!" Her lips set in a bitter line. "He just tried to have me killed, he did."

"It would seem so." Andrew jammed the pistol into his belt. "So what now, Maggie Donnevan?"

"It's back to camp, if my brothers will welcome me back."

"There is some reason to doubt that, I am forced to agree. However, given your persuasive powers . . ." His glance strayed to the buxom girl by Maggie's side. "And who might this be? I haven't been introduced."

"This is Flora Jenkins, my maid. No," Maggie said strongly, placing her hand on Flora's arm. "This is Flora, my *friend*. Flora, meet Andrew Kane."

"How do, sir," Flora said demurely, curtsying.

"Maggie . . ." Andrew shook his head. "You do have a talent for picking up strays."

Maggie was not listening. Instead, she was staring at the beached tugboat, frowning in distress. "The poor *Belle*! It's sorry I am, Andrew. All because of me and my foolishness!"

"All to a good cause then," he said gallantly. He turned, taking his first good look at the *Belle*. The boat, bow buried in the sand, looked like a beached, mortally wounded whale. He sighed. "She has a stout hull and since there are no rocks along here, it's my hope she has sustained no permanent damage and will float free again with the tide." He raised his voice. "Tod, I would appreciate your remaining on board and standing guard until I return."

Tod Dorsey's head and shoulders appeared at the rail. "All right, Mr. Kane."

Andrew stepped between the two women, and offered them each an arm. "Shall we go, ladies? It's a brisk walk to the camp, if we are to make it before dark."

Lord Ramage was in the study with a glass of brandy when Fargo and Snake came back just before dark. Realizing that he had been drunk earlier and dangerously close to making an ass of himself, he had been nursing the brandy, just nipping at it. When Thomas ushered the two men in, he stood up.

One look at Fargo's crestfallen face told him all he needed to know. Anger shook him. In a tight voice he said, "You botched it, didn't you, Fargo?"

"It wasn't our fault, Your Lordship," Fargo blustered. "Whilst we were chasing the two bitches, that Kane fellow and his men jumped us. He drew down on us. We had no choice. He would've killed us if we hadn't backed off."

Lord Ramage got his temper under control. "Kane! Another error I will not make again!"

"We were chasing the pair along the beach, you see," Fargo was going on. "He spotted us. The next thing we knew, he'd run that damn tugboat of his upon the beach and we hadn't a chance."

"Damme, I have been balked enough!" Lord Ramage hurled the half-full brandy glass against the wall. It shattered, staining the wall with brandy. "Thomas, come in here and clean up the mess!"

While Thomas cleaned up the study, Lord Ramage strode into the sitting room, and stood with his hands locked together behind his back, staring blindly out the window, his blood boiling.

When he returned to the study, he had himself under iron control. "This tugboat of Kane's . . . you say it's beached?"

"Yes, indeed." Fargo smirked. "And he ain't about to get it off there until the tide comes in."

"The pair of you hasten back there, and scuttle that boat. See that it never floats again."

"Yes, Your Lordship," Fargo said, grinning "Let's go, Snake."

"Wait, Fargo. After you've done that, gather all your men together, armed to the teeth. Tomorrow, we move against the Donnevans in force. When we are finished, I want them all either dead or driven off their property and into the channel."

Chapter Twenty-one

By the time Maggie reached the camp she was stumbling with weariness and leaning heavily on Andrew's arm for support. It was after dark when they arrived and the first one to spot Maggie was Kevin.

He came running toward her. "Maggie! You're back!"

She dropped to her knees, opening her arms to him. "Kevin, dear Kevin! Yes, I'm back, hopefully for good . . . "

"Kevin!" Patrick's voice came booming out of the darkness. "I thought we had agreed that we had no sister, so who is this strange woman you are after slobbering over?"

Maggie stood as Patrick and Dan stepped into the spill of light from the open cookhouse door.

"Patrick, please," she said beseechingly, "let me try to explain . . ."

"No, Maggie," Andrew said, ranging alongside her. "*I* will explain. Knowing you, you'll make a bad job of it, ending up with everybody angry and hurt. No, Maggie," he placed a hand on her shoulder, restraining her, "for once in your life, shut up and be patient. I know it's hard for you, but this time only, all right?" Without waiting for a response, he faced around. "Patrick, Dan . . . your sister married Lord Ramage for your sake, to save the Donnevans from harm. To save me, and . . ." He hesitated, then raised his voice, "And yes, I would think you, too, Lars Jorgenson!"

Lars, Maggie thought, startled; *Lars has come back!*

A growl came from Patrick. "I don't believe it! I have heard this tale before with Kathleen. The same lies I'm not after listening to again."

"No lies, Patrick Donnevan," Andrew said without equivocation. "You Donnevans have become well acquainted with me these past two months. Many things I might be, but I am *not* a liar. Why do you think you have been able to operate without problems from Lord High and Mighty? Why do you think I have been able to steam back and forth with the *Belle* without hindrance? It's all because your foolish sister here put herself into Lord Ramage's filthy hands to prevent it!"

Patrick took an uncertain step into the light. "Is this true, Maggie?"

Before Maggie could speak, Lars also stepped into the light. In a firm voice he said, "It's true, Patrick. While I have been away, I have thought of

478

little else. I know Maggie well and I finally reached the conclusion that she could have acted as she did for no other reason. . . ."

"Oh, Lars! Dear, dear Lars!" Tears burning her eyes, Maggie rushed into his arms. Against his chest she said, "Will you ever be able to forgive me for hurting you so?"

Lars' confirmation apparently placed the seal on it, for Patrick, Dan and Olaf gathered around, all barriers broken, welcoming her back into the fold without restraint.

After the excitement of the reconciliation had ebbed, Maggie looked around for Andrew. He wasn't in sight.

Dan said, "If you're after wondering about Andrew, Maggie, he left. He said he had to get back to his tugboat."

Maggie sighed, stood on tiptoe to kiss Lars on the cheek. "Whisht! I need a wash and some rest. Patrick?"

"Yes, sister?"

"Lord Ramage will not remain idle, you may be sure. He'll come tonight or tomorrow certainly. Keep the men posted. We don't want to be caught asleep again."

"Back five minutes and you're after giving orders again," Patrick said in a grumbling voice. Then he grinned. "But it's happy I am, Sister. Running this company is too much of a burden on my shoulders, that it is. Now I can get back to falling trees. That's my true calling, not giving orders." He frowned at her. "It's sure you are that I shouldn't take the boys into Port Ludlow and teach His Lordship and his buckos a lesson?"

"I'm sure, Patrick. We'll fight, when he comes, but it'll be on our own ground. Flora, come. You can sleep with me in my cabin."

Andrew came back during the night. When Maggie emerged from her cabin the next morning, she saw him leaning against the cookhouse, morosely smoking his pipe. She hurried toward him. Then her step slowed, as her glance went past him. "The *Belle* . . . she's not in the cove!"

"No, Maggie," he said, his face gray and drawn. "The *Belle* is dead as is Tod Dorsey. When I got back there last night, I was too late. Dorsey had been clubbed to death and the *Belle* set afire. The *Belle* will sail no more."

"Ah, Andrew!" she said in a stricken voice. "I'm so sorry. So much trouble I have caused everybody. Another foul deed of Lord Ramage's, you can be sure."

"No doubt." Andrew spread his hands. "But there is no way to attach the blame to him."

"What will you do now, Andrew?"

He scrubbed a hand across his whiskered chin, smiling slightly. "At this moment, I have no idea. Every cent I had was tied up in the *Belle*."

"On that, you need not worry. It was through my doing and I will see to it that your *Belle* is replaced. You have my promise on that! Meanwhile, you can work here."

"Logging?" He looked startled. "I know nothing of logging. The water is my home. I think I would find logging dull after being at sea so long."

"Logging wasn't exactly what I had in mind. Not right now, anyway." Her face settled in grim

480

lines. "Lord Ramage is not done with the Donnevans. He will move against us and I can use you to fight him. Whisht! Surely you would not think that dull?"

"Hardly." He grinned faintly. "And it will give me great pleasure to fight Lord Ramage and Fargo. I am with you, Maggie."

"Let's have a quick breakfast and get to work."

It was indeed a quick breakfast. Maggie gave the loggers hardly enough time to eat before she was after them to get to the trees.

Patrick protested, "Maggie, if it's Lord Ramage you're expecting today, maybe we shouldn't log, but arm all the boys and put them on patrol."

"No," she said decisively. "We must appear to be going about our work as usual to any men of his sneaking around. That'll throw him off-guard, causing him to think we're not expecting him." She smiled, remembering. "Two things Lord Ramage said stick in my mind. One, he said the Irish are an arrogant race, heedless of any danger to themselves. Let him keep thinking that. Besides, we have to work harder than ever." She looked at Andrew. "I'm responsible for the loss of Mr. Kane's boat, and I want to buy him one to take its place as soon as possible."

"What was the second thing he said?" Andrew asked.

"He said that I didn't have the courage to die in defense of myself, or else I wouldn't have agreed to his sorry bargain. I intend to show him he is wrong. Andrew . . ." She pointed to his boots. "We have to find you a pair of hobnail boots.

Those might be fine for the deck of a boat, but they are dangerous for working in the woods."

An hour later the trees up on the mountain echoed to the sound of chopping axes, and logs were whistling down the chute.

Andrew and Maggie patrolled the chute, Andrew armed with his Colt.

"I'm not good with firearms," Maggie told him, "but at least I have good eyes and ears, and can keep a sharp watch."

The morning seemed peaceful enough and the scouts Maggie had out came to her from time to time to report that there had been no sighting of the enemy.

In mid-morning, Andrew said, "Maybe he's not coming today." They had stopped for a few moments while Andrew lit his pipe. Drawing on it, he leaned against a pine trunk. They were within a few yards of the chute, and about halfway up the mountain. "With his devious brain, he might decide to let some time pass, lulling you into thinking he's given up."

"No, I have a feeling they're coming today. You don't know His Lordship as I do, Andrew . . . yesterday he was almost out of his mind with rage and he'll make his move while still ablaze with that anger, I'm thinking."

"Perhaps you're right." He grinned, that devilish light dancing in his eyes for the first time today. "As you say, you know the man better than I do. . . ."

He was interrupted by Maggie's scream. She was staring past him in horror. "Andrew! Look out!"

Andrew moved instantly, instinctively ducking down and to one side. He caught a flashing glimpse of the figure of a man running at him. Light glittered off a raised pickaroon.

Jake Fargo!

Andrew left his feet in a headlong dive. The pickaroon missed him by scant inches, thudding into the earth. Andrew hit the ground on his side and rolled over several times before coming to his feet.

Fargo was tugging the pickaroon out of the ground. At that moment a shot rang out in the trees behind them. Apparently it was a signal, for gunfire began at once all up and down the mountain.

Andrew reached for the Colt in his belt, feeling no compunction whatsoever about shooting Fargo down like the animal he was, but the Colt was gone. It had been jolted out of his belt when he hit the ground. He looked around in search of it.

At a cry from Maggie he looked up to see Fargo charging at him again, the pickaroon raised. Fargo's mouth was open, and he was roaring, a wordless shout. He was a fearsome sight—pickaroon hoisted high, scarred face a mask of hate, eyes blazing with blood lust.

Andrew, hesitating for a second, debated with himself whether or not he should close with the man. Then Fargo was almost upon him. Deciding that discretion was the better part of valor, Andrew ran, sprinting toward the log chute, praying that he could find something there he could use as a weapon.

Much fleeter of foot than the larger man, he

reached the chute before Fargo. He looked around frantically, but there was nothing in sight that he could use to defend himself. He risked a glance behind and saw Fargo bearing down. Without further hesitation Andrew left his feet, hurtling the log chute, landing in a crouch on the other side. He spun about.

In his raging fury Fargo had apparently been blinded to anything but Andrew. His legs hit the side of the chute and he lost his balance, arms flailing. The pickaroon came to rest in the chute, wedged between a moving log and the side of the chute. It landed sharp end up.

Fargo came to his feet, blinking around. He saw the pickaroon moving away from him down the chute. The logs were jammed up, end to end, and moving slowly. With a grunt Fargo ran along the chute after the pickaroon.

Andrew was already following. This was his best chance. If he could tackle Fargo before he got his hands on the pickaroon . . .

Drawing up even with the big man, Andrew leapt, catapulting his body across the chute. He wrapped his arms around Fargo's hips. He had expected the tackle to knock the other man off his feet, but it was like trying to bring down a great tree. Fargo staggered a few feet, but he kept moving, beating his fists against Andrew's encircling arms, as he would against the coils of a reptile.

Andrew lost his grip, falling to the ground, and Fargo ran on until he had almost reached the pickaroon. Andrew scrambled to his feet and raced after him. He caught up to him again just as Fargo was stretching out his hand for the weapon. Again,

Andrew threw himself at Fargo, hitting the other man around the middle. This time Fargo was caught off-balance. For a moment both men stood swaying, then tumbled heavily into the chute.

As they hit the logs, Andrew's grip was broken and he and Fargo were flung apart. Andrew found himself riding down the chute between a log and the chute's wooden side. He could feel skin being scraped from his arms and he struggled to his feet, just as Fargo also stood upright. Grinning evilly, Fargo balanced on the slowly moving log, his hobnail boots biting deep. Andrew could see the pickaroon still riding along a few feet behind the big man.

Fargo took two short steps along the log and raised one foot, the hobnails resembling wicked teeth. Almost too late, Andrew realized the other man's intention—the boot was coming at Andrew's face. He moved back just in time and clawed his way up onto the log. Now they were both riding the same log, only a few feet separating them.

Andrew sensed at once that he was at a disadvantage. Being unfamiliar with the calked boots, he couldn't get a good grip on the log with the hobnails.

Still grinning, Fargo moved toward him, hands reaching. Above the sounds of the moving logs and the sporadic gunfire, he roared, "There is no getting away from me now, Kane! No more will you torment me! Go to your death thinking what I'll do to the Irish bitch after you're done for!"

Taking advantage of the momentum of the log under his feet, Andrew tried for purchase with the hobnails. He felt the spikes on his right boot catch

485

momentarily, just long enough for him to lower his head and drive forward, ramming his shoulder into Fargo's midsection.

Caught in mid-step, Fargo's feet were knocked out from under him and he fell backward. Andrew, thrown aside by the contact, was flung over the side of the chute. A moment before he struck the ground, he heard a strangled scream from Fargo. Andrew sprang to his feet the instant he stopped rolling. He couldn't see Fargo anywhere, and he stood blinking about in disbelief. Had the man disappeared by some magic trick? Then he saw an arm trailing alongside the chute. He ran toward it.

Jake Fargo was lying between the log and the side of the chute; the sharp end of the pickaroon protruded from his chest, driven all the way through from the back when he had fallen on it. His scarred face was horrible in death. Due to the bouncing of the log along the chute, Fargo's body jogged up and down, as though he was still alive and trying to climb out of the wooden trough.

Sickened, Andrew turned away. He saw Maggie running toward him and he heard a new outburst of gunfire up near the logging site.

Maggie reached him, breathless. "Are you all right?"

He nodded wordlessly.

Maggie stood on tiptoe to stare after Fargo's bobbing body. "Jake Fargo?"

"Fargo is dead, Maggie."

Maggie started to speak, then went silent, listening to the sounds of gunfire. "My brothers! Little Kevin, he's up there!"

Andrew took her hand. "Let's go."

Before they could take a step, a shot rang out closer at hand and Andrew grunted. He reeled, clutching at his left shoulder.

Maggie whirled to look at him. "Andrew! Are you hit?"

"Yes," he said between gritted teeth. "The shot came from over there." He motioned with his head toward the trees.

Another shot sounded, but this time the bullet missed, thudding into the chute boards. Andrew grabbed for Maggie's hand again and pulled her with him over the chute. They hugged the ground on the other side. Andrew ripped his shirt away from his shoulder. It was a clean wound. The bullet had plowed all the way through the fleshy part of his upper arm. It was painful and bleeding heavily, but he could still use his arm.

"Is it bad?" Maggie asked anxiously.

Andrew hastily covered his arm. "Just a flesh wound."

All the while the unseen gunman had been firing steadily, the bullets striking the other side of the chute. Finally, silence fell.

"He must have given it up as a bad job," Andrew said.

He waited a few minutes, then cautiously lifted his head. There was no sound from the trees. He stood up, helping Maggie to her feet. Again, the sound of gunfire came from up the mountain.

"Let's go, Maggie!"

Lord Ramage had never been a particularly good shot. In his anger and frustration at seeing Jake Fargo dead and Kane and the Irish strumpet unharmed and in plain sight, he had started firing with the pistol Fargo left with him.

"I won't need it, not to handle this Kane, Your Lordship," Fargo had boasted. "You use it to fire the signal the very instant I jump the bastard!"

Now the pistol was empty and there was no spare ammunition. Lord Ramage threw the pistol from him in disgust.

It had been a frustrating, maddening day from the very beginning. To start off, a number of Fargo's crew had defected. When Fargo had shown up at Ramage Hall this morning, he had only ten men with him.

"I'm sorry, Your Lordship. The others say they won't work for you anymore. They tell me they think you're not doing right, hounding the Donnevans this way. They say the citizens along the Sound are getting tired of your ways and are talking of getting the law in. I threatened to break a few skulls with my pickaroon, but they just scampered off." Fargo had frowned at him in doubt. "Maybe we should wait until you can scrape together more men? Offer enough money and you can be sure to find all the rough fellows you need."

Lord Ramage had not hesitated. "No, I will brook no more delays. We move against the Donnevans as planned!"

"We're gonna be outnumbered, two to one."

"We will have the element of surprise on our side. They're a careless bunch."

"Well, I'm game if you are, Lord Ramage. I'm itching to get at them, especially that Maggie. When Jake Fargo is through with her, she'll beg me to smash her skull for her, that she will!"

When they had arrived at the Donnevan camp an hour earlier, it was just as Lord Ramage had predicted. The Donnevans and their crew were busily at work, no posted guards in evidence. Lord Ramage had divided the men into two groups of five each, dispatching five to attack the camp, the other group to assault the crew at the logging site, while he and Fargo went in search of Maggie—their prime target. "The instant we clap eyes on the woman, either I or Fargo will fire a single shot. That will be the signal to commence your attack."

Now it had all gone wrong. Fargo was dead, Kane and the Irish woman were unharmed, and Lord Ramage had a feeling that all was not well with the rest of his forces. With the element of surprise in their favor, they should have won the battle with the first skirmish. Yet gunfire was still sounding up the mountain and that could only mean one thing—the Donnevans had not been caught by surprise and were giving a good account of themselves.

Lord Ramage ground his teeth in frustration.

Suddenly, yesterday's scene with Maggie flashed across his mind's eye. Fire! Fargo had said that the people here were deathly afraid of fire. That was the answer!

Lord Ramage tested the wind. The breeze was blowing in the direction in which Maggie and Kane were headed. With good fortune on his side, the wind should blow the fire to the area where the whole sorry Donnevan clan were gathered! He delved into his pocket, closing his hand around the matchbox tin. Taking it out, he found that it contained three sulphur matches. That number should be more than enough.

There was a lot of dry, brown underbrush about. Chuckling to himself, Lord Ramage knelt and struck a match, holding it to a bush. The dry leaves caught fire and he moved on to another. Within a short time, the matches were all gone, but several fires were going. Lord Ramage was disappointed at the slow spread of the flames. His glance lit on a gallon can hanging from a pine branch. He reached for it, popped the cork from the spout, and put his nose to the opening. The contents had a rank odor, and Lord Rammage smiled to himself. Grease for the log chute! Just what was needed!

He tilted the spout over a burning bush and poured a generous amount onto the flames. The fire flickered and for a moment he feared he had doused it. Then it blazed up and began to burn fiercely.

Lord Ramage hurried from bush to bush, until the can was empty. Now the flames were shooting high, vaulting up into the small pine trees, eating their way inexorably toward the dark, towering growth of trees to the south. He stood back, gazing at his handiwork with pride. By the time the fire had made its way up the mountain, the whole forest would be aflame and the Donnevans would be roasted alive.

A cloud of smoke engulfed him and he coughed wrackingly. Waving at the smoke, he looked around anxiously, looking for a path through the flames, feeling the first gnawings of fear. It would not do to be caught in his own trap.

Another heavy wave of smoke obscured his

vision. When it had passed, he found to his horror that he was completely encircled by flames. Eyes burning, lungs laboring, he whirled, desperately looking for a way out. The air had grown thick and hot, difficult to breathe. He had lost all sense of direction. A rift seemed to open momentarily to his left and he caught a glimpse of blue sky. With a glad cry he started for it at a run. Ahead of him was a clear space, not yet aflame. He had almost reached it when a tongue of flame licked out at him, caressing his back with warmth. He could smell the stench of burning cloth over the scent of flaming wood and he heard the bright crackle of flame close at hand, as his hair ignited. And then came the pain—searing, excruciating!

Lord Ramage screamed in agony, trying to protect his face from the flames. He did not see the root that tripped him; he saw nothing but the hell of deadly fire that began to consume him.

And then, after what seemed a very long and painful time—darkness!

At the logging site Lars was the first one to spot the fire raging up the mountain.

Patrick had just come bounding into the clearing with a whoop. "We've routed the bully boys! They're all dead or gone, that they are, the scalawags!"

The loggers gathered around, clapping Patrick on the back. Lars stood apart, smiling to himself. As had proved so often true in the past, Maggie had been right again. Her plan had been to keep most of the men working, as they would on any normal day, but with weapons concealed near at

491

hand. A few of the younger, faster men were sent out as scouts, keeping themselves concealed. The instant they spotted anyone skulking about, they were ordered to inform either Patrick at the logging site or Dan, whose group was down the mountain protecting the camp and the sawmill, or Maggie on patrol along the log chute. The news had been relayed to Patrick first and so they had been prepared when the attack came.

Breathing a sigh of relief that it was all over, Lars stepped to the head of the log chute, gazing down its length.

That was when he saw it—billowing rolls of smoke, changing colors as they rose, from white at the bottom to gray as they climbed and to black at the top. Leaping flames were eating their way across the stumps and small pines of the logged-over hillside. The fire was burning its way toward them and edging closer toward a fine stand of trees on the far right.

Lars whirled about. "Fire! Coming up the mountain right at us!"

The others came running. Lars tilted his head back, sniffing the wind. "The wind, I think it's shifting!" The wind had been coming from the east off the channel, but now Lars had noted the subtle shifting toward the north and west. Fortunately, the wind wasn't very strong or the fire would already have been on top of them.

"If we start a backfire partway down the mountain, along that logged-over swath," he pointed a finger, "we may have a chance of stopping it before it reaches here, or gets into that stand of trees over there."

Beside him, Olaf was sniffing the wind. "Dad-damnit, boy, I think you're right!"

"Then let's get at it!" Patrick yelled.

Lars led the way about two hundred yards down the slope. The fire was coming on toward them, but slower now with the shift in wind direction. Smoke clouds rolled up, the leaping red-and-orange flames swallowing the underbrush and small trees like the mouth of a huge beast.

"This should about do it!" Lars shouted. "Spread out in a line across the mountain, on both sides of the chute, and start your fires, fanning them toward the cove!"

The loggers stretched out in a thin line, stopping to start small fires. Several men made torches out of dried branches and ran along the straggly line, whooping and using their make-shift torches to scorch the earth.

The backfire, small at first, but always growing, inched down the mountainside toward the bigger fire. By the time the lines of fire met, clashing in battle, the backfire was still small in comparison, but it had left a ragged strip of scorched earth some fifty yards wide behind it. The bigger fire slowly died, deprived of fuel to keep it going.

For a half hour more the men ran along the fire-line, stomping at small patches of still smouldering underbrush.

Finally Lars straightened up, weary to the bone, smoke-blackened, his clothes scorched in several places. He heard a shout from below. Moving forward through the patches of smoke still hovering, he saw someone hurrying along the chute. Or what remained of it, Lars noted absently. A hundred-yard section of the chute had been burned away. But they were fortunate if that was all the damage they had sustained, he thought.

He focused his attention on the man hurrying toward him. It was Dan.

"Thank God, you've whipped the fire!" Dan said, puffing from the climb.

"We beat it," Lars said laconically. "How about down at camp? Did you stand off Lord Ramage's crew?"

"Yep." Dan laughed. "There were only a half-dozen of the boyos and we were waiting for them. We don't have a single wounded man. How about up here?"

"Couple of loggers were shot, but nothing serious. The fire was more of a threat . . ." Lars broke off "Where's Maggie? I thought she would be with you."

"I haven't seen her. She wasn't with you?" Dan looked alarmed.

"No, the last time I saw her she was along the chute here. I thought the fire would have sent her bustling down to camp . . . Oh, dear Jesus!" Lars went numb as Maggie's possible fate struck him forcibly.

The same thought occurred to Dan. "She was caught somewhere in the fire! We have to find her, I'm thinking!"

"Yes." Lars looked in both directions. All he could see was scorched, blackened earth, devoid of all life. He raised his voice in a shout. "Maggie! Where are you?"

Maggie and Andrew had gone about fifty yards

from the spot where they'd been shot at, proceeding slowly because of Andrew's wound. He kept saying that it wasn't serious, but Maggie could tell it was giving him considerable pain.

Abruptly, she smelled smoke. She halted Andrew with a touch on his arm, looking back over her shoulder. "Fire! And it's coming toward us!"

Andrew looked around. "We'd better hurry on up the mountain."

They began to run, but had only progressed another fifty yards when Maggie halted Andrew again. "Look!" She pointed up the mountain at the line of fire coming down, moving much more rapidly than the one behind them. "They've started a backfire! We're trapped, Andrew!"

She looked both left and right. To their left, the main fire had leaped ahead of them, curling like a whip. The other way, to their right, was still clear. She pointed. "There, that stand of pine is still safe." She tugged at his hand.

Andrew held back. "Maggie, we'll be trapped in there, too, before long."

"No, there's a small stream in there, one I've been thinking of diverting into the log chute. It's not very deep, but a boulder has made a small pool about three feet deep. I just remembered something Olaf told me once, a way to save yourself if you're trapped in a forest fire with a stream near. Come on!"

Holding his hand tightly, she hurried him along. Once in the stand of trees it was cooler and dark, giving the illusion that they were free of the fire. Yet Maggie knew that the grove of trees could turn into a death trap if the flames leapfrogged into

495

it. Even as she thought this, smoke billowed into the trees in a choking cloud and the roaring of the approaching flames had the sound of a great wind.

She pulled Andrew on. Ahead, she saw the boulder and then the pool formed by its blocking the passage of the stream. Her heart sank. The dry weather had reduced the size of the pool; the water had dropped at least a foot since she had last seen it. But it would have to do.

She let go of Andrew's hand and searched frantically along the sides of the pool. Finally she found what she was looking for—a clump of tall weeds. They were dead, yet the stalks still stood. She broke off two, about three feet in length. The stalks were, in effect, hollow reeds. She put each one to her mouth and blew, making sure they were hollow all the way through.

She ran back to where Andrew stood, and gave him one of the stalks. "The way Olaf told it to me, you stretch out in the water, on your back on the bottom, and put this reed in your mouth to breathe through."

Andrew gave her a dubious look. "You sure you know what you're doing?"

"Whisht!" she said impatiently. "What choice do we have? If we stay in the woods, we're sure to be burned to death. This way, we at least have a chance, I'm thinking."

He made a wry face, shrugged fatalistically, and took her hand. They waded out into the pool. At the deepest part the water came to just above Maggie's knees. It seemed to provide scant protection. What she hadn't told Andrew was the fact that if a forest fire became hot enough, it could bring any water to a quick boil, cooking all life in it. She threw a despairing glance back the way they had come and saw, through gaps in the trees, flames eating their way toward the grove.

She leaned toward Andrew and kissed him, clinging fiercely for just a moment. Then, without a word, she closed her eyes and lowered herself into the water. When she was in position on her back, she put the reed in her mouth, closing her lips tightly around it, at the same time pinching her nostrils closed. Tentatively, she breathed in, and was relieved when a trickle of precious air came through the reed.

In a moment she felt a body settle next to hers and a groping hand. Maggie closed her hand around Andrew's and squeezed.

She had no way of knowing how long they should remain under the water, but it wasn't long before she felt the water surrounding her begin to grow warm. Or was it her imagination? She lay still, heart pounding furiously. Another interminable time passed.

All at once, her curiosity became too much. She cautiously raised up, until just her face was out of the water, steeling herself against a blast of heat searing her skin.

It was all right. The air was warm, but not too hot. She came to a sitting position, looking around. The fire was gone. The tops of a few trees, she saw, had been burned, but the rest of grove was intact. The backfire had been successful.

"Andrew!" She tugged at his hand, pulling him up. He surfaced, spluttering and spewing water. "It's over, we're safe now."

She heard a distant voice, "Maggie! Can you hear me?"

It was Lars! She stood up, shouting, "In here, Lars!"

She waded toward the bank, calling again. Dripping water, dress clinging to her body, her hair a mess, she emerged from the pond just as Lars burst into the small clearing and saw her.

"Thank our Lord! I was hoping you would have sense enough to head in here."

Lars opened his arms and Maggie ran into them. Against his chest, she murmured, "Was anybody hurt? Is everything all right?"

"Nobody was seriously hurt. We lost some timber, but not a great deal." He stroked her streaming hair. "We routed Lord Ramage's crew and I doubt he'll trouble you ever again."

"Oh!" She pulled back from his arms. "Andrew! I forgot about him."

Lars looked at Andrew Kane, who had pulled himself out of the water and was sitting propped up against a tree trunk, his eyes closed, face ashen.

"Andrew, Andrew! Darling!" Maggie flew to him.

Lars heaved a sigh as he watched her kneel beside Andrew, gently touching his face. He had lost her. He supposed he had known that for a long time and had been living in a fool's paradise to ever think he would win her. His thoughts turned to Nancy Woods. Would she welcome him back? Nancy loved him, he was certain of that. The question was, would she forgive him? There was some hope, he concluded. He had forgiven Maggie, hadn't he?

Lars turned away, and trudged through the ashes, leaving Maggie and Andrew alone.

Kneeling beside Andrew, Maggie stroked his cheek tenderly. His eyes fluttered open. "Are you all right, my darling?"

"I'm gunshot, half-drowned, and came close to being burned to death . . . aside from that, I'm fine."

She laughed suddenly. "You still think logging is a dull life?"

He drawled, "I've had enough excitement this one day to last me a lifetime."

"Then you will stay here, work with me?"

A curtain descended over his face, and he said guardedly, "I'll think about it."

"I could make it even more exciting for you."

"Which means?"

"Which means I love you, Andrew Kane."

He grinned. "Whisht! And here I was after thinking you'd never get around to realizing that fact. Damnation, woman, I've known that for a long while."

"You! The conceit of some men!"

Andrew looped his good arm around her shoulders and drew her against him. "Will you for once shut up?"

"I will not!"

Andrew rolled his eyes heavenward with a sigh. Then he pulled her closer and silenced her with his lips on hers. He could feel her lips moving under his, as she smiled.

PREVIEW

LOVE'S PAGAN HEART

by
Patricia Matthews

(The following pages are excerpts edited from the first chapters of this new novel scheduled for publication in November 1978.)

All through the long afternoon the ceremonial drums had been throbbing like the pulse beat of a giant heart, and Liliha Montjoy, in the semi-darkness of the thatch hut, felt her own blood surging to the drum-beat.

Her hair and body had been sleeked by scented oils, in preparation for the honor that would soon be hers. Nothing remained save for the donning of the new *kapa* cloth, which her mother, Akaki, had made specially for the occasion.

After the ministrations of her mother and the other women, Liliha felt beautiful, and more alive than she had ever felt. She moved her head gently from side to side, enjoying the feel of her hip-length, silken black hair as it moved across her bare, golden skin.

Her nostrils widened as the tempting odors of roasting pig seeped into the hut. Since she was a woman, Liliha would not be partaking of the succulent meat; the women would not be able to eat of the white shark meat, or the bananas, for these foods were *kapu,* forbidden, to women.

Liliha smiled secretly to herself as she thought of the stolen bites she had tasted, in defiance of the *kapus.* Even though the punishment for such daring was often death, she, and many of the other girls and women, often broke these laws, which were, of course, made by men and so caused much difficulty for the women.

And then her thoughts turned to one man, Koa, whose wife she would be, within a few hours. Koa, who was beautiful and strong, with wide shoulders to bear the burden of rulership, and strong arms to fight his enemies and to hold her close.

The scent of the flowers in her hair was sweet, and her blood ran warm as Liliha thought of Koa. She was very fortunate to have been chosen for a wife by an *alii,* or chieftain. Of course she knew that she had been a natural choice, since she was of royal blood on her mother's side, and her father was said to have been a prince of sorts in his own land. With their union, their *mana* would be increased, and they would be sure to have healthy, strong children to carry on the line.

The light from the doorway was blocked as Akaki's huge figure entered the hut.

Liliha looked up and smiled at her mother. The tall woman beamed back, her heavy but still beautiful features breaking into a wide smile.

"Are you ready, little one?"

Liliha nodded.

"Here are fresh flowers."

Akaki kneeled down, and removed the flowers from Liliha's hair, replacing them with fresh blossoms, and putting a circlet of flowers around the girl's slender throat.

Liliha then rose, and her mother fastened the *kapa* cloth around her daughter's supple waist. Lastly, Akaki opened her palm to show Liliha what she had hidden there. It was a small carving of a female figure on a cloth string, made from hardwood.

"Pele," Akaki said softly. "She will protect you, as she has me, and my mother before me."

Liliha, eyes glistening with bright tears, pressed her cheek to her mother's, and embraced the older woman.

"May I be as good a wife and mother as you have been, my mother," she said formally.

The two women again embraced, and then Akaki and her daughter stepped out of the hut, into the warm, island sunshine, and moved toward Liliha's wedding litter, a whaleboat.

Liliha felt a great surge of happiness as the boat tilted under them, and then was borne aloft by the men. Then they were moving forward to her future as the bride of Koa, and queen of Maui.

* * *

In the shadows of the gathering darkness, two men, the only white men on the island of Maui, stood well back, observing the arrival of Liliha in the elegantly decorated whaleboat, fastened to light spars. It was a ponderous vehicle, and required seventy strong men to bear it. Liliha and Akaki rode in serene, queenly grace under the damask umbrella.

"Putting on airs for a pagan bitch, ain't she, Reverend?" said the slighter of the two men.

"I do not take kindly to such language, Mr. Rudd," said Isaac Jaggar.

"If you think she's so high and mighty, Reverend," Asa Rudd said in a sneering voice, "why are you helping to spirit her away then?"

"No matter what I may think of Liliha Montjoy's morals, or her lack of faith in the Almighty, she is still a woman, one of God's gentler creatures, and as such should not be profaned."

"Gormy, Reverend, you are a case, you are!" Rudd laughed.

Jaggar winced, but managed to refrain from comment. Rudd, in Jaggar's opinion, was a vulgar, godless man, but Jaggar had allied himself with the man in his effort toward saving the immortal souls of the islanders, and had to endure. Worse than Rudd's coarse nature was his laugh—a high, screeching sound, reminding Jaggar unpleasantly of the cackle of barnyard fowl.

The two men, except for their common goal, were direct opposites. Rudd was shorter, and dark, quick, and darting as a cockroach scuttling away from a candle flame.

502

He was a product of London's noxious alleys. On the other hand, Isaac Jaggar was large, gangling, raw-boned, with knobby joints and a prominent nose set in his austere features. In contrast to Rudd's alley whine, he spoke with a New England twang, his speech liberally flavored with biblical quotations.

Now Rudd said plaintively, "Where is Lopaka? We can't make a move without him. He said he would be here."

"I am here, Asa Rudd," said a guttural voice behind them.

Startled, both men whirled about. In the darkness, Lopaka loomed menacingly. He was a tall, powerfully muscled man of thirty.

With his coppery skin and burning black eyes, Lopaka reminded Jaggar of American Indians he had seen once on a missionary excursion to the Great Plains of the United States. Lopaka had the same brooding savagery about him, and by nature he was cruel, vicious, and utterly without scruples. When Jaggar's conscience nagged at him for siding with this islander, he reminded himself that the Lord moved in strange and mysterious ways, and if aligning himself with Lopaka furthered the Lord's work, so be it.

Beady eyes darting, Rudd said eagerly, "We ready to move, Lopaka?"

"*I* am ready, Asa Rudd," Lopaka said in his deep voice. Dressed in nothing but a *kapa* cloth, there was something majestic about Lopaka, even in his near nudity, lending credence to his claim to the rule of Maui. "The instant the ceremony begins, I will give a single war cry. That will be the signal. Be prepared."

With that he strode away, not furtively, but with measured steps. Nonetheless, within a few short yards, he was gone from view, becoming as one with the night.

"Gormy," Rudd said, "he spooks me, that he does!"

"Lopaka will make a powerful convert to the Almighty," Jaggar intoned.

"That one? The Devil's convert, that's more likely!"

*　　*　　*

It was time.

Liliha stepped out of the hut into the light provided by

the many fires ringing the wedding ground. She saw Koa, tall and breathtakingly handsome, emerge from another thatch hut across the circle, in his feathered headdress and cape of office. The firelight, catching the hundreds of tiny feathers, caused them to glow like jewels. A heavy silence fell, even the drums going still, as the two lovers moved toward one another.

A high, piercing cry rang out, violating the respectful silence. Liliha recognized it as a war cry, a cry almost forgotten with the coming of peace to the islands.

Liliha came to a stop, a scream clogging her throat. Behind Koa, she could see a feathered lance flying toward him out of the darkness. She screamed then, but it was far too late. Koa arched back, hands clawing at the lance, which had struck him in the middle of the back, driving all the way through, the bloody point protruding from his chest.

Shouts of alarm erupted from the crowd, and they surged forward toward Koa as he fell, dropping out of sight. Liliha, sobbing, fought her way toward the spot where he had fallen.

She managed to get close enough for one last glimpse of Koa's face—half-turned, one side pressing into the ground. Then hands grasped her arms, and she found herself pulled out of the crowd into the shadows. Before she could cry out, a rough cloth was bound tightly around her mouth, and she was lifted, as if she had no more weight than a coconut, onto a man's broad, muscled shoulder.

Her struggles were as useless as those of a fish against a net. Her captor began running along the sand now, and as Liliha looked back despairingly, the night swallowed up the wedding ground, and Koa.

* * *

With Koa dead and she herself captive, Liliha felt that her whole world had ended. And, indeed, she would soon discover an entirely new world far beyond the horizons of Hawaii. Liliha's innocent concepts of love would be both debased and enhanced as men discovered the magic and beauty she reflected in every mood. But Liliha would not only survive the cruel shafts of fate, she would triumph and prove to herself and to her enemies that love and dignity could conquer all!